WATER'S WRATH

BOOK FOUR OF AIR AWAKENS

ELISE KOVA

Silver Wing Press

Water's Wrath

Book Four of Air Awakens

ELISE KOVA

Published by Silver Wing Press
Copyright © 2016 by Elise Kova

Cover Artwork by Merilliza Chan
Editing by Monica Wanat
Proofing by Kate Anderson

ISBN (paperback): 9781619844254
ISBN (hardcover): 9781619844261
eISBN: 9781619844247

Library of Congress Control Number: 2016900112

2020 Five Year Anniversary Edition

For the two who joined me at the journey's start:
Monica and Meril

TABLE OF CONTENTS

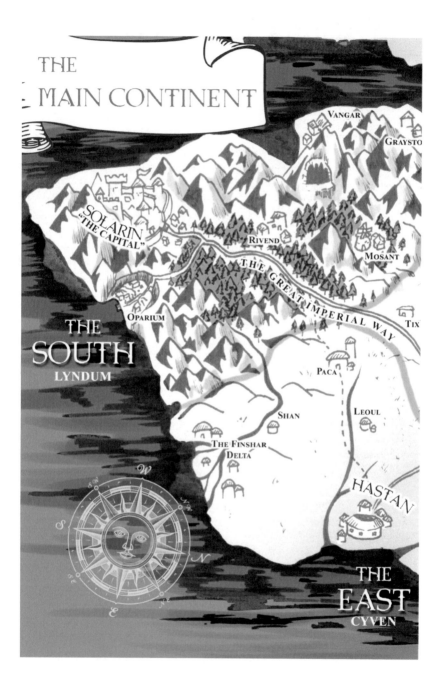

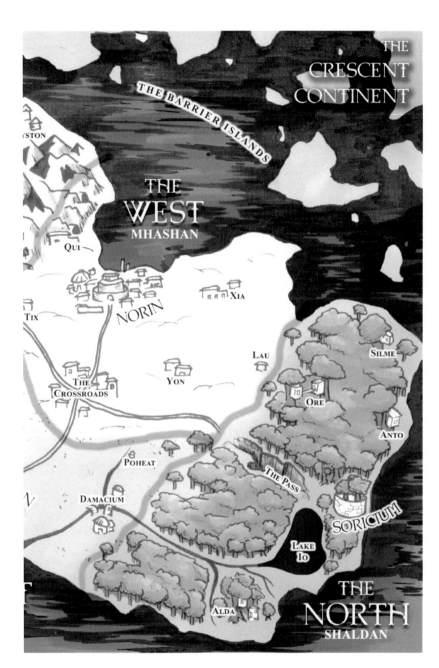

CHAPTER 1

*N*O MATTER HOW *far she ran or how many people she met, an invisible hand pulled Vhalla back to the crown prince of the Solaris Empire.*

She couldn't escape him. Even when she slumbered while half a continent away, her mind joined with his. Mixing, mingling, torturing her with the worst and most beautiful pain she'd ever known.

It wasn't the first time she'd dreamt of him since the war in Shaldan ended, but in all the previous memories she'd witnessed, he'd been a boy or young man. Now she invaded the memory of an adult prince, a prince she knew well enough that her fingers could point to every scar that marred his alabaster flesh under the tight buttons of his military regalia.

In this dream, Aldrik's clothing had been washed as best as could be expected on a warfront. But his shoulders sagged as though he could no longer fill out the mantle of his station. Eyes that usually shone like onyx, illuminated by an undying inner flame, had dulled to coal and sat in dark, sunken wells. His raven hair was dishevelled, falling limply around his face; it was in need of brushing. Dark stubble shadowed his chin and cheeks, accentuating an eternal scowl.

He looked every one of his twenty-five years, plus twenty-five more.

In stark contrast, the golden prince stood next to his elder brother. Baldair glanced often at his sibling from the corners of his eyes, a large palm resting on the hilt of the broadsword strapped to his hip. His face rotated between genuine sympathy and the very real concern that he may have to subdue the fearsome sorcerer known as the Fire Lord—again.

They waited before a giant fortress. Tall trees peeked over the perfect, magically created walls. It housed the head clan of a nation once called Shaldan, now reduced to the Solaris Empire's "North." Shaldan's capital, Soricium, was mostly levelled, save for the stronghold before her. Vhalla knew its walls and passages well. She'd been an executioner in this fortress. She'd helped deliver the final death blow to this former nation.

A large stone drawbridge groaned to life and lowered slowly, revealing four sorcerers—Groundbreakers—on either side. Behind them stood another group of three people surrounded by even more warriors. They all had tanned skin and curled hair, features of the North. A proud and beautiful people Vhalla had been forced to help bring to their knees.

The Head Chieftain was tall and lean, and two women flanked her. One was an archer known as Za, a warrior who'd tried to kill Vhalla. The other was a young girl, pretty with soft curves already budding on her hips and bosom. She'd be a fine woman when she grew into the promises her body was beginning to make.

Emperor Solaris strode forward, meeting the head clan at the end of the drawbridge. He engaged in a brief exchange with the Chieftain, but Vhalla couldn't hear the words. The man whose memory she occupied let them become muffled, as though he was submerged underneath a great lake. Aldrik stood as rigid as a sword. He narrowed his eyes at the silken-clad girl standing at the Chieftain's right.

The child who was to be his future wife.

Vhalla awoke in a cold sweat. The dreams were never easy, and shrugging him out of her mind afterward continued to be a challenge. She panted softly and listened. The air was still and silent, telling her that she hadn't cried out in her sleep or thrashed violently enough to shake her small cot; she hadn't disturbed the woman whose home she occupied.

Her fingers ghosted over the chain she wore about her neck, resting on a small watch. The sun and wing engraved on the watch's front embedded itself into Vhalla's clutched palm. It ticked away the early morning, the light changing the colors of the curtain over the glassless window that dominated her bedside wall.

It had been nearly four months since she had last seen the prince of her dreams, the man who had promised his future to her with the token she clung to. But no amount of time or distance could dull the Bond that they shared. It was a magical connection that only a once-in-a-lifetime magical event could form, and it was enough to make Vhalla want to scream in frustration at the oppressive silence that dared to surround her body when her mind and heart were full of his emotions. It meant that, until the end of her days, she could be haunted by his visage, his memories, his dreams.

No matter how far she ran, her phantom would be there.

Knowing she wouldn't sleep again, Vhalla dressed. A loose linen split-skirt was held in place by a belt around the waist. Overtop, she buttoned a long jacket made of the same breathable fabric. Her last adornment was a wide scarf looped around her head and neck.

Everything she'd ever read about Western fashions held true. Keeping the sun off bare skin was the most sensible way to survive the oppressive summer heat, and the fabric readily breathed in the constant winds. Cutting her hair again would also keep her cooler and would trim away the last of the faded dye that lingered around her frayed ends. But Vhalla was intent on growing it long once more and had yet to allow someone to take shears to it.

In the corner of her tiny room, Vhalla pulled open a trapdoor. She put her feet to the rungs of a narrow ladder before taking a breath. Clenching her fists, Vhalla opened her magic Channel. Gripping the opening, she slowly pulled her feet from the rungs so she was only hanging by her hands. And then let go.

Rather than falling quickly, Vhalla eased down like a feather. Her hands hovered, ready to catch herself should the descent go awry, but that precaution proved unnecessary. Today was slower than yesterday, three times slower than a week ago. Her magic was becoming stronger—or Vhalla was better at managing it. Keeping the same pockets of air around her feet like boots made of wind, she padded across the small living space, not allowing any footfalls.

She relaxed her magic when she had descended most of the way down a side stairway into the dim bookshop below. Vhalla ran her fingers along the spines in the narrow bookshelf walkways. Some of the books were tall, some short, some old, and some new, but every book carried its own story, and she'd already devoured most of what the small shop had to impart.

Throwing back the shutters allowed the dim morning's light to filter into the narrow space. After her first two weeks in the shop, her duties had become engrained. Now at nearly six weeks, she went about the shop keeping with little thought. First came pushing back the shutters, then wedging the door open so the store didn't become an oven. The wind wasn't optional to surviving the day. But it carried in sand that settled on the books, horrifying Vhalla, and she set to dusting first thing every morning.

Her hands rested on one of the manuscripts on the end of the tallest shelf in the back corner, and her dust rag was quickly forgotten. Sliding it out, she ran her fingertips over the embossed cover, *Kishn'si Coth*. It was written entirely in the old language of Mhashan, and Vhalla had overlooked it for weeks as a result. It wasn't until she'd devoured most of the books in Southern Common that she turned to language study, which finally allowed her to translate the title of this particular work.

"That one again?" a portly woman asked with a yawn, standing in the stairway.

Vhalla nearly jumped off her stool. Gianna wasn't a Windwalker, but she knew her home and shop well enough not to make a sound coming down the stairs.

"I think I can almost read it." Vhalla tried to shrug nonchalantly, slipping it back into its place on the bookshelf.

"*Yae, tokshi.*" The woman chuckled.

Vhalla wasn't about to take "not yet" as an answer. "*Vah da.*"

Her careful pronunciation put a wide smile on the woman's features. "What is your obsession with *The Knights' Code*? I can't even pay someone to take it off my hands."

"Curiosity." It was the truth, in part. *A small part.*

She'd come West, to the Crossroads, to escape everything—to go to a place where she could be no one and nothing. But when she came across mention of the Knights of Jadar in a manuscript on Western history, she'd set out to devour as much information about the group as possible.

Vhalla had only known the broad facts about them before, that they were a mysterious and unquestioned force founded by King Jadar in old Mhashan during the genocide of Windwalkers—the Burning Times—with the purpose of executing the king's will. She hadn't given the Knights much thought before the war against Shaldan, when she'd learned the Western zealots had been working with the Northerners against the Empire. Thanks to her reading, she was finally filling in more of the blanks, which was yielding some answers about why the group seemed to be bent on hunting her down.

"Breakfast?" the woman asked.

"Not hungry," Vhalla replied, true to form. After the first week together, Gianna had given up trying to make her eat. Vhalla never felt hungry first thing in the morning. There was too much to think about, too many things to get started for the day.

Vhalla already held a wet quill when Gianna left the room. With diligent accuracy, the sorcerer recounted the dream she'd had the night prior. *Perhaps with too much accuracy*, Vhalla furiously scratched out the portion of writing about Aldrik's hair, the gauntness of his face, and pallor of his skin.

The prince was a memory. Her hand clasped the watch. He was a remnant of another period of her life, and she had to learn to leave him there. *Though, such a thing seemed more impossible by the day.*

With a shake of her head, Vhalla dislodged the memories, returning to her work. The days in the bookshop had done more than remind her how much she loved the smell of parchment or the feeling of bound leather. They had given her time. Time begot thought. And thinking for herself was something she hadn't had time for in far too long.

It was after her first dream that she started her journal, the record of her dreams of Aldrik. Originally, it had been out of a sense of obligation because she had promised to tell him when she dreamt of him. With time, she began writing all the dreams she'd ever had of him and expanded from there. She filled pages upon pages that culminated to the sum record of the memories he told her, the ones she'd witnessed when she slept, and the total of her knowledge on the history of the Empire.

With it all, she began to notice connections.

Her grey quill circled new words as she flipped through the pages, marred passages with arrows and circles and lines and more notes. Vhalla was connecting dots that she wasn't sure she hadn't invented. But a picture was taking shape, *too easily to be chance.*

Prince Aldrik Ci'Dan Solaris—born to Fiera Ci'Dan and the Emperor Tiberus Solaris, a prince of two worlds, the man known as the Fire Lord to his enemies and an aloof, off-putting royal to his allies—had much to hide.

Vhalla knew he'd tried to kill himself before he became a man. She knew he'd killed for the first time when he was fourteen—he'd told her that much. She knew the man she hated as much as the Emperor—the Head of Senate, Egmun—had been behind the first blood on the prince's hands. Her quill rested on a date.

Standing, Vhalla walked over to the small section where they kept books on history. It was mostly Western, but there was a single general story she'd been relying on. Back at the desk, Vhalla flipped open the book and thumbed through the pages. *The War of the Crystal Caverns,* her fingers paused by the year the war started.

Three-hundred and thirty-seven.

It was significant. It couldn't possibly be chance. Aldrik's hate for crystals, for Egmun, the guilt he shouldered . . . *But, how?*

"Excuse me?" a patron called, drawing Vhalla's attention back to her duties.

Her days progressed much the same, split between bookkeeping, research, and language study with Gianna at night. Two more weeks slipped through her fingers before Vhalla finally cracked the spine of *The Knights' Code*, and even then it was rough reading.

"*Tokshi.*" Gianna rested her hands on the desk.

Vhalla straightened to attention. Her back hurt from being hunched over and her fingers ached from the furious notes she was taking.

"Dinner is ready. Close up shop." Gianna's tone was enough to indicate that there was more to say without her needing to hover as Vhalla pulled the shutters. "Why do you read so furiously?"

"I like reading." Vhalla smiled. *It wasn't entirely a lie.*

"You do," Gianna agreed. "But you do not like this book." She tapped *The Knights' Code* and put it back on its shelf.

Vhalla glared at the tome, as though the bound parchment had somehow betrayed her and told Gianna of Vhalla's real intent in reading it.

"Why do you read something you don't enjoy? Why *this*?"

"Do you know about the Knights of Jadar?" Vhalla asked.

Gianna visibly tensed. "Why would you ask that?"

The woman's eyes darted to the open door, and Vhalla eased it closed, granting her host the illusion of privacy. "I want to know."

"That is not something you, of all people, want to look for." Gianna knew who Vhalla was. Vhalla had never lied to the kind woman who was putting her up, and she'd told the broad strokes of her own history over the countless dinners they'd shared together. Perhaps because Gianna knew exactly who Vhalla was, the woman respected the Windwalker's privacy and wish to remain anonymous, preferring the Western term for student—*tokshi*—over Vhalla's actual name.

"Why?" Vhalla knew why, but she wanted to hear Gianna's reasons.

Gianna sighed.

"Tell me."

"Dinner is ready." The shop owner turned, starting for the stairs. "Come and eat. The wind will carry you away if you don't put food in your stomach once in a while."

Vhalla obliged mutely. She allowed the silence to stew after they both had settled at the table and started into the rice hash Gianna had made.

"I will tell you one story," Gianna said finally. "And then you must put that book aside."

"I can't promise you that."

"Try?"

"It depends on what the story is." Vhalla played a game of mock carcivi with her hash.

"You are something else." The woman chuckled and shook her head. "You could just lie to appease me."

"I've had enough lies for a lifetime." Vhalla's eyes drifted upward.

Gianna paused, searching Vhalla's face. She took a deep breath before beginning. "The Knights of Jadar have been around for over one-hundred and fifty years, and they weren't always the hushed organization they are now, zealots clinging to the old ways. The stories tell of a different time. A time not so long ago, when they would ride in the streets and women would reach for them, men would cry their names."

Vhalla leaned forward in her chair. The way Gianna told her story had a certain reverence, a nostalgia for something that Vhalla had no real connection with. Gianna couldn't have been more than a young child at the start of the war in the West and the fall of the Knights.

"They were the best of the best. They protected the weak and fought for Mhashan, defending our way of life. To be counted among their ranks was the highest honor."

Vhalla bit her tongue on the fact that the Knights had put countless Windwalkers to death long before, during the Burning Times, at the will of the king who had founded them.

"But when the last King of Mhashan was slain, when the Ci'Dan family bent the knee before the Emperor, and when Princess Fiera married into his family . . . The Knights were spurned. They tried to raise a rebellion. The princess and Lord Ophain did their best to discourage such, but they were fighting a losing battle."

"Why?" Vhalla's food was forgotten.

"The Knights claimed to have the Sword of Jadar." Vhalla shook her head, indicating she didn't know what the woman was speaking of. "King Jadar was a great Firebearer, but only passed his magic to one of his sons."

"Magic isn't in the blood; it can't be passed on." A fact Vhalla knew all too well from being born from two Commons.

"No . . ." Gianna agreed half-heartedly. "That's true, but . . . There's something special about the magic that lives in families. Certainly, sorcerers are born to Commons, but there's usually magic somewhere in the family tree. It's not impossible, but it is less common to find it without.

"Either way, King Jadar was said to have crafted a sword that harnessed his power and gave it to one of his sons. That son became the leader of the Knights of Jadar, and as long as he wielded the sword he was rumored to be undefeatable."

"So what happened to the sword?" Vhalla asked.

"Who knows?" Gianna shrugged. "I doubt it was even real to begin with. King Jadar is quite the legend in his own right."

Vhalla pursed her lips, a physical reminder to keep silent. Gianna was as proud as most Westerners she'd ever met. While she was fairly forward-thinking, enough so to not harbor any hate toward Vhalla as a Windwalker, Vhalla didn't want to push the woman's kindness by speaking ill of the infamous Western king.

"What happened to the Knight's rebellion?" Vhalla asked.

"I assume they'd grown tired of it." Gianna clearly had not given it much thought. "After the death of our princess, no one in the West thought much about anything for a while."

Gianna didn't speak of the Knights again after that, and Vhalla didn't ask. She did, however, return the next morning to *The Knights' Code*, scouring for any mention of a sword, of the will of Jadar, *anything*. Two days of tedious translations yielded nothing other than rankling her fraying nerves.

"Gianna," Vhalla called and stood. The woman appeared from upstairs. "We're running low on ink. I'm going to buy more."

"I'll give you coin."

"No need." Vhalla shook her head, grabbing her bag off a peg from behind the desk.

"You could at least let me pay you." Gianna placed her hands on her hips. "You've worked for weeks."

"I have gold." Vhalla patted her bag. "And I used all the ink for personal reasons."

"Can't argue with either," Gianna said lightly.

Vhalla slipped out of the store and onto the dusty street, adjusting her hood to hide her Eastern brown hair. It was average by many Eastern standards, but practically golden compared to the black hair of Westerners. The Crossroads held all peoples, sizes, and shapes. But the past few times Vhalla had been to the market she was beginning to notice more soldiers returning home from the warfront, and the last thing she wanted to be was recognized.

Sidestepping around carts and tiptoeing over bile from the prior night's revelries, Vhalla made her way to the main markets. Pennons fluttered overhead, and Vhalla made it a point to ignore them. For every two of the West, there was one of the Empire. And for every two of the Empire, there was one black pennon bearing a silver wing—a silver wing that matched the one on the watch around her neck, a silver wing that had somehow become synonymous with the Windwalker.

Stories traveled as fast as the wind, and Vhalla had listened in on conversation after conversation about the Windwalker. A woman given shape on the Night of Fire and Wind, partly her own air, partly flames of the crown prince. A woman who brought Shaldan to its knees and made fire rain from the sky during the North's last stand.

It was fascinating to Vhalla. She had learned long ago that rumors and reputation could be crafted as easily as armor. But underneath it all, she was still very mortal. A mortal who bled if she was cut too deep, a mortal afflicted with life's great curse: death.

"Are you closing shop?" Vhalla arrived at her preferred sundries store, only to find the owner locking the door.

"For the day." The man nodded, recognizing one of his common patrons.

"May I get ink?"

"I'm afraid it's already late—"

"Two silver for it," Vhalla interjected.

The man's keys paused in the lock before turning in the opposite direction. "Be quick about it."

That wasn't hard. Vhalla knew exactly where his writing supplies were stored and raided them liberally. Within a minute, her bag was two ink blocks heavier and two silver coins lighter.

"Why are you closing so early?" Vhalla hovered, curiosity getting the better of her.

"You haven't heard?"

Vhalla shook her head.

"Lord Ci'Dan is coming ahead of the Imperial army. He'll be holding audiences open to the public." The man started toward the center of the Crossroads, and Vhalla fell into step alongside him. He eyed her up and down, taking an extra step ahead. "But nobles will be given priority, then land owners, then merchants, then Westerners . . ." The man accounted for her brown eyes. "I doubt there will be time for others."

Vhalla's lips twitched with the makings of a smirk. "Don't worry, I wouldn't cut your place or try to go against convention."

She strolled with the merchant. Soon, they walked alongside half the Crossroads as the masses poured into the sunlight at the center of the world. Vhalla adjusted her scarf once more and found a perch atop one of the pedestals bearing a lamppost. She waited with the rest of the crowd, and then watched as a group of nobles trotted in to all the cries and the pomp and circumstance the Crossroads could muster.

Atop the largest Warstrider was a man with short-cut black hair, greying at the ears, and a closely cropped beard along his chin. He was an older image of a royal she knew well; the family resemblance between him and Aldrik was uncanny. Vhalla gripped the lamppost tighter, the only one not screaming the Ci'Dan name.

Aldrik had told her to seek out his uncle if he died in the North because he trusted the man to see to her well-being. Aldrik had told her she would be safer with his uncle than anyone else because Lord Ophain knew the movements of the Knights of Jadar. Her chest ached at the memory, but Vhalla ignored the pain. She needed to know if it was true.

She needed answers.

CHAPTER 2

THE LINE FOR hopefuls seeking an audience with Lord Ophain was long, wrapping around the center of the Crossroads and snaking down the main market and out of sight. Vhalla wondered how many people Lord Ophain could possibly see in one day. She watched the steady flow of people entering and leaving the lavish hotel, which had a front dominated by three large, circular windows.

It reminded her of the day her father had brought her to the palace seeking to trade his place in the Palace Guard following the War of the Crystal Caverns for an apprenticeship for his daughter. That day, Vhalla had felt much the same as the commoners' faces appeared now as they anticipated meeting the Lord of the West: excited, hopeful, and enthralled with avid anticipation. She slid down the lamppost to sit on the base, kicking it lightly with her heels.

She was older now, more versed in the world. Lord Ophain's advisors were hard at work prepping every person. By the time people were brought before Lord Ophain, he'd already been told what his council thought the best decision was and echoed it after the person had their moment to speak. Leadership, Vhalla had learned, was about illusions. The people were happy because they felt their voice was heard by their lord, but their fate was decided before they even stepped foot in the same room as he.

She'd come with the mission of asking questions, but now Vhalla wasn't sure how she'd go about it. Certainly, she could just stroll in, and he'd make time for her. She was Vhalla Yarl, Duchess in the West, Lady of the Southern Court, Hero of the North, and the Windwalker. *Her name had become such an unnecessary mouthful.*

But doing so would draw attention to herself. It would shed the thin veil of anonymity that she'd attempted to don by coming West rather than the East or South. Beyond that, her questions weren't going to have short answers, which would mean she'd take time from all the excited Westerners who were patiently waiting their turn.

The sun drifted lazily through the sky and finally forced Vhalla off her perch, but it wasn't enough to deter the determined people out of their place in line. Vhalla found a shaded nook and adjusted her satchel. It made a soft clinking sound as she sat. Vhalla scowled at the gold as she pulled her notebook from the bag.

She had discovered that by raising her to ladyship, Aldrik had gifted her an incomprehensible quantity of wealth. They didn't even bother counting how much gold she took out from the Imperial Bank; she had enough for ten lifetimes. Her fingers ghosted over the black notebook she'd been using to keep her records of Aldrik's memories and histories.

What was she doing?

The question crept upon her regularly. She had severed ties with everything and everyone that had brought her to the North. She would always hold the friends she had made along the way dear to her heart, but she had come into so much coin that she could go back East and rebuild her family's home, make sure they had enough hands to help her father and his aging joints with the harvest every year, with still enough left over to never worry about drought or blight. She had enough to buy a ship and sail away. She had the option to go anywhere and do anything she wanted now. *She didn't have to return South.*

Vhalla stood.

The one place she wanted to go was to the place she could no longer be. It was a place surrounded by lies and treachery. It was a place so warm that even the heat of the Waste's sun would seem cold in comparison.

The Crossroads had become quiet with the afternoon heat. Fewer people were being taken inside and fewer new folk were willing to line up in the sun to wait.

Aware of this, a well-dressed nobleman walked to the center of the square before the hotel, tapping a cane on the ground for attention. "The Lord Ophain has taken to rest out the midday heat. Audiences will resume in the evening." The man tapped his cane again over the disapproving mumbling that ripped through the crowd. "Do not hold the line, we will form a new system upon your return."

Vhalla watched as the people begrudgingly gave up their coveted spots. She wondered how many would come back and how they would be re-sorted. Many seemed discouraged enough that she'd bet they wouldn't return. She overheard speculation that the Lord of the West was likely done for the day.

Realizing this was her opportunity, she strolled over to the hotel, easing past the few guards and excusing herself up the steps. No one questioned her in the small shuffle of the last nobles leaving. A group went out, and Vhalla slipped in.

It only took a moment to figure out which room the lord was in. His voice made the walls hum with its velvety tones.

"Excuse me." Hotel staff stopped her. "What do you think you're doing?"

"I am here for an audience with Lord Ophain," Vhalla stated imperiously, like a noble would. It was a mantle that didn't quite fit.

"He's in the middle of a conversation right now. You should

come back later with everyone else." The woman looked Vhalla up and down.

"He'll want to talk to me. I suspect I outrank the man he's talking with now."

"Do you?" She was sceptical. But not so sceptical to ignore the fact that if Vhalla's words were true, she'd need to defer to the higher ranked guest. "What is your title?"

"Duchess of the West," Vhalla replied, using the title Lord Ophain had placed upon her.

The woman paused a moment, trying to process why a non-Westerner would have such a title. She squinted and leaned slightly to get a better look at Vhalla's face under her hood. The woman's eyes went wide in surprise. "You must be . . . You're—"

"Let's not say any more." Vhalla held up a hand with a smile. "I would very much like an audience."

"Of course, of course!" The woman ran off.

Vhalla adjusted her scarf carefully. She liked it when people had to bend over to see her eyes; it meant she knew when she was being identified—one perk of being shorter than most people. Her hands paused on the scarf as a major was led out of the room. Vhalla's jaw went taut, and howling wind filled her ears.

Major Schnurr was most known for his mustache. But Vhalla knew him for other reasons; he'd made a sport of undermining her and being her appointed executioner if Aldrik hadn't bought her freedom with his hand in marriage to the Northern princess. The major turned, and Vhalla pursed her lips together. She watched his eyes widen and his lips curl into a snarl.

On his arm, he sported a band of Western crimson, something many soldiers did to show their pride to their homeland. However, printed upon it was the sun phoenix of the West with a sword clutched in its talons. The symbol was an adjustment on the Western Standard and was notably favored by the Knights of Jadar.

It was a bold display, and Vhalla fearlessly scowled, radiating her disapproval. The Knight was unbothered. If anything, he was amused. *Mother*, she had suspected Schnurr was the rat in the council at the warfront; she should've found a way to kill him in the North. *Now he could be a problem.*

"Enter," a deep voice reverberated.

Vhalla turned pointedly on her heel and strode toward a side room to meet the Lord of the West.

Paper screens had been pulled open to a small inner garden that Vhalla had not known existed during her previous visits to this particular hotel. Riding the wind, the scent of roses filled the room. Vhalla nearly lost her step as it assaulted her senses. Her chest ached, and she suddenly struggled to breathe. The Western crimson flowers tangled and grew, oblivious to the power they could command over her.

Aldrik. Her heart ached.

A man's silhouette contrasted against the brightness of the garden. Lord Ophain wore a sleeveless jerkin atop linen pants that were not unlike hers in cut. However, his were crafted of far finer fabrics. Dyed and embroidered, laden with beads and gems in intricate and bright patterns that reminded Vhalla of the way the sun could hit a pool of water lilies.

Lord Ophain turned, and the air became thick with the question his eyes asked. He had supplied the magical shackles that had been used on Vhalla in the North. It seemed irrelevant whether or not he knew that they had been placed upon her wrists. The Lord of the West was clearly unsure how to meet the Windwalker before him.

"*Fiarum evantes,*" Vhalla enunciated the Western greeting delicately. She held a firm gaze, but her words were soft enough to convey her intent.

"*Kotun un nox.*" The lord's shoulders relaxed, and his lips turned upward into a small smile. "It is good to see you again, Lady Yarl."

"I can honestly say the same, Lord Ci'Dan." Her mouth eased into a smile of its own, remembering with bittersweet fondness the last time she had seen the man. "And Vhalla is fine."

"Then I must insist upon the same, just Ophain." As if sensing her instinct to object, the lord continued, rendering the matter no longer up for discussion, "What a sight you are. You wear the clothes of my people, speak our tongue with adept pronunciation." He appraised her thoughtfully. "And you are adorned in the mark of my nephew, despite what I hear of his engagement to a Northern bride."

"I'd like to speak with you." Vhalla tried to remain focused despite her hand seeking out the watch instinctually at its mention. *It must have ended up above her scarf while she was playing with it as she waited.*

"I surmised as much." The lord nodded.

The door opened, and a servant hurriedly delivered a tray of food and the black tea Westerners preferred, served over ice.

Vhalla took the time to compose herself, swearing she was not going to be lost in the intense familiarity of the lord's endlessly black eyes. "I suppose I should apologize for not arranging time with you in advance."

"You are one who is *always* welcome in my presence." The lord gave her a tired smile that spoke volumes as he motioned at one of the chairs positioned around the table where the food and drink sat.

Taking the offered seat, Vhalla pulled the scarf off her head and became distracted once more with the roses.

"They weren't always so popular." Lord Ophain followed her attention out to the garden. "My sister loved them, and she became known for it. Their color, combined with the princess's favor, made them synonymous with Mhashan."

"Princess Fiera?" Vhalla asked, making the easy assumption that he wasn't talking about his two living sisters.

He hummed in affirmation. "Her garden in Norin is one of the most beautiful in the world."

"It's why Aldrik has a rose garden, isn't it?" Vhalla mused softly.

"It is." She hadn't been expecting an answer, but Lord Ophain gave her one, and then some. "The Emperor built it for his wife as a welcome present for when she moved to the South, though she never got to see it."

Vhalla turned her attention inside, meeting the lord's gaze. "I have some questions for you."

"And I have questions for you, as well." Lord Ophain helped himself to some of the tea sweating heavily in the midday heat.

She shifted in her seat. It hadn't occurred to her that he might be curious also. The military host had yet to return from the warfront, and whatever information he possessed must be relegated to delayed letters and reports from soldiers returning home. None of them would know what she knew.

"I'd like to go first," she said hastily. If the lord asked her a question she didn't want to answer, Vhalla wanted to leave this visit with at least getting one inquiry answered.

"I have no intent to rush this meeting." Ophain motioned for her to continue.

Vhalla chewed on her bottom lip, thinking about the most elegant approach to her question. She knew Aldrik had learned from Lord Ophain, which meant the man was well versed in avoiding giving answers he didn't want to give. And, unlike Aldrik, she couldn't just demand he tell her the full truth of everything she wanted to know.

"Is the Sword of Jadar real?" Vhalla finally decided on. It was the one thing she couldn't find conclusive evidence of in any manuscript. And, if the legends were to be believed, there would be no way he could answer her without mention of the Knights.

Lord Ophain leaned back in his chair, an appreciative grin teasing at the corners of his mouth. "You want to know about the Knights."

It wasn't phrased as a question, and Vhalla did not hide her intentions; she gave a definitive nod. "And the sword."

"What makes you think I know about them?"

"Aldrik told me you would." Their words were like a dance of rapiers. Sharp, pointed, elegant, and prepared to cut to bone.

"What happened between you and my nephew?"

Vhalla knew the question would come, but she couldn't keep in the heavy sigh. "Tell me first: is the sword real?"

"It is," the lord finally relented.

Her world stilled. That was an answer she hadn't been expecting. "Do the Knights have it?"

"Perhaps," Lord Ophain answered vaguely and continued before she could persist, "You and Aldrik?"

Reaching forward, she grabbed for the dark Western tea that she had little taste for and let its bitterness wash away the harshness of the memories of Aldrik. She wished it had something a bit stronger mixed in.

"He traded his freedom for mine," she whispered. "He was a reckless fool, and I was a girl pulled along by puppet strings. The fire burned too hot, and we didn't notice until it consumed everything." Vhalla passed the ice-cold glass between her hands.

"I have worried deeply for him," Lord Ophain began. "The sparse letters I received gave me concern for his mental state. My granddaughter's reports offered little hope, for a time."

"For a time?" Vhalla wasn't surprised to learn Elecia and Ophain had been in correspondence. She assumed it meant that Elecia was still well, and Vhalla was genuinely relieved to hear it.

"I hear he gave up the bottle. Or, rather, he is still working on such." Lord Ophain took a sip from his own glass, allowing that information to sink in. "Once he got through the weeks of shakes, sweats, and general sickness, he has been more active in leading his men. He is handling things with a more tempered grace."

Vhalla laughed bitterly. "So ending us was the best thing that could've happened to him."

"Loving you is." Lord Ophain stilled her with three words. He had used present tense. *Is, not was.*

"You said the Knights have the sword?" Vhalla navigated the conversation back to safer waters.

"I said 'perhaps,'" the lord insisted.

She frowned. "How is something 'perhaps' owned?"

"It is not something you should worry about." His expression mirrored hers.

"Ophain—"

"I concern myself with keeping madmen like the Knights in check so my subjects and honored guests of the West, like you, do not need to worry."

"I do not know what misplaced protection you think keeping me in the dark will provide, but you are ill-advised, my lord." Vhalla placed her drink on the table delicately, sitting straighter. She elongated her words carefully, as a noble would. "The Knights have concerned themselves with me, and I do not foresee any future in which they will leave me be. Trying to keep the truth from me is a disservice."

"You will pursue this no matter what I say?"

"I will," Vhalla affirmed.

The lord sighed heavily, stroking the stubble along his chin. "Very well. The sword was not created by King Jadar, as the legends say. The King was merely the one to find it."

Vhalla subconsciously moved to the edge of her seat as Lord Ophain spoke.

"He became so obsessed with its power that he wanted to do whatever was needed to make more weapons like it, to equip an army with them, to use them to conquer the world. That pursuit drove him mad.

"The son who succeeded him entrusted his brother with hiding the sword for good, after it had driven their father to madness. But his brother kept it secretly for the Knights of Jadar." Lord Ophain paused, clearly choosing his words carefully. "It remained in the care of the Ci'Dan family through the Knights of Jadar until the War in the West ended—and it went missing."

"So the Knights could have it?" Vhalla knew there was something he wasn't telling her.

"Perhaps, but I strongly doubt it," he answered cryptically. "It is far more likely to have been lost to time."

"How can you be certain?"

"If it was in anyone's hands, it would have long since tainted them by now, so I have little cause to worry," Ophain proclaimed definitively.

Her eyes widened in shock. "It was a crystal weapon," she breathed. It made gruesome sense. Crystal taint combined with the allure of power could drive a man to genocide.

"You know of the weapons then?" Lord Ophain regarded her cautiously.

Vhalla nodded, suddenly hesitant of the glint in the Western man's eyes. It wasn't dangerous, but deeply cautious and heavy with fear.

"Does Aldrik know you are aware?" he asked.

"He wouldn't believe me if I told him." A seed of worry for where her pursuits may lead her burrowed under her skin.

Lord Ophain stood and folded his hands at the small of his back—*a distinctly Aldrik-like motion*. He walked over to the open paper screens and surveyed the garden. She let the silence hang until he spoke again.

"I must agree, there is no benefit to dredging up the shadows of my nephew's past. After all, there are no crystal weapons left to be concerned about."

Vhalla thought a long moment about her next words. "Would the Knights seek the weapons if they believed them to exist?"

"Relentlessly." The lord turned. "Just as they seek you now in the pursuit of crafting a greater power with your sorcery."

"Major Schnurr—"

"Came to me asking for you." Lord Ophain frowned. "The world is asking where you are."

"They don't need to know."

"They will find out. The Knights are becoming bolder, as I'm certain you saw." The lord crossed back to her, looking at her as though she was a child and he was the concerned parent. "The army will be at the Crossroads within the next few days. When this happens, there will be a celebration in my nephew's honor. All the Western nobles will be there, and Aldrik will have no option but to be in attendance."

Vhalla's heart began to race.

"You must be present," he demanded. "Speak with Aldrik. He will use his title to give you protection no one else can. Return South with him and—"

"No!" She jumped to her feet. Despite being a head shorter, she somehow managed to look down at the lord. "I do not need his protection. I can protect myself."

"You are speaking folly."

"No more than you are," she said sharply. The lord was visibly taken aback, clearly unused to such boldness. "His protection comes with a price I am not willing to pay." *Her heart had nothing left to give him.*

"Vhalla, I am only trying to help you." Ophain's features were overcome with sorrow. "You *and* him."

"There is no help for us." Vhalla gave a small bow. "Thank you for your time today, and for your answers."

"Wait."

She halted stiffly.

Lord Ophain crossed the room to where she stood before the door. Slowly, he pulled at the scarf around her neck, carefully folding it once more around her head. The nearly familial touch smoothed some of the roughness in her heart.

"Keep yourself hidden, at least. Be careful and, by the Mother, consider what you are doing."

Vhalla nodded.

"And if you are ever in need, come to Norin. My protection has no price. Though I can only do so much against the Knights; they are quite the nuisance, even for me."

Her face cracked, and she folded her bitterness into a smile. His protection had the same price as Aldrik's. To accept it would mean to accept his family. It would invite Aldrik into her world. It would inevitably gravitate her into his orbit again, and they would both collapse in on each other like dying stars. She wasn't ready for it.

"Thank you," she said, and left.

Vhalla kept her head down on the way back to the bookstore, her satchel heavy. She fingered Aldrik's watch around her neck, feeling its warmth against her palm. On the way, she stopped to buy new clothes. She'd need to get rid of the ones she was wearing. Major Schnurr had seen her in them, and Vhalla had no doubt he had imprinted them on his memory.

For the hundredth time in a few short weeks, Vhalla thought about returning home. Her feet dragged up the stairs of the shop, Gianna making no motion to switch places on shop duty with the distracted woman. *But if she returned East, they would only hunt here there, too.*

As long as she was a Windwalker, as long as people knew she could be used for their gains, she'd never be free. Vhalla knelt at her bedside, shifting through a pile of clothing packed underneath. Her fingers fell on a solid bundle of rough cotton.

Retrieving it, she stared at the familiar parcel. Vhalla remembered when Daniel had cut off his shirt to help her hide it. Distance had helped her sort a little through her heart, and Vhalla didn't like the woman she saw when she replayed her interactions with the swordsman. She didn't like her reliance on him or how she had abused the fact that he would be there for her without question.

But, clarity in the present would not remedy the chaos of the past. And, the one thing that remained true at the end of it all was that he was someone whom she valued in her life. *He'd understood when she'd left.* The final look on his face had told her as much. And, if she was lucky, whenever she met the swordsman again, he would be someone she'd consider her friend without the pressures of war and loss pushing on them both in odd directions.

Reverently, she unfolded the cloth, moving it aside. The axe was carved from a single stone, glittering like the cosmos underwater in the dim light of the setting sun. Vhalla now knew it may be the last of the legendary and mysterious crystal weapons—if the Knights didn't already have one in their possession. She had been told it had the power to sever a soul.

Vhalla held it up, feeling the weight of it. A deep power coursed through her, seeping into her bones. She didn't need it to cut through souls. She only needed it to cut through the shadows that threatened to swallow her whole. To cut down those who would use her. To hack away at the oppressive darkness that continued to try to smother her so she could defend a new dawn.

CHAPTER 3

THE IDEA OF finding a single Southerner in the Crossroads was complete and utter idiocy. Still, Vhalla waded through the sea of people flooding the streets and markets, foolishly hopeful. She saw soldiers she felt like she should know. Men and women who still donned the dark scalemail of the Black Legion. But the messy-haired man that she sought eluded her.

Cautiously, she ventured back to the center of the Crossroads. She'd not been there in the three days since speaking to Lord Ophain, and now it seemed all the riskier knowing the royal family was present. Yet Vhalla lingered, watching the other hotels and inns around the center of the world. Men and women came and went, but she didn't see Fritz.

Then again, even if she found her friend,

she wasn't sure what she would say to him. She wasn't ready to return South yet. She still had more to learn about the Knights, and she had to ensure they knew she wasn't easy prey to hunt—to dissuade them from their foolish mission of furthering the cause of the long dead King Jadar. Truthfully, she didn't want to say anything to him, she just wanted to listen to Fritz talk. She wanted to hear her friend's voice.

Vhalla adjusted the hood on her newly acquired cape. The plain garment was the second most important thing she'd purchased recently. Strapped tightly around her waist and buckled around her thigh, just above her knee, was a specially made axe holster. Vhalla hadn't brought the actual crystal weapon to a craftsman to measure, of course; she'd purchased an axe of similar size and shape. As such, the fit wasn't perfect, but it kept the weapon concealed and on her person at all times.

There wasn't any other safe place for it, she reasoned. The longer it stayed with her, the more Vhalla wondered how she could've ever been foolish enough to think of leaving it unattended for weeks, hidden beneath her bed.

Finally giving up her hunt, Vhalla wandered back in the direction of Gianna's bookstore. The sun was low in the sky by the time she arrived, and the shopkeeper was already closing up. Vhalla said nothing and started for the stairs.

"You haven't been the same since the day you went off for ink."

"A lot on my mind." Vhalla paused, halfway up the stairs.

"That much is apparent." Gianna appraised her helper thoughtfully. Something in the Western woman's gaze reminded Vhalla of another set of eyes; a dark pair that also missed nothing, a pair she would never be able to look into again for as long as she lived. "You haven't been working as much on learning the Western language. It's going to go stale if you don't practice."

"It's only been three days," Vhalla pointed out.

"For you, three days away from books means something is terribly wrong." The woman gave Vhalla a sweet smile. "Come, we'll go somewhere you'll be forced to practice."

Vhalla fell into step alongside Gianna as they walked away from the now locked and dim store. She hadn't put up much of a fight and didn't bother questioning where they were going. Gianna hadn't ever done anything to slight or harm her. In fact, when Vhalla had arrived in Gianna's shop on a whim weeks ago, the Westerner hadn't kicked the younger woman out after Vhalla had huddled up in the corner for hours, reading as much as she could.

Vhalla had slept on the street that night, then returned to Gianna's the next morning. Gianna had shared her lunch and let the odd patron stay the day again, despite Vhalla not actually buying anything. By the fourth morning, Gianna had figured out her latest 'customer' had nowhere else to be and put Vhalla up in the small attic in exchange for an extra pair of hands in the shop.

It'd taken three weeks for Vhalla to realize that Gianna had no need of a shop assistant. Now, it'd taken over six weeks for her to say anything about it.

"Thank you," Vhalla blurted suddenly.

"For what?" Gianna's question reminded Vhalla that her companion could not actually read her mind.

"For taking me in."

"Hon, you know that is nothing to thank me for." Gianna laughed. "My girl is gone and grown and married and raising kids of her own in Norin. It's good to have company in the house again."

The statement made Vhalla think of her own father, which only brought a fresh wave of shame over having yet to return to the East. No matter how much gold she sent, it wouldn't make up for her absence. But that absence had lingered on so long that now Vhalla had no idea how to break it.

Gianna led them to a restaurant that specialized in Western foods. Proud of its authenticity, the entire staff and most of the patrons spoke exclusively the language of old Mhashan. Vhalla's tongue curled and rolled off the words, doing her best to pronounce them as carefully as Gianna had taught her.

Their conversation fluctuated between Southern Common and the old tongue. Vhalla was relieved by the time food arrived, using the excuse to busy her mouth as an opportunity to listen to Gianna's description of the great castle of Norin rather than speak.

". . . though, I suppose it's nothing like what you're accustomed to."

"Me?" Vhalla had explained her humble beginnings to Gianna; that, despite her current status and wealth, she wasn't accustomed to luxury.

"With having grown up in the Southern Palace."

"Ah," Vhalla uttered a noise of comprehension.

"When will you be returning?"

Food paused on Vhalla's spoon halfway between her mouth and the bowl. That was the one thing Gianna could ask that Vhalla wanted to avoid discussing at all costs. "I don't know."

"Don't you miss it?"

"I . . ." Vhalla wanted to object. She wanted to say she didn't miss the palace and its winding passages. She didn't long for the chill and crisp mountain air, more refreshing than the coldest water she'd ever drank, even if it did set into her bones too quickly and made her shiver. She wanted to claim she didn't want to run through the Imperial Library again like a rebel child, running her fingers gleefully along the spines of the books.

But it would all be a lie.

"I do," Vhalla confessed.

"But there's something keeping you from returning." Gianna's dark eyes regarded Vhalla thoughtfully.

"There is." Vhalla sighed, frustrated. It'd been so long since she'd talked with anyone openly about the heaviness in her heart; Vhalla wasn't sure if she could remember how. But everyone else in Vhalla's life had a reason to be kept at arm's length. Gianna, however, was a neutral third party. "There is a man."

Gianna burst out laughing, and she only laughed harder at Vhalla's scowl. She quickly reduced her voice to a wheeze. "Vhalla Yarl, the Windwalker, the champion of the North, terrified about seeing a *man*?"

Vhalla's eyes darted around for any who may have heard the name said aloud. Spying no one, she rolled her eyes. Just saying the name of the man would've explained the cause of her concern.

"We were *involved*," Vhalla started delicately. "Things became complicated. His family wanted him to be with someone else, and now he's betrothed."

"I take it he's a noble?" Gianna questioned.

Vhalla gave a gesture of affirmation. It was an easy assumption to make since only nobles considered arranged marriages. It was a trend that was going out of style across the continent.

"And he still loves you?"

The question stilled her. As much as Vhalla didn't want to think about it, she had to ask: *was that the truth?* Her eyes didn't want to see it, her mind wanted to ignore it, but her heart knew it with every certain thrum.

"I think so," Vhalla sighed softly.

"And you clearly still have feelings for him." Gianna leaned against the tall back of the booth they sat in. "I don't think you should be so worried."

"But—"

"Listen," Gianna demanded, and Vhalla obliged. "Whatever bride his family strapped him with cannot be better than the woman sitting before me. If I were you, I would gamble on going back. You may discover that they are more amenable to changing their minds when the Hero of the North stands before them."

"I doubt it." Vhalla thought of the Emperor, which immediately soured her appetite. She couldn't settle with just normal people loathing her existence. She had to have some of the most powerful leaders in the world craving her demise.

"Then show them what they're missing," Gianna suggested with a shrug.

"What?"

The Western woman laughed at Vhalla's startled expression. "Show his family what they lost in you. Spread your wings, *tokshi*, and fly. Soar above them, make their eyes tear as they stare into the sun to watch you reach new heights."

The idea turned itself over in Vhalla's head, settling like wet cement curing into a firm foundation. *Show them*, she thought, *show them what they are missing*. The watch felt hot against her chest, and the axe on her thigh seemed to thrum with power.

Vhalla opened her mouth to speak, but words failed her.

Her eyes drifted over to the entry. A man with a bushy mustache stood in the doorframe. The notable facial feature sat atop a triumphant sneer.

Vhalla glanced around frantically. She had been found and there was only one exit. Schnurr may not attack with all the witnesses currently enjoying their dinners. But all he had to do was wait, wait for his prey to finally leave and follow her like a hunter on a blood trail.

"Gianna," Vhalla whispered, thinking frantically. "Listen to me."

"Wha—"

"*Don't turn around*," Vhalla hissed, trying to keep her voice level. "You're going to get up, and you're going to go and not look back. You're going to pretend like this was a casual meeting, we happened upon each other—you don't really know me or who I am.

"Go back to your shop and burn everything of mine. But, most importantly, find my black ledger and destroy it, burn it, make it so that no one can ever read its words." Her heart was racing. "By the Mother, do not read its contents, do not put those words anywhere inside your head."

"*Tokshi*, you're not making any sense." Vhalla's sudden intensity and fear wavered Gianna's usually strong voice.

"Go now. Go now and pretend you never knew me," Vhalla pleaded. Gianna's kindness would not be rewarded with the same ill fate that befell those foolish enough to befriend the Windwalker. "This was all a dream. If anyone asks, deny it all."

Gianna opened her mouth to protest once more.

"Gianna, *now*," Vhalla snapped.

The woman did as she was ordered. Vhalla could commend her for only looking slightly rattled as she stood and strolled out the door past Major Schnurr. The major gave Gianna a long stare before turning his attention back to Vhalla.

Vhalla stood, slowly raising her hood. She made for the door, looking past Major Schnurr the entire time. The man half-stepped in her way, forcing Vhalla to pause. From the corner of her eye she saw a group of men standing from a table, presumably men Schnurr had been coming to meet.

"You know what happens now, don't you?" he purred.

"You and your friends eat a nice meal and pretend you never saw me. You want bellies to fill again tomorrow?" Vhalla threatened.

The major laughed ominously as Vhalla strolled into the night.

She didn't know where to go. She breathed a sigh of relief when she didn't see Gianna anywhere. If the Knights were going to pursue the other woman, it seemed they'd missed their chance. Vhalla hoped that Gianna would heed her warning and do her best to forget the time she'd spent with the Windwalker—for their relationship had just come to an abrupt end.

The Knights were already at Vhalla's back. Men who wanted to take and use her for a madman's dream. Men to whom she needed to send a clear message, a message that they could not force her into a corner.

Vhalla started forward and intentionally walked down the first mostly-empty alley she found. The crowded street was slowly reduced to questionable curiosity shops, gambling parlors, and sellers of flesh. Clenching her fists, she listened carefully to the four sets of footsteps behind her as they trod lightly over the packed earth. They didn't make any motion toward her, however. Too many eyes were still on them and the alley was too narrow for movement.

A dilapidated square was straight ahead of her. The narrow passage between buildings would open up into enough room to move—to fight. Vhalla fingered the weapon on her thigh, popping open fasteners.

She had a choice to make. *Did she fight them with the axe or rely solely on her magic?* If she brought out the axe, they would know it was real. It would be a waving banner that at least one crystal weapon still existed. She should be able to take them on with her magic alone.

But she'd never used the weapon before. It was a strong temptation just to see why so many people had spilled so much blood and furthered so much hatred for it. Vhalla surveyed the area as she crossed into the small junction of alleyways. There were no onlookers as far as she could tell—so the only ones who would know about the axe would be the Knights. *Assuming any made it out alive.*

"I'll give you one chance." She shifted her feet, pulling at the ties on her cloak. "Leave and live. Stay and die. Tell this to your comrades, and we will each go on to see all the dawns of our natural lives."

The men looked at each other and laughed in amusement. "You think that will work, Windwalker?"

"I don't want to fight you." *It was the first lie she'd told in weeks.*

"Then make this even easier for us—submit willingly," Schnurr demanded. "You were destined to help us return to greatness."

"Help?" she scoffed.

"Yes; with you we will finally gain access to the Caverns."

"Never." Vhalla tensed and her fingers curled around the hilt of the axe.

The first of the men moved, sending out a tongue of flame. Vhalla was already two steps ahead. Her feet walked on air, and she moved like an otherworldly entity, flowing from one attack into the next.

The wind pulled the unlaced cloak from her shoulders. Vhalla spun, bringing the axe hard into the man's face. *He didn't have a chance.* The blade cut clean through the man's skull, as if understanding and multiplying Vhalla's murderous intent. It offered nearly no resistance, and Vhalla blinked as the man crumpled with only half a head attached to his neck.

"The axe." Major Schnurr instantly recognized the faintly glowing blade that Vhalla wielded. Where any sane person would look on in horror, the major looked as though he had just been handed the greatest gift of his life.

Something quietly snapped in her at the sight. The thin dam she'd built to hold back her utter loathing for the Knights vanished, and Vhalla didn't hesitate. She thrust out her hand to grab the nearest man's mouth. Power roared and howled from within her, the wind screaming to be unleashed. It poured forth in a tempest that was so violent it both startled and scared her.

The Knight's face exploded under her palm.

With a cry of rage, the third Knight was upon her. Vhalla ducked, narrowly dodging his blade. It sliced down along her arm; blood sprang forth, setting a faint beat to echo in her ears. It had been weeks since Vhalla had heard Aldrik's heartbeat reverberating through their Bond. It was a surge of magic and of overwhelming strength—Vhalla did nothing to hinder it.

The third Knight crumpled like a paper doll, cleaved nearly in half from shoulder to chest by the axe. Vhalla barely had more than a second to relish in the strength flowing through her veins. Adjusting her grip on the axe, she prepared herself for the satisfaction of skinning off Schnurr's face with it—only to find him gone.

The mad beat in her ears faded into confusion. *The coward had run.* She stared in shock, paling to horror, as Vhalla realized the depth of her error.

The major had seen the axe and fled with the knowledge.

A Knight now knew that the axe was real and that she possessed it. She had to find the major and kill him before he could tell anyone. Vhalla quickly sheathed the axe, fumbling with the latches as cries began to rise from the street.

Her mind whirred as Vhalla tried to think of Schnurr's next action. Schnurr wanted her for the Knights; they needed her alive, and subduing her would require more than a small group. Vhalla looked on at the corpses oozing crimson onto the dirt.

He'd need a mob.

Vhalla snatched up her cloak and donned it frantically as she ran. Men and women stumbled from the parlors, blinking in confusion. Her hands were slick with blood, her heart thrumming frantically. If she could find the major, she could stop him before he acted. Before he had time to spin the situation to serve him best.

Vhalla emerged into a dense crowd that was circled around the man she sought. "Down that alley, there!" he shouted while pointing.

Vhalla pressed herself against a wall, trying to be as inconspicuous as possible. "The Windwalker—the Empire's monster—has returned to wage war upon the West!"

The crowd hummed in confusion.

"Look down there and find your brethren lying in pools of their own blood. Faces ripped open as only she can do."

Vhalla stared at her feet, realizing blood splotched the bottom of her cloak. She couldn't kill Major Schnurr here and now—it'd confirm everything he was saying, and the longer she lingered, the more likely it was for someone to notice the panting and battle-stained woman. Vhalla began to move, heading down along the outside of the crowd.

"It's true!" a new voice cried. "Th-there's three! They're dead!"

More whispers, more nervous glances.

"Go, find her! Give her to the Knights. We're the only ones who have ever been able to tame *her kind*. Clearly Solaris cannot be trusted!"

Vhalla slipped into a narrow space between two buildings, climbing over crates and working her way away from the crowd being whipped into a frenzy. *What was she going to do now?* Her fingers ran up and down the leather sheath of the axe, as if it held the answers she sought. As if it could solve all her problems by cutting, cutting, and cutting everyone who opposed her . . .

So engulfed in her thoughts, she missed hearing the footsteps growing behind her. Two arms suddenly snatched her and a palm clamped over Vhalla's mouth. Magic was swift under her fingers until a familiar male voice hastily spoke.

"Finally found you."

CHAPTER 4

VHALLA TWISTED ON her toes, pulling herself from the man's grasp. Her heart raced. She didn't know if it would've been worse to have a Knight of Jadar or the man she faced. *If he was a Knight, she could've at least killed him and been off again.*

Her eyes absorbed the tall shape, the Western olive skin, and the long dark hair that was pulled back into a bun.

"Jax."

"You never disappoint, do you?" The man gave her a wild grin and a shake of his head. "The Windwalker disappears for weeks, and when she shows up, it's to murder Western lords. Didn't you see enough blood at the warfront?"

Vhalla scowled murderously. *How dare he?* "What do you want?"

"You don't seem happy to see me." The man cocked his head to the side. "Here I thought we were friends."

"What do you want?" she repeated, her hand twitching for the axe. He'd better not make her repeat it again. He was her friend, but her patience ran thinner with every beat of her heart.

"To help you." Jax folded his arms over his chest.

She laughed and turned. "I don't have time for you. Go back to the Guard."

"Where are you going?" Jax fell into step behind her.

"Away." Vhalla's eyes darted over her shoulder. No one was following them, but she could see frantically running silhouettes of men and women on the street.

"Did you kill those men?" Jax's tone turned serious.

"I said I don't have time for you."

To his credit, he moved fast enough to catch her off-guard. Jax's palm gripped her shoulder, turning them both, forcing her against the wall. Her back hit hard and Vhalla glared, prepared to give him a string of insults. As was the man's nature, he stilled her with a look that whispered of something deeply troubling.

"*Did you kill them?*"

"I did." There was no remorse and no hesitation.

Jax cursed under his breath. "All right, come. Baldair or Aldrik will fix this."

Vhalla twisted her arm out of his grasp the moment he reached for it. They locked in a staring contest that Vhalla broke with the first word. "I'm not going back to them."

"Vhalla—"

"No. I'm not running to the princes at every turn. If I did, the Knights will never see me as someone they need to fear."

"If you run, then those same princes will be forced to brand you a murderer." Jax leaned against the wall with a sigh. He seemed more exasperated than horrified by her insistence.

"It's not the first time I've fought for my innocence," Vhalla retorted smartly.

"You will be hunted."

"I already am."

"They will condemn you. If you do this, you may never be able to return to the life you had."

Vhalla's shoulders shook, and she freed haunted laughter into the air. "Return to the life I had? That option left me long ago." Her hand rested on the axe holster once more. "If I want a future, I'm going to have to cut it from the hands of fate myself."

Jax stilled, assessing her. Vhalla took a step backward, giving him a half-mad smile of her own. The man was indeed kind, in his own way. But she was too old to have people mothering her.

"If you insist." He adjusted his bun and straightened away from the wall. "Then I'm coming with you."

"What?" That was the last thing she expected to hear. "No, I need to do this alone—"

"Save me the speech." Jax rolled his eyes. "Guards have already been called, and they're going to be scouting the city. You have blood on your hands—literally—and I'm going to venture a good guess that you have nowhere to go. The Knights will move fast. You need a Westerner to help you navigate these alleyways."

Vhalla knew what he was offering was more than help escaping through the narrow passages between buildings. He was offering her his knowledge of Western culture. His insights into the seedy shadows, which she could lurk within and be lost. His wisdom was gained from years of time spent around princes—and the very same lords Vhalla was determined to slay.

"You will become my accomplice," she pointed out.

Jax grinned madly. "They can only strip me of my nobility once—for murdering a lord."

Vhalla blinked, blindsided.

"You didn't know?" Jax chuckled darkly. "I suppose you wouldn't; you never drank much with Western majors, never heard the fantastical stories of the golden prince's Black Dog. You didn't think you were the only monster on an Imperial leash, did you?"

Vhalla stared, frozen. She'd known it in the warfront—she'd realized they were both tied to the crown, but she'd had no idea why. Her innocence had led her to being turned into the weapon she was now, which ultimately led to the surrender of her freedom. But for Jax, his crimes were of a different sort, the sort that had put a noose around his neck where Baldair, or the Emperor himself, held the other end. He hadn't managed to free himself in however long his service had been for.

"Murder?" she asked.

"Don't ask questions if you aren't prepared for the answers," Jax advised ominously. "For now, come this way, my little monster."

Jax set off deeper into the narrow back-alleys of the Crossroads, and Vhalla followed on blind faith. She tried to process what Jax had told her and everything she'd seen. Certainly, the Western majors hadn't been fond of him. He'd insulted the West's noble traditions from the minute she'd met him. But he was friends with Elecia, the granddaughter of the Lord of the West. He was close with Aldrik, and the way he interacted with Baldair in no way resembled slave and master.

As they passed through an intersection, Vhalla heard guards running through a nearby street.

"Stay alert for the Windwalker. If the Windwalker is found, bring her to the royal hotel!"

"You're sure about this?" Jax paused to ask again.

Vhalla only nodded. She wasn't going back to the Emperor and letting him chain her, chains that he would vow to exchange for her freedom if she gave him another part of her soul. She would confront her crimes and the royal family with her innocence apparent, when none would question her—whenever that ended up being.

The buildings became danker, darker, more flimsily built and even more poorly maintained. Mostly everyone on the street wore large cowls that hid their faces so no one would witness their presence in this questionable area of town. Jax stopped and knocked three times on a small door, waited ten breaths, and then knocked again. The door slid open, and a man with beady eyes and a scruffy chin blinked up at them.

"We want to stay." Jax knelt down.

"What will you trade me?" the man asked.

Jax unclipped the golden bracer he wore over his shirt, a symbol of his membership in the Golden Guard. Beady eyes lit up, and the little man was over-eager for the token. Jax pulled it away as the man reached for it.

"You found this," Jax spoke low and slow, flames glittering around his fingers. "If anyone asks, you don't know where it came from. Understand?"

Beady eyes nodded furiously.

"We want two weeks."

"Fine, fine. Give it here." The small man snatched it from Jax's fingers and crawled out of the door.

Jax motioned and Vhalla hunched down to pass through the tiny portal, dropping onto a step, and then onto the packed-earth floor of a truly disgusting room. The small window looked more like a sewage chute that had been used by the people who lived along the streets above. The sleeping palette in the corner smelled of mold and damp. A small fire burned in the opposite corner near some hard tack and salted meat, which she wasn't sure was good enough for the rats she suspected also shared the space at night.

"What is this place?" Vhalla was breathing through her mouth, trying to get used to the stench.

"It's a hiding hole." Jax pulled off his cape, dropping it by the door. "They're used for more colorful dealings here in the Crossroads. Prostitution, gambling, human trafficking."

Vhalla's stomach churned as she stared at the stains on the bed.

"But no one will think to look for you in the underbelly of the Crossroads. It's generally something only Westerners know of, and you have to then be aware of what to look for to find one."

"Are you worried about the man selling your cuff?" There weren't many in the world like it. Whatever merchant he sold it to would certainly realize who it belonged to.

"I'm planning on it. The buyer will take it to Baldair, likely gleeful to win a favor, maybe even one which shows the Fallen Lord has returned to his old ways of noble killing." Jax reached his hands up, letting down his bun. "But then, Baldair will know I'm with you. That's the only real explanation. He'll know I'm keeping you safe."

"Keeping me safe?" Vhalla asked.

"Baldair gave the Guard an order before we left Soricium. That we were to be the ones to find you, and when we did, we were to protect you at all costs. I found you by luck, but that's why I was looking."

Vhalla sunk onto the bed, too tired and confused to care about the dank smell that assaulted her nose. "Why?"

"Because he said he considers you his sister."

Her hand shot up to her necklace, clutching the watch tightly. *What did that mean?*

"Craig went South, Erion went to Norin, Raylynn stayed with Baldair, and Daniel went East, to try to find you."

"How is Daniel?" she asked softly.

"Oh, Baldair put quite the fire under him." Jax chuckled, sitting next to her, his back against the wall. "He felt nothing but guilt for being the last person you spoke to and for letting you go. He agreed with the prince that by not insisting he accompany you for your protection that he let down his honor as a man and a noble."

Vhalla rolled her eyes. Jax laughed, which she gave him a look for.

"You aren't the type of woman who wants manly strutting nonsense." Jax reached out and took her hand, almost contrary to his statement. But the touch was purely chaste as he began to inspect the superficial cut on her arm. "And even if you did, you already know what you want, don't you?"

"What I want . . ." Vhalla whispered. She shook the thoughts of Aldrik from her head, her hand falling onto the axe sheath. Jax's eyes followed the motion, considering it for a long moment, but said nothing as Vhalla continued. "I want to make the Knights pay. I want to know what they have and make sure they know a new Burning Times will not begin with me."

"Very well. How do we do that?"

They launched into brainstorming a plan, which continued on and off over the next few days.

Jax confirmed that the princes were going to be involved in a formal gathering for the Lords and Ladies of the Western Court.

Vhalla remembered what Lord Ophain said and immediately began thinking. "All the lords and ladies will be there, right?"

"They should be." Jax nodded. "They wouldn't miss a chance to lie through powdered lips."

Vhalla snorted. "I think we should hit then."

"But who?"

"Major Schnurr," Vhalla replied without hesitation. She didn't know if he was the highest mastermind, but he had created enough problems and given enough orders that Vhalla was forced to assume he was at least someone important.

"Major Schnurr then," Jax affirmed, a little too eager. "He lives on the far southern end of town."

Waiting stretched the next two days into eternity. In their limited conversations, Jax never asked about the leather holster always buttoned and strapped tight against her leg. Vhalla thought about telling him, but she didn't want to make her friend any more nervous and lose his help. She was, however, careful not to touch or interact with him on a physical level more than necessary. Vhalla remembered Jax cautioning Aldrik once about touching her when she was under the influence of crystals. Her friend didn't seem to mind the lack of contact.

On the night of the event, the whole Crossroads glittered gleefully. Men and women paraded around in their best clothes, admiring and hoping to be admired. Though only the nobles were invited to the Imperial party at the royal hotel, it seemed everyone wanted to be involved in the revelries. From what Vhalla knew of the Crossroads, within an hour it would be nothing but drinking and dancing.

An alcoholic haze suited her goals for the evening. She wanted people to have blurred senses and relaxed postures. Vhalla had dirtied her cloak to the point that the blood was no longer recognizable and the stench it held from that dirtying process prompted people to turn up their noses and walk away as quickly as possible. No one wanted to pay attention to her or her companion.

"You smell like shit," Jax mumbled.

"I worked with what I had. And it's working well."

"Yeah, you're the Crossroads's last candidate for a Lady of the Court right now," Jax teased.

Vhalla looked around nervously, but no one seemed to register his comment.

They walked against the flow of people, as most were heading to the center of the Crossroads. Vhalla and Jax continued down the southern road to a large estate. Giant walls framed it in, a single iron portcullis its only entry. They made two laps before stopping on a side street.

"Well, it appears no one is home," Jax mused into the quiet. "Isn't it nice he sent out his servants as well?"

"He doesn't seem like the nice sort . . ." Vhalla stared at the wall that was nearly twice her height. *Was it too quiet?* "We need to get over this."

Jax pressed his fingers against the tightly fitted stones. "Difficult to climb."

"You're taller than me." She turned and braced her back against the wall. Vhalla laced her fingers, ready for his heel. "I'll help you up first."

"But then what'll you do?"

"Just trust me on this." She needed his trust, because she wasn't quite sure if she trusted herself.

Jax put his foot in her hands. After a moment or two, they managed to lift him high enough that he could grip the top of the wall, pulling himself up the rest of the way. Stretched flat, he put his hand down to her.

Vhalla clenched her fists. She may be able to jump to his hand, but what was the point of training for weeks with Gianna's ladder if she didn't try something a bit different? She was a Wind*walker*, after all.

She raised a foot and felt the pocket of air appear underneath it, resisting her, holding her in place. She raised another foot to meet a higher pocket of air. Her toes wiggled as she stepped upward, uncertain atop the shifting currents. It was a trick to trust her magic over her instinct.

In short order, Vhalla sat on the top of the wall next to Jax.

"Why didn't you do that for me?" he finally managed through surprise.

"It's hard for me to do to my own body. I wouldn't trust myself with getting it quite right for someone else," Vhalla explained. *What if she used too much air and sent him flying backward, head-first into a wall?* She could instinctually self-correct for herself, but not for another person.

Jax accepted the information with a nod. Vhalla was relieved he didn't press too much. She didn't have all the answers; she was still making up her magic as she went. And they needed to be moving.

They descended into a quiet corner of a rock garden that spiraled around the entire home. Vhalla blinked her eyes, activating her magical sight. She stretched her hearing along the wind.

"There's no one here," she announced after a quick survey.

Jax relaxed a bit. "Good, we should have time then."

They let themselves into the main building of the estate, the door now partly burnt from Jax's gentle coaxing. Vhalla turned right for a study. She grabbed a canvas bag from a desk, dumping the writing supplies contained within and began to rummage through the books. Unsurprisingly, there was ample material on the Knights of Jadar; Vhalla intended to steal such books and learn everything she could before turning them in to Lord Ophain.

When full, Vhalla began to wander into other rooms. Luxurious parlors were adorned with Western crimson and an emblazoned phoenix holding a sword. Vhalla grimaced at the sight.

"Jax, was the man you killed a Knight of Jadar?" she asked as they headed upstairs.

"No, just a famous lord . . . and a couple innocents," he replied as though they were just talking about the weather. *If one rehearsed talking about the weather.*

"Would I know of him?"

"Do you want the answer to that?" Jax gave her a broad and toothy grin.

Vhalla paused a moment and shook her head. "Not now." It shouldn't make her uncomfortable to think of Jax as a murderer. Those who survived the War in the North were all murderers and madmen. But it was a side of him she wasn't sure if she wanted to see just yet. There was something different about this, but she had yet to put her finger on what it was.

On the third floor was the room Vhalla had really sought all along: a trophy room. Her hand lingered on the hilt of the axe, as if the crystals could call out to one another. She walked through the shelves, running her fingers along glass boxes and placards.

"I found it," Vhalla breathed in despair. *She'd wanted Lord Ophain to be right.* She'd wanted her expedition into the heart of the Knights of Jadar to prove that the sword was safely hidden in the obscurity of time.

"Found what?" Jax walked over, reading what was inscribed upon a plate affixed to the empty armor stand. "The Sword of Jadar." He lurched away as though he'd been hit. "*The Sword of Jadar?* That's what this is about? Vhalla, it's a legend."

"It's clearly not. And someone has it," Vhalla insisted. "We need to find out who."

Jax gave her a skeptical look and opened his mouth to speak.

The sound of the portcullis grinding open had them both sprinting to a window. Jax and Vhalla both spouted profanities. Major Schnurr and four Knights had returned far too early.

"I'm sure they just forgot something," Jax mumbled hopefully.

Vhalla's eyes went wide as she remembered the canvas bag she'd emptied and used to rummage through the study to the left in the entry. Perhaps the Knights would overlook the singed mark on the door and slightly melted metal in the darkness, but they wouldn't be able to ignore signs of Vhalla raiding the bookshelves. "The books, downstairs." She moved to go get them, but Jax pushed her back.

"You stay. *Hide*. I'll sort it so they don't notice."

"But—"

"Stay!" Jax scowled at her and sprinted down the stairs. Vhalla looked around the room for places to hide. Her fingers caressed the leather buckles on the axe. One by one, they came undone. *Why did she have the axe if she wasn't going to use it?* Why carry it if she wasn't going to carve the Knights into little nubs, useless for anything? Her fingertip touched the crystal and pure power shot up her arm.

She heard steps coming up the stairs and turned, expecting to see Jax.

Schnurr led two other men into the trophy room. The two men firmly held Jax's arms. Their fingers pulsed purple and blue across Jax's skin. His tongue had been turned into ice, spilling out of his open mouth. Her friend shivered and shook, every now and then a spark of fire would lick away at the ice forming around his hands and arms. It seemed all he could do was keep his blood from freezing.

"Let him go," Vhalla ordered quietly.

"You're not in a position to make demands." Major Schnurr ran his hands along the trophy tables. "What did you come here looking for, Vhalla Yarl?"

"Your knowledge and your life." She fearlessly threw her threat at his feet.

Major Schnurr didn't even trip. "Did you want—this?" He dropped on the table the book he'd been holding. It was one Vhalla had decided would be useful when rummaging through his study. Schnurr deftly opened it to a page.

Vhalla read the old Western tongue with ease. "The Sword of Jadar." She raised her attention to the major. "Do you have it?"

"The weapon was stolen from us and destroyed." Major Schnurr snapped the book closed.

"When?" Vhalla asked, not believing him for a moment.

"About ten years ago," the major replied. "Solaris's minister began tampering with powers that he had no idea how to tame. Though I'm surprised your *dear* crown prince didn't tell you of it," Major Schnurr sneered.

She faked anger at Schnurr's verbal jab, but was really focused on Jax. *How were they going to get out of here alive?* Vhalla's hand dropped to the last of the fasteners on her thigh.

"I wonder if you'll figure out—I don't need the sword." Vhalla drew the axe, and the whole room stopped in breathless wonder and horror. She saw the look on Jax's face; it was pure fear and loathing. The Knights wore expressions of ominous glee.

"You will let us go." Vhalla held out the axe toward the major.

"Vhalla, you are poor with your numbers." The man chuckled. "You forgot our two Northern friends who escaped the Night of Fire and Wind. The same two that we decided to help smuggle West in order to try to bring you to us later."

Her arm trembled. *The Knights were behind the Northerners who'd killed Larel at the Crossroads?*

"And you've forgotten again, or didn't really look, I came with four men."

She turned to the Knights holding Jax. Jax's eyes looked down the stairs.

"There is no way out of this, Vhalla Yarl." Major Schnurr took a bold step forward. "If you attack me, he dies. If you think you can save him by attacking the two holding him first, he dies from the archer and Waterrunner at the foot of the stairs."

The major rounded on her. Vhalla tried to put together an alternative solution. A different approach than what she was handed.

"Or you kill us all, and accept his blood on your hands."

She stared at the axe. *Kill them all.* She could save Jax. *She would kill them all.* Vhalla looked up at her friend. She'd be gambling with his life, and the odds weren't on her side.

"Or—give yourself to us and save your palms from being washed in more blood. Let your friend live."

Vhalla looked down at the axe. It seemed to shine brighter, as if it knew it could soon gorge itself on life. Vhalla wanted to give in, to satiate its need—*her need*—its need.

Then her eyes found Major Schnurr, in all his joyous triumph. If she gambled with Jax's life, win or lose, she'd be no better than the men she loathed. She'd be trading in whatever scraps of humanity she still clung to.

Jax scowled at her and shook his head, making muffled protest noises.

With a soft sigh, she closed her Channel and dropped the axe. Live or die, she'd do it with some shred of principles.

Major Schnurr slammed his shoulder into her back, knocking her forward. Vhalla caught the table to try to right herself, and he quickly grabbed her wrists. Vhalla felt the sickening, unnatural cool of shackles, and she was forced to watch as they were clamped once more on her. The shackles buzzed quietly, the crystals activating, blocking her Channel and even the faintest possibility of a magical resistance. *Of course he still had crystal cuffs in his trophy room.*

Fire rode on a scream up Jax's throat, hissing through the ice. Vhalla couldn't stop herself from trying to reach him, but Major Schnurr kicked her down, placing his boot atop her temple and causing her to see stars.

"He's a liability and a smear on Western nobility," Major Schnurr mused. "Kill him."

"You said you'd let him live!" Vhalla cried. But her words were lost as a Knight buried an ice dagger to the hilt between Jax's ribs. The Westerner wheezed and coughed up blood as he slumped.

"You think . . . that'll stop me?" Jax laughed and lunged, his side already soaked to his waist with blood.

"*Jax, stop!*" Vhalla screamed. *She didn't want this.* She didn't want to watch another one of her friends die.

A second ice dagger pierced his back. Jax was thrown to the floor and didn't get up. He wheezed and stared at her with dulling eyes.

"You said you'd let him live!" she raged at Schnurr. "You said you'd let him go!"

"No, I said I'd let him live, never that I'd let him go. And I never said how long I'd let him live, either." The major laughed. "Leave him. We have the Windwalker and the last crystal weapon. We set out for the Caverns tonight."

Vhalla struggled and fought; she bit and scratched and kicked. She was helpless without her magic, the Bond, and the axe. But she still struggled against her fate. Finally frustrated, the pommel of a Knight's sword met the side of her head, and Vhalla went limp between the men holding her.

She'd tried to stop the Knights, but she'd failed. She'd tried to save Jax, but he'd died. She'd tried to make a deal with devils, but she'd forgotten that devils lie.

CHAPTER 5

VHALLA OPENED HER eyes and heaved up the sparse contents of her stomach.

The light speared searing, blinding pain into her brain, which sent her body into rebellion. The second time she heaved was the moment she tried to move. Now, sitting in her own sick, Vhalla struggled to blink away the blazing sun. Blood coated the side of her face. Her whole body felt like it'd been carved from lead. Her mind struggled to churn, but it only made the ripples of nausea turn into waves.

"She's awake," a man called.

Vhalla stopped moving to spare her energy, convincing her eyes to focus. She was rewarded with marginal success as a hazy blob transformed into a Western man.

The swaying of the animal she'd been tied to, however, reduced him once more to a sickening blur.

Her throat was dry. Her lips were cracked. Her wrists were heavy. She felt ropes around her waist and shoulders, tying her upright to a saddle. Vhalla tried to flex her fingers, the sunburn agonizing. Easterners had a tendency to tan before burning, so if she was reddened, she must've been exposed to the harsh Western sun for some time.

A horse rode up beside her, and Vhalla felt tugs on the ropes that bound her. She struggled to piece together what was happening, her circumstances coming back in a hazy blur. Another Western man came into focus beside her as panic slowly bubbled up within her.

He noticed her attention and patted her head. "Good morning, oh great lady."

Vhalla went to swat away his hand only to find her wrists tethered together. She looked down and felt sick all over again. But it wasn't the same nausea as before. It was a cold and crawling dread that felt like glass against her bones, which made her skin prickle and her shoulders quake.

Locked firmly around her wrists was a familiar pair of shackles. Shimmering unnaturally around their circumference were crystals. They pulsed with magic-blocking power. She remembered them being snapped over her wrists by Schnurr.

"For our safety." The man tapped on her shackles. "We can't have—"

Vhalla shrieked in anger and swung her whole body. She brought the irons—*hard*—into the side of the man's face. The ropes binding her bit into her skin and drew blood at the motion, but Vhalla ignored it. Raw instinct took over, and she swung again with murderous intent before the man could completely recover—his nose shattered.

"Get it under control!" a voice demanded.

Another horse rode up beside her. Vhalla snarled like an animal, baring her teeth dangerously, ready to fight for her life. This man, well-armored and clearly well-trained, didn't hesitate to go right for his sword.

"I've seen you fight." She stilled as he held his sword at her throat. "You may be made of wind, but steel will cut you."

Vhalla panted, straining against the ropes. She clenched and unclenched her fists over and over, trying to summon magic that wouldn't come. The shackles seemed to glow brighter, fighting against her magical struggle.

"We won't kill you, *yet*, but we can make you hurt a lot more than you currently do." He waited until she eased away, panting in the saddle. "Good girl."

"Where are we heading?" she demanded.

The man glanced forward, and Vhalla followed his stare. At the head of the small caravan was a bushy-mustached man. *Major Schnurr.*

"You may tell her," Schnurr called. "It will change little now."

"We are going to use you as the tool you were born to be."

Vhalla attempted a bold laugh to sell her lie. She'd known what they sought for weeks, more or less. "You all are larger fools than I thought. I can't manage crystals any better than any other sorcerer."

The Knight actually seemed doubtful for a moment.

"Don't listen to her." The man immediately in front of her shook his head. "All Windwalkers are the same; not one was ever found who couldn't manage the crystals."

"I can't," Vhalla insisted. "I can't, and you are all going to face Imperial judgment for this as I am a Lady of the Court. High crimes for no returns!"

The two men exchanged a look.

"Ignore the Wind Demon's lies," Major Schnurr scolded. "She'd say anything to save her skin, and the Empire hunts her presently for justice, not us. We'd be heroes for turning her in."

"But, sir—"

"If she can't manage crystals, her skin would've already begun to turn to leather and her eyes red with taint from carrying the axe as long as she has." The major patted his saddlebag and returned his attention forward, talking with another man. There were six Knights in all. Two in the front, the two talking to Vhalla, and two behind, one of whom was nursing his wounded face.

"Are you mad?" she screamed. The desert was vast and empty. She saw nothing but sand for miles. She didn't even know how they were making headway. Roads were nowhere to be seen. But if someone was close by, she'd cry loud enough that they would certainly hear. "The Crystal Caverns have only ever spelled disaster!"

"Our forefathers were close to unlocking their secrets," the man beside her proclaimed arrogantly.

"They would have unleashed a new reign with the Sword of Jadar, were it not for the Ci'Dan bitch," the other snarled.

Ci'Dan bitch?

"This is insanity. What do you hope to accomplish?" Vhalla cried to the major. "The last time people went to the Caverns they unleashed the taint that started a war!"

"Do not lump us in with Southern fools." Major Schnurr had finally decided she was worth his attention. "We have centuries of studying your kind." He chuckled. "A war is just what we want to start, and the Emperor was so ready to be rid of you he delivered you right into our hands."

The ropes dug into Vhalla's shoulders as she strained against them.

"Solaris is getting old, losing his edge. Who would have thought he would get so worked up over the son of the Ci'Dan whore finally finding something to squeeze beneath the sheets," one of the men near her sneered.

"The time to strike is near," another Knight agreed.

Vhalla stared at nothing, trying to process an escape, a solution, *something*. She'd tried to stop the Knights and only gave them what they wanted. She'd led Jax to his death in the process. The horse swayed and it caused the ropes to dig farther into her slumped shoulders. They rode the entire day and into the first part of the night before stopping. Vhalla spent it in silence, keeping company with the shade of her friend.

As the other men dismounted, Vhalla was left strapped in place. They sparked a campfire—at least one of them was a Firebearer— and broke out rations, laughing and joking as though she wasn't there, as though they weren't on a fool's mission.

Eventually, Major Schnurr stood and strolled over to her. He wet a cloth and held it up for her to suck upon. Vhalla scowled at the demeaning suggestion.

"It's this or we tie you down and pour water over your mouth and nose until you have no choice but to drink." His tone implied he didn't care much either way.

She scowled. "That sounds like a waste out here in the desert."

"We'll reach the Southern forest by tomorrow night, the day after, maybe. We have supplies and Waterrunners." The major shrugged. "We can't have you dying on us."

Vhalla stared at the dirty cloth another moment. Her throat practically screamed for the moisture that darkened it. But the last thing she wanted to do was give the Knights the satisfaction of lowering her further. The major waited just long enough, as if he could sense her breaking point nearing. Vhalla took the cloth from him, awkwardly with her shackles, and tried not to seem desperate as she sucked the sour liquid from it.

"You have been a hard one to catch, surprisingly so for a once library girl." The major placed his hands on his hips as though appraising a prize buck that he had shot down. "Our comrades in the Senate tried to snag you right off, but the Emperor was too fascinated by your power."

Vhalla hadn't even known who the Knights of Jadar were at the time. It had gone overlooked for months. But she suddenly remembered the senator who had demanded she be given to the Knights because they would "*know what to do with her*" on the day of her trial.

"Then we thought the march would be the moment for us to ensnare you; after all, you came right through the Crossroads. We worked carefully with the North after the Night of Fire and Wind to hide our movements. It was easier to let them create chaos, to let them capture you and throw Solaris and Ci'Dan off our trail. But they didn't seem to quite grasp the idea of needing you alive." Vhalla shifted the rag in her mouth, letting Schnurr ramble on his self-serving tale. "The two at the Crossroads quite missed the mark."

Vhalla stilled. It was the second time the major had mentioned the Northerners who had attacked her the last time she was at the Crossroads. The night Larel Neiress had died was burned upon Vhalla's heart.

"We couldn't make a move ourselves, not then. The Knights haven't survived centuries by being reckless. But the Crossroads served us well enough when it became clear that we needed to remove the son of the Ci'Dan slut to get to you." He sighed dramatically. "And the North couldn't do that right either, even when we fed misinformation to lead the army right into their attack at the Pass."

Larel, then Aldrik in the Pass.

"We were at a loss when you arrived in the North. I never even contemplated the Emperor would be the one to push you away after he had you in his hands. Then again, I've never seen the whore's son so taken with anyone. Power, or the loss of it, makes men quite illogical."

"You're one to talk." Vhalla spit out the rag, letting it fall to the sand below the mount. "You were going to kill me for power, for the Emperor's favor."

"I would've made quite the show of seeming to do so." The major stroked his mustache with a wicked smile. "It's a special skill to carve a human carefully enough that nothing vital is damaged beyond repair while still having them appear to be quite deceased. It would've been my honor to see your corpse carried away only to have my men put you back together."

"You're disgusting," Vhalla muttered caustically.

"You don't get to say that." The man's eyes gleamed with dark pride. "You're less than human. You're nothing more than a tool. And it's been a frustrating century and a half trying to hunt you down in the East."

"Hunt *me* down?"

"The East has become quite good at hiding creatures like you; they don't even speak of magic any longer. It's been nearly twenty-six years since we got our hands on the last one. But we won't mess up this time." The major ran his hand up her thigh. "Not with you."

Vhalla shivered as he left her, despite the residual heat of the desert still hanging in the air. She'd been hunting for connections, to see the bigger picture between seemingly unrelated events. *But was she ready to see what was bubbling to the forefront of her mind as truth?*

Why was everyone so ready to believe that no Windwalkers were being born when it made so much more sense that the East had simply perfected the art of hiding them? The laws following the

Burning Times, the outlawing of all magic, the urge to forget, it was all to hide people like her. She stilled, and the pain of her bindings was ignored for the briefest of moments. Vhalla suddenly had a thousand questions she wanted to ask her own father. How determined he was to go fight in the War of the Crystal Caverns, how outspoken he had been about sorcerers tampering with the crystals.

Vhalla remembered her mother instilling a fear of magic in Vhalla from a young age. A distaste for it that ran so deep Vhalla had never questioned or thought twice about it. She remembered the first time she'd fallen off the roof after climbing up fearlessly, *unharmed*. The argument of her parents she had overheard. She had never thought of it before, it seemed so normal. Her parents had been afraid for her wellbeing. They believed in fearing magic like the rest of the East; they'd never think their daughter was a sorcerer.

The shackles around her wrists suddenly felt heavy, and Vhalla blinked at them bleary eyed. What if it hadn't been as normal as she thought? *What if she had been hidden?*

The thought echoed in her mind through the long ride the next day, sobering her to a withdrawn silence. The Knights made jokes about clipping the Windwalkers wings and how easy she'd been to break. Schnurr made it a ritual to impart knowledge of the twisted practices of the Knights of Jadar. He told her of the experiments conducted on Windwalkers with such detail that it soured her stomach and stilled its growling.

They never untied her from the saddle, never removed her cuffs. Someone could cut off her feet and Vhalla doubted she'd be able to tell. Her lower body had gone numb from the ropes long ago.

The Knights had the arrogance to think they were breaking her, but it couldn't be further from the truth. Every waking hour, she plotted. She wiggled, tugged, and worked at her ropes. She watched as Schnurr checked his saddlebag every morning and night, leaving Vhalla no need to guess where the axe and key to her shackles were hidden. If she could remove her shackles, she would have her wind and her Bond with Aldrik—she could make them suffer.

But how to get the key?

Vhalla settled on biding her time. The only plan she could think of was trying to launch an attack during one of his brags—if she could get her ropes loose enough. But she suspected he kept the key in the same saddlebag as the axe, and he never let it go far from his side.

The smell of the Southern forest nearly overwhelmed her with nostalgia when they'd crossed into it from the Western Waste. They made headway into the mountains without roads and pushed onward and upward until dusk began to settle. The nights were already cooling, and it made a stark contrast with the heat of the desert.

A year had passed—Vhalla realized with the changing seasons—since she had met Aldrik and everything began. *A year that felt like a lifetime.*

"We'll stay there tonight." Major Schnurr pointed to a windmill fashioned of stone and wood.

It sat high on the edge of a small town. She suspected the cluster of homes to be the town of Mosant or one of its outskirts. If Vhalla and her captors had progressed as the crow flew from the Crossroads straight for the Crystal Caverns, it would put them right in Mosant's path.

A generally noteworthy town, Vhalla stared at the houses down the mountainside from the windmill as they made their way toward it. If she screamed, would her voice carry far enough? Could she slip away in the night? Even if she could slip away, it didn't solve the issue of the cuffs. Vhalla had a suspicion that a blacksmith couldn't just break off magically enhanced shackles. If she drew attention to herself, the Knights would certainly overwhelm any villagers who came looking, forcing them to flee before more could follow.

That much was proven true as they arrived at the windmill. A tired-looking village woman came out to greet them, and Schnurr wasted no time putting his sword through her eye. Vhalla stared at the gaping hole the blade left behind in the woman's face as the Knights untied their prisoner. War had taken its toll, and she was beginning to struggle to feel anything toward the death of innocents.

The windmill had one entrance up a short flight of stairs, a place horses couldn't go. Schnurr decreed that she was too valuable to leave outside, so Vhalla was finally untied and carried inside. She tried to find her legs, to stand on her own, but after nearly a week of being stuck in a saddle, they were useless from stiffness and sores. They threw her unceremoniously atop bags of grain. The dust sent her dry throat into a coughing fit. But when she could breathe again, Vhalla took solace in the smell of the wheat. It reminded her of home in the fall, when the barn was full; it gave her some measure of comfort in spite of her newly conflicting feelings about her upbringing.

She waited in silence as the men settled. They relaxed, talking and laughing. Schnurr had forbidden a fire given the dry contents of the windmill, and Vhalla knew that meant they would not stay up late and instead tuck underneath blankets to fight off the mountain chill.

Vhalla lay unmoving as the last of them began to settle. She counted to a thousand and listened for any indication that any were still awake before sliding off her sacks of grain. Vhalla kept her wrists close so that the shackles wouldn't clank together.

She crept through the dim moonlight, holding her breath. She'd get one chance. Schnurr had made it quite clear that while he wouldn't kill her, he could do a laundry list of other horrible things that would make her wish she was dead. If this attempt failed, Vhalla had no doubt he would be starting at the top of that list.

Vhalla stood over the sleeping man, debating if she should try for the saddlebag he clutched in his sleep—for the key she knew would be in there alongside the axe, or if she should take his sword and slit his throat first. Vhalla glanced at his weapon. Drawing it was likely to make enough sound that someone would wake. She crouched down and reached out slowly.

The man shifted and Vhalla stiffened, but he didn't waken. Her fingers wormed their way through the flap of the saddlebag, feeling within. The crystals on the shackles almost burned her skin as her fingers brushed against the axe, and Vhalla winced. It was as if they waged a magical war with each other and her flesh was caught in-between.

Reaching forward, Vhalla continued her slow rummage. She was about to give up when she touched something iron and distinctly keylike. Her breath wavered with the rush of anticipation of removing the cuffs. Like a viper, fingers closed suddenly around her elbow, tight enough to pop bones, and Vhalla met Schnurr's wide eyes.

"You are a bold little cur," he growled.

Vhalla gripped the key and tugged herself free. Schnurr was moving as well, and Vhalla fumbled with her hoped-for salvation, but she couldn't quite get the right angle of the key and lock while shackled. He lunged for her—sending the saddlebag sliding across the room—and their tumbling woke the other Knights.

Schnurr grabbed for his sword and Vhalla tried to wrestle it from his hands. She leaned forward, biting one of his wrists hard enough that blood exploded into her mouth. Cursing, Schnurr instinctively pulled away, and Vhalla won the weapon.

Still sheathed, she drew it back and twisted her body—*just as Daniel had once shown her*—to put all her momentum in the thrust. The tip of the scabbard sunk into Schnurr's neck and Vhalla watched his eyes bulge as he gasped for air. It was blunted, but the force crushed his windpipe.

The other Knights were nearly upon her. Vhalla looked around desperately, trying to reason if it made more sense to try to fight them off or spend the seconds she had left trying to get the shackles unlocked. She dropped the sword and scrambled for the key.

"Wind scum!" one of the Knights shouted as he kicked her, the heel of his boot digging into her shoulder.

Vhalla was sent rolling, but she clutched the key so tightly her nails left bloody arcs in her hand. She was back to trying to unlock the shackles. Her magic would mean her freedom, her longevity. The axe was already in the hand of one of her assailants.

"We should just kill you," one snarled as he looked at the corpse of the bushy-mustached major.

"Kill her! Take the axe," another said, brandishing the weapon. "We can find another Windwalker in time. We have the axe and that is more important."

Vhalla watched the man as he spoke, twisting her hands against the cuffs.

"We stick to the plan and head to the Caverns."

"Why?" Mutiny rumbled between the now leaderless Knights. "I say we kill her."

A Knight grabbed for her and Vhalla plunged her heel into his groin. The man instantly let go, a string of foul language spilling from his lips. She spun face-to-face with the man wielding the axe.

"Kill the wind bitch!" Two strong hands grabbed her.

Vhalla struggled valiantly against the man's hold on her. She watched as the axe-wielding Knight raised it. *If only she had her magic.*

Fire suddenly erupted over their shoulders at the door.

"What the?" The men turned.

"Get that under control!"

A man held out his hand, and the flames swayed as they roared against his command.

"I said put it out!"

"I'm trying!" The sorcerer struggled.

The fire was magic. Vhalla blinked at its warm heat. A Firebearer would be able to assume control of any normal flame without any trouble. But a flame created by another sorcerer became a battle of power, and clearly these flames were crafted by a Firebearer of fearsome skill.

The flames caught the dry grain, and the wooden inside of the windmill was quickly going up like kindling. The men scrambled like rats, trapped between stone and flame.

It was impossible. Vhalla blinked as more of the room caught. She'd been forgotten about as the men tried to charge for the door, for escape. They sweated, they screamed, they shied from the heat. Vhalla watched them as they burned, even the Firebearer was overcome by the magical inferno.

And she felt little more than heat.

Vhalla walked toward the flames that blocked the door—there was no change. There was only one man's flames that wouldn't harm her, but it couldn't be him. *Aldrik couldn't be here.* She was so entranced by the predicament that she didn't notice the structure beginning to collapse around her until a large beam cracked.

She unshackled herself and snatched up the axe from where it sat in the fire, ignoring the charred remains of the Knights. Vhalla plunged into the flames. Fire licked around her, it burned her clothes, but it didn't singe her skin even slightly. It allowed her to pass unharmed into the chill night beyond.

Immediately outside, Vhalla looked frantically for him. She cleared the structurally compromised windmill, starting for the horses before they could all spook and flee. The whole time Vhalla's eyes searched the dark forest around her.

"Aldrik?" she dared to call into the darkness.

There was no reply.

Vhalla stashed the axe into a saddlebag, gripping a horse's reins with white knuckles. The rush of her escape was already fleeting; aches and pains were appearing in its wake. Vhalla mounted the horse, stalling long enough to give someone a chance to come forward, for an explanation to the miracle she had just witnessed.

A flash of red caught her eyes and Vhalla peered into the blackness. The hairs on the back of her neck rose as though there was unseen electricity crackling through the air. Barely discernible from the shadow was the outline of a woman, cowled and mostly hidden by the brush of the woods. Her eyes flashed red for one long moment before she vanished into the night.

CHAPTER 6

THREE DAYS HAD passed since she collapsed in the center of the small town known as Mosant. After riding through the woods with a burning windmill at her back, Vhalla's energy gave out, and she was forced to rely on the care of the townsfolk. However, she'd forgotten that she'd once met a woman who hailed from the mountain town she now sought shelter in.

Vhalla sat on the opposite side of a table from a woman she'd never expected to see again. Her fingers curled and uncurled around the steaming mug, from which she happily leeched warmth. Wool covered her arms and legs, basic clothing that offered her a deep comfort.

"If you go back, the Senate will jail you." Tim was a lovely young woman, pretty enough that Vhalla wondered how

Tim had managed to masquerade as her. Though, they had all been wearing a thicker coating of grime during the march North.

Vhalla had grown to love her too-slender proportions and less than ideal hair and height. She'd encountered people who had found her beautiful in spite of those facts and had learned to foster her own love for herself by learning what they saw. But Vhalla knew she wasn't going to win any broad strokes beauty contests.

Where Vhalla had been cut and carved into harsh lines and a strong presence, Tim had been left to develop naturally to be soft and graceful. Neither of them was wrong, neither right. *Simply different.*

"They've already jailed me," Vhalla reminded.

"You could flee to the coast. Or live here; no one will ever turn you in. Not after what you did for all the soldiers in the North and especially not after killing Knights of Jadar; they've always been a menace to our town. Or, go back to the East, maybe?" Tim suggested.

The offer was heartwarming, and Vhalla appreciated it deeply. But she'd made up her mind while recovering and lying low from her ordeal with the Knights. The days that had passed had given time for messengers to arrive and announce that the Lady Vhalla Yarl, the Windwalker, was wanted for murder of Western lords. Should she be found, she was to be turned in for Imperial justice. Vhalla burst out laughing at the thought and shook her head at the curious look from Tim. One would think they would've learned from the first time she'd been falsely accused of murder.

"I need to return to the capital." Vhalla sipped on her tea. The lemongrass and honey reminded her of summer despite the world beginning its shift to winter.

"The Knights of Jadar are demanding your death." Tim sighed. "But the messengers said the crown prince decreed that if the Windwalker were to come forward, he would see to it that she received a fair trial."

Vhalla turned the idea over in her head. Aldrik was protecting her, in his own way. She heard his message loud and clear: *return to me and I will keep you safe.*

Her chair scraped against the hard dirt floor as she stood. She walked over to the fire, still nursing the steaming tea. Vhalla watched the flames dance, her mind replaying the night with the burning windmill. She'd looked for the person who started the fire that saved her life. But Vhalla saw no one in her flight through the forest that night.

That wasn't entirely true. Vhalla remembered the shadowy outline of the woman, the glowing red eyes. But the night was already a hazy memory becoming more dreamlike with each passing day. She knew who had to have made the flames, but the logic didn't add up. Only one person's fire couldn't burn her—*Aldrik's*. But he was certainly in the South.

How would his fire look to her now? She wondered if his magic would still sparkle for her as it once had. She was certainly no longer the girl who had been lost in rose gardens, enthralled by tongues of flame slithering between his fingers.

"I suppose," Vhalla whispered, "I've run long enough."

The axe was hidden along with the cuffs within a saddlebag in the corner of the room, *the only good idea Schnurr had ever had.* Vhalla considered the unassuming bag for a long moment. The longer she had the axe in her possession, the more she realized that she needed to bring it to Victor. He had been the one who had trusted her to bring it South; he'd know what needed to be done to hide or destroy it for good.

"You're going back?" Tim was surprised, but not *that* surprised.

"It's time." Vhalla would go, but not because she needed a prince to keep her safe. She hadn't shown the Senate the product of their efforts yet, the weapon they'd forged out of a library apprentice. "I will need something before I ride."

"What is it?" Tim was ever-helpful. Vhalla had expected the people of the valley to shun her and her magic, but time and tales had healed the reputation of the Windwalker, rebuilding Vhalla in the eyes of the Southerners as their chosen champion. Furthermore, according to Tim, the Knights of Jadar had plagued the citizens of Mosant for decades as the town was on the route from the Crossroads to the Crystal Caverns. They would rather harbor a criminal than do anything that could remotely please the Western group.

"I need a cape." Vhalla thought of the symbol she'd donned at the warfront. If she was the South's war hero, she'd look the part. "I need a black cape with a silver wing on the back."

Vhalla turned to meet Tim's eyes. The woman wore a mischievous grin. Vhalla smiled back. To Tim, it was a game, a fantasy she was playing a part in. But Vhalla's life wasn't a storybook. She was returning to the South and showing herself as more than a piece on the Carcivi boards of powerful men and women—*she was a player*.

She rested for two more days before finally leaving. As soon as the seamstress had finished Vhalla's cape, Vhalla announced her intention. The Festival of the Sun was starting, and the last thing Vhalla wanted to do was engage in the revelries. Spending her time on the road, away from the celebrations, was a far better use of her days.

It was a gray morning when Vhalla said her goodbyes and set off on her mount, stolen from the dead Knights.

"Is it all right?" Tim asked. The white puffs of their breath became fainter as the chill of the dawn slipped away.

"It is." Vhalla gripped the reins and adjusted her cape again. The cloak was a heavy wool, sturdy, made for the mountains in winter, and long enough to drape over the haunch of the horse. For the first time, Vhalla looked like a noble on a journey. Her hand went up to her watch, caressing it thoughtfully.

"I trust you have a plan." Tim settled into her saddle. "A plan to *not* be marching to your death?"

Under the tall pine trees, the soft clanking sound of the stirrups filled the silence as Vhalla mused over how to respond. "Not really."

"So, you're going to ride back into the capital with a target on your back and deliver yourself neatly?"

"That's as far as I've made it in my head," Vhalla affirmed. She really didn't have an idea of how returning to the capital would go. All she knew was that she wanted a public stage to put the Knights in their place once and for all. *What better place than the greatest stage in the world?*

Tim let the silence linger, but Vhalla could almost hear the woman shouting her unasked questions. They'd been together for a few days, but Tim had kept her inquisitions fairly tame.

Vhalla sighed softly. "Go ahead, ask what you want."

"What?" Tim squeaked, startled.

"We have a long ride, and since you've chosen to come with me,

I'm not going to have it be filled with awkward silences," Vhalla explained.

"Oh, sorry." Tim laughed uncomfortably, passing her reins from hand to hand. "I suppose I want to know what everyone else wants to know."

"I don't know what that is." Vhalla could guess, but she wasn't going to hand Tim information mindlessly.

"After the battle, you left. Where did you go?"

"The Crossroads."

"Why?"

"Because I wanted to." Vhalla saw Tim's expression deflate from the corners of her eyes. *She wasn't talking with Ophain or Aldrik, just an average woman with no experience in subtlety.* "I wanted to escape everything for a bit," Vhalla explained further. "I needed to be no one."

"So then, did you really kill those Western Lords there?" Tim ventured.

"I did." Tim's eyes were wide at Vhalla's response. "They would've killed me, or worse, if I hadn't fought them. They weren't just lords; they were Knights of Jadar trying to use my powers to start a new war. More of the same ilk that died at the windmill."

"Oh, that's different then." The woman easily shrugged off the idea of Vhalla committing murder in self-defense.

Vhalla appraised her traveling companion. Tim was soft-looking and girlish, but she had been in war as well. She had killed and carried invisible scars just as ugly as all soldiers did. Yet, despite that fact, Vhalla withheld the information that she'd killed Tim's direct superior, Major Schnurr.

"Why are you really going back to the capital?" Vhalla asked her own unsaid question.

Tim sucked on her teeth in thought. "I want to train with the archers in the guard. They said there'd be a position for me."

"They told you that after the war was over," Vhalla pointed out. "You chose to go back to Mosant instead."

"Oh, fine." Tim laughed. "I want to travel with you."

"That may not be the best idea," Vhalla remarked dryly, watching the trail curve ahead of them.

"Maybe not," Vhalla's companion agreed. "But I feel like my fate is linked with yours." The statement stilled Vhalla. "For a time, I was you. I saw and heard things I'd never seen or heard before. I was there to watch the rise of the Windwalker. Then I found you again. This is your story, but I want to see how it ends."

It would likely end with a violent death. Vhalla spared Tim any further warning and kept the thought to herself.

"Plus," Tim added, "you're a Lady of the Court now, right? If you build out your household, maybe you'll find a place for my set of hands." Tim laughed brightly.

Vhalla cracked a small smile.

The woman's company proved to be more welcome than Vhalla ever expected. Tim already knew much about Vhalla, so when they broke for camp, Vhalla spent the majority of the time learning about Tim. The young woman was transparent, and it was a welcome reprieve for Vhalla's mind. It wasn't necessary to exhaust herself quizzing or dancing with words to find the truth.

The two women spent the night huddled together under a single blanket for warmth, and as time went on, Vhalla allowed the young woman to snuggle closer and closer. Sometimes, she'd lie awake, listening to Tim breathe in harmony with the sounds of the forest at night. Tim was warm, *but not nearly as warm as Aldrik.*

At a leisurely pace, it only took three days to reach the capital. Vhalla hoped she'd missed all the festivities of the Festival of the Sun. They paused at the intersection of the Great Imperial Way and the Capital Road. High above them, the palace glittered despite the perpetually greying sky as winter drew nearer.

"You're sure about this?" Tim asked once more.

Vhalla adjusted her cloak, making sure it was splayed just so over the horse's haunches. "Very."

As they ascended the mountain, it didn't take long for Vhalla to be noticed. Citizens stared in slack-jawed awe at the woman wearing the black cloak. Vhalla held her head high, prepared for their judgment.

After the first series of houses, people began running alongside and ahead of her. More citizens lined the street, but none stopped her.

Word spread far enough ahead that a man had time to prepare to address her. "Is it true?" he called from a second-floor window of a tavern. Vhalla pulled on the reins, slowing her mount, prompting him to continue. "Are you her? Are you the Windwalker?"

"I am," Vhalla announced.

Murmurs rippled through the people lining the road. Vhalla nudged her horse, pushing it forward again. They didn't spout words of hate. Instead, Vhalla's ears picked up words like *hero* and *champion*.

How fickle people were, she smirked to herself. Sorcerers were scary; she still had no doubt that such was the reigning perception in the South. There was too much history surrounding the Crystal Caverns that she was beginning to understand better for that hate to root into. But she had become something more than a sorcerer. She'd become the Windwalker. Which was something different than all who had ever come before her and had a reputation to match.

By the time she was crossing the gate of the capital city of the Solaris Empire, horns were heralding her arrival. Vhalla was certain it was in warning; she knew guards were being called for her arrest. This only forced her to ride faster into the city.

Men and women blurred together, but no one stopped her. Vhalla saw bold black pennons bearing the silver wing displayed, like she had seen in the Crossroads. She wondered if the soldiers who had returned home from the war had kept the mantra that the winds of the Windwalker were lucky.

Vhalla was nearly standing in her saddle now. Her heart racing as she sped through the streets. She was over halfway to her chosen destination when a guard made a dash to try to stop her.

Tim sped up and stopped, blocking the man's progress to Vhalla. "Go on!" she called.

Wind picked up the mountainside behind her as Vhalla crossed under an archway to her final destination. Her gamble had paid off, and she pulled hard on her reins, stopping the horse with a whinny and a loud clamor of hooves before the sunlit stage. A long row of guards was positioned before the stage, blocking the path between her and the Imperial family.

Emperor Solaris stood center. Baldair and his mother stood

back and to his left, a Northern girl hovering half a step away. Guilt
surged through Vhalla at the sight of Baldair. She wondered if Jax's
body was ever found or if the Knights of Jadar had hidden it. She'd
have to tell the prince the fate of his loyal guard herself, but now was
not the time. Vhalla's eyes swept to the Emperor's right.

There he was.

He looked nothing like the haggard man she'd dreamt about. His
hair was not only styled, but it had been cut as well to taper neatly
at the nape of his neck. His face seemed less gaunt, though there
were still dark circles beneath his eyes. Vhalla suppressed insane
laughter. He wore the same coat as when they had first met.

"Emperor Solaris!" Vhalla shouted, using her magic to amplify
her voice so the mass of commoners could hear her. "I have come
for my justice."

The Emperor's eye twitched slightly at her getting in the first
word. "For your justice?"

"The Knights of Jadar have laid false accusations against my
name." Vhalla sat tall in her saddle. "As a Lady of the Court, I
demand a fair trial before the Mother to prove my innocence."

Just as the Emperor was about to speak, a man entered the stage,
followed by several others. Vhalla's eyes narrowed slightly as the
Head of Senate stepped into the sun. He regarded her with equal
disdain, and Vhalla seriously weighed the options of freedom and
justice versus the satisfaction of killing him on the spot.

"Senators," she addressed those who had just arrived. "I have
come to prove my innocence."

"Guards, arrest this woman!" A Western man stepped forward,
casting his finger toward her. "She is a slayer of lords and ladies! A
wind *witch!*"

The guards glanced between the Emperor and the senator,
seeking confirmation of orders.

"Arrest her!" the man raged.

"If she has accusations of murder against her, then she is to be
taken into custody," Egmun finally spoke. "Fetch irons."

Vhalla shook her head, laughing softly to herself. A hush fell
over the people as they strained to hear the reason for her strange
reaction. Vhalla reached into her saddle bag.

"If it is irons you desire to put on me," she said as she straightened, "then make sure they are stronger than the ones the Knights of Jadar shackled me in!" Vhalla threw the crystal cuffs, propelling them with the wind to the feet of the Senators.

Chaos erupted.

"Lies!" the Western senator raged.

"Citizens of the Empire," Vhalla cried. "I am not your enemy. I have never been your enemy."

"Order!" the Emperor boomed.

Every man, woman, and child focused on Vhalla with avid attention.

"On the Night of Fire and Wind, I fought to save you." Her heart was beating so hard it hurt, so hard she could choke on it. "I went to the North in good faith of the Empire, as punishment for crimes I did not truly commit. I fought against the Knights of Jadar when they sought to bring down our army on the march. *They* were behind an attack that nearly caused the death of our future sovereign."

Murmurs erupted.

"Lies! She lies!" The Western senator's face was red with rage.

"Enough, Lady Yarl!" the Emperor called. His words went unheeded again.

"I fought for your Empire, and when the Emperor saw fit to grant me my freedom for my service, others sought to chain me." Vhalla jerked her head in the direction of the Western senator. "Yes!" she screamed. "Yes, I killed those men at the Crossroads because they sought the tainted powers within the Crystal Caverns!"

The crowd was worked to a near fever pitch.

"They sought to bring a new war upon the Empire." Vhalla met the Emperor's eyes. "Once more I have defended the Empire, and my reward is to be more chains?"

"Justice for the Windwalker!" a woman screamed.

"Justice for the Hero of the North!" another cried.

The Sunlit Stage filled with their demands.

"Are you going to let her spout these lies?" Her ears picked up the strained words of the Western senator.

Those upon the stage were quickly losing their control of the situation as the crowd slipped into anarchy. Wind howled through the archways, *howled for her justice.* Vhalla met the Emperor's eyes with a level stare and waited.

Fire arced across the sky. The crowd was silenced as they shied away from the wave of heat. Aldrik had taken a step forward.

He stared down at her, and Vhalla met his gaze as an equal—for the world to see. *What was to become of them now?*

"It seems a trial is not necessary." His voice filled the square. It filled the cavernous volume of her chest as two perfectly dark eyes met hers.

"My prince!" Egmun was aghast alongside the Western Senator.

"Senators, you exist so that the will of the people may be channeled to my father and to me." Aldrik motioned to the masses that were growing by the second. "The people have spoken."

"But a trial—"

"Is not needed for one who is so clearly innocent." The crown prince pointed to the crystal-laden irons. "Unless you have an alternate explanation for those?"

The Western senator fumed in silence.

"She is a Lady of the Court." Aldrik shifted his focus back on her. Everyone could've screamed at once, and Vhalla was certain she'd somehow still hear the frantic pulse in his neck as he stared at her once more. "She was given her freedom by the Emperor. And I, as the future Emperor, will pardon her for any crimes that were committed in her own self-defense against the Western madmen who call themselves the Knights of Jadar."

The crowd did scream then. It was deafening, but her ears were already ringing; they were echoing Aldrik's words so loudly that Vhalla felt the resonance of his voice in her bones.

The prince's eyes soaked in her form for one moment longer before he turned, starting alone for the palace. The rest of his family followed behind him. Vhalla caught the Emperor's eyes only briefly, but long enough to see the cautionary stare.

Swinging her leg over, she dismounted gracefully. Vhalla grabbed the saddlebag with the axe, holding it tight against her as the crowd amassed to welcome her back. She didn't want their false smiles and misplaced praise. It had suited her when she needed their love to cement her freedom, but she knew better than to take it to heart. The people would just as easily shift against her once more if Vhalla wasn't careful to keep the wind blowing her way.

The silence of the palace hallway was welcomed, and Vhalla breathed a sigh of relief the second she was free of the crowd. She clutched the saddlebag tightly to her side, setting off in the hall toward the center of the palace. She didn't know quite where she was, but she knew the general direction. Nostalgia crept into her mind, welcoming her despite her disorientation.

It was a sweet dulling of the senses. The way her feet sounded against the floor or the candles that dripped years of wax over their sconces; it was all familiar. It felt like home.

But it was a façade. She'd seen first-hand the ugliness that festered in the hearts of the people who had built this palace. She was now one of them. And the illusion could only last for so long before it was broken.

"Look at you," a voice sneered.

Vhalla reeled in place.

Egmun stepped slowly from a side hall. *Had he been following her?* "Put a title on her and she becomes bold. Do you think yourself powerful?"

"I know I am." Vhalla did nothing to hide her scowl. There was no one around, and it seemed Egmun had no interest in "playing nice" either.

"You should've never left this palace alive." Egmun took a step closer, and Vhalla took a step back. "I should've killed you myself when I had the chance."

"Another step closer and I will be the one killing you," she threatened.

He paused, chuckling darkly. "We both know you won't."

"You have no idea what I'm capable of," Vhalla whispered.

"Oh, I have more idea than you realize." Egmun bared his teeth in a wide grin. "But you won't kill me, because you would do anything to avoid giving me what I want, even if that means denying yourself that particular satisfaction."

"You want me to kill you?" That was a turn she hadn't been expecting.

"Oh, dying like this would be less than ideal. But I would hope the Knights, the Emperor, someone, would put on a better showing of getting you condemned for the death of the Head of Senate." Egmun pinched the bridge of his nose with a sigh and the distinctly Aldrik-like motion threw her mentally off-balance. "The Knights were a failure. But it all comes down to the fact that I will do whatever it takes to see your end, ended in such a horrible way that no one will dare speak the name *Vhalla Yarl, the Windwalker,* for years."

"You're mad." She'd never been more certain.

"I was, once. Now I'm the only sane one here," Egmun observed quietly.

"What is your obsession with me?" she finally asked. The question was out, and Vhalla held her breath to await what she knew would be a terrible answer.

"Oh, you already know," Egmun hummed. "I want you to die. I thought the Knights would do it, or the North would, or you, in your feebleness, would be broken by the trials of war. Disappointments, the lot of them; now here we are."

"Why do you want me dead? I never did anything to you!"

"You existed!" the senator snarled. "No, it's worse than that. You let your existence be known. You, you didn't stay put. They should've never let you out of the East."

"What do you know?" Vhalla whispered.

"I know you will be the death of us all." It seemed to be the most level thing he'd said and for that it was all the more terrifying. "I know, I know better than any what you are capable of."

"How?"

"I sought wisdom that was never meant for mortal men, and I traded my magic for it. No one else will pay that price, and now I am the only one who can protect our world."

"You're mad," Vhalla breathed. Something was seriously broken within the Head of Senate. A god-complex, a power-hungry madman, a deranged lunatic stood before her and affirmed it with every word.

"I am the only one of us who isn't." Egmun frowned.

"So why don't you kill me now then?"

"You've made yourself untouchable." The Head of Senate finally took a step away. "You have powers that I cannot compete with.

You've put a spell over the people. You've crawled into bed with a prince."

Vhalla clenched her fists and gritted her teeth.

"And now you'll return to the Tower to study under the puppet-master of those powers that be." Egmun shook his head, starting in the opposite direction. "I have only one final thing I could try."

Vhalla braced herself for an attack. She readied for an ambush, for Egmun to turn and lunge for her. But the senator only glanced over his shoulder, his eyes glittering with crazed and broken amusement.

"Ask yourself, Vhalla Yarl . . . Ask yourself: is your life worth more than this world?"

With that, the senator departed.

Long after he'd vanished, Vhalla contemplated the hall where he had disappeared. She took a step, stumbling over her feet and leaning against the wall for support. She was shaken down to her soul. Egmun, her most hated entity in the world, had shown her an emotion she didn't know he'd had: compassion. Not for her, but for the people of the Empire.

She gripped the saddlebag with white knuckles, holding an axe that could sever souls. Another piece fell clearly into her mind as Vhalla realized she'd just succeeded in bringing the last crystal weapon back to the South, nearly back to the land of the Crystal Caverns.

The North had just been the battle. There was a much greater struggle at play here, and people had yet to show their true hands. The war still raged on.

CHAPTER 7

A LL THINGS CONSIDERED, Vhalla hadn't really spoken much with the Head of Senate. But it seemed every time she did, the impression was destined to linger, and Egmun's words repeated in Vhalla's mind, imprinting themselves as she made her way for the bottom entry of the Tower of Sorcerers. She clutched the saddlebag, her fingers tracing the outlines of its stitching in thought. *Egmun.*

Egmun had been the Minister of Sorcery, and then *something* changed. He said he had traded his magic; was it taken from him somehow? If so, by what? Vhalla's mind went down every dark path when thinking of the Senator and came up with a memory that wasn't even hers, of Egmun egging on a boy Aldrik to commit his first murder.

The questions circled like a tornado, faster and faster, until all other thoughts were destroyed by their repetition. Vhalla pushed open the door to the Tower of Sorcerers, completely absorbed in trying to recall every word she'd ever written in her journal on Aldrik and deeply wishing she'd taken it with her from Gianna's. It took her five steps to notice she wasn't alone.

The large, circular lobby was filled with people, as it had been the last time she'd been there. But now they weren't wearing armor, and there wasn't the tension of dread. Hope glittered in every flame bulb. Hope for a future that they would see because they were the ones who had survived the battles. Their eyes looked to her in admiration, as though she was the foundation of those dreams.

Vhalla hastily took in those assembled, and her eyes fell on a man. Words and thoughts and emotions tangled into a knot and lodged themselves in her throat. She had cried so many tears of sorrow that it made the moisture at the corners of her eyes burn sweetly with joy.

Fritznangle Charem, Waterrunner and friend of the Windwalker, stood opposite her, already crying like a babe. The room blurred until only he remained in focus. Fritz took a step forward, and Vhalla matched his sprint.

There was only one thing that could've made her part with the bag containing the axe, and that was the man she threw her arms around. The saddlebag was forgotten on the floor, and Vhalla clutched Fritz as though he was nothing more than an illusion about to fade on the wind.

The room was congratulating her; there may have even been cheers. But Vhalla focused on her friend's face, wiping away the rivulets of tears streaming around his wide grin with her thumbs.

"I missed you, Vhal," Fritz hiccupped.

"I missed you, too." Vhalla leaned forward and rose to her toes to give her friend a light kiss on the forehead.

The room hummed around her, and Vhalla took stock of the other sorcerers. Their robes bore the seal of the Tower of Sorcerers, a dragon curling in on itself as a circle, split in two and offset. But above the standard insignia, were pins of a silver wing.

"We knew the Windwalker would return to us, heralding her good fortune." A man rose his hand to his chest, explaining the pin.

"I don't know about that." Vhalla laughed.

"Do not discredit yourself, Lady Yarl." Vhalla turned to the source of the voice. A man with sharp blue eyes and a neatly cut goatee stood in long black robes, different from the rest of the apprentices. Victor, the current Minister of Sorcery, smiled down at her. "You have brought much good fortune, without even being here, by helping ease tensions between sorcerers and the common folk."

"Tensions I made worse with the Night of Fire and Wind." Vhalla couldn't let herself just take the compliment.

"That debt has been repaid, and then some." Victor proceeded down the sloped walkway. "I can imagine you are exhausted after your ordeal at the Sunlit Stage. The chill is still on your cloak, and you've yet to shake the dust from your hair. Let us all give our Windwalker the best welcome home we can and allow her to take a much needed rest."

As the room began to empty, the minister took a half step toward her, placing his hand on the small of her back. He leaned forward slightly to speak only for her. "When you are refreshed, come to my quarters. We have much to discuss of your time at war and your future in the Tower."

Vhalla nodded, starting to speak when Fritz interrupted her.

"Here." He held out the saddlebag. "You dropped—"

"Don't!" She snatched it away in horror, and the wounded look on Fritz's face left no question for Vhalla as to the expression she'd given him. Vhalla fumbled for words, turning to the minister for assistance, but he had already departed. "Don't touch it, Fritz."

Fritz's brow furrowed in confusion.

"Sorry, I . . ." She didn't want to lie to him. She didn't want to lie to her friends. She had sworn off lying. *But what else could she tell him?* Her hands tightened around the saddlebag. "There's something precious inside."

"What is it?"

"Just something I picked up along the way," Vhalla muttered, grabbing at straws for a new topic. Her eyes fell on an Eastern man who had been lingering by Fritz's side since Vhalla had first seen him. "Grahm? Right?"

"Welcome home." The man beamed at her. "I'm surprised you remember me."

"Of course I would! I heard so much about you."

"You did?" Grahm seemed honestly surprised.

"Vhal!" Fritz was redder than scarlet.

"Just that you're quite talented," Vhalla spoke to Grahm, giving Fritz a knowing wink while the other man's eyes were averted. Clearly, Fritz had been making slow use of his time when it came to the man he was so obviously pining for. Vhalla paused. "Where's Elecia?"

"Still in the West." Fritz pouted, affirming Vhalla's suspicion that she wasn't in the Tower. If she had been, Vhalla had no doubt that things with Grahm wouldn't have faltered so.

"Wasn't she coming to study here a bit?" Trying to recall details between the final battle and leaving the North was a struggle, it all blurred together into one ugly mess.

"In spring." Fritz sighed heavily. "She doesn't like Southern winters."

"You can't blame her." Vhalla thought back to the time she'd spent in the West. If she'd grown up in such a climate, she'd truly loathe the chill that was already slipping into the halls.

"I can blame her and I do!" Fritz grumbled. "I've missed her, and you."

"Tell me what I've missed." Vhalla pulled her friend close, enjoying having him at her side once more.

They strolled leisurely and began what would be the long process of catching up. *How she had missed her favorite Southerner.* His laughter was like sunlight, and his heart was more golden than his scraggly hair.

"You remember where your room is, right?" Fritz asked, pausing with Grahm at a door.

"You're not coming with me?" Vhalla blinked. She expected Fritz to be glued to her side, demanding all the details of their adventures apart. But it seemed he presently had other priorities.

"To your room?" Fritz laughed. "No, I figured you'd want some time to wash up alone. Unless you want me to scrub your back?"

Vhalla grinned. "I doubt you'd be let into the women's baths."

"Grahm was beginning to teach me the process of making vessels, you see," Fritz explained, taking a step closer to the other man. "I want to keep studying."

Fritz was studying something, all right.

"I'd enjoy learning more about vessels, from an expert." Vhalla smiled nicely at Grahm.

"I actually need to speak with you on the subject, now that you're back." Her fellow Easterner was completely oblivious to the silent but certain exchange between his two companions.

"Oh?"

"Yes, but it'll keep for now. Go and relax," Grahm encouraged.

So Vhalla finished her journey as it had begun, in silence and alone. Her future felt as equally uncertain now as it had the first time she'd entered the Tower. Vhalla ran her fingers over the nameplate that was on the door of one of the highest rooms in the Tower of Sorcerers. Her name had been engraved in tight, slanted script.

With a deep breath, she opened the door and was hit with an unexpected wave of nostalgia. This had not been her home for long. She'd only slept in the bed for a few nights between her trial and departing for war. But it was her home now. It had been the place she had dreamed of returning to with Larel and Fritz. She'd been the library apprentice everyone expected—and hoped—would die. Now she was the Windwalker, a lady and hero, and this was her home.

Vhalla ran her fingers reverently over the small table, the bed, and stopped at the wardrobe. Opening the doors, Vhalla stared at the contents for a long moment before promptly closing it. Her clothes were folded and hung on pegs, *exactly the same as Larel had left it.*

Closing her eyes, Vhalla pressed her forehead against the shut doors, as if she was locking a specter of the other woman in the wardrobe. As if she could protect herself from it entering her heart once more and consuming her soul. *Then again,* Larel had given her Serien, and Serien had become part of the woman Vhalla had grown into. She opened the doors again.

Vhalla knelt and carefully plucked a silver bracelet from atop a stack of carefully organized notes. If she were a Firebearer, she would have burnt them. But Vhalla resigned herself to living a little longer with the notes that Aldrik had exchanged with her a lifetime ago. She ignored any whisper in her heart that her reason for keeping them had little to do with whether or not she could start a fire.

She decided to proceed directly to Victor's office. Despite all the grime that coated her, Vhalla didn't want to wait a moment longer to deliver the axe to the minister. The conversation with Egmun was still fresh, and she had some questions for the current Minister of Sorcery.

The minister's quarters were higher than hers, and there was almost nothing close to it, save for one more door that was completely unmarked. If Victor's office had been farther down the Tower, Vhalla might have missed the heated conversation under the noise of sorcerer apprentices coming and going about their daily duties. But this high up, the halls were empty and silent. Vhalla clenched her fists, heightening her hearing by opening her magic and inviting the air into her.

". . . she is too bold, Victor." *The Emperor's voice.*

Vhalla looked around frantically. Swallowing the knowledge of whose chambers she was about to hide near, she sprinted up to the shallow alcove, pressing herself against the unmarked door at the top of the Tower. It would've been too far for anyone else to hear, but the silence and still air allowed her to magically stretch out her hearing, and she heard as clearly as if she was standing with her ear pressed against the door.

". . . bother you. She was only saving her skin from Egmun."

"Yes, Egmun has given me counsel on what he thinks we should do with her." Footsteps stilled and Vhalla could only assume the Emperor had been pacing. "You think she can be controlled?"

"I told you as much when you last returned from the war. Aldrik has command over the girl, you have command over him; she is yours," Victor said easily, setting Vhalla's heart to racing.

"I sought an end to that. He was actually *involved* with the creature," the Emperor spat.

"You knew that was a risk, my lord, given Aldrik's history with the women he chooses."

The axe seemed to pulse with a nervous energy that matched her heartbeat. Vhalla clutched the worn saddlebag tighter.

"My son does not always make the best choices; he has his mother's heart. It troubles me deeply, as I shall leave this continent to him so that I may continue my expansion," the Emperor muttered. "Though, since removing the distraction from his attentions, he has improved significantly, putting our Empire before himself. He may just have hope as a ruler yet."

"The Crescent Continent? Such is still your plan?" Victor asked, somewhat cautiously.

"As long as you are confident we have the girl," the Emperor retorted.

What? Vhalla was screaming the word in her mind. She didn't understand. *No, she understood it perfectly.* She just didn't want to.

"You want *me* to guarantee her cooperation?" Victor seemed surprised.

"It hardly matters if it is willingly or not, as long as she plays the role I have scripted for her. It has taken long enough to find a Windwalker, and the axe is the last of the Goddess's weapons. It must be her, or I cannot turn my campaign across the sea while my army is primed. Without the power in the Caverns, we do not stand a chance against their magic."

"Did you manage to get the axe?" Victor's voice held a tension to it that wasn't there before.

"Not yet," the Emperor seethed. "The Northerners think they will be able to keep it from me. But I will have it, even if I have to squeeze its location out of their princess myself."

Her nails dug into the saddlebag. Blood, the man wanted blood and more blood. He wanted to feast upon it until he was bloated. Vhalla stared at the flap of the bag. If she killed the Emperor now, she would be put to death. *But would it be worth it?*

Vhalla never thought that out of everything the Head of Senate had said to her, that his final question would linger—but now she found herself weighing the life she'd fought so hard for against allowing a murderous madman to travel to new places and bring war in his wake.

"I see. Well, you must keep me informed as to your successes, my lord," Victor hummed.

"I *must*?" The room seemed to still.

"A figure of speech," Victor spoke cautiously. "You know I am nothing but your humble servant. Though I do hope you continue to include me in your plans so that I may advise you to the best of my abilities."

"I hope so, Victor." The Emperor's voice could turn water to ice. "Because I had one errant Minister of Sorcery, and I do not care what you know or can do, I will not tolerate a second."

"You have nothing to fear, my lord."

The door swung open, propped by Victor, for the Emperor to stride out from the room. She had thought he would head down the Tower, but she had guessed wrong. As his footsteps neared, her heart raced and Vhalla pressed deeper into the door behind her.

A cold dread swept over her, and Vhalla held her breath, wishing she could be invisible and thinking of every frantic excuse. The Emperor passed by, so quickly he blurred before her eyes and didn't even glance in her direction. Vhalla blinked, her fingers nearly trembling with nerves, as the Emperor's footsteps faded away and disappeared.

Closing her eyes, she breathed a sigh of relief, only to open them and discover herself face to face with the Minister of Sorcery. Victor stared her down with his cerulean eyes, and Vhalla scowled up at him. *How could she have thought he was on her side?*

She pushed herself away from the door, to be caught by icy-cold fingers and wrenched back by force. Vhalla raised a hand, prepared to attack.

"I think we have much to discuss." Victor leveled his eyes with hers, stilling her immediate aggression with a look.

"I have nothing to discuss with you." Vhalla narrowed her eyes at him.

"You must let me explain."

"I mustn't do anything you say, *traitor!*" she seethed. She shouldn't have been surprised that he was her enemy, too. *They all were her enemies.* Vhalla clenched the saddlebag tighter.

"You heard." Victor looked utterly deflated. He took a deep breath, still holding her in place. "I remember, I remember you don't do well with force." The minister slowly relinquished his grip on her. "So let me bargain with you."

"What could you possibly have to bargain?" He had nothing he could offer.

"Here's my deal." The minister glanced down the hall nervously. "Give me a chance to explain, to tell you everything I know and show that I am not your enemy. If I succeed, your trust is my prize. Should I fail, then you should go and hide that bag and tell no one what I suspect are its contents. And I promise to never ask on it or tell a soul."

"Like I would ever trust you," she spat, pushing away from the wall and starting down the hall.

"Why do you think I used an illusion to make you invisible?"

Vhalla stopped, turning to face him.

"If I wished you ill, don't you think I would've let the Emperor see you? That alcove isn't small enough to hide you. I saw your robes from my door; he would've seen you without trouble were it not for me."

She swallowed, trying to counter the logic. "Fine, you have your deal."

Vhalla threw open the door to his office, stomping in without permission. By the time the minister closed it behind him, she'd stormed over to the window, gripping the sill with a hand. He stood silently, letting her work through the words.

"You had me bring it here for *him*?"

"Not for him," Victor denied.

"No, I heard you, you—you had me find it so he could turn his bloodlust on a whole new continent? A whole new people?" She whirled in place. "*What does he want?*"

Victor shrugged. "What does any man want when they have tasted power? To rule the world."

"And he wants me to help him do it," Vhalla filled in the blank.

"He does."

"He wants me to open the power of the Crystal Caverns. He wants me to use this." Vhalla held out the bag. "He wants to make monsters and perform feats of magic men should never perform."

"He does." Victor's cool responses were working her to a fever pitch.

"And you, you bend to his will. You're going to hand me over to do it for him. To be his thing, his tool, his *wretch of death!*" she shrieked.

Victor crossed the room and placed an arm around her shoulders, leading her to one of the two chairs that sat opposite his desk. His touch cooled some of the heat in her veins, and she sank into one of the chairs.

"I wouldn't." His palms rested on her shoulders a brief moment before Victor rounded the chair to lean against the desk in front of her, arms folded. "I wouldn't give you to him."

"You're his loyal servant," she snapped. "You're just like him, like all of them, looking for power, looking to use me—"

"I am not like him!" Victor slammed his open palm on the desk and leaned forward. "I have watched that man use sorcerers as tools. I have seen him degrade our people for the power that flows through them. I have endured him taking my students and teachers to be nothing more than cutthroats! I have watched him take a library girl and turn her into a "wretch of death" for no other reason than it suited him best."

For being a Waterrunner, fire was alive in Victor's usually icy eyes.

"I have balanced protecting my Tower, my sorcerer kin, against his aims and not lost my head in the process. For if I die, there would be no shield for people like us." Victor sighed, his shoulders slumping.

The minister knelt before her and rested a palm on her knee. She stiffened at the contact; it was part fatherly and part not—combined, it felt entirely wrong. "My dear girl, do you really think I'd let him have you again?"

"So what do you want?" Vhalla asked finally. "What are you risking everything for?"

"I want to protect people like us." Victor met her eyes. "I want to fight for a world where sorcerers aren't feared, but revered by Commons for our powers. Where no one would think to use us. Where a sorcerer would never have to hide."

Vhalla searched his face for a trace of insincerity. Finding none, she asked, "What do you want with the axe?"

"I want to return it to the Caverns and see that no one will be able to think of using it again." Victor's face was overcome by an intense severity. "Do you trust me on this?"

She ran her fingers over the saddlebag, searching for the buckle on the front, searching her heart for the answer. *Did she trust him?* If anything, out of everyone, Victor was the one person who'd only helped her at every turn. He healed her after her fall. He stood up for her in her trial. He trusted her with knowledge of the axe, with the task of bringing it to him safely and keeping it from the Emperor or the Knights of Jadar.

Vhalla unlatched the saddlebag as her answer. Victor stared intently as Vhalla produced the legendary crystal axe, *achel*.

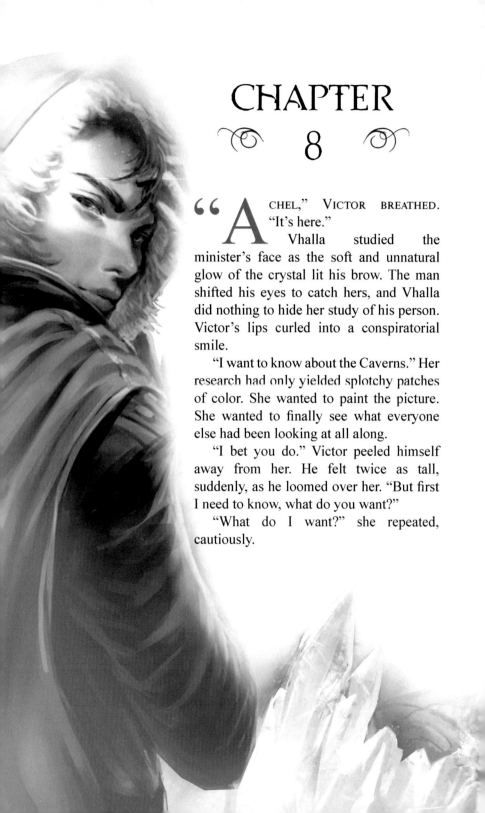

CHAPTER 8

"ACHEL," VICTOR BREATHED. "It's here."

Vhalla studied the minister's face as the soft and unnatural glow of the crystal lit his brow. The man shifted his eyes to catch hers, and Vhalla did nothing to hide her study of his person. Victor's lips curled into a conspiratorial smile.

"I want to know about the Caverns." Her research had only yielded splotchy patches of color. She wanted to paint the picture. She wanted to finally see what everyone else had been looking at all along.

"I bet you do." Victor peeled himself away from her. He felt twice as tall, suddenly, as he loomed over her. "But first I need to know, what do you want?"

"What do I want?" she repeated, cautiously.

"I told you my dream. I told you the world I'm prepared to fight for. What do you want?"

Rather than speaking the first thing that came into her mind, Vhalla remained silent, introspective. She mulled over the question, letting it settle across her mind and stretch into the cracks where she'd pushed her hopes and dreams into—things that had been too dangerous for her to engage in while she had been property of the Empire.

"I want . . . I want a future again. I want peace. I want freedom. I want to be free of people trying to use me for my magic."

"So we want the same thing." Victor beamed. "I'm relieved to know we're aligned in this."

"What are we aligned in, exactly?" Vhalla settled back in her chair, watching as Victor rounded his desk to a workbench in the far corner.

"The world we want to strive for—a world where sorcerers aren't used as tools, a time and place where we are revered and left to our own, rightful sovereignty." Victor paused his motions. "Tea?"

"Sure," Vhalla agreed cautiously. "How do you think we can get to your future? And what part does the axe play in it?"

"We will use it to make sure no one will be able to access the Crystal Caverns ever again." Victor placed a steaming cup of tea on the desk before her.

"How?" Vhalla took the item in question from the saddlebag, placing it on the desk next to the steaming tea she sipped gingerly.

"How much do you already know about the Crystal Caverns?" Victor sat.

"Not nearly enough. The literature is disappointingly sparse." Vhalla pondered all the books she'd managed to read about the Caverns while working at Gianna's. "I know the Knights of Jadar needed the axe—or, at least, they thought they did—to tap into the power of the Caverns. I know they needed the axe even more than a Windwalker . . ." A thought suddenly hit her. "Wait, Victor. Am I truly the first Windwalker?"

The minister set his own cup of tea down thoughtfully. "The first to be known again. The first to return to the world as far as the general populous is concerned."

"But, not the *first*?"

Victor shook his head, and Vhalla stared, baffled. She'd been revered, hated, desired, for being the *first* Windwalker. But there were more? She spoke as if Victor could read her suddenly tumultuous thoughts, "Why me?"

"Because you were in the right place at the right time." Victor frowned slightly. "Or the wrong place at the wrong time, depending on how you look at it."

"The East outlawed all magic following the Burning Times to avoid another genocide. It pushed the Windwalkers into hiding." Victor stood and ran his fingers along the spines of books lined up on a shelf behind his desk. "You see, there were never *that* many Windwalkers to begin with, not when compared to the other affinities. That just seems to be nature. But Windwalkers disappearing? That was the greatest act of self-preservation the world has ever known."

Victor placed a thin ledger on the desk between them. There were only a few pieces of parchment inside, some names and dates scribbled on a few lines. Victor flipped through them, the dates increasing until they stopped at the most recent date—*and her name*.

"It's a record of Windwalkers," she said softly.

"An incomplete one, for sure." He sat down once more.

"You told me I was the first . . ." Vhalla honestly felt relieved to know she wasn't. *Maybe she could return East and find others like her.*

"Everyone who wasn't actively hunting Windwalkers would believe such. Aldrik believed it, and I saw no reason to correct him or tell you differently." Victor pressed his fingertips together thoughtfully. "Whatever happened with you, I felt my actions would continue to protect your kin by not sending the world into another Windwalker-hunt."

"He doesn't know this exists?" Vhalla gaped at the notion of coming across some knowledge the prince didn't already possess.

"No, there are only three people who know this exists." Victor counted on his fingers. "Myself, the Emperor, and Egmun."

"*Egmun*," she seethed instantly. "Why isn't he the Minister of Sorcery any longer?"

"There was an accident." Victor scowled. "The man was mad,

insatiable for knowledge, and lusted for something beyond his reach."

"You mean crystals." It always came back to crystals. It seemed the world's every orchestration had the same, underlying harmony. Notes that one's ears had to be trained to pick up, but once one heard them, it was a cacophony of sound that drummed to a singular beat, pulsing the world forward.

"Yes. The Emperor wanted the power in the Crystal Caverns and set Egmun to free it."

Vhalla stilled, a memory flashing across her mind. She spoke without thinking, "You and Aldrik, he worked with you and Aldrik and crystals."

The minister's gaze suddenly went stony and guarded. His hands settled on the desk as he leaned forward slowly. Vhalla wasn't about to allow herself to be intimidated, but the minister was doing his best to make a case for it.

"Tell me what you know about that." Vhalla could hear the whisper of a threat hovering under his words. She didn't have a good answer, and the minister continued in her silence. "The rumors *are* true then."

"What rumors?" she whispered.

"Aldrik took you as his lover."

Vhalla was on her feet, snatching the axe faster than Victor could blink. She meant to only take it so that if she was forced to leave, she would leave with it in her possession. The watch she wore around her neck burned hot on her chest. "Don't you dare speak about him."

"If you cannot take my remark without brandishing a weapon at me, then you shouldn't go anywhere near the Court." Victor frowned, leaning back in his chair.

Vhalla looked at her hand. It clutched the axe in a white-knuckled grip. Muscles taut and ready to swing. Slowly, she eased it back onto the desk, mentally forcing herself to uncurl her fingers from it.

"What does it feel like for you?" Victor blinked at her a few times and Vhalla could only assume he was observing her with magic sight.

"I don't want to talk about the prince and me," Vhalla mumbled.

"Not the prince, I meant the axe." Victor tried to lighten the mood by smiling.

"Oh," Vhalla hummed, staring at the weapon. "It feels . . . Good? Powerful. Like I really am as strong as the wind." Vhalla considered it for the first time. "Is that how all crystals feel?"

"Yes." Victor nodded. "They taint sorcerers by trying to widen their Channels unnaturally. For Commons, it takes longer because the crystals actually forge new Channels."

Vhalla blinked. "Sorcerers can be *made*?"

"Not really." Victor shook his head. "The Channels they make in Commons seek out the magic in the Caverns. Sorcerers' Channels are widened to allow for it. But our race wasn't meant for such a power. It taints us. It twists our minds and deforms our bodies as it consumes us. It turns men into disfigured monsters."

"Except for Windwalkers." Victor nodded at her addition. "Then how could anyone but Windwalkers want to use the Caverns? It brings taint for everyone else."

"It does, if the crystals aren't managed properly," Victor elaborated. "Windwalkers can work with the crystals. Hone them, adjust them, alter their magic to fit better within a sorcerer's Channels, or to try not to leech onto a Commons and create something that isn't there.

"With a Windwalker, and enough training and time, you could outfit an army of Commons with magically empowered weapons," the minister concluded.

"And the Emperor wants this."

"He *needs* it if he wants to take the Crescent Continent." Victor sipped his tea for a long moment. "Our magic on this continent is fractured, diluted. Our sorcerers can only manage the elements. Across the sea, magic is part of the various peoples; it's of a different and greater nature that defies the laws we know."

Victor's explanation reminded Vhalla vaguely of the magic she'd seen the Northerners use. They had spoken of the South being out of touch with the "old ways," and the North was closer to the nearest point of the Crescent Continent, if her cartography knowledge wasn't failing her.

"Their magic is more like the crystals," she reasoned.

"Indeed," Victor confirmed. "At least, the little we know of it. Our traders are limited in what they are allowed to see. But we have a few reports from sailors."

"So, how do we make sure the Emperor doesn't get what he wants?" Vhalla rounded back to their original topic.

"You help me close off the Caverns." Victor stood again, returning the Windwalker ledger back to the shelf before hunting for something else. "You have the magic, the skill, the affinity that allows you to touch the crystals. But I—" he placed a worn and unassuming journal between them "—I have the knowledge required to do it."

Vhalla reached out, gauging the minister's reaction as she gingerly took the black, leather-bound book. Flipping it open, a script that Vhalla was utterly unfamiliar with graffitied the page. Her eyes skimmed the words, and her heart seized.

"Subject One has been displaying some issues with his Channels and an increase in headaches. An instructor reported a violent outburst. Further exploration is postponed until symptoms subside," she read aloud.

"I was Subject One," Victor interjected.

Vhalla stared back at the page, her fingers paused at a new paragraph farther down. "Subject Two was Aldrik?"

Victor affirmed her assumption, and Vhalla's skin crawled with horror. The Emperor had allowed his son to be turned into a test subject. He'd risked Aldrik's body and mind for his insatiable thirst for subjugation.

The minister pulled the book from her limp fingers, closing it. "I know more than nearly anyone about the crystals. I worked with them myself. Let me make some good of this knowledge?"

Vhalla stared up at the man. She guessed he was only older than Aldrik by four or five years. That meant he'd only been a boy as well when Egmun began his nefarious research.

"Tell me what I must do." Her words were soft but stronger than steel.

"For now, go and actually rest. Sleep well, because tomorrow we will begin work."

CHAPTER
9

*W*IND HOWLED, SWEEPING *fast up the mountainside. Vhalla stood on a painfully familiar rooftop, side-by-side with the crown prince. Aldrik was fixated on something below, muttering to himself over and over.*

"No, no, this is wrong. No!"

Vhalla took a masochistic look at what commanded his attention with such horror. She knew what she'd find. Her own body bounced off the rooftop, flying into the open air. She watched as the Vhalla that lived in Aldrik's memory struggled to right herself in the wind. She saw the moment her power began to come to her, as she twisted and turned unnaturally and out of control.

Aldrik cursed loudly, pulling at his hair and storming down the Tower. Only a guest in his memory, she followed along at his side without trying, watching the prince's actions play out before her.

He sprinted as fast as his long legs could carry him, bursting out of a dark hall and into a lavish parlor. Unlatching a window, Aldrik strained his neck out, looking for her. Vhalla wondered if somehow his magic called to hers through their Bond, even then, as her body smashed against the side of the building.

The prince pointed toward a pennon, burning away the supports in such a way that the pole it was supported by fell in her path. Her body hit it too violently for her to have any hope of catching herself. A futile and unexpectedly ill-thought gesture.

Another gale swept up the mountain, and Vhalla watched as her body unnaturally—magically—began to slow. The wind kept her from dying in its embrace. Vhalla knew that she would live, but this Aldrik clearly feared otherwise. His heartbeat reverberated in her ears as he was on the run again.

The prince skidded around a tight corner, pushing open a window and jumping over the sill into the small interior courtyard where she'd landed. Vhalla saw her body, bruised, bloody, broken and unnaturally bent at sickening angles.

"N-no . . ." Aldrik couldn't take another step as the sight of her tripped him. "This wasn't supposed to happen."

Vhalla felt him mustering his strength, retreating emotionally into the sheltered safe haven of his stony, battlefield shell. Training clicked in. Instinct clicked in. And the horrified, guilt-crippled man became the Fire Lord. Through his memory, Vhalla felt it happen.

"Breathe, breathe, you frustrating girl." Aldrik knelt at the side of Vhalla's body, putting a hand at her neck.

The noise of relief was almost a whimper, and the prince was on the move again. Vhalla watched as Aldrik scooped her up. She watched as he began running again, blood darkening his fine jacket.

"I miscalculated," he admonished himself, cursing. "I miscalculated."

This was an Aldrik no one had seen before, Vhalla suspected. How the man acted when no one was around, when he thought himself alone. She bore witness to the words he spoke when he thought no one would ever be there to listen.

"*Hang in there. Let me save something, make it, instead of break it.*" *His hands tightened around her.*

Aldrik burst through a door that clicked and locked behind him. Vhalla saw the flame bulbs line the hall, and she knew they were now in the Tower. He ran upward, his long strides carrying them higher.

He finally stopped at a door with the broken moon engraved onto its surface. Aldrik kicked at the door with his boot.

"*Victor,*" *he called.* "*Victor, now!*"

The door opened to a disheveled and confused Minister of Sorcery still wearing his sleeping gown.

"*My prince, do you have any idea—*" *Victor stopped himself the moment he saw the frantic prince and his burden.*

"*She needs help,*" *Aldrik panted.* "*Help her. I need you to help her.*"

"*Come.*" *Victor swept past him and began leading him down a familiar path.* "*Is that Vhalla Yarl? What happened?*"

"*Doesn't matter,*" *Aldrik attempted.*

Victor stopped short and stared Aldrik down. "*You do not knock on my door at ungodly hours of the night with a bloody mess— literally—and tell me this 'doesn't matter.' I expect an explanation!*"

Aldrik scowled, and the minister rolled his eyes as they began to nearly run down the hall again. The prince held his tongue until they were in the room Vhalla knew all too well. He gently set her body down onto the bed.

"*She's a Windwalker,*" *Aldrik whispered, finally.*

"*What?*" *Victor hissed, turning away from her corpse-like form. "Have you lost your mind?*"

"*No,*" *Aldrik said sharply. She heard the princely inflection slip into his tone.* "*I have not, she was Awoken tonight.*"

"*What in the Mother's name do you think you're doing?*" *Victor stepped closer to Aldrik.*

"*You cannot speak to me that way!*"

"*Don't play the prince with me, Aldrik,*" *Victor snapped. To Vhalla's surprise, it worked.*

"*It was under control.*" *Aldrik tried to smooth back his now-hopeless hair.*

"This is not 'under control!'" Victor shouted, pointing at the bed. Vhalla saw she had already bled through the sheets.

"So help me fix it!" Aldrik's voice rose as well. The two men stared at each other for a long moment before the prince's facade crumbled into the panic she'd seen earlier. Betraying the history that Vhalla knew the men had, he sighed heavily. "Victor, I need you—please."

"I'll need help." The minister began rolling up his sleeves.

"What do I need to do?" Aldrik pulled off his heavy black coat, revealing a fine black silk shirt underneath, also sticky with blood.

"I will need someone around the clock. Your hands are fine at this moment, I need them now, but I will need someone to stay with her." Victor stormed into the other room, furiously selecting concoctions.

"Who do you have in mind?" Aldrik asked.

"You pick. I know you want to choose who's by her, just do it fast." Victor went back into the room to begin working on Vhalla's corpse-like body.

Vhalla followed Aldrik out as he ran down a few Tower levels, stopping at an equally familiar door. She felt his tension, his hesitancy. The prince knocked. Aldrik waited stiffly as shuffling was heard from within, the door creaked open a sliver.

"My prince?" Larel yawned.

Aldrik stepped in and shut the door behind him. "Larel," he whispered, nearly collapsing against the wall. "I need your help."

"Aldrik, what is it?" Just like that, Larel knew it wasn't the crown prince addressing her, but her friend.

"I made a mistake," he breathed heavily.

"I am always at your disposal, Aldrik. What do you need?" Larel's caring manner shone through.

"It's Vhalla, come." Aldrik opened Larel's door, slamming it closed behind them.

A blistery fall gust rattled Vhalla's window in the early dawn, calling her from sleep. She blinked away the haze of dreams, Aldrik's memories lingering as sharply as the morning's chill. Running a hand through her hair, Vhalla tried to tease away the tangles and find motivation to face the day.

Like a petulant child, the wind rattled the window again, and Vhalla pulled herself from the bed, unlatching the glass. *Fall was heavy upon them*, she thought as she observed the trees rustling in the breeze far below her. Vhalla rested her elbows on the iron railing lining the small balcony that turned the large window into a doorway to the outside world. Her eyes scanned the greenery making its annual shift to red.

Vhalla turned away the second she caught herself searching for a certain garden with a rose-filled greenhouse. She remembered her promise to the prince—that she would tell him of all the memories she witnessed in her sleep. Vhalla debated the scope of the promise as she began dressing. Technically, the memory was one that involved her, one she knew about, and it held no real secrets.

She ran her fingers over the dark apprentice robes of the Tower. *When will I see you in black?* Aldrik's words echoed in her mind.

Vhalla shook her head and shrugged on the robes. The palace was full of too many memories—memories of other lives, of a man who was capable of both hurting and loving her, of a man who had promised his future to her when he asked her to be his bride.

Determined, Vhalla ignored the Tower kitchens as she strode down the curving, sloping hall. If she was going to drown in memories, then there was somewhere in particular she wanted to do it in. Vhalla knew many of the unlabeled doorways in the Tower were passages into the palace at different levels and places, secret to all Commons. But Vhalla had never had an opportunity to learn them. She'd only ever come and gone out of one location.

It took a long time to reach the library, longer than she expected, as Vhalla had become turned around at one point along the way. The main Tower entrance was on a much lower level than the Imperial Library, and winding up toward it from the Tower of Sorcerers was something she'd never done before.

Vhalla paused at the large doors of the library. Like the soft breathing of a slumbering beast, she felt air pulsing through the crack between them. It was inviting, a heady dose of too-sweet familiarity.

Her hands shook as she rested them on the wood. She'd been to war. She'd fought off a zealot group known as the Knights of

Jadar. She'd stood up to the Emperor countless times. But there was nothing more terrifying than confronting her guilt.

A rainbow of color splashed across the floor down the middle of the central walkway. It drew Vhalla's attention, as it always had, the moment she opened the door. It carried her eyes straight to the main desk where two people sat—the two people Vhalla sought.

Master Mohned, as ancient and sagely as he ever was, could barely be seen over the top of the desk. Next to him were the ringlet curls that Vhalla had admired for years. They were as beautiful as ever, but Vhalla no longer felt the same jealousy toward them. She had seen the world beyond the South in all its shades of beauty and would no longer trade her mess of brown hair. She no longer longed to be anyone more or less than who she was.

She was over halfway to the desk by the time Roan's head turned up. Vhalla froze in place, her heartbeat frantic, her breathing stuck. Roan's expression betrayed nothing.

The master stood slowly, following Roan's attention to the dark-clad woman haunting their library.

Clenching her fists briefly to invite her magic to give her strength, Vhalla closed the remaining distance to the desk. She stood, alternating between looking at the master and at her childhood friend, her mouth trying to form words.

"Welcome home, Vhalla," the master spoke up and spared Vhalla the toil of breaking the silence.

"Thank you, master." She let the man's warm nature soothe her nerves.

Roan still hadn't said anything.

"Roan—"

"Vhalla—"

They spoke over each other, silencing instantly.

"Roan, my eyes are bleary already. Why don't you give me a small rest and stretch your legs," the master encouraged.

Roan pursed her lips together briefly, looking between Mohned and Vhalla.

"I'd like to speak with you." Vhalla didn't want to lose the opportunity the master placed before her. "Please?"

"All right," Roan sighed. "I'm stiff anyway."

The blonde looped around the desk, crossing her arms over her chest. Closer, Vhalla noticed the slightly darkened patches of skin that marred her flesh. *Scars*. The sight brought the memory of Jax back to her, bleeding on Major Schnurr's floor. *How many more of her friends would have to suffer or die because of her?*

Vhalla turned quickly, starting down one of the rows of books. Roan thankfully followed, and they disappeared into the shelves.

"How's the library been?" Vhalla forced.

"Fine."

"Has the master been well?"

"He's fine." Roan clearly had little interest in actually conversing.

Vhalla stopped, leaning against one of the bookshelves for support. "Roan, I'm sorry."

Despite the flush of pain those words spread across Vhalla's chest, she managed to look the other woman in the eye and say them. Roan squinted marginally. Whatever pain Vhalla felt from guilt or shame could hardly be a fraction of what Roan had experienced.

"I'm sorry I didn't tell you what was happening, about my magic." Vhalla didn't know where to start. "I was going to tell you, really, but then—"

"You lied to me."

"I didn't!" Vhalla wished she could catch the hasty defense and swallow it back.

"You hid the truth, which is basically a lie." Roan frowned. "You hid it from me, and from Sareem. Unless you told Sareem?"

Vhalla nodded meekly, finally breaking eye contact.

"Oh, so you told him but not me?" Roan's hatred only seemed to grow. "You told him and the knowledge got him killed."

"I never meant for that to happen," Vhalla pleaded for Roan to understand. "He knew, yes, but he hated it. He wanted to see me Eradicated. Him knowing had nothing to do with him dying. And how could I bear to tell anyone else after the way he acted? Plus, you were so over the sun for him that you were blinded to anything else. I thought that I'd join the Tower and it'd sort itself out."

"Isn't it nice to be Vhalla Yarl?" Roan's words cut deep.

"It's not."

The other woman snorted and rolled her eyes. "The world

revolves around you and what you want, doesn't it? The great Windwalker decides for the rest of us what we can know and when we can know it."

"It wasn't that, Roan. You know it wasn't."

"I thought you were my friend." There it was—the deepest wound that still seeped blood. "I thought you were my friend, and you didn't trust me with any of your secrets."

Roan couldn't have known the depth of pain that her words caused. For all Vhalla had angrily faulted Aldrik for keeping her in the dark, she had done the same to Roan. She knew that feeling of being shut out by someone she loved, and there was no heavier guilt than that feeling.

"I'm sorry. I'm really, truly sorry. If I could do it again and fix it I would," Vhalla said honestly.

"You don't get that luxury." Roan frowned. "And you don't get my forgiveness either."

"Roan, please—" Vhalla tried to stop the other woman as she began to head back to the desk.

"No, Vhalla Yarl, I don't want anything to do with you. You made your choice. Go back to your Tower." Roan looked over Vhalla's robes. She shook her head and continued on her way.

Vhalla buried her face in her palms. But she didn't cry. She allowed the air she breathed to echo through the hollow that ballooned in her chest.

This was her true punishment for the Night of Fire and Wind.

On the march, Vhalla had gained Larel and Fritz and Daniel and the rest of the guard. She'd learned the love of a prince. At war, she'd become betrothed. She'd paid the cost with her humanity, and that seemed enough to satiate the Senate.

But this—this was the final ember of the Night of Fire and Wind finally flickering out. It was extinguishing the last light of her life from before she had become *the* Vhalla Yarl. There was no beacon back to the past, no warmth to keep her lingering. There was only forward now.

Roan ignored her again at the desk.

"Master." Vhalla wasn't about to let her trip be a total failure.

"Yes?"

"Before I left, you had me bind some books from the East. I was wondering if I might read them?"

"You didn't before?" The master was honestly surprised.

"No . . ." Vhalla had been far too distracted with other things at that point.

"I expected you had." Mohned stroked his scraggly beard in thought. "No trouble. Come."

He took the library's keyring from its hook behind the desk and began the slow shuffle toward the archives. Vhalla followed silently, adjusting the sleeves on her robes in thought.

"Roan took it very hard," the master stated the obvious. "Sareem's death, your magic, you leaving." Mohned sighed. "I was worried for her recovery."

"I'm sorry." Vhalla felt like her apologies would soon mean nothing if she kept offering them left and right.

"Sorry will neither change nor help now." Mohned's weathered voice was as soft as flipping pages. "Be patient, instead. Be kind in spite of her outward hostility. She still has a place for you in her heart."

Vhalla shook her head. "I don't think so."

"She asked about you. To every person who even breathed a word with a messenger from the North. She hung on Court gossip. She began to read books on magic."

She couldn't believe the same person the master was describing was the icy woman whom Vhalla had just faced.

"But presented with you, in the flesh . . . I think some wounds are still too fresh."

"I know how that is," Vhalla sighed.

"So give her time."

"How long?"

"It could be weeks, months, even years. You'll know when it begins to feel right again. When her pain has been softened by love once more." The master paused at the door to the archives. He gave Vhalla another long look. "I am glad, truly, to see you well."

"'Well' may be a matter of perspective," Vhalla muttered. She felt thin and empty, filled with ghosts.

"From my perspective, a girl I watched grow up is finally coming into her own." Mohned smiled tiredly. "And your hair is shorter."

"Oh." Vhalla's hand went up to the ends of her hair, caught off-guard by the sudden change in conversation. The master hadn't seen her since she'd cut it. "It used to be a lot shorter." It now was almost back to her shoulder blades.

"I prefer it long, if you'll permit this old man's opinion," Mohned offered with a chuckle.

"As do I." Vhalla smiled as Mohned unlocked the door to the archives.

She followed him down the center iron staircase to where she remembered the books to be, helping him draw back curtains for light.

"I had given you this task so that you would read," Mohned explained as Vhalla pulled the books carefully from the shelf. "You mean to tell me the one time I intended for you to give into the distraction of reading, you were actually working?"

"It seems so." Vhalla's hands paused on the large tome. She remembered what Aldrik had said on the last day of her trial. "Aldrik went to you, when he knew I was a sorcerer."

Mohned stilled, and Vhalla inwardly cringed, realizing she forgot the prince's title. The master let it slide. "He did." Mohned nodded. "I've known the crown prince since he was a boy. His obsession with books is not unlike your own. He quickly devoured the contents of the Tower's library from an early age, discovering the manuscript I penned on the Windwalkers."

"He suspected I was a Windwalker before he'd met me." She'd dreamt countless times of meeting the prince in the library, only to learn later that she was Projecting in her sleep.

"He did, and I confirmed."

"What?" Vhalla's hand slipped from the tome in shock.

"Vhalla," Mohned sighed and adjusted his spectacles. "You remember when you fell off the rolling ladder getting me a cartography book?"

"No . . ." She shook her head. "I fell so many times that—"

"Exactly," the master interrupted gently.

Vhalla's eyes went wide.

"And you were never hurt." Mohned rested his hand on the book. "I had begun to suspect the possibility long ago. You Manifested gracefully, so subtle and small that no one would know unless they knew what to look for. But I did. Knowing you came from two Eastern parents, it was all too much to just be chance."

"Why didn't you tell me?" Vhalla sunk into a chair. She'd had the same thoughts about that possibility when she rode with the Knights. But to hear it from the man who'd been like her father. "Master, why didn't you put me in the Tower?"

"Because I wanted to protect you. Vhalla, I was a boy when I first learned of the atrocities committed against Windwalkers. I knew if you were found, you would be hunted." The master sighed heavily. "I am loathed to say that I was proven right. I thought you would be safer here, hidden in the library, kept in the palace."

Vhalla stared at nothing, trying to piece it together. The childhood she'd thought she known was a shadow play.

"Does my father know?" Vhalla whispered.

"If he does, it is not because I told him." Mohned rested a hand on her shoulder. "Vhalla, forgive me?"

"For what?"

"For keeping this from you."

Vhalla raised a hand, gripping the Master's for a brief moment. "You were only doing what you thought was best."

She was wounded. But unlike Roan, she was used to secrets. Vhalla had grown accustomed to the forces lurking behind corners that pulled at the threads of fate, tying together the world and moving her without her knowing.

"Come to me, if you need." The master withdrew, starting up the stairs.

"I will," Vhalla called after him, "and thank you."

Silence was her reply.

Vhalla stared at the motes of dust floating through the beams of sunlight that pierced the windows. She ran her fingers over the manuscript before her, remembering vividly the last time she'd touched it. She'd been disappointed then, when Sareem's boots had appeared on the stairs instead of Aldrik's. Now she'd give anything to see those soles stepping down the stairs again.

With a sigh, Vhalla flipped open to the first page.

The work was an old collection of stories from Cyven. From short rhymes that Vhalla knew well, to long tales that she'd never heard. It was easy to read, and Vhalla found the pages slipping by one after the next. She allowed them to lull her into a quiet comfort by reminding her of the smell of wheat or of rain on her family's fields.

It was such a subtle trance that she'd fallen into that Vhalla didn't notice the one thing that began appearing in every other story—more frequently in older ones. The word suddenly lit up on every page. Vhalla stood slowly, flipping the pages quickly. The next random page the word was on. Again on the one after.

It was there in the story of harvesting the first grain. It was there in the story of a farmer defending his land from raiders. It was there in the tale where a man used it to scare away the clouds themselves.

Vhalla closed the book and returned it to the shelf as quickly and carefully as possible. She sprinted out of the archives and thanked the master with a panting breath before she was out of the library.

CHAPTER 10

"VHALLA!" GRAHM CALLED out. She skidded to a stop. The man must be part psychic and part hawk to pick her out when she was nothing more than a blur up the Tower.

"Vhalla, do you have a moment?" He emerged from the Tower library where he had been sitting with Fritz before stepping into the main hall.

"I was actually on my way to see the minister . . ." Vhalla glanced upward. *What she needed to talk about would keep.* She knew it would, so she didn't need to avoid taking time for Grahm. But the Eastern book had lit a fire under her, and now Vhalla had a lot of questions that she just wanted answered.

"Is it urgent?" Grahm asked, as if reading her mind. "I needed to speak to you about vessels."

"Oh, well, if it's that, could we do it another time?"

"I suppose." Grahm rubbed the back of his neck. "It was something Larel asked."

"Something Larel asked?" Vhalla repeated. *That was the last thing she'd been expecting.*

"What does this have to do with Larel?" Fritz joined them in the hall.

"This was something she asked me to do if . . ." The Easterner looked between them; a sorrowful expression overcame him. "If she didn't make it back."

"What is it?" One hand sought out the comfort of the watch under her tunic, the other gripped Fritz's tightly.

"She came to me with a bracelet she had made for you. Do you still have it?" Vhalla nodded at Grahm. "She wanted to make a vessel of it, a vessel of words. She said she knew Fritz and I were close and she could trust me with this, as a friend of a friend."

"Larel did?" Fritz jumped in.

Larel had seen it, Vhalla realized. She had seen Fritz's affection for the other man. She had known Fritz would go back to this person and trusted him with her message. Because those were the kinds of things Larel had been able to see—the inner mechanics of other people's hearts.

"Do you have the bracelet?" Grahm asked.

"I do," Vhalla answered eagerly, thinking of the beautiful metal cuff Larel had given Vhalla for her birthday.

Her heart raced as they started for her room. Vhalla wanted to break out into an all-out run. The world was moving far too slowly for her liking. Larel, her mentor, her guiding hand, her sister and confidant—she had something more to give. Vhalla's feet picked up speed, and the men silently followed.

The bracelet was exactly where Vhalla had left it when she had marched to war. Vhalla wondered when Larel had taken the time to spirit it away to Grahm, but Vhalla hadn't been paying attention to much of anything in the days leading up to the march.

Retrieving it, Grahm led them down into a center workroom. Along the perimeter were a handful of small doors. A couple of men and women worked at stations littered with books, focused on the magic that sparkled around the tokens they were focused intently on.

"This is where Waterrunners learn about vessels," Fritz explained upon seeing Vhalla's confused expression, keeping close to Grahm as he led them to one of the doors along the outside.

Grahm flipped a disk hanging by the door, from black to silver. "You know what to do, Fritz."

"You won't come in?" Fritz blinked.

Grahm shook his head. "I think it's better if it's just the both of you."

Vhalla's curiosity silenced her confused questions.

"But, I always—" Fritz began uncertainly.

"You will be fine." Grahm rested a palm on Fritz's shoulder. "You have a problem recording to the vessel still, yes, but you should have no problem drawing out the words that are recorded within the magic."

"I'd feel better if you were there," Fritz insisted.

"Larel would have wanted you to do it on your own," Grahm countered. There were no more arguments that could be put forward. "I'll be out here when you're finished."

Grahm opened the door, and Vhalla followed Fritz into a small chamber.

There was a single flame bulb overhead, casting the room in light shadow. It was little more than a closet, barely large enough for two people to stand around a center pedestal. Fritz squeezed around to the far side, and Vhalla stood opposite with the door to her back. Square in shape, the pedestal had a shallow indent in the center that was filled with water. It looked almost like a birdbath.

"Place it in the center of the water," Fritz instructed.

Vhalla did as she was told, gingerly putting down her precious possession with two hands.

"Fritz," she whispered.

"Yeah?" His eyes were glued onto the bracelet.

"What's going to happen?"

"Oh, right." Fritz shook his head. "I forget you're still technically new to the Tower. Vessels can store magic. But with a skilled Waterrunner—like Grahm—they can also hold words."

"Words?" Vhalla stared at the unassuming piece of jewelry.

Fritz nodded and lifted his hands, placing his fingertips into the edge of the water. Her friend took a deep breath and closed his eyes. Vhalla watched as his magic pulsed outward, generating shimmering ripples in the water. At first, the ripples bounced away from the bracelet in small waves, as they would any normal object. But the pulsing changed, and eventually the ripples hit the bracelet, stopping as though they were absorbed.

Vhalla waited expectantly, clutching the watch around her neck tightly. *Larel had been Aldrik's friend, too . . . Should he hear what was about to be said as well?*

The water hummed from the speech of a speaker who wasn't there, silencing all of Vhalla's thoughts.

"*Vhalla, Fritz.*" It was Larel's voice. Vhalla's hand flew up to her mouth. She took an unsteady breath at the sound of her dead friend's voice once more filling her ears, as though Larel stood with them once more. "*I know what it means if you are listening to this. It means I walk the Father's halls.*"

Vhalla looked at her friend. Fritz's expression was equal parts pain and joy. She was certain hers matched.

"*It's all right. I want you to know it's all right.*"

Vhalla wanted to scream at Larel that it wasn't. That it was Vhalla's fault Larel had been on the march in the first place. Vhalla had been given a gift in Larel, and she had never fully appreciated it before it was lost.

"*I knew before I left what it may mean for me. And, if you are listening now, then it means one or both of you survived, and I so pray for the latter. That alone brings me joy.*

"*I hope no one is doing anything silly like blaming themselves for my death. It doesn't matter how it came to pass. Please don't waste your thoughts on such nonsense.*" Larel's voice was as gentle and kind as it always had been. "*My life was borrowed from the moment Prince Aldrik found me. My existence was given an extension, a chance to really live. And live I did. It was simply my time to return what the Mother gave me.*"

Vhalla closed her eyes and breathed, absorbing every word.

"*I wanted to tell you both not to worry. I wanted to make sure you both knew."* There was a wavering pause that nearly stopped Vhalla's heart altogether. *"Fritz, it was always us, wasn't it? When the prince disappeared from my life for a time, you were the first one to be there for me.*

"All the rest of them told me it was about time I was no longer the prince's favorite. You never seemed to care. You were there when I needed you most, and I never forgot. I love you, my friend. I would gladly die for you—and if I did, I know I am content that I could give my life for my brother."

Fritz hung his head, and Vhalla bit her lip. It was not this well-loved friend who had taken their dear Larel from them. It was Vhalla who bore that curse.

"Vhalla." She looked at the bracelet at the mention of her name. *"I have only known you for a few months, and then not entirely intimately. I don't know what will happen on this long march—what has happened—where we will be. But if I want to leave you with one thing . . . It is that I am, and have always been, honored to be your mentor.*

"You are strong. You are a chick that has burst from its shell, and you are already struggling to fly long before you should ever be pushed from the nest." Vhalla heard the touch of sorrow in Larel's voice. *"I want you to know that I have always helped and protected you because I wanted to. Not because Prince Aldrik asked me to."*

Vhalla laughed softly, shaking her head at all that had transpired. There was no question in her mind.

"You will do great things. Call it my Firebearer's intuition. But never lose faith, never lose your beautiful heart. Don't let them win, those wicked men and women who would do anything to cage you or kill you." Larel's voice was strong and Vhalla let out a small hiccup, struggling to keep the tears under control. The day had already been emotionally taxing.

"Both of you, live long and wonderful lives. I know I will be looking at you from the far realms of the dead. My life was better because you were in it. I know, no matter how horrible the act could be that brought my death, I will die happy, for I lived with my friends." Larel's final goodbye echoed through the room.

Fritz grabbed the sides of the pedestal for support. Vhalla swayed slightly, trying to stop her head from reeling. Neither said anything.

"Damn it, Larel." Fritz's voice was at the verge of tears. "Why, why didn't—why couldn't you . . . I don't want a goodbye."

"Fritz," Vhalla said softly, seeing through the words that the pain put in his mouth.

"I miss her," he whispered.

"I do, too." Vhalla stared at the bracelet. "But she's still here, right?"

"Yeah." Fritz pulled himself together. "She'd be the type to haunt us 'til the end of our days if we didn't keep her in our hearts."

Vhalla smiled hopelessly at her friend and wiggled around the pedestal to the back of the room. She pulled her friend to her, taking a deep breath. "Fritz, thank you for being such a good friend to me." Vhalla hid her face where his neck met his shoulder.

Fritz mimicked the gesture. "You don't have to thank me for that."

"I do." Vhalla pressed her eyes closed and held him tighter. "The next time I wander away from the world, I want my friend with me. If you'll come."

He laughed weakly. "You know I will."

They stood together in a few long moments of silence. Eventually, Fritz pulled away and turned to the bracelet. Vhalla nodded in unspoken agreement, and they listened to their friend's last words again, and then for a third time, arms wrapped around each other to remind themselves of what they still had before them in spite of all their loss.

Fritz's eyes were red when they finally emerged. Vhalla rubbed hers but had managed to keep things together. They had both been to war, but Fritz had somehow emerged with his heart intact. Vhalla was almost jealous that he could still cry as easily as he did.

Grahm warmed her heart and brought a tired smile to her lips as he hugged Fritz tightly without a word. Vhalla watched the two men holding each other and wondered if they had any idea how they looked locked in an embrace.

"I think I'm going to go to my room for a little," Fritz announced finally. Watching him pry himself away from Grahm's embrace was almost painful for Vhalla. She wanted to scream at them to hold each other for a little longer, until it finally clicked for them. "Just sit for a bit."

"Do you want me to come?" Vhalla asked.

Fritz shook his head. "No, I think I'll be alone for a bit."

"All right." Vhalla gave him a friendly squeeze, and the once-again mourning man departed down the hall.

Grahm followed Vhalla up to her room. Vhalla shot him a curious glance, and he motioned for her to proceed. Clearly the man had something on his mind, and Vhalla didn't feel like filling the silence for small-talk's sake.

The man followed her into the room without a word, softly clicking shut the door.

"Grahm?" Vhalla inquired as to his uncharacteristic melancholy.

The man took a deep breath, his eyes searching. "I want to help him. How can I help him?"

Vhalla shook her head. These two were hopeless. It wasn't her place, but it didn't seem like they'd get anywhere without a little nudge.

"You should go to him, be with him, *hold him.*"

"But he said he wanted to be alone . . ." Grahm floundered.

"And you think he really meant that?" Vhalla crossed her arms over her chest with a tired grin.

"So, why didn't you go with him?"

"Because maybe he was sincere." She shook her head with a small laugh. "Or maybe I can see that I'm not the one he wants right now." The man actually blushed, and Vhalla wasted no time driving the point home. "He cares for you. You make him happy. You must see that."

"I . . . have."

"So what are you afraid of?" Vhalla touched her watch thoughtfully. "It's worth it, the chance is worth it. Love is always worth taking the challenge."

The words were real before Vhalla even realized it. *She didn't regret her time with Aldrik.* Her heart began to race, and she struggled to stay in the moment with Grahm. Vhalla's own affections were a known mess that continued to fall into hopelessness; she'd have ample time later to confront it. For now, she'd focus on her friends.

"Love is far better to know, even if it slips from your grasp or doesn't bear fruit like you'd hoped. People who say they regret love, true love, are just bitter liars."

Grahm looked at her for a long moment. Vhalla gave him an encouraging nod.

In that moment, she felt like she had lived a thousand lifetimes and loved a hundred times. She realized her own advice was true, and something about it made her yearn with sweet longing. In that moment, she wanted to see her prince more than anyone else in the world.

Grahm excused himself, and Vhalla watched him walk down the Tower. She wondered if he would head to Fritz's room. Vhalla walked on air, following Grahm down the slope of the Tower, a couple paces behind. The second she saw the man pause at Fritz's door, she turned and started back upward before her friend answered and she could be spotted.

Knowing Fritz was cared for, Vhalla walked past her room, continuing on. Silence settled into the Tower, and the doors became sparse. Vhalla caressed Larel's bracelet, thinking of her friend's words, of how Larel would advise Vhalla's tumultuous soul.

Vhalla bypassed the minister's office, going to an unadorned door that bore a black lock when others in the Tower were silver. She pressed both her palms to the door, leaning forward and pressing her ear against the wood. Vhalla stretched her hearing, listening for any signs of life in the room.

Silence.

Vhalla pushed away with a small sigh. *It was better if she didn't meet the prince again, privately.* It was better if she stopped thinking about the man with whom she had been briefly—secretly—engaged to. It would all be better if the watch at her neck would stop giving off phantom heat at the mere thought of the man she loved.

Vhalla knocked on the minister's door. Fritz may need time, but there was work to be done, and she couldn't waste hours mourning a woman who had long been lost. Vhalla had done her mourning and made it a part of her. She'd carry it with her forever.

"Ah, Vhalla." Victor smiled at the sight of her, holding open the door.

"Is now all right?"

"Certainly, come in." He clicked the door closed behind her, heading back to his low table before a window. "Tea?"

"Why not?" She assumed the previous day's chair, already settling into what felt like a routine.

"It's a little different," Victor proceeded with small talk. "I bought some lemongrass today in the market."

"I like lemons."

"Do you?" Victor passed her a steaming mug. "That's good to know."

Vhalla indulged in the steaming cup for a moment, deciding it was time to get to business. "Where do you hide the axe?"

She watched as Victor opened a secret panel in one of his cabinets, pulling out a locked box that the axe was hidden within. "No one else knows of that hiding spot."

"Well, now someone else knows," Vhalla remarked smartly, earning herself a chuckle. "Victor, the crystal weapons, each nation had one, didn't they?"

"So the stories and evidence indicates," Victor affirmed with a nod.

"Shaldan had Achel." Vhalla motioned to the axe. "Mhashan had the Sword of Jadar. And Cyven had a scythe."

"How did you come across that information?" He sounded impressed.

"I went to the library this morning," Vhalla explained. "I was reading some old Eastern books in the archives and noticed every story held mention of a scythe of great power. Now that I know about the weapons, I didn't think it could be chance."

"It's not." The minister preempted her next question. "Though if it still exists, it's not been mentioned in hundreds of years."

"Did Lyndum have a weapon?"

"Lyndum was rumored to not have a weapon, but a crown." Victor pressed his fingertips together in thought.

"A crown?" It made no sense.

"In some lore, the weapons were wielded by the Goddess herself as she forged and cultivated the earth and life. The crown was the symbol of her dominance over all things." The minister paused to sip his tea, collecting his thoughts. "But if it's true, the crown has been lost to time as well."

"What about the sword? The Knights of Jadar said it was stolen by a Minister of Sorcery."

"Egmun got his hands on it," Victor affirmed, confirming her worst fears.

"He took it to the caves," she continued. Something began to creep on the edge of her memory. Something about this story was familiar, despite having never heard it before.

"He did." Victor watched her carefully.

"And then he . . ." Vhalla placed a palm on her forehead. *A sword. A crystal sword.* The axe glowed faintly before her, as though the whole universe was contained within it and all she had to do was discover its secrets.

"He tried to unlock the Caverns. But he miscalculated, and the fool started the War of the Crystal Caverns," Victor finished bitterly.

The knowledge was distracting enough that Vhalla ignored the feeling that it wasn't what she had been about to put together.

"How is he the Head of Senate if he caused the war?" Vhalla frowned. It sounded like he should've been long dead.

"Because Egmun craved knowledge in all its forms; he collected it, hoarded it. And some of that knowledge was inevitably the sort that other people didn't want to be made public." Victor sighed and stood. "His foolishness cost him his magic. But it did yield information that we will be able to use."

"How?"

"Egmun needed the sword because with it he could access the heart of the Caverns. The crystals have a single heart from which their power stems." Victor was back to rummaging. "Every other crystal's power comes from being spawned by this center, like tiny looking glasses into the Caverns themselves. Hence the Channels they build in search of that magic, which taint sorcerers and Commons alike."

Vhalla was reminded of the Northern ruins where she'd procured the axe. The moment she freed the weapon from amid the crystals, the others had darkened into dormancy and fractured. "The crystal weapons are like smaller hearts, aren't they?"

Victor turned and gave her an approving look. He rested a box with Western writing on its lock on the desk between them. "Exactly so. Because of that, they are the only thing that can access the true power of the Caverns—which is one reason why they've been so sought after. But I also theorize that they would be the only thing that can destroy that power as well."

"An axe that is legendary for cutting anything, even a soul." Vhalla stared at Achel.

"Perhaps, the soul of the Caverns, if you will." Victor sat, opening the box of crystals he'd used on her after her fall. "You'll need to cleanse it, sharpen it." He motioned to the axe. "Look at it with magic sight."

Vhalla obliged. The axe was a tangled mess. Dark colors overlay lighter ones, a swirling mass of lingering traces of magic.

"Those are remnants, like a vessel; the axe has been dirtied with the leftovers of things it's been used for."

"Like magic blood," Vhalla reasoned.

"That's certainly a way to think of it," the minister agreed. "We will have one chance at this, Vhalla, and I want to set us up for success by removing all the possible variables that could get in our way. I want no magic reacting in ways we don't expect."

The minister spent the rest of the afternoon going back and forth with Vhalla on the properties of vessels and how they were created. He educated her on how a Waterrunner could draw out the magic from a person by tapping into their Channels.

The theory was the same for what they were seeking to accomplish, but the execution was completely different. Victor tried to help as best he could, though there were some things that were left to trial and error. Vhalla ran her fingers through the magic that hovered around the axe, imagining them to be threads fluttering on the wind.

With this imagery, she pushed them upward, focusing on one at a time. It was wind without wind, a level of magic that she had never tried to tap into before, and it was utterly exhausting. Once she had a thread free, the minister provided her a crystal to store it within. That was much easier than the brow-dampening process of untangling the magic from the axe.

She managed three threads before she felt utterly spent. Vhalla blinked away her magic sight and collapsed back into the chair. Victor wordlessly began to clear his desk of the tools they'd been using all day.

"You did well," he encouraged.

"I will be an old maid by the time it's cleansed," Vhalla lamented.

"Your second was faster than your first, and your third faster than your second." Victor smiled, rounding his desk. "Think of it as learning magic all over again."

"I just finished learning magic the first time." She stood, stretching.

"Then the process is fresh in your mind." Victor chuckled. "Thank you, Vhalla," he said sincerely. "You're going to be the catalyst for a new age."

"One step at a time." She shrugged. As all she sought was lasting freedom and peace; Vhalla kept her eye on the prize.

"We should work again tomorrow, if you feel up to it." The minister started for the door.

"I have a feeling this is how I am going to spend my days," she murmured.

"It is. I want to move quickly, but not so quickly that you burn out . . . so rest in the morning. I don't want you pushing yourself on trivial things; this will be taxing enough for you. When we are not working, focus on giving your magic ample time to recover."

"I'll be certain to take it easy," she agreed lightly.

The minister paused, unappreciative of her tone. "I am quite serious. We are working with advanced magic unlike anything you've ever seen before."

Vhalla held her tongue about the magic she had seen in the North.

"Don't fret." She shrugged off the minister's worry as fatherly concern. "I'll keep up my strength."

"I trust your judgment," Victor said finally the disapproving glint to his eyes vanishing. "Though, I request that you tell no one of what we are doing."

"By the Mother, no." Vhalla laughed. "I'm not stupid."

"No." The minister smiled, "you're not."

When Vhalla finally returned to her room, the window was dark and the moon was already cresting the horizon. Utterly exhausted, she wasted no time bathing. The baths were mostly empty due to the unconventional hour, and Vhalla greedily soaked in the warmth of the water.

By the time she crawled into bed, she expected to fall asleep instantly, but her mind lingered in wakefulness. There was a smell on her pillow, on her blankets, so faint that Vhalla was certain she was imagining it. Real or not, it brought back memories of the last nights she'd spent in the bed, with Larel soothing her nightmares away.

Vhalla passed the watch around her neck from hand to hand. She'd returned home, she was surrounded by almost everyone she'd ever known, but she still felt very, very alone.

CHAPTER 11

Two days later, Vhalla escaped the Tower with determination—she could only spend so many hours with Fritz and Grahm making eyes at each other and saying nothing about it. There was somewhere else that she knew she had to venture. And, while she'd find friends there, it would also force her to confront the truth she'd been harboring since the West.

Swords rang out above shouting and laughter. The palace training grounds were full of veterans from the Northern war, and with them came a whole host of new recruits for the palace guard. It seemed Tim had been at it again, spreading stories about her, as most of the guard had a wing painted on their breastplates. It didn't take long for Vhalla to be noticed by some of the men and women, and she was greeted like an old friend.

It was the reception she would've wanted from the librarians and would've never expected to find among swords, bows, and drills. But the encouragement was welcomed. Plus, once she was spotted, it made fleeing in absolute terror much more difficult.

Her eyes scanned the dusty training field. Archers sent arrows toward targets, and men assaulted wooden dummies with what would be lethal slashes. Vhalla found Daniel among the latter. *Breaking the news about Jax to one of the Guard would mean breaking the news to them all.*

"If you want to say hello, I think he'd appreciate it," the voice nearly startled her out of her skin.

"Erion," she breathed the second she met the Western eyes. "Erion!"

Vhalla threw her arms around the man's shoulders. They'd never been exceptionally close, but the Golden Guard felt like family. The feeling must have been mutual as his arms wrapped around her waist for a brief squeeze.

"You are all sorts of trouble, aren't you?" Erion pulled away quickly, his Western nature getting the better of him. "It's no wonder Jax likes you."

Vhalla swallowed hard. "Erion . . . Jax is . . . ." Vhalla gripped her fingers, emotions running high. "He was trying to protect me."

"Oh, he told us."

"What?"

"When he got back to the palace a few days ago, not long before Daniel, he told us all about how you got him stabbed." Erion laughed.

Vhalla didn't share the same emotion. "He's here?" she asked, deadpan.

"Yeah, right over there." Erion pointed to a group practicing grappling.

Vhalla stormed across the training grounds like a little vortex, her hands balled into fists as she stomped toward the tall figure of a Western man.

Jax turned with a laugh, breaking away from his conversation and noticing her for the first time. He put his hands on his hips and tilted his head to the side. "No blood, no weapon, no armor? This may be the first time you've disappointed me."

She debated between punching him and kissing him the second he was in arm's reach.

"You've been back for *days,* and you didn't think to tell me you were alive?" Her voice couldn't make up its mind either, and it alternated between cracking with rage and relief.

"I figured someone else did." Jax shrugged. "It's not like it makes that much of a difference."

"Of course it does!" Her intensity startled him. Vhalla spoke over his loss for words. "You think that you dying 'doesn't make a difference?'"

The Easterner in her finally won out, and Vhalla wrapped her arms around his waist. The hug was awkward, but she persisted all the same. His hands fell on her shoulders, but he didn't instantly push her away. It seemed as though he was at an utter loss for what to do when someone showed him affection.

Vhalla broke the short embrace, staring up at him. "I'm glad you're okay, Jax. I thought I'd killed you."

"You don't need to worry about someone like me," Jax replied. He glanced around, catching the eyes of the other guards staring curiously. The man thumped the top of her head with a fist in a brotherly fashion. Laughing, he spoke loud enough for everyone to hear, "Bleeding heart Easterners! You don't need to worry so much about us tough Western stock. Right, Erion?"

Erion gave a marginally committal grunt.

Some of the men chuckled, and Vhalla let them have their laugh. The look she received from the corner of Jax's eyes spoke volumes of his true feelings toward her concerns.

"How did you survive?" Vhalla was still trying to process that the man before her was real.

"One of Schnurr's servants found me," Jax explained. "I was able to cauterize most of the wounds myself, so I didn't bleed out entirely. Unsurprisingly, they had little love for their *most generous* lord, and helped me get back on my feet."

Her presence had been enough of a break from the normal routine that others were noticing. Among them was the golden prince, Raylynn at his side, with Craig and Daniel in tow.

"Vhalla!" The Eastern man nearly sprinted over to her.

If Vhalla hadn't pushed wind at her back, the force of his embrace would've knocked her over. But Vhalla locked her arms around him tightly for a long moment. Daniel pulled away, beaming.

"It's such a relief to see you're all right." He hooked an arm around her shoulders and shook her lightly. "You had me so worried!"

"Jax told me you were foolish enough to feel responsible for letting me leave alone." Vhalla grinned, appreciating the now effortless atmosphere time had created between them.

"If it isn't the troublemaker herself." Baldair joined the group.

"You're one to talk." Without hesitation, Vhalla hugged the youngest prince tightly. Baldair squeezed her in reply. "How many hearts have you broken while I was gone?"

"Me? I never break hearts!"

Raylynn snorted.

"At least five," Erion outed the golden prince.

"No, no, only three."

"*Only*," Vhalla teased.

"It's not my fault if they think there's more to it than a night! I never advertise any differently," the prince defended himself with a laugh.

Vhalla decided it was true after a moment's consideration. He didn't seem to have many *repeat offenses*. Her eyes shifted to the blonde at Baldair's side. *Maybe he had one repeat offense.*

Raylynn rolled her eyes. "The paragon of innocence."

"I'm about to make all of you run double drills," Baldair threatened.

"Speaking of," Erion said as he caught Daniel and Craig's attention, "where are they at so far?"

The men began conversing on the status of the swordsmen. Vhalla was quickly forgotten, until Baldair took a step closer to her.

"Take a walk around the grounds with me, Vhalla? I'd like to show them to you."

She knew by his tone, by the way that the rest of the Golden Guard seemed to take a step away, that the prince showing her the grounds was a front for other intentions.

"Certainly. I'd like to see them," Vhalla agreed with grace.

The prince offered her his elbow, which she took without hesitation.

"I remember a time when you wouldn't be seen touching me." He chuckled softly.

"How times have changed." She smiled in bittersweet fondness at the unconventional start of their relationship.

"You are the only woman who ever was of such an opinion. I should've known then you were already practically family."

"Jax informed me that you told the guard to protect me as if I was kin." Vhalla glanced at the Western man, reaffirming he was actually alive.

"I heard you were to be family." Baldair's usually booming voice was soft and rich with sorrow.

Vhalla couldn't stop her hand from flying to the watch at her neck, confirming his words with a single action. "How did you know?"

"It wasn't hard to put together when I saw that watch. And, when Aldrik came to his senses, finally, he went to Father and begged once more for you."

"*Begged?*"

"He said that he loved you and that he had already promised his heart and future to you."

Vhalla stopped in place with shock. "He said that, to your *father*?"

"Not one of his finer ideas, I agree. I wouldn't have been surprised if Father's eyes had fallen out of their sockets as they bulged with rage." Baldair shook his head, and they continued their walk. "We all should've known what that token meant."

Vhalla focused on the dusty ground, not even bothering to pretend the prince was showing her the regimen of the palace guard. "How is he?" she breathed.

"Rough, beyond rough, for a while. He snapped, broke completely in a way I'd never seen him break before." Baldair paused, chewing over his words. "Then, one morning, like magic, he woke up and changed everything. Or, at least, he started *trying*. It was like he finally got it, what everyone had been trying to tell him all along. He worked to put a stop to all his nasty habits, he endured the shakes, the sickness. He withdrew more, but it tempered his anger."

"Ophain said much the same," Vhalla recalled.

"Aldrik's uncle? You met with him?"

"In the West," she confirmed.

"Right . . . Were you really ambushed by the Knights?"

Vhalla shook her head in exasperation. "You think I'd lie about that?"

"I suppose you wouldn't." The prince laughed. "The fools, like you could ever be chained. If my father couldn't do it, no one could."

She never thought she'd laugh about the Emperor trying to enslave her. The conversation reminded her of what she'd learned about Jax's history during her brief time on the run.

Before she had a chance to ask, Daniel interrupted them. "My prince, were you still planning on heading to Court?"

"Oh, by the Mother," Baldair groaned as he glanced at the sky. "I was, but I have no time to change."

"Neither do we." Daniel shrugged. "I thought we might present the Lady Vhalla to the Court today."

"Present me to the Court?" Vhalla wasn't sure if she liked the sideways look Baldair was giving her.

"I suppose you haven't been here since the last Court day," Baldair murmured. "If the lady wishes it, I'll come for moral support. But, Mother, don't make me speak more than I must."

"What does being *presented* entail?" Vhalla asked uneasily.

"You're just formally announced as a new lady," Daniel answered easily. "If Baldair doesn't wish to speak, I'd be honored to do the announcing."

He held out a hand, and Vhalla considered it briefly before taking it. "Couldn't hurt, right?"

"It's easy!" Daniel encouraged.

"By the Mother," Baldair muttered under his breath. He turned and raised his hands to his mouth, calling across the field. "Ray, we're going to Court."

The blonde let out a monumental groan at that information.

"That's not encouraging," Vhalla said uneasily.

"Raylynn's just dramatic. She hates Court."

"For good reason." Baldair actually frowned.

"It's not *that* bad," Daniel insisted.

Vhalla stared at the prince until he yielded an explanation, "I've been around the Court for too long to see it with an entirely optimistic view. Just know going into it that there really are vipers."

Daniel escorted an apprehensive Vhalla through a short series of outer hallways and then across a lavish series of gardens to the building in which Court was held. Vhalla knew of the place conceptually, but she'd never had reason to explore it before.

She knew instantly what Baldair had meant about dressing once she saw the nobles strolling into the building. Lucky enough for her, it wasn't the first time she'd worn unconventional attire to a noble function. Vhalla adjusted her black robes proudly and squeezed Daniel's arm tightly as they crossed the threshold of the Imperial Court.

They were noticed within seconds. Clipped whispers echoed through the assembled nobles, and the hum of conversation was quickly snuffed. Curiosity, fear, resentment, admiration, the expressions they gave her crossed the spectrum. *And were no different than what she was used to receiving.*

Daniel cleared his throat. "I'd like to have the honor of presenting the Lady Vhalla Yarl to the Court."

The expected convention observed, the first man stepped forward to play his role. "May the sun shine brightly on your house, Lady Yarl."

The next person said some similar equivalent, the person after said another. Vhalla feared they'd have to go through every person assembled, but Daniel explained later that the ten or so nobles who greeted her were the heads of some of the oldest families on the continent. Naturally, not every noble family was in attendance. Court wasn't a mandatory function, but nobility often had little else to do to pass the hours and were kept happy and complacent toward the Empire by milling about and gossiping with each other.

"Vhalla, I'm glad you're here," Daniel spoke the moment they were free of the initial party that was brave enough to break the ice with the Windwalker. "I did a lot of thinking after the North . . ."

"I did too," Vhalla said quickly. His expression mirrored her heart and Vhalla was inclined to spare them any awkward moments. "It's good to be home." *Whatever home had now become.*

"Speaking of home, I have something I want to show you."

"What is it?" Vhalla tried to decipher his cryptic words.

"Lady Yarl." A man interrupted their conversation before Daniel had time to elaborate. "I heard word of your ordeal in the West. Appalling, really, that Lord Ophain allows those zealots to run so freely."

Vhalla turned to face the Western man, trying to gauge his sincerity. "Lord Ophain does what he can. He's worked to make it clear where the West now stands toward Windwalkers."

"And where do you think that is?" The man gave her a slow smile.

"I think—"

Another hush fell over the crowd, and Vhalla was stilled by the man and girl standing, hand in hand, in the back doorway to the large hall. Vhalla tried to look at anything else. She tried to look at the vaulted ceiling with carved archways. She tried to look at the patterns the stained glass printed on the alabaster floor. She tried to look back at the lord and strike a conversation.

But she was trapped, her eyes focused on the hand wrapped in Aldrik's.

She had seen the princess before. She'd stood on the Sunlit Stage upon Vhalla's return. But she might as well have been half a world away from Aldrik then. Now she stood poised and tense at his side, and in them Vhalla saw the future Emperor and Empress.

She wanted to leave. She didn't want to see any more. She didn't want to confront the mess his perfect façade created in her heart.

Aldrik scanned the crowd and his lips parted to speak, freezing halfway open the second his attention found her. She saw his confusion at her presence, a similar feeling to the panic she was already drowning in.

The nobles missed nothing and hastily pointed out the awkward exchange between the prince and the newest lady.

"Prince Aldrik, so good of you to join us today! The Lady Yarl was presented by the Lord Taffl earlier," came a voice that broke the silence with malicious excitement, the same Western man whom she'd been speaking to a moment before.

"Lady Yarl." The prince's lips formed her name with such

precision that it sent a shiver up Vhalla's spine. "It is an honor to have you as a member of this Court."

The words were stiff and formal, but his eyes were alive.

"Thank you, my—" Her voice wavered as she caught herself before she could use her former term of endearment. Aldrik's eyes widened a fraction, and she could hear him hold his breath. "Prince Aldrik."

Disappointment attempted to pull his shoulders down. *What did he want from her?* What did he think would happen?

"I believe this is the first time the Lady Yarl has met the future Empress," a woman tittered. "She wasn't there for the presentation of our dear prince's betrothed during the Festival of the Sun."

Vhalla's hand went to her neck. Baldair had been right; these people were awful. She sought him out, and the younger prince looked on helplessly.

"Lady Yarl, *Hero of the North*, why don't you introduce yourself to your future ruler?" the woman suggested.

Vhalla was tempted to show them all exactly how she'd gotten the title of the Hero of the North. She'd reaped destruction and rained hellfire upon her enemies. Vhalla straightened, holding herself taller. But she'd also earned her title and freedom by playing this noble game. *If they wanted her to play, then she would show them how to play to win.*

All eyes were fixed on the Windwalker as she crossed the room to the prince and princess. Her feet echoed across the floor, the only thing breaking the silence. Vhalla swallowed her frantically fluttering heart. She would do not only what she had to do, but what was right, what she wanted to do.

"Princess—" Vhalla didn't even know the girl's name and was forced to leave it as such. The young royal pursed her lips slightly, but didn't betray any other emotions. In that way, perhaps she was a fitting match for Aldrik. Vhalla was honestly loathed to think it. "You truly grace us with your presence."

No one moved a muscle.

"Your poise in the face of those who have committed such transgressions against your home is beyond your years." Murmurs swept through the room. "Your poise in the face of the people who no doubt gossip over the massacre of your innocent people, as though it were sport, is a grace that I clearly cannot command!"

"Treason!"

"Truth!" The word was as fast as a whip from her lips, and it silenced the noble who had interrupted her. Vhalla turned back to the girl, her expressionless mask cracking with shock. Vhalla pressed her eyes closed with a sigh. "If this is the grace by which you will rule, then the Mother has smiled upon the Solaris Empire with your union."

Vhalla braved a look at Aldrik. The prince wavered between the look he got when he was about to tell her off, and when he wanted to sweep her into his arms and kiss her until she saw stars. Vhalla took a cautionary step away.

"My presence is likely uncomfortable for you, so I will excuse myself and set the example for any who seek to foster rifts in our Empire, an Empire for *peace* now, by leaving."

Vhalla turned and didn't look back. She strode out the Court's meeting hall and into the sunlight. She walked, hands clenched, until she was out of eyeshot and then broke out into a run. Her lungs burned from the sudden sprint, and her eyes stung. *Aldrik, Aldrik, Aldrik,* her heart screamed. *What had she done?*

Vhalla slowed to a stop, sighing. She'd heard the footsteps not long after she'd left the Court and turned, expecting to tell Daniel not to worry so much. Vhalla froze, face to face with an emerald-eyed Northern woman.

"*Gwaeru.*" It was fitting that the first word she spoke to Vhalla was the same word that had confirmed that this woman had tried to shoot her down in the North.

"Za," Vhalla replied curtly.

"You know my name?"

"I do."

"You know who I am?"

"I do." At least, Vhalla could assume the woman was here as some guard for the princess. "I didn't see you in the Court."

"You wouldn't notice a fire if the Fire Lord did not start it."

Vhalla ignored the jab. "What do you want?"

"Sehra wishes to meet."

"Sehra?" Vhalla put it together after only a second. "The princess?"

"Child of Yargen and future chieftain," Za corrected, setting Vhalla's mind to whirring around anything she knew as to the significance of the first title.

"Why in the name of the Mother would she want to meet me?" Vhalla asked cautiously.

"She has deal."

"What kind of a deal?"

"Meet tonight. Same place." Za started back for the hall of the Imperial Court.

Vhalla went to call for Za as she disappeared in a side alcove.

"Vhalla!" Daniel broke the moment, jogging up to her. Vhalla glanced between the Eastern man and where Za had disappeared. He watched her attention shift. "What is it?"

"Nothing," Vhalla mumbled.

Daniel escorted her back to the Tower, apologizing for what happened and explaining how his first day at Court was nothing short of magical. He could've made all the excuses in the world, but they wouldn't make Vhalla forget what had transpired, and they wouldn't make her any more interested in returning.

At least, not when Court was in session.

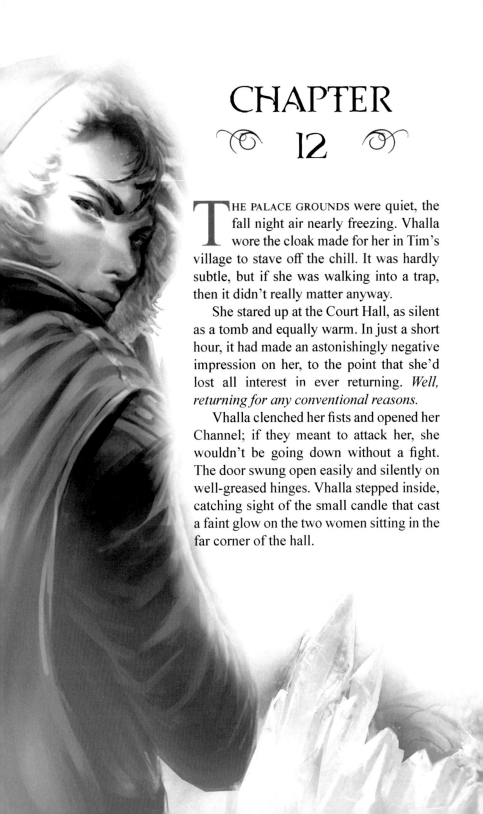

CHAPTER 12

THE PALACE GROUNDS were quiet, the fall night air nearly freezing. Vhalla wore the cloak made for her in Tim's village to stave off the chill. It was hardly subtle, but if she was walking into a trap, then it didn't really matter anyway.

She stared up at the Court Hall, as silent as a tomb and equally warm. In just a short hour, it had made an astonishingly negative impression on her, to the point that she'd lost all interest in ever returning. *Well, returning for any conventional reasons.*

Vhalla clenched her fists and opened her Channel; if they meant to attack her, she wouldn't be going down without a fight. The door swung open easily and silently on well-greased hinges. Vhalla stepped inside, catching sight of the small candle that cast a faint glow on the two women sitting in the far corner of the hall.

Both of their heads turned, and Za stood from where she had been busy fletching arrows, sending scraps of feathers and wood fluttering like tiny sprites in the candlelight. Princess Sehra didn't stand, she merely turned, watching Vhalla warily. She was garbed in a loose and warm looking dress, reminiscent of patterns that Vhalla had seen on the Northern warriors' tabards, rather than the Southern fashions she'd been wearing in court.

"You've come alone?" Za called.

"I have." Vhalla didn't move far from the door, ready to run if needed. Though she didn't really know what these two women could do to hurt her. Vhalla outclassed them both in combat—unless they had some secret prowess Vhalla didn't know about—and they were severely outnumbered in the South. Vhalla suspected that the Southern people would jump on any excuse to remove a Northerner from their throne.

"What do you want?"

"I have a deal for you." Her voice was gentle and bright, like morning dew.

"What could you possibly want with me?"

"Sit, share our light, and I will tell you." Sehra motioned to the circle of light the candle cast on the floor.

Cautiously, Vhalla crossed the room, sitting on the outer edge. Za sat stiffly as well, close to her princess.

"You know who I am, what I am." Vhalla didn't want to mince words. "You know what I've done against your home, your people."

"I do," Sehra affirmed. Her eyes flashed dangerously in the candlelight. "And for it, I hate you deeper than any I have ever hated before."

"You didn't call me here to tell me that." If the girl had meant to wound Vhalla, she would've done so already.

"No, but I don't want you to think you will make an easy friend in me." As Sehra spoke, Za shifted closer to the princess, her hands busy fletching arrows in as threatening a manner as possible.

"That would never be something I'd be confused about." Vhalla shook her head. "Though I harbor no ill will toward you and your people. The Empire invaded you without cause, no matter what is said here."

"Not without cause," Sehra corrected. "You know the cause."

Vhalla met the girl's green eyes, suddenly seeing a woman much older than her years staring back.

"Perhaps." Vhalla wasn't going to be the first one to bring up the axe.

"Do not lie," Sehra scolded. "I can sense the magic on you. You have touched Achel."

Vhalla stiffened and blinked her eyes quickly, shifting her vision into magic sight. The girl looked no different from Za, whom Vhalla knew was a Commons. *Did she have a closed Channel?* Had Vhalla somehow been misled that Aldrik's bride wasn't a sorceress?

"My mother speaks to me; she tells me the achel has been stolen. But the Emperor rages daily for it to be given to him. It is gone, but not into the Empire's hands. Only your hands have its shimmering remnants upon them."

"How are you so certain?" Vhalla asked uneasily.

"I am a child of Yargen." Sehra sat straighter at the word. "I know the old ways. I know the old magic that has long been forgotten by those to the south of Shaldan."

"Why does Shaldan want the axe?" Vhalla hoped the question didn't confirm or deny her possession of it.

"Because it is our history," Sehra answered as Za shook her head in disgust at Vhalla's question. "Because it is not yours to take, or have, or use."

Vhalla had no argument to any of those. "You wish to use it to fight for your sovereignty?"

She couldn't exactly fault the North for it. She personally knew what it felt like to be chained under the Emperor. She couldn't imagine a good leader's agony at the knowledge of their entire people being reduced in such a way.

"Not fight." Sehra shook her head. "Make a deal for it."

"With me?"

The princess nodded.

"What do you think I can do?" Vhalla hardly had any say in the future of the North, even less the power to give them their sovereignty.

"You hold no more love for this Empire than my people do, this much I have seen. It gives me faith for you. However, with the axe in hand, you are a danger to us as a tool of the war-hungry men who sleep in these stone walls," Sehra said, revealing nothing Vhalla didn't already know.

"Yet," the princess held a long pause, "you also hold the future of Solaris in your hands."

"How?" Vhalla frowned.

"Not hands, perhaps. Around your neck would be a better way to say it?"

Vhalla's hand went up to the watch, buried under the cloak and layers of clothing. Vhalla knew that Sehra had never seen the token, and even if she had, there was no reason for her to be so certain as to its origin. "How did you know?"

"His heart sings for you, his eyes search for you, his magic calls for and embraces you. Even a fool could see it, and I am no fool." Sehra raised a finger, pointing at Vhalla's chest. "He may not even realize what he has given you."

"What?" Vhalla's curiosity got the better of her.

"His magic sleeps within." Sehra was gracious enough to inform Vhalla, in not so many words, that Aldrik had given her what was well likely an unintentional vessel. "Do you deny the rumors of your involvement with the crown prince?"

Vhalla remained silent. It was an odd thing for a bride-to-be to ask about her groom. But the whole night so far had been anything but conventional.

"No . . . One who screams for truth cannot turn and deny her heart." Sehra leaned slightly against Za. "You can have him. I give him to you."

"What?" Vhalla blinked.

"You cry for an Empire of peace; here is your chance, Vhalla Yarl." Sehra narrowed her eyes slightly, a challenge carried in her words. "Give me achel. Let me return the weapon to its tomb to await its true master's return. I will disappear, return to my home from your frigid, barren mountaintop. The North will write me off as dead so long as the Empire relinquishes its hold on my people."

Vhalla processed this for a moment, and somehow managed to keep in insane laughter. "You want me to make a deal, that if I give you the axe and convince the Empire to give up the land the Emperor has just won at the highest price, I can be with Prince Aldrik?" She commended herself for remembering the prince's proper title.

Sehra frowned at Vhalla's amusement.

"You're delusional." Vhalla stood. *As if she would ever try to bargain for Aldrik's heart.* Vhalla ignored that part and focused on one of the many other reasons why the girl's proposal wouldn't work. "There's no way the Empire could, or would, let go of Shaldan now. To do so would admit failure, which no one will do."

"And I thought you were different, that you had reason and a sense of justice."

"Those are luxuries we cannot afford. We're all trying to survive in a world that doesn't give a damn about reason or justice, so learn well, princess." Vhalla sighed. "Even if I wanted to take your deal, I'd never be with the crown prince. The Emperor would refuse it. Nothing is ever that simple."

Za engaged in a quick series of harsh words punctuated with nasty glances at Vhalla. Sehra nodded a few times, frowned, and held up her hand.

"Then help us kill the Emperor."

Vhalla's head jerked around instinctually at the deeply treasonous words, looking for someone to spring from the shadows and lock her up. She returned her attention to the princess once it was clear no one else had been in the empty hall for hours. Vhalla clenched and unclenched her fists. She should be appalled. But the thought settled easily upon her mind. It complemented the dark history she had with the Emperor Solaris and the utter hatred she generally held for the man.

Sehra took Vhalla's hesitation as an invitation to continue. "If the Emperor dies, then you could be with your prince, and our deal could stand."

"Aldrik would never love someone who killed his family." Vhalla frowned. "And I thought my dismissal would be clear, this is about more than me and him."

"And here I thought you would be foolish enough to make a deal for love." The princess grinned briefly before sobering once more. "You don't need to swing the axe. Za will."

"Then why haven't you already?"

"You would help us escape," Sehra explained.

Vhalla turned, finally letting out mad laughter as she started for the door. "Princess," she called, her voice echoing through the empty space, "I realize that you are doing what you must to defend your people. But I have no interest in actually committing one of the crimes the Senate has been trying to pin on me for months."

"If you do not help us, we will consider you our enemy."

Vhalla paused with a sigh. "Frankly, I don't care if I am your enemy." She met the child princess's eyes once more. "But if you brought a deal to me that wasn't rooted in wishful thinking and delusions, I could be willing to help you. I meant what I said today, I hold no ill will toward your people. But I'm tired of senseless bloodshed, and that's what your resistance would end up bringing."

The princess didn't like hearing this, her guard even less. Vhalla didn't care, the truth wasn't always easy or beautiful. Often, the only joy Vhalla had found since growing up was in spite of the truth. She left the other two women to their thoughts.

The walk back to the Tower was lonely and cold. Vhalla kept her hands under the heavy cloak, passing back the watch from fingertips to fingertips. She'd learned two things. The first was that the princess and her bodyguard were unsurprisingly mutinous against their new sovereign. The second was that she held a vessel of Aldrik's magic, strong enough that the princess could sense it with whatever strange magic she wielded.

Now Vhalla was presented with the debate of what to tell Aldrik, if anything. Had he intended to give her a vessel? Should she tell him about Za and Sehra? Certainly he already knew . . .

Vhalla focused on the sloping floor of the Tower, counting the cracks between the stones. She paused as the ghost of light illuminated the otherwise dim hall. Vhalla turned to see a mote of fire shine through the bookshelves of the Tower library, following some late-night patron.

She didn't know if she truly believed in all the utterings of the Goddess. Of fate. Of a grander meaning to the world. But in that moment, it felt like something greater had shown her a light.

The flame reminded her of Aldrik's, and Vhalla knew that

whatever she did next, she had to somehow restore some lines of communication with the man she had once promised to marry. She had things that she needed to say and, if his expression at Court was any indication, so did he.

CHAPTER 13

THE MAGIC OF the axe shimmered around her fingertips, and Vhalla focused on it intensely. She delicately pulled and pried, separating the layers of foreign magic entangled around the blade. The more her own power mingled with the axe, the cleaner it became, the waves of power radiating outward.

It had been three days since she decided she needed to speak with Aldrik. Instead of seeking the prince out, she'd spent the majority of her time throwing herself into her work with Victor. It was a cheap diversion from what she really needed to do, but Vhalla could insist to herself the importance of cleansing the axe and destroying it—especially after her conversation with Za and Sehra.

She was so exhausted by the time she called it a day that her body nearly ached from magic depletion. But she wasn't too tired to miss spending time with her messy-haired friend. So in the late afternoon, Vhalla found herself leaning against the wall of the alcove she shared with Fritz, reading in the Tower library.

Fritz broke the silence with a stretch and a yawn. "Vhal, I've been wondering."

"Wondering what?" Vhalla's eyes continued to scan the words of the book she was reading.

"What do you do with the minister?"

Vhalla knew the question would come eventually. She should've thought of some kind of response before being put on the spot. But she hadn't, and there she was, struggling to form an answer. *Lying would be easiest.*

"We're working on something."

"What?" Fritz couldn't just let it be.

"Something involving my magic."

"So, special Windwalker training?" Fritz hummed.

"Something like that," Vhalla replied with a nod, flipping the page.

"Do you like it here?" His question surprised her, and the silence prompted him to continue. "In the Tower, do you like being part of the Tower?"

"Where else would I be?" She had nowhere else to go. If she went home, she was likely to bring danger to her father. She was safest in the Tower and could help the most there also. *Maybe she'd go home after the axe was destroyed.*

Fritz frowned slightly. "You never leave. You're tired all the time, on edge."

Vhalla rubbed her eyes, instantly annoyed with her friend for being right.

"You're almost as bad as you were on the march."

"I just have some things on my mind." Vhalla closed her book with a sigh.

"Talk about them? We're friends, talk to me."

She smiled sadly at her friend. Fritz had such an innocent hopefulness about him, despite the fact that Vhalla knew he had just as much blood on his hands as she. How he had managed to salvage his soul from the Northern campaign escaped Vhalla, but she wished he could've taught her before the war ended.

"It's nothing." Vhalla squeezed Fritz's hand encouragingly. "I'm trying out some new Windwalker things with the minister, so I am exhausted."

"All right." Fritz still looked skeptical.

"Tell me, how have things with Grahm been?" Vhalla knew just what change in topic would shift the Southerner's focus completely.

However, she still felt a little guilty for not being entirely honest with him. It was the least she could do, she felt, to heed his words and escape the Tower for a bit. So after Fritz had gone off to work with Grahm on vessels again, Vhalla wandered out for the first time since the Court day.

She wasn't going to head to the Imperial Library, not without purpose, given her last confrontation with Roan. So Vhalla headed to the only other place in the palace she knew she would find friends— the training grounds. The Golden Guard was present, as expected. Raylynn worked with archers, Daniel was drilling swords again, and Erion sat behind a table under a sunshade propped up by four posts.

"I hear you caused quite the stir at court." Erion glanced up at her as she crossed out of the sun. He had papers spread across the table with times and names written on them. Vhalla could only assume it was some sort of schedule for the guards.

"I tend to cause a stir wherever I go." Vhalla leaned against the table and looked out over the training grounds.

"That you do." Erion chuckled. "Are you here to interrupt my training, then?"

"Maybe," Vhalla mused. "Why, do you need a stir caused?" She grinned back at the Western man.

"Oh, I'm sure I could find something for you to do." Erion made some marks on the papers, pressing the parchment down to the table as the wind tried to carry it away. Vhalla waved a hand and the wind stopped. His eyes jumped up to her.

"You looked like you were having trouble."

"Practical as ever." Erion spoke in between scribing.

A thought occurred to her as she stared across the men and women practicing at war. "Why don't the Tower sorcerers train here?"

"They have their own training grounds in the Tower," Erion answered.

"These are better. Why don't they use this?"

"If I had to guess, it's because of tensions between the soldiers and the sorcerers."

"Foolish," Vhalla muttered. "Let me train with them?"

Erion glanced up at her, gauging her intent. Finding her serious, he spoke, "What would you like to do?"

"Just some sparring would be sufficient, I think. You said you could find something for me to do." Vhalla smiled. Baldair had once told her to ride with the men so they saw her with him. That didn't stop now that the march was over, she resolved. She'd be seen among the soldiers, and she'd work to bridge the gap between them and their brothers and sisters in black.

Vhalla was put into the main ring with Jax. It had a short wall built around the perimeter with a ledge above for spectators. Erion sent swords and pole arms in batches so each would get a round with the two soldiers in black. Being a member of the Golden Guard, Jax had trained with them before. As it was Vhalla's first time, it took coaxing and encouragement of the soldiers who remembered her from the front in order to get the other soldiers into the ring with her.

Vhalla leaned against the side wall, catching her breath while Jax trained. His fighting style was a rough and wild combination of jumps and kicks. His flames soared through the air and crackled along the ground. It was different from the close-ranged combat Aldrik preferred. Jax kept his opponents at bay with bursts of fire, finishing with him plucking a dagger from some hidden location as soon as his opponent was prone on the ground.

"I need a breather, fight the lady." He waved off the next soldier, crossing over to her. "All yours." Jax motioned for her to enter the ring.

Vhalla adjusted the jerkin she'd been lent, shaking out the stiffness in her muscles. It'd been too long since she'd last trained, and she made a vow to do so more often.

"Daniel?" Vhalla blinked.

"I heard the Windwalker was sparring." The Easterner gave her an easy smile that removed the awkwardness the Court had created during their last encounter. "Thought I'd see if I fared any better than the last time I went against your winds."

"I'm not so sure you will," Vhalla replied coyly.

"No?" Daniel chuckled. "Let's make a wager then."

"Of what sort?"

"If I win, let me show you my home?"

That certainly wasn't what she'd been expecting. "And if I win?"

"I'll do any one thing you ask of me." Daniel drew his sword, a beautiful rapier with a golden pommel in the shape of wheat.

"*Anything?*" Vhalla raised her eyebrows.

"They say make love, not war," Jax shouted down from the spectators' ring that lined the training pit. "I frankly don't care as long as you two get to one or the other."

The peanut gallery burst into laughter.

"Is that how you treat a lady, Jax? There's more to it than just saying hello and putting a sword through her eye!" Daniel jested back.

"Mate, if you're going for the eye, your sword is in the wrong place!" A roar of laughter threatened to deafen them.

Daniel rolled his eyes and Vhalla found herself joining in laughter with the rest of them. It was all lighthearted jesting. He eased himself into a fighting stance and held his sword as gently as she would a quill.

"You have your deal!" The words rang out. *What could it hurt?*

"Enough stalling. Fight!" Jax cried.

Daniel waited for her to charge. Vhalla pressed the wind against her heels and targeted his face with an apparent attack. He swung his sword upward, and Vhalla nimbly stepped out of its arc, dropping and sweeping her foot. The soldier did a half jump-step to avoid being tripped.

His sword cut through the air, whistling slightly as he wove it like an orchestra conductor's baton, keeping her at length with a series of slashes. Vhalla realized he was cutting closer than he had before. *He had more faith in her magic.*

Daniel's eyes caught hers, and Vhalla grinned. He grinned in return, and Vhalla rewarded him with a gust straight to his chest.

The soldier tumbled, head over heels, regaining his feet with a lunge off the ground.

Vhalla was too fast for the blade and nimbly sidestepped. It was a good fight, but he was outclassed against her magic. With a flick of her wrist, the wind ripped his blade from his fingers, leaving Daniel prone and shocked, his blade hanging over him in the air.

"I yield!" He raised his hands, and the soldiers cheered at their display.

Vhalla helped him up from the ground, easing the rapier back into his palm. "You said you would do anything I wanted."

"I'm a man of my word." Daniel sheathed his sword.

"Well, I want to see your home." There was still some air that she wanted to make sure was cleared and settled between them. It seemed as good an opportunity as any.

His face lit up. "I must run some more drills, but I'll be available soon. Can you wait?"

Vhalla smiled and nodded.

She passed the time alternating with Jax in the training ring. The other sorcerer began to feed her advice between rounds, and Vhalla heeded it with a keen ear. However, he did the same with her opponents, and their skill showed marked improvement. Jax was experienced in combat, and he'd worked with her enough to tell people exactly where the Windwalker's skill was lacking.

Vhalla was on her fifth consecutive opponent when there was a commotion from the spectators' walk around the ring. She glanced up, unable to make out the source of the fuss with a blade swinging by her face. Vhalla dodged backward, turning her attention to her attacker.

And then she stopped. It all stopped.

She felt his eyes on her, cutting into her soul. Everything slowed, and her gaze rose. Aldrik stood atop the spectators' wall. His hands were folded behind his back. He looked down at her with guarded eyes, his expression betraying nothing.

Her vision shifted. His betrothed stood two steps away. Her emerald eyes fixed on Vhalla as though Sehra was once more looking at the crystal magic that she claimed lingered on Vhalla.

Her opponent was smart enough to capitalize on her complete

distraction. The dull training blade came down on her shoulder, and she called out in surprise as it dug into her joint. Vhalla bent her knee and tilted to the side, trying to absorb the shock of the impact. "Vhalla, you should know better. Don't take your eyes off your opponent in a fight!" Jax shook his head, strolling away from the wall he'd been resting against. He glanced behind and gave a small nod to the prince before quietly adding, "Not for anything."

"Of course." Vhalla glanced away. She felt the weight of Aldrik's stare remain on her.

"Why don't you take a breather?" Jax patted her shoulder, and she winced. "Are you all right?"

"Fine, fine." Vhalla brushed by him, barely remembering to thank her opponent before she walked out of the ring. She didn't know where she was heading, but she knew staying anywhere close to Aldrik was not a sound idea. There were too many things unsaid right now, and this was not the forum to say them.

Familiar footsteps crunched the ground behind her, and Vhalla didn't even have to turn to know the prince was there. Aldrik strolled by, his future wife in silent company. He didn't look back at her once.

Vhalla retreated to the tall table underneath the sunshade. Erion no longer occupied the space behind it. Now Baldair was managing the guard and working on schedules.

"I heard you were here." Baldair assessed her thoughtfully.

"With how often people speak of me, I sometimes think I can exist in multiple places at once." Vhalla massaged her shoulder.

"My brother heard as well."

That explained it.

"What's going on with you and him?" Baldair's voice was thoughtful, but it carried an unusual weight.

"Nothing is going on." Vhalla frowned. "Everything is over between us."

"Really? And, does he know that?" Vhalla narrowed her eyes at Baldair's remark. It didn't dissuade the prince from continuing. "We all know what happened the last time you both tried this path. But that will be nothing compared to what will happen if you try to get in the way of his engagement."

"Good thing I'm not trying then." Vhalla pursed her lips, barely refraining from remarking how, despite her general hatred for the Emperor, *she* had never tried or suggested his assassination—*unlike Aldrik's current betrothed.*

Daniel appeared shortly thereafter, putting a blissful stop to the conversation. "Sorry to keep you waiting."

"And what's this?" Baldair glanced between his companions with a tiny smirk.

"Two *friends* catching up," Daniel responded easily.

"Sure, *sure.*" The prince held the word for emphasis. But the tease was empty. It lacked the weight of any real suspicion for things going on between them.

Daniel led her away from the prince, and Vhalla found herself breathing easier the farther they got from the Tower and the training grounds—the farther she got from the princes and the axe. They walked out of a side entrance into the common area of town. Daniel immediately turned to the right, and they strolled up a small street to the section where nobles and dignitaries lived. In the distance, Vhalla could see the high walls surrounding the water gardens around the golden ballroom. Vhalla smiled faintly.

That was a different time. The dance she had shared with Aldrik was the last night he had just been a prince and she had just been a girl. She'd yet to learn of the depth of their Bond, and she'd yet to be known as the Windwalker.

"Have you ever been to the mirror ballroom?" Daniel asked, seeing where her attention was.

"I have, once," she sighed wistfully.

"It's quite the spectacle." Vhalla hummed in agreement as Daniel continued. "I hear that's where they're holding a gala following the wedding."

"The wedding?" Vhalla repeated, her voice revealing no emotion.

"Yes." Daniel's voice was soft as he spoke. He knew what he was saying to her, what she was hearing. His words were the nails in the coffin of a love she'd once coveted above all else. Her hand went to the watch around her neck. "It should be sometime just after the new year; all the Court will be invited. They want to make it a wintertime ball."

"It'll be lovely, I'm sure." Vhalla forced a smile.

"But you don't think you'll see it with your own eyes." Daniel gave sound to the meaning between her words.

"I doubt I'll attend," she agreed.

"I'm not surprised." He brought his eyes away from the towering walls of the water gardens. "I wouldn't want to go, if I were you." Vhalla regarded him cautiously. She didn't know how to respond to the sentiment, so she kept her mouth shut and waited for him to give it more color. Daniel obliged.

"You know, I was engaged." Vhalla nodded, prompting him to continue. "She still lives in Paca. And, I *still* haven't had the courage to go back there yet. Not even when I went East looking for you. I had thought, if I'd found someone new. . . If I could show that I had not been nearly as devastated from losing her as I was that it would be easier."

Vhalla realized he was talking about her. He had been her crutch, and she had been his validation.

"Then again, I built a bit of home here instead." Daniel quickly put an end to his prior train of thought.

"Built a bit of home?" Vhalla was unfamiliar with the expression.

"You'll see. It's what I wanted to show you."

Daniel finally stopped before an iron gate leading into a narrow alleyway. It was tucked between two large buildings, and Vhalla glanced around curiously. He produced a key, unlocking the gate and motioning for her to go ahead.

The alley was so narrow that they could no longer walk side-by-side, and Vhalla was forced to take the lead. She ran her hand along the stone walls on either side of her, utterly overcome with curiosity about where they'd end up. The walkway opened into a courtyard that stole Vhalla's breath.

It smelled like Cyven.

A large tree stretched upward to the watercolor sky, and tall Eastern grasses grew untamed at its base and across the ground to where she stood at the end of the stone alleyway. River rocks created a pathway to a building nestled against the others, which made up the courtyard his home was hidden within. It was construction she was familiar with; the roof was thatched instead of shingled with tile or wood like the West or South. She was frozen in time, unsure of how she'd stumbled across the alternate world in which she now stood.

"What do you think?" Daniel leaned against the corner of the building behind them, a bittersweet expression overcoming his face.

"It's amazing, it's like, like . . ."

"Home," Daniel finished for her. He started for the house. "No one wanted this plot because it had no real street access. Nobles couldn't get their carriages or horses to it easily. They also couldn't put their wealth on display. So they built up on the perimeter, and somehow the middle was left untouched while they fought over who would get to enlarge their house. No family could agree on who had the best claim, so my wanting it offered the city a solution."

Vhalla followed behind him as he spoke, the grasses tickling the fingertips of an outstretched hand.

"I had intended my future bride to make her home here, with me. I thought it would ease her transition from the East."

"Do you ever intend on going back to Paca?"

He shook his head. "Baldair needs me here. My future is here, especially after what happened."

Vhalla grabbed his elbow, stopping Daniel in his tracks. The motion made her shoulder hurt where a bruise had formed from the earlier training, but Vhalla kept the pain away from her face. She looked him in the eye and spoke slowly, hoping his heart would hear her every word.

"You don't need her. You have so much to give."

"I could say the same to you," he whispered in reply.

Vhalla's chest felt hollow. Somehow, the weird circumstances that had brought them together had given them insights into the uglier portions of the other's heart. They'd never been that different. They'd both been wanting to fill the gaps in their life. Perhaps they'd went about it the wrong way, but with someone who could have been the right person.

"Show me your home." Vhalla released his arm.

"Gladly."

Daniel led her through the decently sized, two-storey home. There was more than enough room for a small family, which made it feel all the emptier. It was modestly furnished with the trimmings of a lord still building his name and his wealth.

He stoked a fire, and Vhalla found herself baking bread. Daniel sliced cured meat and honored her as a special guest by bringing out spiced cheese from his larder. It made her homesick, as Vhalla remembered going through the same motions growing up.

"I think I should go East," Vhalla mused aloud.

"I was wondering why you hadn't yet." Daniel pulled out a chair for her at the roughly crafted table that sat before the stone hearth of the kitchen. "I rode out to Leoul and asked for you after the North."

"It didn't feel right," she confessed. "I'm a danger to myself and others. I've changed so much. I just haven't been ready." Vhalla leaned back, watching the world darken outside the window. "But this reminds me of how much I miss it."

"I didn't want for this to cause you turmoil." Daniel rolled up his sleeves before carefully extracting the loaves from the oven.

"You haven't. It's almost so peaceful it feels wrong," Vhalla admitted with a laugh.

"Don't you think you deserve a little quiet?" Daniel placed the steaming bread between them.

"Maybe," Vhalla confessed. She burned her fingers slightly, as she always did on the hot bread, too impatient to wait. "But I still have things to do."

"What more could the world possibly expect of you?" Daniel shook his head. "You've given enough, you know."

"Thank you." Vhalla smiled tiredly at him. She couldn't tell him what she still had left to do. "For now, though, I'll settle for the taste of home you've given me."

"You're welcome to it anytime."

"I wouldn't want to impose on you . . ."

"Craig isn't shy about occupying a room when things at his family's home are less than ideal." Daniel shrugged. "Jax has also slept in a bed many nights when he was too drunk to make it back to the palace."

"If I ever do stay, you are not allowed to make me sleep in the same bed that drunk Jax has," Vhalla teased.

"On my honor!" Daniel laughed. "But, truly. If you ever need to escape the palace . . ."

The unspoken words hovered and Vhalla claimed them with a small sigh. "Things are a *little* awkward." She tore a piece of bread into crumbs. "But it's my home, too. I need to learn how to be around him."

"That's fair. But the offer remains." Vhalla was relieved that there was nothing in Daniel's words or stare other than friendly compassion.

After their meal concluded, Daniel insisted on walking her back to the Tower. He explained the process of joining the palace guard, how the training was for the new recruits and for guards seeking to move up in rank. Daniel had the job of deciding who the best swordsmen were to be sent out into the Empire as keepers of the peace.

"Oh, one more thing." Daniel shifted uneasily.

"What?" There was something about his face that nearly called into question her entire understanding of the evening they'd shared.

"I want you to know, that I didn't lie to you then."

"Lie to me about what?" Vhalla's voice had fallen to a whisper.

"I *did* still look forward to seeing you return." Daniel clearly struggled with putting his emotions into something tangible. But her heart was already beating in time with his. She already understood. "You really weren't just something to 'fill the hole in my heart.' You're more than that. And, while sometimes I wish the stars had aligned for us just in a slightly different way . . ."

"You don't have to explain it." Vhalla took his hand and squeezed it lightly. Relief eased its way into his eyes and smoothed the tense line his mouth had been. "I enjoyed myself tonight. Actually, I've always enjoyed time with you. And, it's easier now, now that we've had that time and there isn't death on our doorsteps."

Daniel's fingers closed around hers for a brief moment. "So, come and visit me again?"

"Soon, I promise." It was a promise that Vhalla's heart had no hesitation making. And, it was only affirmed as he pulled her in for one more quick embrace before departing.

Daniel was everything that could have been. He was the

embodiment of a simpler time and place where she was only a girl and he was a farm boy, where the only crowns in their lives would be the ones he'd braid for her out of field flowers. It was no wonder that they had both wanted to play at such a fantasy. But, neither of them were pretending anymore.

Vhalla headed up the Tower. For the first time in a long time, things were starting to feel simple. She caressed the watch around her neck, passing a faint glow in the library.

But nothing would ever be simple for long.

Vhalla saw the rose on her desk before the door even clicked closed behind her. Attached with a black ribbon was a note, in the same fashion as one she'd received once before. Her fingers traced the delicate velvet of the petals before flipping open the message.

Her eyes skimmed it twice, though it was only four words in a familiar, slanted script.

We need to speak.

CHAPTER 14

VHALLA RESIGNED HERSELF to no sleep. She wasn't going to sleep even if she stayed tucked in bed, so she decided to wander into the quiet palace.

There was no location on the note, no time marker, nothing other than four words. The only words with which he dared to intrude upon her world again. He'd trusted her to understand, and she did.

She had to stop to catch her breath as she stood at the window overlooking the Imperial garden. She hadn't laid eyes on it since leaving for war. The last time she'd seen it, she'd snuck in to meet him for a lunch that had seemed so harmless at the time. Now she was sneaking in again to meet with that same prince under the cover of darkness.

Vhalla walked on the wind; she barely touched the ground, and the gravel didn't crunch under her boots. As silent as a wraith, she slunk toward the central greenhouse, mindful of all the windows that overlooked the garden overhead. She doubted that any held watching eyes, *but if there were* . . . Baldair's words of warning no doubt had merit.

She composed herself briefly, reminding and reaffirming what she was doing, before slipping into the greenhouse. The air was hot against the chill air outside. Her clothes instantly felt too heavy. Vhalla squinted into the dim light of the greenhouse.

Her eyes met another set, dark as the night sky. They belonged to a figure who was swathed in moonlight and shadow. His clothes were plain and comfortable, but stitched to perfection upon his lean form. *Always the prince, ever perfect.*

He watched her watching him. Vhalla studied the man who could still set her heart to racing.

"Are you real?" A voice, deep as ever, broke the silence; eternal, yet fleeting like the midnight hour.

"You've asked me that before," Vhalla replied.

Aldrik looked away, thought knitting his brow. "I have, haven't I?"

"When I first met you here," she affirmed softly.

"I owed you an apology then also." Aldrik let nothing be forgotten. He wasn't the type to let a single detail slide. It was the right thing, but Vhalla resented the notion of confronting their last explosive time together. "I'm sorry for how I acted in the North."

Vhalla swallowed, hard. "There may come a time when your apologies aren't enough, Aldrik."

The use of his name, plain on her tongue, gave him pause. He searched her face. "Is now that time?"

"No." She didn't string him along; there wasn't any point to it. She was tired of playing games and hiding feelings. "What I said to you then, about the Bond—"

"And that you had no romantic feelings for my brother? Was the truth," Aldrik finished bluntly. "I was too wrapped up in my world of lies to see it, even when you confessed it to me. By the time I was ready to admit it to you, you were gone, and all I could do was admit it to myself."

Vhalla leaned against the door, her eyes fluttering closed with a sigh. Everything seemed out of time and place. Someone should've told her about her magic before it had spiraled out of control. Daniel was the one she should've met long before the prince. She should've split her time between swords and books. And the Aldrik standing before her was the man she'd needed months ago.

Nothing happened when she needed it to.

"I told you once," Aldrik continued, "that I am not a good man."

"You did." Vhalla met his eyes once more.

"That I have never been a good man." Aldrik took a step forward, moonlight outlining his form in silver. "But I realized that I was only the man I've let myself be. That if I want something beautiful in my life, if I wanted *you*, I had to make myself a person that could be the soil in which such beauty could take root."

"It doesn't work that way; you don't just get to change and then we are something once more."

"I know," he spoke hastily before she could get too far down her train of thought. "I didn't do it for you." Aldrik paused. "Maybe, at first. But then I continued because I wanted to, for me. And every day I still struggle with that goal. Vhalla, I want to see if I can be a man that I can look in the eye when I look into a mirror."

"How's it working out?"

"Some days are better than others." Aldrik shrugged. "I can still be an ass."

His deadpan remark sparked laughter in her. The notes were still heavy, but it was enough to tug the corners of his mouth into a small smile.

"We're hopeless, you and I," Vhalla whispered.

"If I am going to be hopeless for anyone, let it be for you, Vhalla Yarl."

Vhalla's hand reached for her watch, her heart doing acrobatics. This feeling was one only he could instill in her. It put everything else to shame, and it rose every warning flag and rang every alarm.

Aldrik watched her motions thoughtfully. After a long internal debate, he crossed the remaining distance between them. A half step too close, every part of him was easily within reach. He reached out a hand, hesitantly, slowly. He searched for permission, and Vhalla wanted to deny him, she wanted to push him away. *She wanted to hold him so hard her hands would leave bruises.*

His fingertips fell gingerly on her neck, lightning striking in their wake as they slid down to her collarbone. His elegant hand hooked the metal chain and pulled free the watch from under her clothes. The prince hardly touched her, and yet it was the most intimate act Vhalla had experienced in weeks.

Aldrik's eyes smoldered as he confirmed what her hands perpetually sought was indeed the watch he'd given her. Vhalla watched a flame alight at the knowledge. He turned his attention to her face, and Vhalla knew what he sought.

"My . . . lady?" he breathed.

"We can't," Vhalla reminded him.

"Do you still love me?" He'd gone from glancing blows straight for the kill.

Vhalla frowned slightly. "It doesn't matter."

"It matters to me." His words were quick and breathy. "Tell me, Vhalla, do you still love me as you once did? Do you hold any feelings for me in your heart? Is there a single ember of love that I might, honorably, fan to life once more?"

"You are engaged," Vhalla whispered weakly. "I've seen you with her."

"With her? Publicly, yes." Aldrik laughed, a deep and sorrowful sound. "Do you think I love her because I have to put on a show? Because I tolerate her as I must?" He met her eyes, and Vhalla witnessed the unfiltered truth as he spoke it. "Vhalla, you should know, out of everyone, you know I chose the woman I wanted to be my wife long before I knew the Northern girl even existed."

Fire raged through her veins, flushing her skin at his words.

"I made my choice. And, while I cannot honor that choice with my hands, I shall honor it eternally with my heart." Aldrik leaned forward, almost close enough for her to feel his breath. "If you will not say it, then I will. Vhalla, I—"

"She means to kill your father," Vhalla blurted out. Somehow, confessing to knowledge of treason was less frightening than knowing, beyond all doubt, that Aldrik still loved her.

"What?" Aldrik straightened away. "How do you know that?"

Vhalla swallowed. If it had been anyone else, she would've been afraid of telling the truth. But she knew Aldrik wouldn't subject her to a trial, use her knowledge as an opportunity to jail her—or worse. "She and Za called me for a meeting."

"When?" Aldrik's expression darkened.

"After my day at Court." Vhalla launched into a quick recount of the evening, ending with the princess's suggestion that Vhalla help them escape after killing the Emperor.

"We expected this." Aldrik began to pace. "I'll have to shift the guards on her room, change the watch patterns so she can't learn them." He paused, as if remembering Vhalla was there. "Why did you tell me this?"

"Why wouldn't I?"

"You, of all people, should hate my father," Aldrik pointed out.

"I do," Vhalla had no hesitation in affirming such. Her bluntness brought some amusement to Aldrik's expression. "But I'm tired of the bloodshed. If she kills your father, then she'll be put to death, and it'll likely spark a rebellion in the North. You'll be forced to subdue them because the only other alternative to appease them, possibly, would be letting the North go from the Empire. That may cause a different sort of civil war from people who would rebel against freeing them after so many lives were lost to bring Shaldan into the Empire."

He watched her with sorrow that matched what she felt in her heart.

"It's why she *must* be the future Empress . . . There isn't another way now that doesn't end in blood."

The truth they both were loathed to admit was out, and now they had no choice but to face it. Whatever Aldrik had been playing at was nothing more than a fool's dream. It was the same dream they'd indulged in during the war in the North. Vhalla knew how quickly it could become a nightmare and had no desire to linger over it further.

"Speaking of Northern rebellions," Aldrik paused, clearly struggling with his words as he became suddenly uncomfortable. "The axe, the one Sehra asked for . . ."

Vhalla dreaded what Aldrik was about to ask her next, so much so that her skin crawled.

"You have it, don't you?"

"How do you know?" Vhalla breathed. She heard it in his tone, the way he asked, and the way he moved. The question was only a formality, as he already knew the truth.

Aldrik frowned and cursed slightly under his breath. "Does anyone else know?"

"Yes." She braced herself for what she expected would devolve into a fiery confrontation.

"Who?"

"Daniel was there when I found it in the North," she confessed.

"*Daniel?*" Aldrik said the name as though it was sour on his tongue. "My brother's Easterner?"

She nodded.

"You and he . . ." Aldrik looked at her hopelessly.

Vhalla fought to suppress her instinctive response that Daniel and she were nothing more than friends. *Maybe it was better if Aldrik believed her heart could belong to another.*

"Never mind," he muttered. "Does anyone else know?"

"Victor." She was in too deep to hold anything back.

Aldrik pinched the bridge of his nose with a heavy sigh. "That's it?"

"That's it," Vhalla affirmed with a nod.

"Baldair's Easterner." Vhalla noticed that Aldrik wouldn't use his name. "Will he tell anyone?"

"He hasn't told a soul so far; I don't know why he would now."

"Pleasure, pain, power—men have many motivators." Aldrik ran a hand over his hair.

"Daniel won't," she insisted.

"I leave him to you, then." Aldrik glanced at her from the corners of his eyes. She let her expression betray nothing. "I'll take care of Victor."

"Do you trust him?" Vhalla asked quickly.

"Victor? I do," Aldrik affirmed. "He was my mentor. We went through a lot together."

Vhalla bit her lip and refrained from bringing up the crystals. Aldrik had been fairly level-headed throughout it all, surprisingly so. But she knew there were some things that would likely trigger his anger. And now that she knew more of his history, she could see why crystals may be one such thing.

"Aldrik." She jarred him from his planning once more. "How did you know I had the axe?" Vhalla had a few theories, and the prince was quick to prove them all wrong.

"The Bond."

"What?" The explanation made no sense.

"*Think*, Vhalla. What is the Bond?" He crossed to her once more, waiting for her to put it together, acting the teacher he had once been.

"It's a Channel between us . . ." She shuddered in horror, looking up at the dark eyed prince. "An open Channel. Then you . . ." Vhalla couldn't bring herself to say it. The guilt was suddenly too overwhelming.

"I know what the early stages of crystal taint feels like," he whispered solemnly.

Vhalla moved without thinking. She grabbed his hands in hers, clutching them tightly and assuaging the need to feel him, to hold onto and protect the man before her. "Are you all right?"

"I'm fine." He smiled tiredly at her, squeezing her hands in reply. "I'm fine."

She was suddenly too close again, so she quickly withdrew. The man was a dark star, brilliant and terrifying, and she was constantly being pulled into his gravity. "I should go."

"Must you?" Aldrik couldn't keep the frown from tugging down his lips.

"Yes," she insisted.

"When will I see you again?"

"You know we can't make a habit of this," Vhalla cautioned.

Aldrik opened his mouth, and she felt his protest. But he quickly caught himself. "I can't sleep, you know I can't. Most nights I'm in the Tower library."

"It was you?"

"Me, what?" Aldrik clearly didn't understand.

"Never mind." She didn't want to explain how she'd seen his firelight on more than one occasion.

Silence settled upon them. It was the calm lurking at the edge of a raging storm that would be there for as long as they lived, threatening to swallow them whole. Vhalla moved to the door. It was time to leave. They'd run out of "business" and any continued interaction now would be a dangerous indulgence in pleasure.

"Vhalla." Aldrik stopped her one last time. He crossed over to her, holding her in place with his stare. Vhalla swallowed past a dry throat as Aldrik rummaged through his pocket. "You're better than the cutthroats my brother tries to pass as soldiers. Don't let them surprise you again."

Vhalla laughed softly at the small vial in his palm. "Thank you."

His hand closed around hers as she retrieved the vial. "No, thank you." Aldrik opened and closed his mouth, searching for words. "For never giving up on me."

"I left you," Vhalla blurted.

"But you didn't give up on me." Aldrik paused, giving her an opportunity to object.

Vhalla stayed quiet. "I never could, even when I was as angry as I was that day." She gave him a small smile, which he returned in full. Vhalla resisted the urge to kiss him, then stepped away. Aldrik's eyes followed her as she slipped back out into the night.

Vhalla created pockets of air beneath her feet and walked her hands up the wall to scale back up to the window she'd left cracked open. Vhalla waited, watching the prince leave a short time later through the iron gate that led into the Imperial quarters. No one noticed her on the way back, and Vhalla downed the clerical potion for the bruise on her shoulder before crawling into her bed alone just before dawn.

She didn't bother with bathing or changing clothes. In her mind, she made the excuse she was too tired. But the truth was her heart wanted to have the scent of roses on her skin for just a little longer.

CHAPTER 15

VHALLA'S EYES WERE fixated on the axe. She sat in her usual chair, and Victor was fixing his usual tea. But her attention remained solely on the weapon as he went about his business.

"Vhalla."

Could she continue going on as she had been? Aldrik was in the forefront of her thoughts.

"Vhalla."

The steam tickled her nose, rising from the mug that Victor held in front of her face. It brought Vhalla back to life.

"Oh, sorry, yes?" Vhalla took the mug carefully, her eyes returning to the axe at the earliest possible moment.

"What is it?" The minister sat slowly behind his desk. "You're out of sorts."

Vhalla's nails scratched lightly against the mug. She couldn't deny it, and she wanted to broach the subject that was burning brightly in her mind. But how could she without revealing what had transpired with the prince? Even if Victor was on her side, she didn't want anyone to know of her meeting with Aldrik.

"Is there another way?" Vhalla finally asked.

"Another way to do what?" Victor leaned forward, his elbows on his desk.

"Destroy the axe, the caves. Is there another way to do it?" Vhalla whispered.

"There is no other way, Vhalla." Victor frowned. "I have been researching this my whole life. I was the *product* of such research. Why the sudden hesitation?"

"I just want to be certain," she mumbled, not wanting to explain herself further. "It is crystal magic, after all. I want to be careful before I get too far . . ."

"Too far into what?" Victor laughed lightly and sat back in his chair. "Vhalla, what is the real root of this? You don't think I really believe that you're suddenly hesitant about taint after you carried this halfway across the world, do you?"

Vhalla pressed her lips together. She couldn't say and decided to busy her mouth with the tea to give her a chance to think of a different approach.

"Is it because of the crown prince?"

Vhalla nearly spit out her tea. She looked at Victor in shock.

"He came to me asking very pointed questions. *I know you spoke to him.*" The minister's voice was low and slow, a frigid edge to it. "I need you to trust me, Vhalla. I'm trying to help us all."

"I know, I do trust you, Victor." Vhalla placed the cup on the desk, leaning back in her chair.

"Above all else, I need your unquestioning faith."

"*I do* trust you." She frowned, unappreciative of his tone.

"Which is why you felt the need to tell the prince about the axe." Victor's words were sharp and clipped.

"He asked!" Vhalla snapped back. "But even if he hadn't, why can't he know? He's the prince and the ultimate head of the Tower."

At her final statement, Victor's brow furrowed, and he opened his mouth for some hasty retort—then paused. "He asked?" Victor mulled this over. "Aldrik doesn't ask unless he's fairly certain he knows the answer. How did he know?"

Vhalla looked away.

"Vhalla, *please*," the minister sighed, pleading. "Tell me the truth. I can't help anyone if you don't grant me that."

She sat at a crossroads—her personal vow to remove lying from her life, as much as possible, against the desire to keep one of the most personal aspects of her life private. *Perhaps the minister was right,* and she only needed to trust him. "We're Bonded."

There was a long stretch of silence where Vhalla wasn't even sure if Victor had heard her. The man stared at her in shock. "Excuse me?"

"The prince and I, we're Bonded." Vhalla wanted to explain as little as possible, but she'd already come this far. "He knew because he felt the magic of the crystals through the Channel between us."

"A Bond . . ." Victor breathed, as though the veil had suddenly been lifted from a great mechanism he'd been trying to understand for ages. "You and Aldrik have a Bond."

Vhalla nodded, uncomfortable.

"His ability to see you Projected, his surviving the fall in The Pass, the feats of magic that I hear you two performed together." Victor pressed his fingertips together in thought, as though he was running through every possibility that surrounded the idea of her and Aldrik being Bonded. "It's more than a Bond, isn't it?"

"Joined as well," she confessed like a child who was put on the spot.

"Bonded and Joined . . ." Victor stood, walking to the window. He surveyed the gray sky for a long moment. "So then, is it safe for me to assume you have his magic in you?"

"I think so."

"You think so—or you know?" Victor turned and looked at her with an intense expression.

"His fire doesn't hurt me, so I'm fairly certain," Vhalla insisted.

"Without doubt?"

"Yes!"

"This is excellent," he breathed, turning back to the window, tapping the sill. The Minister of Sorcery was suddenly overcome with barely contained energy. "Most excellent, indeed."

"What is excellent?" Vhalla asked when it became apparent that he wasn't about to expand upon his mutterings.

"Oh." He turned quickly, as if remembering she was there. "Because you don't need to worry so much!" Victor clapped his hands with a smile. "Whatever Aldrik is feeling now should be the worst of what he will feel."

"Are you sure?" She wasn't nearly convinced by the minister's optimistic words.

"You know Aldrik's and my history."

"More or less."

"He'll act as he needs to avoid taint," the minister continued, avoiding giving her any more of the aforementioned history. "But this means we can move faster. The Emperor is pressing hard for the axe. I don't know why the North hasn't told him yet that they don't have it, but the Emperor will eventually find out it's gone. I thought we would have to stall until spring, but now—no, we can push, we can move. I've found the other pieces. We can end this vicious cycle we're trapped within."

"Other pieces? What vicious cycle?" Vhalla tried to remember if she'd ever seen the minister before her; something was alive in him, and he seemed like a different person as a result.

"The oppression of sorcerers." He ignored her initial question.

"Minister?" she asked, suddenly cautious.

He was at her feet, kneeling before her. "Vhalla, you can remove the possibility once and for all of being used by the crystals. You can set us all free."

"Right . . ." Vhalla wished she could move the chair away from him. The man before her made her uneasy. He had a glint to his eye that Vhalla recognized. It was the same glint the Emperor had, that the Northern Chieftain had, that Major Schnurr had had. The look that would overcome a reasonable and sane person when presented with power.

She would not be used again.

"How are we going to use the axe to close the Caverns?" Vhalla asked as the minister stood.

"I'll tell you once we get there. For now, let's get to work."
Vhalla hid her reservations and did as Victor instructed. She needed to speak with Aldrik. But she didn't think she could even tell her prince everything since it involved crystals. Day by day, it came more abundantly clear that she was the only one truly fighting for peace. Not a peace anchored in blood and power, but a lasting peace that would benefit the people of the Empire. A peace that would focus on the citizens more than their leaders.

She'd learn Victor's knowledge. She'd destroy the Caverns herself.

At each of their meetings, she worked to learn his greater plan. If Victor suspected she was trying to procure information, he didn't change his actions. Vhalla continued to cleanse the axe and probe the minister gently.

She didn't disagree that the faster it all happened, the better they'd be. Vhalla prayed that the minister was everything he said he was. That she could trust him. As the days passed, Vhalla began to believe it more by the lack of any note from Aldrik. Surely, if the prince was ailing from her labors with the axe, he would inform her?

At night, she would go to the training ground and relax with Baldair and the guards. It was a different atmosphere from the Tower, and Vhalla relinquished her concerns in the white puffs of breath she panted in the training pit. She kept it to herself, but she was training for something once more. She didn't know what she'd find in the caves, and she wanted to make sure her body was ready for it.

Every once in a while, Vhalla would take dinner at Daniel's home. She used the opportunity to quiz him about swordplay and, more than once, they ended up sparring in the grass around the tree. The bouts were even better practice than at the grounds, and would go until one of the lords or ladies in the surrounding homes complained about the noise. Vhalla's skill steadily improved.

Winter was upon the world when Vhalla was almost finished with the axe. She knew it would only need one more session, two at most, and she was ready to wash her hands of it. Fear of the Caverns had been so constant that she indulged in her curiosity of what her life would be like when they would no longer be a worry.

She went out to the training ground again that evening. In addition to trying to figure out how to destroy the fount of the most fearsome magic the world knew, she was still determined to bridge the gap between the guard and sorcerers; tonight, there would be more than just the Windwalker in the ring.

"Vhal, I didn't join the guard after the war because I am *tired* of fighting," Fritz whined playfully.

"But you're so good at it with your illusions." Vhalla threw her arm around his shoulders, ruffling his hair. "And it'll do the other soldiers good."

"It's hard," Fritz mumbled.

"I think it's a good idea, also." Grahm nudged Fritz playfully, shaking away the other man's pout. Vhalla had actually gone to Grahm first. He and Fritz were hard to find apart these days, and she knew if she got him on board with her idea, Fritz would be sure to follow.

"You would, you're too hard-working not to." Fritz's shoulder brushed against Grahm's side as they walked, and the Eastern man took Fritz's hand, the one that wasn't wrapped around Vhalla's waist.

They had become so adorable it was blinding.

Erion was behind the main table again. Vhalla headed straight for him. "Erion," she called as they neared.

His head shot up, and he gave her a tired smile. "Here for the ring?"

She nodded.

"And you bring friends, I see." Erion appraised the two Waterrunners at her sides.

"Hopefully the start of a trend," Vhalla replied, making her intentions known.

"It's a trend I'll live with right now." Erion sighed softly. "Can I have you two in the pit? And can I put you with the archers?" He motioned to Fritz and Grahm, then Vhalla, in turn.

"No problem!" Fritz gave a rallying cry and led an amused Grahm over. It was amazing the sway Grahm had on Fritz with such little effort. In the short walk from the Tower to the training grounds, he'd completely transformed Fritz's mood.

"I'll walk you to the archers, outline what needs to be done."

"Is everything all right?" Vhalla asked, falling into step at the Westerner's side.

"What?" Erion was jarred from his thoughts. "Oh, yes, everything is fine."

The man quickly launched into an explanation of what he wanted Vhalla to do. It was a simple enough task, producing wind for the archers to train in. Vhalla listened absentmindedly, her mind churning over the fact that something was definitely wrong with her companion.

But Erion kept his secrets to himself, returning to the center table alone.

At first, the archers were skeptical about her presence, but Vhalla had an unexpected ace. Tim was among them, and the young woman was hasty to tell the grand tales of the Windwalker to her comrades who hadn't been to war and hadn't already heard. So they approached the range with a timid curiosity that quickly vanished into annoyance when most of their arrows shot wide of their targets due to Vhalla's wind.

It ended up being a competition of the Windwalker versus the Empire's best archers. They began taking her seriously, finding ways for their arrows to hit their targets in spite of her winds. Those arrows were points for them, the ones on the ground were points for her.

She could make it so that not one arrow hit its target, but Vhalla kept the sport fair, enjoying the game. The score was almost even when three archers left the shooting line to make room for one more. Vhalla's hands fell to her sides, and the winds quieted.

"*Gwaeru*," the Northern woman called.

Vhalla stared at Za blankly. She wasn't sure what emotion she should summon for the woman who was plotting treason.

"I prefer Lady Yarl, actually," she corrected loudly. Vhalla hardly cared for the use of titles, but she didn't want to give the woman the power of taking her name from her—of reducing Vhalla once more to nothing more than the Emperor's Windwalker.

"Lady Yarl." The woman smiled, which quickly turned into a sneer. "I want to shoot."

"We are practicing shooting in the wind tonight," Vhalla announced.

"Fine." The woman fixed her armguard to her left wrist, adjusting a large wooden bow in her hand.

Without another word, Za reached for an arrow in the quiver at her side. Vhalla raised her hands. A strong wind blew across the range. All arrows were knocked off course—all except for one. Vhalla met the eyes of the Northern archer, a frown tugging at her lips.

The next arrow hit. The wind blew harder. The third almost missed. Vhalla shifted the direction of the breeze. The fourth was knocked off course. She fought a smirk and looked back to the woman. *It had begun.*

Four quivers in, Vhalla was almost breathless, as was the other woman. The ground looked like a porcupine made of arrows, illuminated by the high moon.

"That's enough," Za announced, throwing her bow over her shoulder.

Vhalla shrugged, wiping her brow. She looked for Fritz and Grahm, but it appeared that they had already departed without her. In fact, almost no one was around. Time seemed to have escaped her.

"*Gwaeru.*" Za's voice was close, and Vhalla turned, unsurprised to find the woman a few short steps away. The bow was still in her hand, armguard still on, quiver mostly full. Vhalla eyed them uneasily, keeping the wind under her palms.

"I said my name was Lady Yarl."

Za ignored Vhalla's correction. "Sehra has a new deal."

Vhalla scowled. "I don't want to be involved with either of you."

"And we don't want to be involved with you or the prince," Za hissed. "But you both continue to touch Achel and leave us no choice."

Vhalla stilled, bringing her eyes to Za's emerald ones.

"Sehra knows. She can feel that he has come into contact with Achel now, too."

A quiet horror crept through her, whispering her worst fears. Vhalla's lips were quiet, but her mind was loud. The taint creeping through her bond with Aldrik must have progressed farther if Sehra could pick it up. Or maybe it was just consistent, but no worse?

Vhalla knew she had to find him. She hadn't sought him out once in the weeks since their meeting in his garden. But now she'd haunt the library for a certain sorcerer prince.

"Give us the axe."

"No." Vhalla frowned. She was so close to getting rid of it for good.

"We all know the prince is already half-monster. If he becomes twisted into a whole monster, I will shoot to kill."

Vhalla's arm snapped out, gripping Za's bow before the woman had time to pull it away. Za tugged but Vhalla held fast. The Northerner's gaze met hers, and Vhalla narrowed her eyes threateningly.

"If you as much as think of touching him, I will kill you myself," Vhalla growled.

"Sehra has a new deal." Za smiled maliciously, knowing what she was about to do would drive Vhalla mad. "But she will tell her future husband, no more deals with you."

Vhalla shoved the bow back into Za's hand in frustration. The woman grinned and took a few steps backward before starting for the palace. This was a bigger game than Vhalla and Aldrik. They all knew it. But her love for the prince was being made into an easy pawn.

She stilled.

Her love for the prince.

For the first time in months, Vhalla had admitted it to herself. She gripped her watch tightly. There it was, the truth. *Now, what to do with it?*

Vhalla found herself looking for Aldrik's light on her way up the Tower. She looked for the tiny, flickering mote that stood against the darkness. And didn't find it.

CHAPTER 16

*H*E RAN THROUGH *the halls with a blond-haired toddler on his heels. His excitement for the small bundle he held in his hands was palpable. Aldrik couldn't be more than seven or eight. He had a goofy smile, and his hair was cut straight across the middle of his neck.*

"Do you think she'll like it?" Aldrik asked the boy. Vhalla looked at the little Baldair struggling to keep up with his brother's longer strides.

"Yes!" he said with all the black and white certainty of a child. Baldair carried a little parcel himself.

They ended up at the top of a grand staircase with a large pair of doors that formed a blazing sun between them. There were two guards stationed outside who both gave small nods to the princes. Baldair stood regally tall for his small stature.

"I am here to see mommy!" *he announced. Aldrik actually laughed at his brother's antics.*

A guard chuckled and opened the door. "After you, little prince." The room was massive. The main area was just a sitting room. On the ceiling, there was a large dome with a sun, and on the floor was a mosaic map of the continent made in painstaking detail. More rooms indicated that the Imperial quarters extended beyond, but Aldrik and Baldair ran to a woman sitting on the wide balcony.

"Happy birthday!" Baldair proclaimed.

"Happy birthday." Aldrik stood a step back, fussing with the wrapping on his gift.

"My little Baldair." The even younger Empress was pure radiance. Long golden hair flowed to her mid-back in waves. Her skin was aglow with youth, a soft pink on her cheeks. There was not a single sign of exhaustion or stress upon her face. She picked up the younger boy and placed him in her lap. "Did you remember my birthday?"

"We did," Baldair announced proudly. "Look! Look!" He held out the present, far too close to her face, and she accepted it with a laugh.

"All right, all right, let us see here." The woman wrapped her arms around the boy in her lap, opening the gift.

Aldrik shifted his hands again around his gift, looking up at the woman, his heart beating in anticipation.

"Oh, my little noble prince, this is simply perfect." The woman held a small wreath, haphazardly put together with twigs and sticks. There was twine in some places; in others, it seemed to have come undone and a stick popped open awkwardly.

"It's a crown!" Baldair explained. "A birthday crown!"

"A birthday crown indeed." The woman put it on her head nicely and gave a kiss on the boy's forehead. Aldrik looked on with longing and sadness.

"I-I brought a present also." Aldrik took a step forward.

"So I see." The woman turned to the elder child staring up at her as she stroked Baldair's hair lovingly.

"I hope you like it." Aldrik presented it with both hands.

The woman took in a deep breath and held in a sigh. She took

Aldrik's present with one hand and unwrapped it quickly. It was a little mass of molten silver, like a sun, with a loop around the top.

"I've been study—"

"I have, *Aldrik; speak properly," the woman interrupted.*

"I have been studying my sorcery," Aldrik began again. "I-it's a, it's—"

"It is, and don't stutter," the Empress corrected for a second time. Nervousness radiated off the boy. How could this woman not see the same?

"It is a pendant," the boy Aldrik finally managed. "I thought you would—"

"Yes, thank you, Aldrik." The Empress looked away and adjusted the twig crown on her head. "Did you see the gift Baldair made?"

"I did." Aldrik looked at his feet.

"He helped me, mother!" Baldair grinned, completely oblivious to any tension.

"I am sure you picked up quickly and did it even better, my smart son." The woman kissed his golden forehead again.

Baldair nodded. "I did try!"

"It shows." The Empress gave her child a hug.

Aldrik was left standing alone, staring at his feet, a few steps away.

A rapid set of knocks jolted her from sleep.

Vhalla sat with a start, clutching her watch, the memory of the child Aldrik fresh. Her heart ached for the elder prince. *Aldrik being called the black sheep and him taking it to heart suddenly made a lot more sense.*

More knocks on the door jarred her from her thoughts. Vhalla flopped back on the bed, rolling over and burying herself under the covers. The mornings were frigid now, nearly cold enough to form frost on the glass of her window. The chill combined with her latest dream made her utterly uninterested in company.

The knocking persisted, the person clearly not getting the point.

"What?" she said with a groan.

The door opened a crack, and a pair of Western eyes looked in at her. Vhalla peered at Jax through thin slits. The man chuckled and let himself into her room.

"Lucky you, sleeping past dawn." He wiggled onto the small bed next to her.

Vhalla rolled her eyes and pressed against the wall. The tall man was comically large atop the small mattress, his side flush against hers. But Vhalla had come to an understanding with the strange man known as Jax Wendyll. After their short time in the Crossroads, there was something base, gritty, yet simple about their relationship; it was ugly beautiful.

"I'd like to *keep* sleeping, you know," she mumbled and buried her face into her pillow. It was cramped with two, but having someone next to her again was relaxing. Larel and Aldrik had both been Firebearers, and Jax was equally warm.

"But I need you."

Vhalla cracked open one eye. "How?"

"Oh, in all the worst ways." Jax waggled his eyebrows.

"Mother, you're awful." Vhalla's dry remark earned a laugh. "Jax, really, why are you crawling into my bed?"

"Really, we could use your help on the grounds today." Serious notes had finally worked their way into his words.

"I've been helping you for weeks. Why are you suddenly bothering with asking?" He had her attention now.

"We're short-handed."

"Have Baldair and Raylynn finally run off together?" Vhalla couldn't stop herself. The more she'd come to know the Guard, the more she'd learned who and what the easy targets were for jokes.

"One of those said parties is missing, though not who you'd expect. Ray is actually pulling her weight." Even Jax sounded impressed. "But Baldair is still gone, and Craig woke feeling unwell."

"*Still* gone?" The word had Vhalla wondering when was the last time she'd actually seen the golden-haired royal.

"Oh, you know him. Last I saw he was chasing Lady Imaj around the Court. I'm sure they just ran off." Jax's laugh didn't have the strength it usually did. He quickly rolled off the bed and pushed the topic along before Vhalla could linger further. "So, help?"

"Yes, yes." Vhalla sat, realizing she was done with sleeping. She knew she should go to the minister. They were *so close* to finishing the axe, and then it would be over. But it was one day, and Vhalla didn't want to ignore her friends when they were in need. So, after quickly dressing, her feet carried her to the grounds with Jax.

Erion was relieved the second Jax arrived with her, and Vhalla was quickly put to work. The difference two sets of hands made in managing the palace guard and their training was noticeable. Her practice with Daniel actually qualified Vhalla to help train young swordsmen and women in training, so Vhalla haunted the grounds until dusk.

She ate with the guard after, and lingered until the moon had crested the horizon. Sweaty and exhausted, she finally dragged her feet up the Tower. Her crystal work was taking a lot out of her, and she was on a mission for a hot bath and her bed.

The heavy thud of a book dropping drew Vhalla's attention into the dimly lit library. Footsteps moved across the floor, and Vhalla watched the flickering light of a single flame dance over the tops of the books on the bookshelves. For once, she was thankful for his insomnia.

She needed to talk to Aldrik. She needed to speak with the prince about the crystal taint, about the princess, about making sure his father and the fragile peace that he'd bought with so much blood would last into spring, and about Aldrik's succession as the Emperor of Peace. *It had nothing to do with her admission the night prior,* she assured herself.

She rounded a bookcase, looking at the dark form scanning a high shelf for a manuscript. Vhalla leaned against the shelves, watching him. His hair was limp and messed, his shoulders had an uncharacteristic sway. For a brief moment, she feared everything she'd heard about his old habits was really a lie, that he'd never stopped—or had returned to—his less than healthy ways of coping with a problem.

Aldrik sighed heavily, pulling a book and scanning it. Something was wrong, but Vhalla couldn't place her finger on it.

"My prince," she whispered, not wanting to startle him too badly. It didn't work, and Aldrik nearly dropped the book he was holding. Vhalla realized too late that she had used their former term of endearment; she wondered if her presence or her words startled him more.

"What—when did you get here?" Dark circles blemished the area under his eyes.

"Aldrik." Vhalla took a step closer, noticing his rumpled, extremely casual attire for the man who was usually perfection incarnate. "What's wrong?"

His defensive instinct took over, but only for a brief moment. The tension in his shoulders vanished, and the man swayed, nearly collapsing in on himself. "Baldair. He's sick, Vhalla."

"It's serious, isn't it?" The day was still fresh in her mind, Baldair missing training yet again.

"It started as a cold, aches, chills," Aldrik spoke softly to the bookshelf, unable to meet her gaze. "It's Autumn Fever."

"This late?" The fever normally set in at the first transition between summer and fall. Not into the winter.

"You'll hear more cases of it soon, I am certain." Aldrik looked back to her. "The clerics say the years it appears late are the worst."

"Has he had it before?" She remembered clerics telling her once that because she had contracted the disease as a child, it would not be as severe if she were to catch it again. Aldrik shook his head, and her heart sank. "How long has he been ill?"

"They've had him on bed rest for over a week," Aldrik answered.

"The coughing?" she asked tentatively.

"It is only now beginning to worsen," he answered. "You had it as a girl, didn't you?"

Vhalla stared at her toes, remembering her mother's coughing, *so much coughing and then the blood . . .* "I did."

"Come see him?"

"What?" Her head snapped up, startled at the idea.

"I want you to see him." Aldrik stepped forward and boldly took both her hands. His touch had the same familiar warmth as it always had, but it held no lightning given the subject of conversation. "I don't know how much the clerics may not be saying. I've never been sick with the fever, so my knowledge is limited to second-hand study only. You're at less of a risk of contracting the fever again, having had it before."

"I know . . ." she sighed. It wasn't about getting sick. She didn't want to go into a room and confront that illness. "I'm sure the clerics are doing their best, Aldrik."

"I trust you. I trust you, not them."

Vhalla met his eyes with trepidation. *That was the truth of it.* When the cards fell, when all else was taken away, there remained the assumption that the other would be there—that somehow their existence as unit, as a force, remained.

"I'll go see him," she agreed.

Aldrik scooped up the small stack of books he'd pilfered and started out the library without a word.

"Wait, *now?*" Vhalla fell into hasty step with the long-legged prince.

"Clerics will be in his room without stop when the day comes," Aldrik explained. "Night will be the only time that you can give me an honest assessment without having to dance around the egos of the bumbling idiots that my father seems to think pass for competent."

Vhalla allowed herself a small smile and held her tongue. There was something reassuring about Aldrik being well enough to insult something. He led her down to one of the many doors lining the Tower staircase. Aldrik paused, fumbling to adjust the stack of books into a single arm.

"Give me them."

"They're heavy." Aldrik looked at her uncertainly.

"Oh, yes, you're too right, my prince. I am a delicate flower." She batted her eyelashes for emphasis. "Allow me to do nothing more than stand and look pretty while you struggle."

Aldrik shook his head with a huff of amusement and passed her the stack of books. It was hardly the largest she'd ever carried, and Vhalla adjusted her grip, managing it with ease. With his hands free, Aldrik unlocked the door and led her into a hallway that was completely dark, save for the mote of flame at his side.

Vhalla smiled tiredly at his back. *How many times would she follow the prince into darkness, trusting his light to guide her?*

Upon reaching a dead end, Aldrik pushed on the wall, and it

swung open under his palms. Vhalla followed him into a large room. Moonlight streamed in through diamond-checkered glass doors that overlooked a massive balcony. A four-poster bed with large, black, square posts dominated the space. Around it was a stone hearth, a number of armoires, and doors leading in other directions. Vhalla stopped in her tracks as he closed the secret door, which was concealed as a large mirror. She looked at the gilded ceiling, the white marble flooring, the decorative tapestries and rich textiles that adorned the floor, walls, ceiling, windows, and doors.

"This-this is your room," she stuttered.

Aldrik stopped. "It is indeed."

"Where is the princess?" Vhalla asked delicately.

"Do you think she stays with me?" He gaped. "Scandal aside, I would never let the girl into my haven."

Vhalla swallowed as he crossed back over to her. Aldrik always said more between his words, and she heard him as clearly as ever. His hands rested on hers.

"Let me take those."

"It's fine. You have to open more doors, right?" His soft words coaxed her into whispering.

"I was going to do it alone before."

"But you're not alone, are you?" It was her turn to speak between words, and Aldrik's expression let her know he'd heard her.

The prince's hands fell from hers, and he started for the door to the left. She focused only on him, ignoring the opulent sitting area he'd led her into. *Even if they were never anything more than they were now, would she be happy?*

Aldrik poked his head out of the main door, glancing up and down the hall. He motioned for her to follow, and Vhalla walked on air over the plush white runner that went the length of the hall. They crossed to a door opposite.

As he opened the second door, Vhalla realized that she had been in this hall before. The day Baldair had invited her to the gala, he had taken her to the same room she now faced. But it didn't have the same brightness as then. Now it was cast in darkness, with vials—empty and full alike—littering nearly every surface. The room smelled strongly of herbs and salves.

A blanket was thrown over one of the couches in the sitting area, a pillow keeping it company. A semi-circle of books stood in defense of the cleric's equipment that encroached in on a set of parchments with familiar handwriting on them. As she put the books down with the others, Vhalla wondered how long the elder prince had been living with his brother.

Aldrik held out a length of cloth to her. She noticed he'd already covered his own nose and mouth with one. Vhalla brought it to her nose and covered the lower half of her face with it.

They walked over to a secondary door that was almost entirely gilded. Aldrik knocked twice lightly, then paused. There was rough coughing barely muffled by the door. Vhalla braced herself, as if she was headed into battle once more.

"Enter," came a tired voice from within. Baldair faded into another fit of coughing as Aldrik pushed open the door.

"Brother." The older prince took a few steps in, holding the door open. "I brought a guest."

"A guest?" Baldair wheezed. There was a rough and raspy chuckle after a short pause. "Vhalla, come in."

"How did you?" she mumbled as she inched into the room.

"Who else would my brother bring at this hour of the night? Without prior word? Directly into my room?" Baldair reclined in a large bed with a golden canopy.

Vhalla noticed a chair set by his bedside and glanced back knowingly at Aldrik. *These brothers were impossible*, and it was almost hilarious how the world thought they hated each other. How they tried to insist sometimes that they did.

"How do you feel?" she asked gently, crossing over to the edge of the younger prince's bed, leaving the chair for Aldrik.

The crown prince lit the candles at the bedside tables with a thought, then sat.

"Almost like the time I had a sword through my shoulder." Baldair coughed. "But closer to my chest."

"Here, cough into this for me?" She took a small piece of cloth off his bedside table and handed it to the prince.

"Coughing is not a problem." Baldair chuckled, and it sent him into another fit.

Vhalla sat directly on his bed and held out her hand for the cloth when his coughing subsided. She looked at the mucus; it had a distinctively red tinge. Her heart sank.

"What is it?" Aldrik read her face without difficulty.

Vhalla wanted to scream at the cloth and burn it, as if that would make its truth disappear. Blood, *the blood was starting*. It would get worse from here. She took a deep breath and forced herself to remain calm, to not panic. Aldrik had brought her for her experience, but her experience was only death once the blood set in.

"You need to eat." She looked back at Baldair. His usually glowing face was hollow and pale. "When was the last time you ate?"

"Do I have a new cleric?" Baldair asked his brother with a tired grin.

"She had Autumn Fever when she was a girl, Baldair," Aldrik answered. "She has seen it, she has lived through it. You know how the clerics are."

Vhalla glanced back at the cloth in her hand. *She* had lived through it. She had also lived with her mother dying from it.

"Food," she said again, not entertaining the memories of her ailing mother. "You have to eat, Baldair."

"Vhalla," he groaned. "It hurts to breathe, and you want me to eat?"

"It will get worse, if you . . ." Vhalla shook her head, trying to part the flood of emotions that assaulted her. "Don't stop eating. Keep up your strength," she insisted. "Aldrik, can you get him food?"

"I can find something." He nodded, standing. "Will you stay here until I return?"

"I'll stay with him." Aldrik's concern for his brother was not lost on her, not for a moment. The prince left the room briskly, without further word.

"Vhalla." Baldair struggled to sit.

"Lie down." She placed her hands on his shoulders.

"If I'm going to eat, I need to sit a little." Even his coy grins looked tired. Vhalla relinquished his shoulders and helped him adjust his pillows. The covers fell to his stomach, and Vhalla saw his skin had truly lost its luster. *He was starting to thin.* "What are you doing?"

"I'm helping you." Vhalla had assumed that much to be obvious.

"With Aldrik," Baldair clarified.

"He asked me to come and help." Vhalla sat back with a sigh.

"My brother went to you?" Even exhausted and sick, Baldair managed skepticism.

"Not entirely . . ." She suddenly remembered the original reason she'd sought out the prince. With all that was occurring, how could she broach the subject of crystals, taint, and his family being targeted from within? "I had something I needed to speak with him about, and then he asked me to come here."

"What were you going to speak with him about?"

"It's personal." She avoided answering.

"With you two, I bet it is."

"You know, I don't think you're that sick after all." Vhalla peered at the prince.

"I'm trying to help." Baldair was unrelenting.

"And I'm trying to tell you to focus on nothing other than getting better." She crossed her arms over her chest.

"Fine." Baldair's eyes lingered on her chest and Vhalla knew he wasn't checking out her figure. She tucked the watch under her shirt as she unfolded her arms. "Well, whatever the reason, I am happy to see you around again. I was worried about Aldrik."

"Has he fallen into any . . . bad habits?" she asked delicately.

"Surprisingly not," Baldair praised his sibling. "He's held himself together, done what he's supposed to do and then some. He's the man I always knew my brother could be, and he did it on his own this time. And yet, it feels so empty."

Vhalla stared at the candles, flickering with Aldrik's flames.

Baldair continued in her silence, "When he fought for you, he fought. It was bad, it was ugly, but he *fought*. The man I knew to have fire in his veins now does nothing more than simmer. I know I said everything between you both was a bad idea."

"It was," she interjected.

"It was," he affirmed. "But you did it anyway, and now I don't see him ever being happy again without you. He may be the best

Emperor the Empire will ever know, and he'll be empty inside." He paused before adding, "I know, I am a hypocrite for this . . . But, I've gained some new perspectives since I've been trapped in this bed. Don't leave him now, Vhalla." Baldair wheezed, "Especially, if something happens to me. He'd have no one else who knows that the Fire Lord is capable of joy."

"Don't say that." Vhalla brought her eyes back to the golden prince. "Please, don't say things like that."

"I know what this illness does." Baldair shifted uncomfortably. "Especially in adults who contract it with no history."

"You will be fine," Vhalla insisted bravely.

The outer door opened and closed again. Aldrik appeared in the inner doorway before anything else could be said.

He brought a tray, setting it down on his brother's lap. "Will this do?"

"It's perfect." She nodded, appraising the soup and small roll of bread. "Now, Baldair, will you eat this or do I need to force-feed it to you?"

"I'll eat, I'll eat." He chuckled.

The golden prince ate slowly, and Vhalla and Aldrik both had to push him toward the end. But eventually the whole bowl and bread were consumed. He complained about it sitting uncomfortably, but Vhalla told him to stop moaning about what would make him better. It was followed up with a firm order to eat all of whatever the clerics put before him from then on, no matter how he felt. She could imagine the clerics going soft on the prince when he needed to be pushed.

They helped him lie back once more. The older brother supported the younger as she situated the pillows. Aldrik produced a potion for the cough, and Baldair took it without question. It coated his throat and took effect almost instantly. Baldair was asleep within a few minutes, and Vhalla suspected there might have also been deepsleep potion in the now empty vial.

Vhalla and Aldrik sat for a while, watching the golden prince rest.

"How is he?"

Vhalla turned her attention to the elder prince at his question. He was hunched over, his elbows on his thighs, his hands folded.

"When . . ." Vhalla took a deep breath, forcing herself to be brave. "When my mother fell ill, it took a week for the blood to set in. He's not far." She reached for the cloth, showing Aldrik.

"After the blood?" He looked from his brother's red-tinged mucus to her.

"My mother." She glanced back to the golden-haired prince. "Three days." She reached out to Baldair, placing her palm on his forehead lightly. "But she did not have clerics like you do here. Her fever was much higher by this point. We didn't have a lot of good food either. If the clerics can keep the fever low, and he eats to keep his strength, I know he will fight it."

Vhalla looked back to Aldrik. He had his face hidden in one hand, the other on his knee. Silent suffering summed him up so woefully perfectly. Her hand hovered in the air a brief moment before Vhalla brushed the skin on the back of the hand on his leg with her fingertips.

Aldrik's face snapped up. His gaze was uncertain, but he did not move his hand away. The crown prince's whole body was still and tense. Vhalla's fingers slid and curled in a reassuring motion. His hand closed around hers with sudden force, and they did nothing but look at each other.

"I won't leave again," she whispered. "Whatever ill fate awaits us; I'll wait for it with you."

"I want you with me, always." His other hand caressed the chain on her neck. "Even if you never need me again in the same way, I need you."

His fingertips paused, the metal of the watch the only thing separating his hand from her chest. Aldrik took a deep breath. "I want to start over. Before the heartbreak, the anger, before the foolish words that were said, and before you knew the man I used to be." His dark eyes pleaded with her, his voice breathy beneath his mask. "I want to go back to a time when I could teach you magic. I want the chance to treat you as I always should have."

"I don't think it works that way." Her own mask hid her tired smile.

"We can make our own way; we always have." Aldrik cupped her cheek boldly, and Vhalla didn't stop him. "What have we to lose?"

"Everything?"

"Is that all?" His eyes were alight.

Vhalla gave into that joy for only a moment. Baldair wheezed in his sleep, reminding her where they were, what was happening. Her expression fell as she considered the ailing prince.

"Aldrik, promise me one thing."

"Anything."

"If anything ever happens to me . . ." She remembered Baldair's words. How if she left Aldrik, and Baldair didn't pull through, their future Emperor would be truly alone.

His hands suddenly gripped her shoulders, and the prince was half out of the chair, staring at her with a shocking intensity. "*Nothing will happen to you.*" Aldrik looked right through her, and Vhalla had no idea what he saw, but it terrified him. "I will not let it happen."

"Aldrik . . ." Her brow furrowed in confusion, trying to figure out the source of the man's panic.

He took a deep breath and seemed to remember himself once more. "I-I'm sorry." Aldrik let her go quickly and rubbed his eyes.

"When was the last time you slept?" Vhalla asked him, standing.

"I catch some sleep when the clerics are in with him."

Vhalla translated the Aldrik-speak to mean that it had been a long time. "Rest," she demanded. "I'll sit with Baldair 'til dawn."

She pushed Aldrik lightly toward the other room. Thankfully, he did not give much of a struggle, and he allowed her to herd him toward the couch he used as his makeshift bed during his brother's illness. Aldrik lied down, pulling off his cloth mask, and dropping it onto the floor. Hooking a finger, she lowered her mask to drop around her neck since she would need it again in a moment. Vhalla situated the blanket over him.

"My prince." She dropped to a knee at the side of the couch. Aldrik turned to look at her. Neither seemed to mind her method of addressing him. Vhalla resisted the urge to touch his face. She ignored the desire to run her fingers through his hair. "I don't wish we could start over. Everything that happened, we made mistakes, but-but we loved, and I don't regret that."

His hand reached up and took hers at the edge of the blanket. His fingers intertwined with hers, and Vhalla's heart stuck in her throat as she watched them lace together. "Fight at my side again?"

Vhalla nodded, not finding her voice. She didn't know in what capacity he meant, but she could guess.

"I will be better. I will never push you away again," he whispered.

"I'll never let you." Vhalla laughed softly.

"I vow to honor my promise to you, Vhalla."

Her free hand rose to her watch, a look that affirmed she understood the promise he meant—his promise of a future together. "And I will mine." *Their promises still meant something.*

Vhalla sat with him until his breathing slowed and his body relaxed. Her fingers remained entwined with his, and she watched him sleep. Maybe they would never again be the lovers they were— maybe they'd become something better. They'd both grown apart, and maybe they'd grown into the people they should've been all along.

Love was a simple emotion, Vhalla had learned. Once one experienced it, a person understood it, and there was no doubt when one felt it. If there was no doubt, then nothing would ever serve as a substitute.

Vhalla knew she understood love. Love was throwing herself into a sandstorm. Love was braving her darkest fears and battling her demons. Love was a blind dash through a Northern jungle. Love was hopeful words shared across a pillow in the darkness. Love was bravery and—perhaps most importantly—forgiveness.

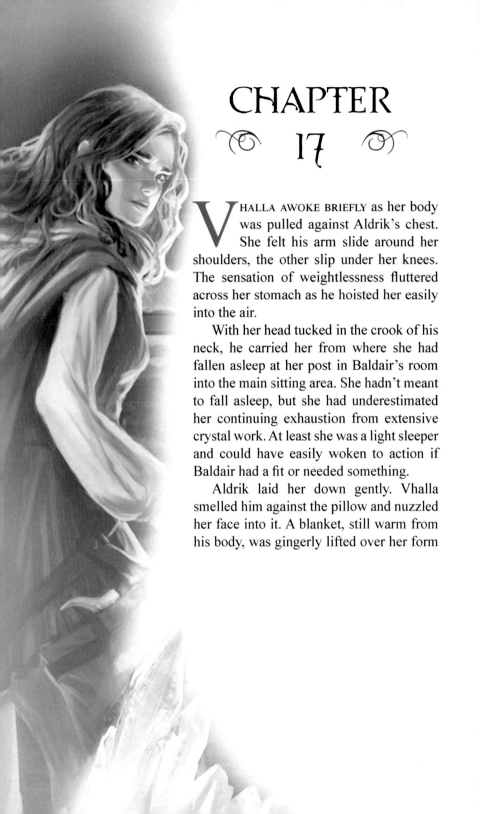

CHAPTER 17

VHALLA AWOKE BRIEFLY as her body was pulled against Aldrik's chest. She felt his arm slide around her shoulders, the other slip under her knees. The sensation of weightlessness fluttered across her stomach as he hoisted her easily into the air.

With her head tucked in the crook of his neck, he carried her from where she had fallen asleep at her post in Baldair's room into the main sitting area. She hadn't meant to fall asleep, but she had underestimated her continuing exhaustion from extensive crystal work. At least she was a light sleeper and could have easily woken to action if Baldair had a fit or needed something.

Aldrik laid her down gently. Vhalla smelled him against the pillow and nuzzled her face into it. A blanket, still warm from his body, was gingerly lifted over her form and tucked around her. Her hand reached upward and found his, in a complete reversal of how they had been earlier.

He stopped all movement and intertwined his fingers with hers once more. Vhalla wasn't certain exactly what every touch meant yet, but she knew how they made her feel. She knew all the wrongs in the world that seemed to be bearable by knowing he was near her once more. The unsettled sickness, one that had plagued her stomach so long that it had begun to feel natural, finally quieted.

Slipping his long fingers into her hair, Aldrik stroked her head gently. Vhalla nuzzled deeper into the warmth and comfort that surrounded her. Eventually his motion ceased, and she felt his hands pull away.

"Don't stop," she murmured in sleep.

"If it pleases," his voice was deep and throaty when he whispered, and Vhalla smiled tiredly at the sound as much as the words. His fingers returned to her hair, and she sighed contently, remembering every time on the march she had fallen asleep to the feeling after practicing her Projection.

Vhalla drifted back into a deep slumber without ever opening her eyes.

Coughing woke her, and she peered between her eyelashes. The brightness of the room pulled her into wakefulness, jolting her upright in a moment. Looking around, her panic was briefly quelled by the absence of anyone else in the room. It was certainly past sunrise, but the world was still quiet. She carefully folded the blanket and placed it at the end of the couch, resting the pillow on top.

More coughing accompanied her steps toward the bedroom. Aldrik sat at the bedside looking rather determined with a spoon in one hand and a bowl in the other. Baldair wore a stubborn glare. She rolled her eyes at the scene before her.

"I told him he needs to eat." Aldrik glanced at her. She saw a glint of amusement in his eyes at the familiar sight of her trying to tame her morning hair. "Vhalla, your mask."

"Your brother is right, Baldair." Vhalla yawned and pulled the fabric from around her neck to her nose and mouth. "You told me you'd eat everything."

"Vhalla?" Baldair's shoulders lurched as he continued to cough. "I don't recall giving you permission to sleep in my room."

"She stayed on the order of the crown prince," Aldrik proclaimed with mock haughtiness. "You said it yourself, you have a new cleric." His dark eyes flicked back to her, and Vhalla shook her head in amusement.

"Don't tell me." Shades of a healthy Baldair returned as he wheezed for breath. "You two did the do on my couch."

Aldrik visibly paled, Baldair smirked, and Vhalla's laughter rang out throughout the room.

"If by 'the do,' you mean slept. Yes, we did." Baldair blinked at her as she crossed to her place at the edge of his bed. "And before you get any ideas or form any assumptions, it was not at the same time."

Vhalla grabbed a roll of bread off the table—Aldrik had continued to make safe choices with food. She tore off a hunk and, as Baldair opened his mouth for some retort, she unceremoniously shoved in the mass of food. Baldair looked at her in shock as he was forced to chew through the soft piece of bread.

"Now eat, oh golden prince." She grinned.

"Don't—" Baldair chewed. "Don't think that when I'm well—" he coughed again "—I won't get you back for these indiscretions against the crown."

"Take it up with the crown prince." She tore off another piece and forced it into the younger prince's mouth with a satisfied grin at his frustration. "I hear he has a wicked temper."

"Oh, I am certain there could be a fitting punishment administered." Aldrik crossed his arms over his chest and leaned back in the chair, content to let her assume the duty of feeding his brother.

Vhalla glanced at him from the corners of her eyes, a sly smile hidden by the mask at the coy nature of the crown prince in a good mood.

"Getting sick will be the death of me." Baldair cleared his throat.

"Don't say that," she insisted gently.

"Oh, don't be so dramatic." The prince coughed, barely managing to keep the food down. "I only meant it in that my being sick has clearly reunited you both, and that is a fact that may be detrimental to my health for many years to come. And I don't need to be fed like some invalid."

Baldair rolled his eyes and snatched the bowl and spoon from her hands. He coughed and sputtered, spilling some. Vhalla stood to clean it up, and Aldrik did the same. He passed her a rag from the table next to Baldair's bed for his coughing. Their fingers touched briefly. Vhalla looked up at the dark-haired prince, their eyes met, and her heart did a strange beat.

Saying nothing, she turned and cleaned up the small spill, ignoring the embarrassment of an apologetic Baldair. She smiled tiredly at the younger prince. *Nothing could possibly happen to Baldair*, she mentally insisted. He was too well cared for and too strong.

"You should go, Vhalla."

"So soon?" Baldair objected like a child. "Can't we just say I invited her?"

"Brother, it's for the best. Her presence would raise too many questions." Aldrik glanced at her. "I don't want us to make her life difficult."

Vhalla knew it was for the best, but at the same time, she was done hiding what she wanted. She simply had to figure out her next move alongside Aldrik. A similar turmoil was written on the prince's face, and Vhalla knew there would be words over what their future would hold sooner rather than later.

"Tonight?" she proposed. "Could I come back after the clerics have left?"

"That's—" Baldair digressed into coughing that cut all words short. He was forced to simply nod.

"Tonight then," Aldrik agreed.

"Perhaps we could play carcivi." She was certain the prince could have a dozen carcivi boards crafted and delivered before the day was out if he didn't already have one. "Something to stimulate your mind a bit."

"It's better than Aldrik's suggestions of books."

Vhalla laughed. "Well then, carcivi it is. I'll be back to beat you wickedly, so eat your food, drink your potions, and get rest. I don't want to let you have the excuse of illness for your loss."

"Ha! We will see who beats who!"

"We should go." Aldrik's palm fell on the small of her back. "Before the clerics come."

"See you, Baldair." Vhalla gave him a small wave as Aldrik closed the door behind them. She crossed over to the bar that had been turned into a medical supply stand and removed her mask completely. "He seems better."

"He usually is after company," Aldrik agreed.

"The Golden Guard?" she guessed and Aldrik affirmed. "You should send for them, then. I think they are quite worried."

"I'll see what I can do," Aldrik mumbled.

Vhalla beamed brightly, for in Aldrik language, that meant he was about to throw around the weight of the scary crown prince on his brother's behalf.

"Wait a moment."

Holding up his hand, he cracked open the door and took a glance down the hallway. Aldrik opened the door halfway, gliding across to his own room. He fit a key into the lock and unlocked it with a soft click. One more glance, and he was motioning for her to join him. Vhalla eased closed Baldair's door and slipped into the safety of Aldrik's haven as he shut out the world.

In the daytime, she could appreciate the stunning nature of his quarters. Vhalla looked up, and she lost all breath. A staircase wound up the far wall to a landing that looped around the circular room. There were more staircases and ladders leading up to additional landings and levels of books. She looked up into the roof area of one of the golden spires she had admired from below so many times, only to discover that it held Aldrik's personal library.

"Aldrik," she breathed, walking into the room. The white marble floor was covered with a large, circular black rug that almost took up the whole space. There were two leather chaises near a couch that was reminiscent of the Crossroads and a desk with chairs to the right side. "This is *yours*?"

"It is." His expression was unreadable.

"It's—" she fumbled for words. Vhalla felt dizzy at the notion.

Aldrik took a step forward to stand at her shoulder, holding his breath for her review. "Amazing."

"Would you like to see the rest of it?" he asked softly.

"The rest of it?" Vhalla blinked up at him.

Three doors led out from his initial sitting room. One he had led her through the night before—his bedroom. The second went into a smaller, cozy office. Vhalla realized the large, dark stained desk in the main room was just for show as she could immediately tell that this office was reserved for his real work. Papers littered the surface in an order only he understood. There was a smaller bookshelf that contained stacks of titles he'd squirreled away for immediate reference.

Vhalla paused. Tentatively, her fingers reached up to a stack of books that rested to the side of the middle shelf. She took one off the top of the stack. Aldrik said nothing as she opened it. Vhalla looked down at handwriting she knew very well.

Earthen magic tends to have deep roots.
The magic can take days or months to remove.
Remove carefully, please, or shock.
Please live. Earthen, magic, can,
create,
please live, sensitivity to cold,
please live - or hot - please live, plaese lvei plselav pl-

Her writing had started neat and tidy but digressed into scribbles. She placed the book down and grabbed the next one. Her note from long ago, when she was doing research on that fateful rainy night, fell out. Vhalla leaned down and picked it up off the floor. It was much the same, though her writing was even messier. She returned it and grabbed the third book. Her note wasn't even legible.

Vhalla looked back at Aldrik, speechless. He had told her what had happened that night. But to see the actual vessels themselves, the ones that carried her magic to him and formed their Bond, brought a whole sense of world-shaking reality that she had not experienced before.

"I wanted to keep them." He gently took the book from her hands and returned it with care to the shelf. He considered the stack of books that saved his life. "They are very precious to me."

"I still have all your notes," Vhalla confessed. "They're in my wardrobe."

"I assumed you would have thrown them away." Vhalla saw through the thin veil of indifference he threw over the words.

"I thought about it," she admitted. "But I couldn't. They, too, are very precious to me."

"Yours are in the bottom drawer of my desk." Aldrik shared a smile. "I look at them from time to time to remind myself of how foolish you were."

"Oh?" Vhalla laughed in relaxed amusement. "Perhaps I should look at yours to remind myself of how much of an ass you are."

"As if you need a reminder," he snorted. It sent her into a fit of laughter.

Vhalla walked around the room, her amusement fading into a bright smile. He did not stop her, and he did not deny her access to anything. The most private man in the world allowed her to lift papers, open drawers, nose through books and more. Vhalla shifted aside the numbers of the Imperial coffers to look at some reports from ministers. He leaned against the bookshelf as she shuffled through them.

"The Minister of Coin didn't agree to half of the funding for the Festival of the Sun this year?" She blinked at Aldrik. She had no idea, missing it during her time away. "Why?"

"He's trying to rein in the spending," Aldrik explained. "We have a lot of soldiers still on retainer. After my demand of spending at least half of the spoils from war on rebuilding the North, we didn't come back with as much."

Vhalla stared at him, her mouth halfway open. *Her words*, those had been her words when she demanded him to help the North. "Why are you helping them still?"

"You know why." The words were gentle, thoughtful.

"They're conspiring to kill your father," Vhalla reminded him.

"Hardly surprising. And I have no doubt that half the North would do the same if given the chance." Aldrik looked over the papers and pinched the bridge of his nose for a moment to collect his thoughts. "But the people of the North didn't start that war, and I cannot blame them for hating the man who did; just as I cannot and will not punish them for it."

Admiration swelled her chest, competing in space with pride for her prince. He was making hard decisions and fighting for peace at the same time. Some would call him foolish for it, but she chose to describe it as noble. Vhalla put the papers back in order, averting her eyes. "I suppose I can see the Minister of Coin's concerns, then."

"Shall we move on?"

He led her back into the main room and through to another room. It opened into a smaller space that was clearly more lived in than the first. It was a room designed for casual entertaining, but Vhalla couldn't imagine Aldrik taking many visitors. Her eyes fell on a bar that stood barren.

"I haven't touched it in months," he admitted as shame deepened the prince's voice. "I couldn't. I promised you I wouldn't and then . . ."

Vhalla watched the prince struggle to continue, neither stopping nor encouraging.

"Then I decided I wouldn't let it have the better of me. I couldn't stop quitting."

She took a half step into his personal space, tilting her head to catch the prince's gaze where it had fallen on a corner of the room. The lump in his neck bobbed as he swallowed hard, awaiting her judgment.

"I'm proud of you," Vhalla whispered. "I know your struggles."

"Better than anyone."

Vhalla stepped away, avoiding becoming too engulfed by his essence. Her eyes scanned the rest of the room, darting over a carcivi board, across another bookshelf, and to the hearth. Around the crackling flame was a low area built into the floor with pillows and a low table in the style she had come to associate with the traditional West. Papers littered this table as well, a looser script across them. Vhalla instinctively walked over, curious.

"Not those," he said suddenly. She stopped, surprised. He had let her learn the Empire's secrets, *but would not let her see what was on those papers.*

"Aldrik, *secrets*," she reminded him, unconcerned if it was or wasn't her place anymore.

"Not yet." His expression softened a fraction. "I'm working through it. I'll tell you when I've written them all."

"Them all?" Vhalla repeated.

"Yes, my parrot." The term now brought a smile to her lips. Something dawned on him, and Aldrik suddenly sported a wide grin. "Come, I wish for you to see something."

Aldrik led her through yet another door that emptied into a hall with his bedroom on one end and had a third door into his bathing room—which was as large as a small house—and his closet. *No, closet was a loose term.* It was an open space with racks of clothes and glass cabinets as big as people—cabinets that displayed gems, jewels, and fine trimmings of the crown prince.

Vhalla ran her fingers along the glass. The jewels weren't tempting in the slightest. They were cold and meaningless.

"Aldrik."

He hummed in reply, fumbling through a cabinet.

"When your father made me a lady, the gold . . ."

The prince paused, staring at her for a long moment, trying to read her expression. "I told you in the North, I wanted to shower you with the trappings the world had so woefully denied my giving you before."

"I thought it may be something like that." Vhalla laughed softly, turning back to the gems.

"Do you see something you like?" Aldrik asked over her shoulder.

"Not really." There were women who would die to be in her position. Vhalla knew she could point at any of the shining jewels, and Aldrik would give it to her without a thought.

"How about this?"

She gave him her attention, her eyes quickly falling to the golden circlet he held in his hands. Vhalla remembered taking a similar, larger crown off the prince's brow during the first night he'd held her, during their dance. Aldrik searched her expression, waiting, his message clear.

"Don't do this," Vhalla cautioned. "Don't do this to us." He was going to shatter the fragile peace. He was going to throw them into chaos again. The madness they always devolved into. She didn't know if she was ready to take that leap just yet.

"I want to save us." The prince stood in limbo. "I want to find a way to honor our promises in more than shadow. You said the princess conspired for my father's life? I'm trying to find proof, to have her—at the least—removed from being my bride."

"She must be!" Vhalla's voice cracked and fractured. "She *must* be, Aldrik." Her hands gripped his and the crown he was holding. "She must wear this or you condemn countless more lives to death. Even though she conspires and everyone knows it, it changes nothing . . ."

"If I could find a way," he whispered.

"You can't."

"Believe in me!" Aldrik's voice rose by a fraction before softening. "I have crawled out of deeper holes this past year. Believe I can do this, because if you will be by my side, I will let nothing stop me." He took a deep breath and continued his earlier thought. "If I could find a way to keep the peace and allow us to be together, would you still take me? Would you forgive me? Would you want me?"

Vhalla bit her lip, containing her cry of, "*Yes!*" She pressed her eyes closed. He spoke of escaping pits, but they were about to be thrown back into one if they did this. *He was risking everything.*

"Vhalla, you are the dawn at the end of a seemingly endless night, and I never showed you enough appreciation for the essential part of my life that you are." He leaned forward and caught her eyes.

"That's not true." She shook her head.

"It is," Aldrik insisted, his tone suggesting how he would feel about further objections. "I kept you too far, and I let you slip from between my fingers. At the end of it all, I do not blame the Northern girl or my father, I blame myself for not being enough of a man at the moment I gave you the papers decreeing your nobility; instead of severing our relationship I should have taken you into my arms and comforted you, promised you that I would find a solution if you only stayed by my side. I should have never been the person I was that drove you to, alone, walk out of those camp doors."

"I wish I could hate you, you frustrating man," she breathed hopelessly.

"And I wish I could stop loving you, my frustrating woman." He laughed. It was an equally hopeless sound. "I wish I could see the sun rise without thinking of how beautiful you are in the dawn, your hair an impossible mess and your body contorted in that weird way you call sleeping."

He shook his head and stared up at the heavens, as if beseeching the Mother for help. "I wish I could go to my rose garden without thinking of sitting there with you, of reading, of just . . . just hearing you breathe."

Vhalla's back pressed against the bookcase.

"I wish I could see you smile without thinking of how it feels when your lips make that shape against mine." Aldrik braced himself with a hand by her shoulder. "I wish I was not utterly, hopelessly in love with you, Vhalla Yarl."

"But you are," she finished for him, searching the prince's expression.

"But I am," he repeated. "And I have promised myself that if I was ever privileged enough to be in your grace again, I would hold you closer to all that I am, more than I have ever held anyone or anything before—that I would never lose you again."

"What do you want from me?" *She already knew*, and she had long since given it to him.

"I need to know what you still feel for me." He swallowed, his words becoming thick and heavy. "Tell me truthfully, what is your heart's design? Do you still see me as the man who is wandering lost in his own darkness?" His breath quivered. "Or . . . could we, could you, see me as the man that I want to be and try to be every morning?"

Vhalla stared into the darkness of his eyes. Absorbing them, falling into them, into *him*. They'd been ensnared in a labyrinth of eternal night. Finding each other again didn't mean absolution; if anything, it likely meant they may be trapped forever.

But it would mean they were together.

It would mean the long hands that slowly lowered the golden circlet atop her hair would seek her out. It would mean that the blazing sun that burned away their fantasies of the night would be a little more bearable. It would be torture. But it would be the most beautiful torture they had ever known.

"I love you, Aldrik, and I always will." He leaned forward, and Vhalla stopped his progress with two palms, flat on his chest. "I love you, I respect you . . . and I respect myself. And, because of that, I will *not* become the other woman. I will not let you take me when you are engaged to another."

Aldrik stared at her, stunned as though he didn't understand what she was saying.

"If you find a way, Aldrik. Yes." Vhalla enjoyed the feeling of his chest, his heartbeat, his breathing, underneath her palms once more. "But before then, we are no more or less than we are now."

CHAPTER 18

VHALLA NEVER DID talk to Aldrik about the crystals. He'd returned her to the Tower hallway after a somewhat begrudging acceptance of her condition. Their conversation put everything else far from her mind.

Vhalla groaned softly at herself, rubbing her now barren forehead. *What were they doing?*

"Vhal . . ." Fritz nudged her shoulder for the second time. Vhalla blinked and looked at him. "What's the matter?"

She shook her head. "Sorry, it's nothing."

"You've been wandering away from the world today."

"I haven't moved from this spot all morning." She motioned to the table they worked at in the library.

"Exactly, you're like a statue. You've

been on that page for over an hour." Fritz flipped the book closed and glanced around the mostly empty library. "Talk to me."

"Fritz," she groaned, sitting back in her chair and burying her face in her hands.

Her friend grabbed her wrists, pulling her palms from her eyes and replacing them with his gaze. Worry marred the usual laughter that lit Fritz's eyes. Vhalla relaxed, and he shifted her hands into his, holding them tightly.

"Vhal, I'm not Larel; I don't magically know the depths of the human heart with a glance at someone's eyes. *So talk to me.*"

She opened her mouth and choked on the truth. Fritz let her work through the lump of confessions that had been building for months. "I've been working on crystals."

"What?" His grip went slack, but he didn't let go of her.

"Victor and I are working to put an end to the Caverns, once and for all."

Fritz blinked as his mind struggled to process what she was saying. "That's . . . not possible."

"It is. It has a heart, and we know how to get to it and destroy it."

"No . . . Vhal, no. This, this is dangerous."

"My existence is dangerous," she countered hastily. "As long as I, a known Windwalker, and the Caverns exist, there is danger. Either I need to be removed or the Caverns do."

"Well, I'm glad you picked the Caverns." Fritz grinned weakly. "I can't believe Victor is letting you do this . . ."

"He has years of research. He's been working toward this for a long time in secret, he's just needed someone like me."

Fritz frowned. "Doesn't it seem a little weird that he was developing a plan for someone that might not have ever come to be? I've heard some of the teachers speak on his theories and opinions of sorcerers in society. They make him sound like he can be a bit radical. Plus, he couldn't have known the Windwalkers would return."

"People always make plans for things that may never come to pass." Vhalla bit her tongue on the truth of Windwalkers. Without knowing the truth about it all, she could see how Victor's musings could come off as a little intense to the average person.

"I don't like it, Vhal. Every time someone goes into those caves, it results in something bad," her friend insisted.

Vhalla wished it didn't, but her friends concerns did put the conversation she overheard between Victor and the Emperor back in her mind. "Has the minister ever done anything to make you suspicious?"

"Me, personally? Not really . . . I just don't like the Caverns, and I don't like that you're mixed up in something bad. *Again.*" Fritz leaned back in his chair, staring at her hopelessly. "Vhalla Yarl, you're going to worry me to death."

"I didn't want to tell you because I didn't want you to worry," she mumbled guiltily.

"I'm glad you did though." Fritz squeezed her knee. "When is all this happening?"

"I don't know . . . It was supposed to be before winter was over, but now . . ." Her mind returned to Baldair and Aldrik—the reasons why she hadn't found the strength to return to Victor that morning.

"Now . . . what?" Fritz studied her carefully. "What else are you involved in?"

Vhalla glanced away. Baldair's condition wasn't common knowledge. She wouldn't lie, but she wasn't going to share it either—it wasn't her place. Beyond that, she wanted to keep it out of people's minds. As if by more knowing, it would condemn him to a horrible fate.

"Vhal . . ." Fritz pressured.

"Aldrik." Her guilt snuck out as a quiet confession.

"Vhal, you can't, you mean . . ." Fritz leaned forward, struggling to keep his voice no louder than hasty whispers. "Vhalla, he is *engaged.*"

"I know!" She shook her head. "It's not right though. His bride conspires against him, against his family."

"Her wrongs do not absolve you of yours." Fritz was gentle, but his words hit her as hard as a battering ram.

"We haven't done anything untoward." *Physically at least*, though Vhalla was certain confessing love and intent edged up to or crossed quite a few lines. "Aldrik is going to find a way."

"What way?" Fritz frowned. "Think through this. What could he possibly do? Kill her?"

"What? No!" She was aghast. "He wouldn't."

"If you have proof she's treasonous, why not?" Fritz countered.

"Do you think so little of him?"

"I think he's had to do worse things to achieve his ends." Fritz wasn't wrong, which only made Vhalla feel worse. "Would you want to be with him, if that's what it took?"

"No . . ." Vhalla slumped in her chair, hating the world. For a brief moment she almost wondered if it would be better if she went off to the caves and never came back. *She should've never stayed in the palace.* "What should I do?"

"Not be the illicit lover of our engaged sovereign," Fritz replied easily.

Vhalla shot him a glare. "We've done nothing physical."

"Infidelity of the heart to some is a greater crime than infidelity of the flesh," Fritz countered, and then sighed heavily. "Vhal, I know you love him," he relented. "But think about what you're doing."

Thinking about it wasn't hard. It weighed on her mind for the rest of the day and into the night when she returned to the library to look for the prince. He had no books today. Aldrik waited, hands folded across his chest and his mouth curling into a satisfied grin the moment he saw her.

Vhalla could feel her face betray her, listening to her heart over her head, as it mirrored his expression. He looked more himself than the previous day. His clothes were tailored and fitted, tucked in and buttoned up. His hair fixed.

"My lady." He pushed away from the table he'd been leaning against and held out a hand.

"My prince." She took his fingers as if in a trance. Their terms of endearment rang sweetly in her mind.

Aldrik gripped her hand tightly, pulling her to him. Vhalla almost stumbled at the sudden movement, but the prince was quick to catch her, one hand on her hip, the other buried in her hair.

"Oh, *Vhalla.*" Her name was a low growl resonating up from his chest, which sent goosebumps over her arms. Aldrik pulled away, smirking at her flush. The arrogant royal knew exactly what he was doing to her. "I missed you."

"Aldrik . . ." Her voice was almost pleading, though she wasn't sure what she pleaded for.

"Come." If Aldrik knew what she was begging him for, he wasn't about to give it.

Aldrik led her boldly, hand in hand, down the Tower. One person seeing them together would be enough to set people to talking. *Walking hand in hand?* Vhalla had no idea what that would incite. She looked at each door that they passed, waiting for someone to catch them. Her fingers nervously closed tighter around his.

Baldair was coughing as they entered his room, and all the magic that filled her chest at the nearness of Aldrik vanished with each of his wheezes and gasps for air.

"How is he today?" she whispered.

"Saw Erion and Jax for a while, until the clerics removed them so he could rest. But that only made him inquire after you. So he must be feeling better." Aldrik gave her a hopeful smile and affirmed the reason for his more jovial nature. Vhalla accepted the cloth he handed her for her nose and mouth. His fingers fell upon the fabric as she tied it to her face. "I'm certain he will come out of this."

"I thought I heard—" Baldair coughed from the doorway of his bedroom. "Talking," he finally finished, managing to slip out a breathless word.

The butterflies Aldrik's happiness had been breeding in Vhalla's stomach lost their wings as she saw the golden prince grabbing the doorframe for support. Coughs heaved his shoulders, and Baldair put a hand around his upper stomach where his ribs were. He winced in-between every relentless attack of the disease that plagued his body.

"Baldair." Aldrik's smile fled from his eyes. "You should not be out of bed."

"Ah, you would like me to soil myself then, dear brother?" Baldair jested. "Perhaps I should, then insist you be the one to clean my sheets."

"Don't threaten the person who brings you company twice in one day," Aldrik retorted. He walked over to his brother and held out his arms. "Let me help you back to the bed?"

"I can do it just fine on my own," Baldair insisted.

Vhalla gave a faint smile at the princes' stubborn kinship. Aldrik did not end up helping his brother to the bed, but he was there adjusting the younger prince's pillows and helping with the covers as Baldair collapsed in a fit of coughing. The elder prince then crossed over to the side of the room.

"Vhalla, help me with this?"

She went to Aldrik's aid, helping him maneuver a small table made at the perfect height to sit between the chair and the bed. It was perfect enough that Vhalla suspected, with a note of sorrow, that it had likely been commissioned during the prince's illness. She sat herself in one of the waiting chairs, pulling up her feet.

"Is that any way for a lady to sit?" Aldrik teased.

"I am a lady, and I am sitting this way; therefore, yes." Vhalla nodded her head to underscore her response.

"I can't refute such sound logic." He placed his hands on her shoulders, standing behind her chair.

"Oh, brother, I think the lady promised me a game of carcivi." Baldair glanced at Aldrik, a slightly odd inflection padding his words. "Will you go get the nice marble one you use?"

"You have plenty of boards here." Aldrik pushed off Vhalla's shoulders lightly, starting for the door.

"But I like yours." Baldair called between coughs as Aldrik shook his head, closing the door behind him.

Vhalla smiled faintly at the prince's departure, turning back to Baldair. "How do you feel?"

"Oh, I'm managing." Baldair gave her a weak smile. "It's nice to have visitors other than Aldrik. Not that his company isn't a bundle of sunshine."

"He's not so bad, and you know it."

"Small doses," Baldair wheezed.

"He said you had Erion and Jax here today?"

"I did. Seems as though they are doing a good job of managing the guard." Baldair settled into his pillows. "They said you were joining them as well."

"I've tried to lend a hand," Vhalla affirmed.

"I appreciate it, really I do." The prince paused for a long moment. "Do you want to join the guard, Vhalla?"

She considered it. "I don't think I'd say no. Erion, Jax, Daniel, Craig, even Raylynn, they all feel like family already."

"But?" He picked up on her pause.

"But . . ." Vhalla didn't know where her hesitation stemmed from. A sense of direction was pulling at her, telling her that the Golden Guard was not what she was meant to be.

"What do you want, Vhalla?"

"Freedom, peace," she breathed longingly. Her mind drifted over the Knights of Jadar, the Emperor, the War in the North. War, bloodshed, turmoil—it seemed her world had been punctuated by them since she was a girl. Before she really saw it all for what it was. "I think real peace begets freedom. So, more than anything, I want peace."

"What do *you* want," Baldair emphasized. "Not for the Empire, for you."

Vhalla thought about it a long moment. "Peace, still?"

"Will you ever find it when my brother marries his Northern bride?" She stiffened instantly at the younger prince's soft words. "What will you do then? Will you always wonder what could have been?"

"Why are you asking this?" Vhalla looked to the door, praying Aldrik would walk in and save her.

"I need to know."

"Why?"

"Because I told you something in that very room," Baldair replied with a nod at the door with a tired smile, evoking memories of the day he taught her to dance. "I told you that you deserved some sort of real thanks for your service to the Empire, and it fell to me to give it to you. If anyone deserves peace, Vhalla, it's you."

"I don't want to talk about this." She grabbed the watch around her neck tightly, her heart aching.

Baldair's eyes focused on the token she held, but his inquiry remained. "Indulge me one question, and I'll ask nothing more.

Would you be with him still, after everything? Does love spring eternal between you both?"

"I—" She relented and didn't push the ailing prince further. "It does. I would stand at his side until my dying day." Vhalla shook her head and ran a hand through her hair. "It doesn't matter. We're not, we can't be anything because my peace, as you call it, isn't worth the Empire's."

"They don't have to be exclusive." Baldair leaned forward, squeezing her hand. He opened his mouth to speak again but devolved into an aggressive coughing fit. Vhalla was up, rubbing the back of the younger prince when Aldrik returned almost immediately after.

Aldrik placed the carcivi board on the table. Vhalla assumed her previous seat, beginning to pull out alabaster tokens from a garnet colored bag. Unlike the carcivi boards she'd used before, these had small sculptures of the warriors, archers, and sorcerers on them.

"It's weird." Vhalla paused, staring at two sorcerer tokens. "I never thought about it before; all sorcerers have the same range. . . But a Groundbreaker would need to attack much closer than a Firebearer."

Baldair burst out with laughter that dissolved once more into coughing. *It sounded wetter.* "Brother, didn't you have the same argument with me once?"

"Perhaps." Amusement lit Aldrik's eyes; his mask hiding the grin Vhalla knew was there.

"You two would think alike." Baldair chuckled.

"Would we?" Aldrik pulled away the partition in the middle of their board, revealing the full field of play to Vhalla and Baldair.

"She's the only one who's ever been able to stand you. It makes perfect sense." Baldair smirked.

"Brother, your words just warm my heart," Aldrik muttered.

"As if you have one," the younger prince said in obvious jest.

"You are quite right," Aldrik agreed. Baldair paused to look at his brother curiously. "I gave it away long ago."

The golden prince wheezed in amusement, his eyes fluttering partway closed.

"Baldair, it's getting late. Perhaps we shouldn't begin a game," Vhalla suggested thoughtfully.

"What? And miss out on this beating that I was promised from you?" Baldair's brave smile looked exhausted.

"You're sure?"

"Now I just think you're scared." Vhalla watched as he made his first move, using it as an opportunity to assess his condition. The prince was worn thin, his cheeks looked more hollowed than yesterday. His skin was almost translucent.

"Perhaps I am a little scared," Vhalla remarked. Aldrik glanced at her, and Vhalla held his stare from the corners of her eyes. For once, he seemed to miss her nonverbal concerns.

"My brother favors the direct approach, if that surprises you," Aldrik commented on the board instead. "Don't be looking for subtlety or finesse."

"Do you play?" Vhalla tried to ignore the worrying panic creeping up her spine.

"To whom do you speak, my lady?" Aldrik smirked at her foolish question.

Vhalla rolled her eyes at the elder prince.

"Brother, I am truly glad I was able to see this." Baldair smiled weakly, countering Vhalla's move.

"See what?" Vhalla heard the caution in Aldrik's voice. After all this time, he still withdrew when it came to publicly acknowledging things that made him happy.

"Seeing you acting like a normal man." Baldair gave his brother a tired but affectionate smile. "It has given me hope for you."

Aldrik looked away in awkward bashfulness.

"When I get better," Baldair wheezed. "I agree."

The crown prince snapped his head back to his brother. Vhalla blinked at the sudden intensity to his eyes. She had no idea what they were talking about. He took a sharp breath.

"Do you mean it?" Aldrik's voice quivered with anticipation, or excitement.

Whatever it was, she clearly wasn't meant to understand. Rather than pressing the matter, Vhalla pretended to consider her move so the princes could have their moment.

"I do." Baldair nodded. Aldrik seemed to be utterly baffled. He fought for words. "Brother, just-just be happy for once." Baldair leaned back on his pillows.

"Thank you." Aldrik jumped to his feet. He hovered awkwardly a moment.

Vhalla realized her presence had been completely forgotten. The elder brother took one step, then another to kneel down at his brother's bedside. Vhalla watched him take Baldair's hand and hold it tightly.

"Thank you," Aldrik repeated, his voice soft.

Baldair gave him a familial and loving smile that held for a long moment. "Come now, Aldrik." Baldair grinned and sat forward again. "Don't get all weird." He punctuated the end of the moment by taking his turn on the carcivi board.

Vhalla tried to focus on the board as Aldrik resumed his seat. *But something felt different*, and she was forced to pretend to not notice the princes' glances. Whatever had just happened between them was a genuine moment that felt like both men were no longer interested in waging war, that they were one team. The last thing she wanted to do was break such a fragile, yet welcomed, calm between them by pointing it out.

"You're not even making this a challenge for me," Vhalla teased, knocking out two of his warrior tokens with a sorcerer token.

"I don't think a sorcerer should be allowed to play with their own tokens," Baldair mumbled.

"Then you'd remove all the warriors from your side of the board?"

"Oh right." Baldair coughed. "You'd want-want—"

Baldair's shoulders lurched as he leaned forward to make his move. Vhalla watched in horror at the moment that the prince's eyes widened in surprise at the blood that she knew suddenly filled his throat. The crimson liquid spilled out, splattering across the board and the table.

"Brother!" Aldrik exclaimed, on his feet.

"Aldrik!" Vhalla snapped. "Don't touch him!" Aldrik stopped mid-step, like an animal before the hunter's bow. "The blood will get you sick far easier than breathing his air. Let me, I've had the fever before. Go get the clerics."

She moved without thought. Vhalla grabbed the clerics' rags, wiping Baldair, her hand around the prince's shoulders, feeling the tremors that signified another cough. The younger prince shuddered and coughed into her waiting hand. The fabric was saturated and as she reached for another rag, Baldair coughed a crimson puddle into her lap.

"Aldrik." Her rough voice snapped the elder prince back from his horror. "I can't, I won't leave him like this. Get the cleric you trust most who won't say anything about my being here." Vhalla took a deep breath through her nose, forcing herself to remain calm through the memories of being covered in her mother's blood. "Now! Aldrik, *now!*"

The crown prince ran from the room, and Vhalla turned back to Baldair. She wiped his mouth, moving her clean hand from his back to his forehead. *He was burning alive.* "Sit back on your pillows."

"Vhalla," he wheezed.

"I know, it's an awful taste, isn't it?" She allowed him to slump into her. "Try to stay upright, it comes up easier that way."

"I-I've been worse . . ." Baldair gave her a foolish grin. It would've been more convincing if he didn't have blood dribbling down his chin.

"Don't talk, it'll only aggravate the coughing." Vhalla tried to sound brave as she made another attempt at cleaning his face. "I know being quiet is hard for you."

The door to the outer room slammed open and shut again. Hasty footsteps made their way to the bedroom door, and a man with graying hair and bushy eyebrows darted into the room. He fearlessly set his clerical box down upon the table, sending the carcivi pieces scattering. Vhalla stood, giving him room to access Baldair.

"Excuse me, Lady Vhalla." The man stepped around her. "Prince Aldrik, I will need you to fetch the full team."

"With haste." Aldrik's voice was level, but his eyes betrayed his panic for his younger brother, who began coughing again.

Vhalla followed him out of Baldair's room, dripping a trail of blood onto the pristine carpet. She took two steps for every one of Aldrik's long strides and still fell behind.

"Wait for me here," he whispered, ushering her into his room.

"Go help him," Vhalla encouraged bravely.

"Wash, get the blood off you before it can infect you. Help yourself to whatever you may need." Aldrik looked fearfully at the crimson stains on her lap and sides.

"I will. Now go."

Aldrik needed no further prompting. He stepped back into the hallway, locking the door behind him.

Vhalla stepped back into the room and took a deep breath. Her inhale was weak. Her exhale quivered. She turned and sprinted for the bathroom. *She had to wash it away.*

She leaned over the side of the large, golden tub in Aldrik's bathing room, turning on only the faucet for hot water. It came out steaming, and Vhalla nearly burned her hands in it. The blood fell in large droplets down onto the floor of the tub. Vhalla wrung her hands even after they were clean.

Putting in the stopper, she stripped off her soiled clothing and tossed it into a corner of the marble-tiled room with a cry. The night air was icy on her bare skin as Vhalla plunged herself into the water, still shivering.

Her mother had been thinner, she had been weaker. They didn't have the food or the medicine available to Baldair. He would be all right.

Not once, in all her racing thoughts, did she give note to the fact that she was naked in the crown prince's chambers. All her contemplations circled around how hot Baldair's forehead had felt, how much blood had come up. Vhalla began to scrub, going over her skin until it was raw, as if she could wash away the memories.

Aldrik still wasn't back by the time her bathwater began to cool, and Vhalla emerged numb to the dull gray world. She pulled a drying cloth over her shoulders before she raided his dressing chambers. Many women would've been satisfied with just one of his oversized shirts as a dress, but Vhalla never felt comfortable without wearing some kind of trousers or leggings.

Awkwardly dressed, she wandered listlessly to his bedroom. His bed was large enough for three people, and it was extraordinarily comfortable. In that moment, it could've been made of rocks and felt the same. Vhalla bundled herself beneath the blankets, shivering against the cold until she fell into a restless sleep.

Long fingers buried themselves in her hair, the bed shifting to accommodate a weight at her side. The scent of the blankets, the heat of the man next to her, the familiar tingle under his fingertips, it reminded her where she was and who was gently pulling her from sleep.

"Aldrik." Vhalla sat, rubbing her eyes with the heels of her palms. The sound of coughing filled her ears and the smell of smoke, sweat, leather, and Aldrik on the sheets was replaced with the tangy metallic aroma of blood that still lingered in her nose. "How is Baldair?"

"The clerics say my annoying little brother is presently stable." There wasn't any bite to Aldrik's words. "They'll be staying with him around the clock now. About time."

Vhalla saw Aldrik's mannerisms for what they were: a retreat. He was withdrawing into the temperamental indifferent front he'd always used to keep out the world, to hide his emotions. A deep sorrow settled into her chest for her fearful prince.

"I swear, Baldair just wants to make a show of this." Aldrik shook his head. "Always, always the showman, that Baldair. He wants all the attention, as if he hasn't had it. He just—he loves when—he loves when people are fawning over him."

Aldrik's words became weaker as he rambled on. Vhalla looked on in torment. It was a pain she knew so well, and yet she couldn't do anything to lessen it. Saying nothing, she took both of Aldrik's hands in hers.

"The clerics say he can still make it," Aldrik finally added, after a short silence. "Elecia should be here soon, too."

"Elecia?" Vhalla asked, surprised. Last she'd heard, Aldrik's cousin wasn't coming until spring.

"I called for her when Baldair fell ill. If she could heal me after the North, she'll make quick work of Baldair and then complain to me for years for bringing her to the South during the winter. Between her and the clerics, he has to make it." Aldrik allowed himself a tired, fragile smile.

"They don't want me going in anymore. They say it's too much of a risk now that it has progressed this far."

"I'm sorry."

"Well, it's not as if I wanted to be there in the first place," he said begrudgingly. "Why would I want to spend more time with my loud, annoying little brother? I was only there because my father insists on having morons in his staff. No one else was watching him, so I had to, right? They should have been there from the start. Complete, utter incompetence . . ."

Vhalla squeezed his hands lightly, and let him hide behind the security of his jabs. She knew just as well as he did the real reason why he had been in his brother's room. She knew from the moment she had seen a pillow and blanket on Baldair's couch.

"Speaking of incompetent nitwits, I should bring you back to the fools who run my Tower." He stood and swayed from exhaustion.

"Will you be all right without me?" Vhalla braved the question. Leaving was the appropriate thing to do, but worry changed the rules.

He sighed, running a hand over his hair, trying to tame the stray pieces that escaped over the events of the evening into place. "I'm always all right."

"No." She stood as well to bring a palm to his cheek. His mask broke under her touch. "Don't hide from me, my prince."

"Vhalla, please," he pleaded, his voice thin and strained. "Come back tomorrow?" He closed his eyes and tilted his head toward her hand. "I need you."

"All you ever need to do is ask," she whispered in thankful awe that he relented so quickly to accept whatever comfort she could offer.

"I'll fetch you when I can," Aldrik affirmed.

"I may be with the minister."

He paused, searching her face. "You're still working on crystals with him, aren't you?"

"I am." Vhalla didn't even try to lie. "I've meant to speak with you further about it but . . ."

"I know, with my brother being how he is," Aldrik agreed with a sigh. "Later, but soon. When Baldair is better, we need to speak on it."

She was relieved he relented. Whatever the conversation would reveal, Vhalla already suspected it would be exhausting for the prince. Perhaps, if she played her cards right, she could have already closed the Caverns for good by the time they had it.

Aldrik led her through the secret passageway behind his mirror. Vhalla returned to the Tower without a word. They'd moved past the point of words long ago. A look was all it took for them to communicate.

Into the night, he weighed on her thoughts. Vhalla tossed and turned in her small bed, a bed that suddenly was cold and uncomfortable and far too small. Exhausted, Vhalla finally relented and closed her eyes, slipping out of her body with ease.

Her Projected form was unhindered by doors and darkness. Unsurprisingly, she didn't find him in his bed as she'd hoped. He was hunched over in front of his hearth, scribbling frantically on the papers that he'd hidden from her.

You need to sleep. Vhalla nearly startled the prince out of his skin.

"What are you doing?" He blinked at her ghost-like presence.

Making you take care of yourself.

"You're so annoying, you know that?" he said after a long pause, the tiniest of smirks curling the corner of his lips.

Pot meet kettle. Go to bed, Aldrik. Vhalla was glad she returned. He was going to exhaust himself, which only increased the odds of him falling ill also.

Vhalla stayed with him until he crawled into bed, watching as his body relaxed, his brow softened. She waited until she saw her prince's breathing deepen, telling her he was asleep. She lingered long after in the darkness, a silent sentry to the crown prince, until her body was too exhausted to maintain the Projection. She finally withdrew into a deep and dreamless sleep.

CHAPTER 19

"**A**RE YOU FEELING all right?" Victor asked, glancing up from his workstation in the far corner of the room.

"I'm fine," she mumbled.

The minister laughed. "Dear Vhalla, you don't think I believe that for a moment, do you?" He crossed over to stand before her, blocking her view of the axe. The minister summoned her attention with a tap on the chin. "Tell me."

Where should she start? The ailing Prince Baldair? The gray area she'd walked back into with the crown prince? Keeping crystal magic a secret?

"It's nothing." It was too much to tell.

"Vhalla, trust me. I cannot protect you if you shut me out."

"I don't need your protection," she

snapped. She was too tired and too weathered to be treated like a child.

"No?" the minister asked slowly. "If I were to dismiss you from the Tower, where would you go? Where could your safety be assured? Where could you remain out of the hands of the Knights of Jadar?"

"I handled myself when it came to the Knights." Vhalla ignored the magic and still mysterious fire that was the catalyst for her escape.

"And Egmun?"

"Were you absent at the Sunlit Stage?" Her ability to manage the Senate should've been apparent.

"What about the Emperor?" Victor folded his arms over his chest. "When he demands you become a weapon in his war, what will you do to refuse him?"

Vhalla's tongue was stilled. *That* required some thought. But she wasn't exactly a novice at defending herself to the Emperor either.

"Perhaps you will use Aldrik for that?"

She was on her feet. "Are you threatening me?"

"By the Mother, no!" Victor held up his hands with a chuckle. "I simply want you to understand how this relationship works."

"Which is?"

"That I have put all bets on you and your skill." Victor placed a palm on her shoulder, squeezing it encouragingly. "That I know you will do what must be done in the Caverns."

"Thank you." She pulled her shoulder away, not wanting to be touched by the minister.

"I think we're both ready to put all this behind us," Victor remarked thoughtfully. "How close are you to finishing the axe?"

"I just finished, actually," she announced confidently.

"You did?" The minister paused in awe. "You're certain?"

"I am."

"Then we could set off for the Caverns tomorrow." The minister turned, going back to his workstation where he was diligently tempering crystals he'd said would be necessary to access the heart of the Caverns.

"Tomorrow." All Vhalla thought of was the ailing Baldair, of leaving Aldrik alone when his brother was in such a fragile state. "Can it wait?"

The world seemed to hold its breath as the minister assessed her.

"I thought you wanted this done as much as I do."

"I do, but . . ."

"So why do you stall?" He scrutinized her once more.

"I have my reasons." And she didn't owe him any of them.

"You have one." Victor held up a single finger, slowly pointing at the watch that rested under her tunic. "A man to whom you remain foolishly devoted, despite his hand being promised to another."

"If you speak about Aldrik again—" Vhalla didn't even think twice about the fact that she had just acknowledged the prince and her being devoted.

"A man who can throw you off a roof, build you up only to cast you aside."

"Enough!" Vhalla cut her arm through the air. The breeze sent the papers on his desk fluttering to the floor, but Victor smiled in the face of the warning shot.

"A man who can hurt you." He started for her. Vhalla's heart was racing in the limbo of fight or flight. "A man who can break you, drive you to madness, only to have you running to his side at a word."

"You know *nothing* about us," she seethed. "Don't come one step closer."

Victor took that step, and Vhalla raised her hand. His arm was as fast as a viper, and his fingers closed around her wrist, crunching the tendons together. His grip was like ice.

"Vhalla," he said in a dangerously soft voice, "you may be incredibly special to me, but *never* lash out at me again."

A shiver coursed through her as his magic reached its icy tendrils into her veins. His magic was numbing, dulling. It was the antithesis to the life Aldrik's exuded, and Vhalla loathed it instantly.

A knock prevented the moment from escalating further. The minister released her at the sound, and Vhalla rubbed her wrist with a shiver. He walked back to his desk, quickly scooping up the majority of the papers, stashing the axe, and smiling as though nothing had happened. "Enter."

The door opened. Vhalla had never been happier to see the pair of dark eyes.

"My prince," the minister spoke first. "To what do we owe the honor?"

"Forgive my intrusion." Aldrik spoke but didn't take his eyes off her. Vhalla could see him working through the silent messages she was sending him.

"Never an intrusion by the crown prince. Tea?"

Vhalla didn't even recognize the man casually talking to the prince as the same man who had just stashed a legendary crystal weapon and threatened her outright.

"Not today," Aldrik thankfully refused. "I need to steal the Lady Yarl for Imperial business."

"*Imperial business*?" The minister smiled, glancing between them. "Sounds important."

"My brother has requested her presence," Aldrik explained. "You know Baldair and pretty girls." Aldrik gave a smirk.

Vhalla kept her mouth from falling agape at how lightly he was mentioning his brother, given Baldair's state.

"I certainly do." The minister nodded, his body language clearly conveying that he knew there was much more beneath the surface. "We'll speak again soon, Vhalla."

"Please follow me, Lady Yarl." Aldrik put on a stiff and formal front. If she didn't know better, she would've thought he had no feelings toward her whatsoever.

Aldrik stepped out first. As he closed the door behind her, she caught a glimpse of the minister. He stood leaning against the back counter, stroking his goatee, a knowing grin on his mouth. Vhalla shook him from her mind, focusing on what was important.

"Baldair?" she asked softly, taking two hasty steps for every one of Aldrik's long strides.

"I did not lie." Aldrik looked forward and kept his voice low. "He has requested to see you."

"What does that mean?"

"Where on the list would you like me to start?" Aldrik muttered. She shot him a look that caused him to sigh. She stopped at the usual door, but Aldrik shook his head. "Not there."

"Then?" Vhalla asked as he continued down a bit more.

"Here." Aldrik opened an unlocked and unmarked door, and they were plunged into one of the many secret passageways that led in and out of the Tower. "You are coming formally, not through the back door."

Vhalla grabbed his hand. Aldrik stopped instantly at her touch. "You still haven't told me what that means."

"It means my father and Baldair's mother know you are on your way." Vhalla didn't miss Aldrik acknowledging the Empress as only Baldair's mother. "It means they know I am with you now, this very moment. It means you will have to endure the delicate dance that is my family, and who knows what that really ever means." Aldrik swallowed and grimaced. "It means you are going to see the girl."

"I already met her, remember?" Vhalla tried to sound brave, unbothered.

"Vhalla," he sighed softly. Time stopped a moment as his fingers intertwined with hers. "They aren't allowing me in still."

"I figured."

"It means, I will—I will be waiting in her company." His tone was apologetic.

Vhalla laughed softly, looking down at their laced fingers. He apologized to her for time spent with his intended. She realized that however good they were struggling to be, some lines had already been crossed.

"It's all right," she whispered. "I figured you to do that a lot. Be in her company."

"I don't," Aldrik breathed, and his other hand found her face. "I don't want to."

"We should go," she reminded him.

Aldrik nodded reluctantly. His hand fell, but he allowed his fingers to remain entwined with hers until they departed through the castle-side door.

Vhalla was led in an upward direction. The staff hall gave way to a more public walkway. This opened into a larger hall that led upward to a pair of golden gates. They had a pattern of suns that were thin and delicate, like lace. Their purpose was clearly more metaphorical than functional, as they'd be useless at actually keeping out anyone trying to forcibly gain entry.

Two guards snapped to attention as Aldrik walked upward. His hands were folded behind his back, his shoulders were tall, and he was every inch the prince. Vhalla looked at him and could see her future Emperor. She had no doubt he would command respect, but she prayed he could do so with love more than fear.

"My prince." The guards saluted in unison, hastily opening the gates.

"Lady Yarl, this way." His voice was detached, and he hardly even glanced back at her.

She tried to play her part and look as uncomfortable as any average citizen would be in tow of the Fire Lord. It still behooved them both to conceal their affections.

They walked through the dazzling central atrium Baldair had led her through months ago, navigating down a side hall that Vhalla recognized instantly. Clerics passed them hastily, their hands laden with crimson rags that made her heart lodge in her throat.

Aldrik led with his cold and distant mask as he brought her into the hive of activity of Baldair's sitting room. Clerics flitted about and mixed potions, but Vhalla's eyes rested on the one outsider to the group.

The princess's hair was tied atop her head with delicate white lace. The girl was swathed in the Imperial color, white fabric trimmed in gold flowing elegantly down to her feet. She turned from her place at the window when Vhalla entered. Sehra and Aldrik must have attended the same school for training their expressions, as her eyes gave nothing to Vhalla's searching stare.

"Lady Yarl," a cleric called for her attention. Vhalla jerked her eyes away from the princess before her stare could linger too long. "Thank you for coming. The prince personally requested to see you."

"It's hardly trouble. An honor to be called on by the family Solaris," she replied dutifully. Vhalla's eyes widened a moment; she recognized the gray hair and bushy eyebrows as the cleric who had come earlier to attend Baldair.

"You see, the prince is quite sick," he explained as though it was Vhalla's first time in the room. "We have been told you have contracted Autumn Fever before?"

She nodded. "I have."

"Excellent; your risk is far lower then. Still, for your protection." The man handed her a mask.

"I understand." Vhalla tied the mask around her face adeptly.

"Given the prince's condition, we ask that you limit your time. We do not want to exhaust him, so please try not to let him talk too much," the cleric explained as they started for the door.

Aldrik settled himself on the couch, a book in his lap as though he hadn't a care in the world.

The bedroom door opened suddenly to reveal the Empress. Vhalla saw the woman's normally youthful radiance had been reduced to red and puffy eyes. Her cheeks were flushed, and her hair was pulled into a single braid. She inspected Vhalla up and down.

"No one other than family," she announced sharply.

"My Empress," the cleric faltered. "The Lady Yarl was only brought here because of his direct request."

She continued to block the doorway. "I did not hear such a request."

"You had stepped out a moment," the bushy-eyebrowed cleric explained.

"Isn't it convenient that the request occurred then?" she murmured with a nasty look to the back of Aldrik's head.

"I don't want to make trouble." Vhalla was sincere, which shone through enough that it made the woman pause. Vhalla could only imagine the pain the Empress was shouldering; now was not a time for Vhalla to insist on her pride. "I am more than happy to depart, if that is best."

The woman opened her mouth to speak, only to be cut off by a tired wheezing. "Vhalla, don't be crazy," Baldair managed from the bed within. "My mother said only family. Clearly—" He coughed, and Vhalla heard the blood come up. "Clearly, the little sister I never had is included in that."

The woman looked toward her son in shock, then back at Vhalla. A lot of eyes were on her at once, and Vhalla gripped her hands more tightly. Clearly Baldair's condition had made him fearless, and

Vhalla knew she had to also be so in order to give the prince what he was asking for.

Vhalla followed the Empress into the room, startled to see the Emperor on the opposite side of Baldair's bed. The Empress assumed her seat next to her husband, and Vhalla awkwardly took the seat on the opposite side of the bed. She tried to ignore her sovereigns as much as possible, focusing on Baldair instead. *His normally brilliant eyes were listless and dull.*

"Come now, Vhalla." He coughed. "Don't give me those sad eyes."

Her hands moved before a cleric could. Vhalla mindlessly picked up the cloth from his bedside table so she could blot the blood from the corner of his mouth gently without a thought, *just as she had done for her mother.*

"Forgive me, my prince." She forced her voice to sound strong.

"Baldair," he wheezed. "I don't have time for pretense anymore."

Vhalla finally glanced at the Emperor and Empress. She couldn't make much from their expressions. The Emperor's was hard and shut off. The Empress's eyes glistened.

"Don't say that, Baldair," she whispered. Vhalla turned her eyes back to him, and the world went away. "Please don't."

"I know." Baldair lifted his hand, and she took it gently. "I can feel it." He coughed again, and a muffled whimper escaped her lips.

"No, *no!* You're going to keep fighting. You've been eating right? I told you to keep eating and—" Vhalla blinked several times in quick succession, her eyes burning frustratingly.

"I'm sorry to disappoint you." Baldair coughed again, and Vhalla's hand quickly caught the blood. The other held his tightly.

She shook her head. "You-you've never disappointed me."

"How foolish is it?" He leaned against his pillows. "The mighty golden prince, felled by a cold."

"No." All she could do was shake her head and refuse. It was a never-ending loop, refusal at the world, at fate. "No, Baldair, please. Don't talk like this. You will get better, you will. My mother couldn't because we didn't have anything, because I couldn't save her. But-but." Vhalla took a shaky breath through her nose, her chest ached. "But they can save you."

"Your mother?" Baldair asked softly.

Vhalla blinked. She wanted to laugh or cry; a strangled noise of pain was her body's compromise. "I had the fever. So did my mother. I got better, she-she didn't." Vhalla hung her head. Before he could say anything else, she looked up suddenly, swinging between emotions. "But like I said, you are much stronger. You can keep fighting."

"Oh, Vhalla . . ." Baldair looked at her sadly. "I am so sorry."

She shook her head, knowing the cause of his guilt. *He wouldn't have a reason for it*, she insisted to herself. He would get better.

He sighed softly. "I'm tired."

"No." Vhalla shook her head. She was completely oblivious to the clerics around her, the hovering healers who did not know how to react to her proximity and actions toward healing the dying man whom she clung to. She did not see the looks from the Emperor or Empress. All she saw was the golden-haired prince, the heartbreaker, wasting away from an evil that could not be fought with swords or arrows or wind. "Please, please . . ."

"Do you remember . . . when we met?" Baldair breathed. "You were . . . so . . . jumpy." He laughed, which only lead to more coughing.

"My prince, please," a cleric finally pleaded.

Baldair shook his head at them and continued, "You had, you have still, a beautiful heart, Vhalla. I'm glad I somehow found a place in it. You healed things, things I didn't think could be healed. I don't think I have spoken as much to my brother in years as I have in these past months. I am thankful for it."

He spoke of her healing things, but she couldn't heal what mattered. She couldn't escape the curse of her existence that threatened to consume everyone and everything she loved. Vhalla clung onto him and his words.

"Tell him—they don't let him in here now—tell him I am sorry; I don't think I'll live up to our agreement." Baldair coughed again.

"It's fine," she whispered. *It didn't matter whatever the brothers had agreed.* "Aldrik just wants you well." Vhalla had completely forgotten herself as she used the name of the crown prince loosely, without title.

"I know he does," Baldair confessed. "I love that idiot brother of mine. Will you tell him that for me?"

"You will tell him yourself," she insisted. Vhalla threw a bold look to the Emperor and Empress. *There should be a fourth.* There was another soul who needed to be present more than she did.

"Don't change," Baldair continued on. "Don't let the world change you."

"Stop saying goodbye!" Her voice was louder than she intended it to be. "Don't you do this! I did *not* come here for this!"

"Vhalla, please." He coughed again, and she was right back to tending to him. "Listen. They do not see you for what you are. Or perhaps, they see you *only* for what you are upon the surface. Don't let them define you."

Vhalla shifted her clean palm to his forehead as Baldair's eyes fluttered closed. Beads of sweat dotted his skin.

"He needs more fever reducer," Vhalla observed aloud.

The cleric shook her head. "We can't give him any more."

"Then cool him with water." Her mind drifted back to the icy feeling Victor had put in her veins earlier. "Are any of you sorcerers? Waterrunners?" They all shook their heads. *Aldrik was right, they were all incompetent.* "Then get someone from the Tower!"

"Who are you to order our clerics?" The Empress's voice was shrill and thin.

"I am the woman who is going to try anything I've ever seen or read to save your son's life," Vhalla proclaimed with ferocity. "Because clearly no one else will step up to the task and try whatever needs to be tried."

"It *is* a method common folk use in situations without medicine." Bushy eyebrows stroked his chin. "Go, tell the crown prince." A cleric raced out of the room.

"Vhalla." Baldair chuckled weakly. "You're scary when you let your ferocity show—a little twister."

"Don't talk too much," she whispered softly and ran her hand through his hair. "Save your strength. Elecia is coming, did you know that? She's so strong, Baldair. She will fix you, I know it."

Coughing was his only response, and Vhalla clutched his hand all the tighter.

Vhalla shouldn't have been surprised when Victor was the one to appear not long after. A mask around his mouth and nose, he walked into the room with purpose. A short briefing from the clerics, a once-over of Baldair, and he set to work. For an hour, the minister lightly cooled the prince's skin, each time colder than the last to not send his body into shock all at once. Vhalla retracted all negative thoughts she had on Victor, mentally sending a sincere apology— if he could save Baldair. *She'd do whatever the man wanted if he healed Baldair.* Eventually, nothing more could be done, and the sorcerer departed.

Baldair shivered. "It's too cold."

"You need it to be," Vhalla soothed gently. "It won't work if it's not."

"Vhalla, let me rest?"

"No, not now . . ." It was the third time he'd asked. "Stay awake, stay with us."

His fever was down, thanks to her idea, and it had allowed enough time to lapse that the clerics could give him another round of potions. Baldair struggled to swallow. The first batch he coughed up, and Vhalla was the one to clean up the mix of blood and potion off his chest. She was going to fight. She was going to lead him by her example.

"Do you remember when I got in trouble on the march?" Vhalla said softly as she cleaned his collarbone and neck. "Grun, he really hated me, didn't he? I guess a lot of them did. They were afraid."

"They didn't know you yet." Baldair looked at her from under drooping eyelids.

"I suppose not," she agreed.

"They didn't know how . . . strong . . . the little girl from the library was." Baldair struggled to keep in a cough.

"No, let the blood come up," she insisted. "Or you'll choke."

He obliged her, and Vhalla set to cleaning again, covered in his blood.

"Vhalla, I am tired," he reminded her.

"Don't sleep yet," she begged again and looked across to the Emperor and Empress. While Vhalla knew they'd never acknowledge it, her presence had saved them from being in the position of calling the shots around their dying son. How she hated her sovereigns. *But this wasn't about her.* "Tell your mother about your favorite memory with her. Tell your father what the best thing he taught you was. Tell them how much you love them."

Vhalla remained as Baldair spoke, cleaning up the blood and helping the clerics shift the prince as he needed. She heard the story of the first time he went riding with his father. She saw the Emperor affectionately put a hand on his son's shoulder. She bore witness to the Heartbreaker Prince apologizing to his mother for never feeling like settling down with any woman she approved of.

Baldair told them everything a son could say to their parents, and then some. He made confessions. He reminisced. He told them of his love.

But something was still missing.

"Can Aldrik please come, just for a moment?" she asked softly. "He should be here."

"No," the Emperor's voice responded sternly. "The health of the *crown prince* cannot be risked."

"Just for a moment, please." Vhalla looked at the blue-eyed man across from her. She braced herself to go against what she believed, that appealing to his humanity was foolish. "He's your son. He's Baldair's brother. He should be—he *needs* to be here. Don't do this to him. Don't make him live without this moment."

The Emperor regarded her thoughtfully.

"My Lord Solaris, this isn't about you or me." She remembered how adamantly the man had gone against her on principle in the North. "This is only about your sons."

"Bring Aldrik in," he commanded suddenly. "But only for a moment."

Baldair looked at his father in shock, and Vhalla gave a breath of relief. A cleric left and returned soon after with a cautiously stunned Aldrik in tow.

"My prince." The cleric paused their step a bit away from the bed as Vhalla was about to stand and give him her chair. "Do not go any closer, for your health."

"Baldair." Aldrik managed. His voice sounded as though he'd been screaming for hours, even though the man hadn't said a word.

"Aldrik." Baldair struggled to sit higher.

"Always the center of attention, aren't you?"

Vhalla heard the crack of emotion to the crown prince's voice.

"Annoying little brother, 'til the end."

"You are stronger than this," Aldrik admonished.

"I know," Baldair wheezed. "I am, aren't I? Isn't that what's frustrating about it all?"

"You don't lose," Aldrik insisted.

"Not normally." Baldair had a tired grin again. "Brother, I never got to finish paying back what I owe to you."

"You are debt free." Aldrik shifted his hands awkwardly as though he was trying to keep from fidgeting. "Get better, that's all I ask."

"We should go, my prince." The cleric turned at a nod from the Emperor.

"Aldrik!" Baldair struggled to sit fully upright. The dark-haired prince turned and looked at his younger brother. They couldn't be more different while still needing the same things. "Aldrik, I love you, brother. I always have, even if I've been awful about it."

There was a pregnant silence, one that Vhalla wanted to scream over at the unmoving crown prince. This was a moment that would live with him forever.

"I love you, too, Baldair," Aldrik managed. It was awkward and forced.

Vhalla's lips pressed together in a heartbreaking smile under her mask.

And the crown prince was ushered away.

The day turned to night, and Aldrik was not allowed back again. Vhalla tried everything she knew about medicine, from real life experience to what she'd read in books. She tried different ways of positioning him or pacing potions with food. She questioned the clerics on everything. But there was one thing that haunted her the whole day.

"Vhalla, thank you, for staying by my side." His voice was little more than a breathless whisper. She knew the words were coming. "But I am tired. I would like to rest."

"No," she choked out. *Nothing was working.* The inevitable truth that she had known from the moment she walked in the door crashed down around her. "You can't . . . I won't let you . . ."

"You tried so hard; you always do. You didn't give up, even when everyone else had." His hand found its way to her cheek. Vhalla didn't care that blood smeared along with his touch. "Please, keep trying. Don't give up. This world needs you, I feel it."

"Baldair, no." She was choking on her words again. "Let's talk—"

"Fine." He sighed softly, settling into his pillows. "Tell me about your home in the East."

"It's so boring, you don't want to hear that." Her forced laughter had a sharp edge, almost crazed.

"I do. Please?" he encouraged.

Vhalla sighed, stroking his hand with her thumbs. All she could think about in that oppressing moment was her mother, and Vhalla told him the story of the token her mother and she had crafted one year together, a token to bring a good harvest. They'd put their hearts and souls into making it before burying it in the field.

Baldair closed his eyes, and she stopped the moment she noticed.

"Baldair, you can't fall asleep. I agreed because you were going to listen." Vhalla nudged his shoulder. Her heart stopped and fell from her chest. "Baldair," she repeated. "*Baldair*."

The Emperor and Empress were on their feet. Clerics rushed in. She was finally, and literally, pushed aside. Vhalla looked at his lifeless form, at the soulless visage of the golden prince.

"Don't go," she whispered to the golden-haired man, stumbling a few steps backward. The clerics were talking, but she didn't hear them. It was just wind in her ears. They were wiping blood from her hands and face and clothes, *so much blood*, but all Vhalla saw was the Empress burying her sobs in her hands as the Emperor took her into his arms. "Don't go . . ."

Vhalla turned and stumbled for the door numbly. *She couldn't save him.* He died, just as her mother had. She was helpless to change it. Her destiny was full of horrible history repeating itself, and her being forced to watch as it happened.

The princess still lingered, reading in a chair away from the group. Vhalla instantly despised the woman for her casual demeanor and relaxed expression. Her emerald eyes rose. Vhalla looked away quickly to hide her hate.

Aldrik was on his feet by the time their eyes met. Vhalla struggled with her mask, casting it aside. The clerics continued to struggle to get the blood off her, with mixed success. *Noise, it was all noise.* Aldrik's eyes bored into her.

Vhalla broke under their weight.

"Aldrik, I-I-I am so sorry." Her sobs came. Vhalla covered her mouth with her hand and hung her head. She fought for control. He needed her to be strong. *She had to be.*

Aldrik swayed, he stumbled. He hovered in the limbo that was living after death, a cage that was crafted by grief and imprisoned the heart. She heard a choked noise rise from his throat. Her head snapped up. His face twisted in torment. He struggled to keep his breathing under control.

Aldrik grabbed her hand and, before anyone could say anything, bolted for the door. Vhalla's eyes caught the princess as the girl's future husband dragged another woman from the room. Aldrik's hand was already in his pocket for a key. His door across the hall was unlocked in a breath. He pulled her in and locked it again behind them, shutting out the world.

Aldrik let her go, and he brought the palms of his hands to his eyes. He leaned against the door and slid down into a ball on the floor. Vhalla's own tears left rivulets down both her cheeks, falling onto the floor at his feet. His shoulders began to shudder.

"*No,*" he whimpered. "Baldair, you, no, *you idiot!*"

Aldrik's voice cracked and broke. The tears came freely, and she watched as he allowed his composure to shatter. Vhalla turned, placing her back against the hard wood of the door, and slid down to meet him. There was no thought or second-guessing as she wrapped her arms around him and pulled her prince to her.

At first, he was a tense ball. But slowly his arms wrapped themselves around her waist. His head found her chest, situated away from the blood, and Aldrik sobbed into her as Vhalla cried softly into his hair.

They did not move from their spot. Not for the commotion that was being raised in the other room. Not for the footsteps that were in the hall. Not even for the Emperor's angry cries and banging on the door at their backs.

It all only made them cling tighter to each other.

CHAPTER
20

"A LDRIK." THERE WAS more banging from the Emperor. "We will not make a scene of this. Open the door."

Vhalla clutched the prince's shoulders protectively. His face was pressed firmly against her upper chest and shoulder. She shifted, wrapping a leg around his.

"Grief can be maddening," the Emperor attempted coolly. "I am certain your *future wife* would be happy to console you."

Vhalla knew from the moment Aldrik had grabbed her that they were headed toward this moment. Vhalla took a deep breath, inhaling the familiar and comforting scent of eucalyptus. *He had chosen her.* And it had been a deliberate and public choice. Now, they would reap the consequences together.

Aldrik drew a slow breath.

"No." She shook her head. "Don't." Vhalla whispered through her ragged breathing. "Just don't say anything."

Aldrik obliged.

They both jumped as the Emperor banged aggressively at the door behind them. Vhalla put her hands over his ears. *Let him be*, she thought to herself. *Let him be*, she prayed to the Mother above. If there was a Goddess or God, surely, they had to take pity on the grieving man.

Eventually, when shouting a few more times did not work, the Emperor stalked away and Vhalla's arms slipped to Aldrik's shoulders. Silence did not greet them in his absence. Preparations were being made; she could hear the clerics calling to each other for cleaning, cleansing, and the handling of the body. Aldrik's shoulders heaved; he let out a rough sob. *Nothing else but the prince in her arms mattered right now.*

"Baldair," he panted softly. "My *little brother*, Vhalla, he's dead. I wasn't supposed to outlive him. I was supposed to be on my deathbed when he also was wrinkled and gray."

Vhalla rubbed her eyes with her palm. His pain was worse than hers, which meant she had to be the strong one now. She had to be in control of herself.

"I was awful to him," Aldrik sobbed. "I-I never, I never forgave him for so much. It didn't matter, Vhalla. I don't care about it all now."

"I'm sure he knew," she whispered softly, trying to find some stability in her voice.

"No." Aldrik shook his head; she made a soft *shh*ing noise. "He knew nothing. He knew nothing because I told him nothing. It wasn't because he wouldn't understand, or because it was safer for him not to know, or because he didn't care, or any of the other reasons I told myself.

"It was because I simply did not tell him. I was too scared or too weak to let Baldair know that he was foremost my brother. That I loved him." Aldrik pressed his face farther into her. His forehead was uncomfortable against her collarbone, but she said nothing. "He never knew why I wore black. He never knew how badly I just wanted to *be him*, just for one moment. How jealous—by the

Mother—I was jealous of my little brother for all the love and admiration he seemed to just have from birth. He never knew that I attempted . . . he never knew why . . ." Aldrik's voice cut itself off with a pained groan.

Vhalla ran her fingers through his hair, not caring that she was messing up the appearance he had so carefully crafted for himself.

"Baldair loved you," she tried to soothe her crown prince's broken heart. "Despite all what may or may not be, he loved you."

"He did not know me," Aldrik spat.

"He knew you were his brother, and that was worth more than anything," Vhalla replied firmly.

Aldrik's weak retort was lost to tears. Vhalla kept one hand in his hair, the other stroking his back lightly. *It hurt*, the world hurt. It hurt to look, it hurt to breathe, it hurt to see. It hurt to be in the place where Baldair had been only an hour before. It hurt to admit that he was gone, forever. His golden hair and charming demeanor were gone from their lives—that hurt the most.

Eventually, Aldrik began to pull away. She heard him choke down waves of grief before they could slip through his lips, and he straightened away from where they had lain intertwined on the floor.

"He-he can't be dead." Suddenly, the prince was laughing. "This is a joke. This is all a joke."

"Aldrik, I saw it . . . he's gone." Vhalla reached out to smooth hair away from his face, but he jerked away at her touch.

"Don't lie to me!" the prince snarled. "Don't you dare."

"I'm not lying," she pleaded, trying to grab for his hand.

Aldrik was on his feet, leaving Vhalla to try to scramble after him. "I'm going to see him." Aldrik stilled, muttering to himself, "I'm going to see him, and he'll laugh at me for believing his grand joke."

"Aldrik, he's gone."

"I told you not to say that!" Aldrik yelled.

Vhalla flinched at his tone, and the involuntary movement brought the sharpness of sanity back to his eyes.

"I'm sorry, Aldrik." Vhalla wiped her face, trying to keep her emotions under control. "If you need to see his body, I won't stop you." She stepped away from the door, gripping her tunic with trembling hands, *the tunic that was still stained with Baldair's blood.* "But I'm certain if you unlock that door, they will take me away—and who knows where, given the circumstances . . . They will make demands of you, and it's too soon. It's all right to grieve."

"Damn it," he cursed. "Damn you, Baldair!" The prince spun in place and unleashed the sound of raw frustration. His hands were alight in flame.

"Aldrik, stop!" Vhalla cried as he lit the first piece of furniture aflame.

"Damn you to the Mother's fiery justice for eternity for giving me hope." He threw out a hand and the flames jumped to the desk. "No, no! You got the last laugh in the end. Aldrik, the heartless prince, bared himself for you on your deathbed."

"Aldrik, it wasn't like that! You must know that!" she shouted, trying to reach the prince.

"You-you agreed to take the throne knowing it'd never come to pass!"

Her heart stopped. *Baldair agreed to Aldrik abdicating his birthright to him?*

"You gave me hope, you bastard!" Aldrik turned up his gaze, and the flames turned white hot.

Vhalla saw the dazzling library that spiraled above them, likely housing countless precious works, given their collector. She realized—in horror—that he was going to burn the books. She opened her Channel and took a deep breath.

Her clothing singed as the fire burned up his forearms and she threw her arms around him. The flames were warm, hotter than any other time they had ever tested their Bond. But the fire didn't burn her. Vhalla clung to his waist, her face buried in his chest.

"Vhalla . . ." The flames vanished, and his arms crushed her against him. "Vhalla, I—I am a monster."

He let her go suddenly, and she swayed without the support. Vhalla watched him listlessly take in the charred remains of the room. She knew he was replaying in his mind the acerbic words he'd just uttered against his brother.

"You're not a monster," she soothed gently. "Hurting, yes. Scared, yes. But not a monster."

"Baldair died because of me . . . I am a curse to anyone who would ever dare care for me."

"You're not." The way he cringed away when she approached him nearly broke her heart.

"Don't, Vhalla. Don't come near me, or I will curse you further." Whatever madness grew in his heart that made him say those words had taken root there long ago. He believed it completely.

Vhalla moved with purpose, taking his face in both her hands and forcing him to look at her. "Aldrik, *stop*," she demanded softly. "Don't push me away, don't even try. The opportunity for it came and went; I didn't take it. You promised you wouldn't."

"And you promised not to let me," he whispered in reply. His hands went up to hers, and Vhalla saw his eyes glisten once more. Tears spilled over his high cheeks and onto her fingers. "You don't know."

"I don't know what?"

Aldrik swayed and took her hand. He led her purposefully into the other room, seating her between the hearth and the low table at their backs. Vhalla made it a point not to look at the papers scattered upon it.

Flames sparked to life in the fireplace, and Aldrik looked to them for answers. "Where do I start with this?"

"We don't have to do this now." Whatever it was, it seemed to be the source of great pain for him, which was the last thing he needed.

"We do," he insisted. "Baldair, brother of my flesh, died and never knew the truth. I won't let the same happen to you."

"I'm not going to die, at least not for a long time." She attempted a reassuring smile.

"I have seen it."

"Seen what?"

"Your death." Aldrik looked at her as though she was already swathed in burning cloth for the Rite of Sunset.

"What?" The word was little more than a breath.

"I have seen it, but I will do all I can to prevent it." His hands were on her face, as if reminding himself that she was real. "I will fight the Mother herself to keep you safe."

"You're not making any sense . . ." That fact didn't make her any less frightened.

"I saw it in a dream."

"It's a small wonder your dreams are consumed with death, with Baldair as he was." Vhalla had her fair share of nights consumed with death.

"They're not just dreams." The shadow of fear darkened his expression. "Vhalla, I can see your future."

"What? That makes no sense."

"Firebearers can see the future in flames."

"I know, but you're not looking in flames." She shook her head, his hands falling onto her thighs. *She didn't want to think of fortune tellers.* "You never told me you could see the future."

"I couldn't." Aldrik emphasized the past tense. "I don't look through the flames. I look through our Bond."

"They're just dreams," she insisted weakly.

"Oh? Like your dreams are always 'just' dreams?" Aldrik's voice found a touch of annoyance. "Do you have any idea how difficult this is for me to tell you? Why would I lie or paint a falsehood? I'm telling you because I'm *scared*. The crown prince of the realm is terrified. As much as it burns me to say it, I will because I need you to believe me. I'm not going to lose you."

Vhalla opened and closed her mouth like a fish above water, fighting for words.

Aldrik turned back to the table, pushing together the papers. He spent a moment shuffling them in his hands before beginning to display them on the floor. He paired one piece of parchment with one another, and Vhalla instinctually began to skim their contents.

"I don't know exactly when it started . . ." he sighed. Despite being stressful, the action seemed to help him continue to move in the wake of his brother's death. "But logically, it would've been after the Joining, since that's when your dreams began."

"How are you not sure?" Vhalla whispered, giving him her attention rather than trying to read the papers.

"I've dreamt about you for so long." His hands ran over her, memorizing her shape again and again. "It wasn't easy for me to tell what were my own wants or paranoia, and what were premonitions."

"If you dream so much, there would certainly be a chance for some of it to come true, right?" Vhalla thought aloud.

"For months, that's what I thought. It wasn't until our last meeting in the garden that I put together that they may be more. When you actually came without my explaining, when you looked as I dreamt, when you said verbatim what I had seen."

"*Are you real . . .*" Vhalla repeated his former words, her eyes growing wide.

Aldrik nodded solemnly. "After that, I set to writing it down. Every dream I could remember with you in it, in as much detail as I could manage. The premonitions are normally hazy, and I can see little beyond you. That helped me narrow it down some . . ." He motioned to the piles. "But I wrote them all, just in case."

Her eyes skimmed the papers, mirroring his own gaze as he struggled with words for a moment. *Riding in the desert,* she read the lines at the start of each page, *blood on her face, reading together in the library, a crown upon her beautiful hair, writhing on the floor, dancing at a gala, holding hands on the Sunlit Stage, first child . . .*

Vhalla reached out and took the paper from where he'd sorted it, and Aldrik didn't object.

She is radiant, even when she has every right to be exhausted. Hair clings to the sweat that's on her brow, and she is tired—I can see she is. But her smile is so brilliant, she is goodness incarnate. She's reclining in a bed, though I cannot discern where it is or who else may be there. It is bright though, and warm. She's reaching out to me, her mouth is moving, and I know what she is asking for. I look down, and perhaps it is the most perfect sight I have ever seen. The tuft of hair upon the babe's head is black, though he has her eyes: bright, inquisitive, and almost yellow. He has more her than me in him,

I can feel it, and I am so thankful for it. I pass him to

her, and she seems almost afraid. I move to kiss her.
There is nothing to be scared of. I will protect them both.

The words became more difficult to read as the paper quivered in her trembling fingers. Vhalla blinked her eyes. Her emotions were too wild to handle this. She curled into a ball, clutching the paper to her chest. Aldrik's arms were around her shoulders, and she wept into her knees, not caring for the folds or wrinkles it put in the parchment.

This was what he'd been silently enduring for months. Each night he went to sleep, he risked a dream. He risked seeing joy, he risked seeing pain. Vhalla realized it was far worse than seeing his memories. Those were cemented in history. But, for Aldrik, the brightest hope could be torture because it may be a guiding light or a false beacon.

"You say you are a curse, but I'm the one who's cursed you. To torture you with such visions." Even before he'd realized his dreams held the future, she knew they would've caused him the rainbow of agony to ecstasy, depending on their subject.

"Hush," he demanded. "Do you know how often I sleep wishing to see something like the paper you hold? It's been the only thing that's allowed me to sleep some nights. It's the only thing that gave me the courage to ask you to be mine." His long fingers wrapped around the watch at her neck.

"You're sure?"

"I am." He coaxed the paper from her hands and began to show her the sets he'd created of his dreams against records of events that had come to pass. His moments of confidence suddenly made more sense. She knew why he had so much faith in getting her to the front as Serien, why he'd easily refused her advances for something more at the last campsite before the North, how he'd known he could accomplish making her a lady. Even if the details were blurry, and the means of it all happening was slightly off, it matched dream to reality.

"Did you know, about—" Vhalla swallowed hard and risked the name "—Baldair?"

"I didn't." He sighed and pinched the bridge of his nose. "Maybe, maybe I saw something. But I only ever see you. Perhaps it's because I don't possess general future sight?"

"My death?" The word was like a curse upon her lips.

"I don't know," Aldrik groaned. "I haven't even written it down, I couldn't manage with—" his voice quivered, and he drew in a shaky breath "—with Baldair."

His hands were on her again. They ran down her cheeks onto her neck. They were over her shoulders, intertwining his fingers with hers and back again. As though he was assuring himself that she wasn't some phantom, that it wasn't one of his dreams.

"I saw you bleeding. You had a gash from your shoulder to your chest." His forehead fell against hers. "I can't lose you. I-I lost my brother, I won't lose you. Baldair is gone, by the Mother, *Baldair is gone*. If I lost you, Vhalla, I would have no one, nothing."

Aldrik pulled her back to him, and she realized how his grief was beginning to manifest. It fed off his paranoia, his mistrust of the world. *If he wasn't prepared to do anything to protect her before, he was now.*

"You won't lose me," she assured him.

"I never thought I'd lose Baldair." *He was crying again*, she realized. "Oh, Gods, Baldair. I am cursed: my mother could not escape, Baldair could not escape, and I will damn you, too."

"Enough of that." Vhalla struggled to pry herself far enough away from his chest to catch his eyes. "You didn't damn anyone."

"My mother did not die in childbirth."

"What?" Every book she had ever read, everything she had ever heard, had said such to be true.

"She died shortly after. The explanation of death in the birthing bed was easier than the truth." Aldrik rubbed his eyes tiredly, withdrawing physically. "Isn't that how it always is, a beautiful simple lie over the ugly truth?"

"I've come to prefer the latter." Vhalla rested a palm on his knee. "Tell me later; this is too much for one day."

"No." He was focused on the dancing flames. "I need to tell you. I did not tell Baldair, now I never will. I need to tell you, Vhalla. I need to do things right for once in my miserable life."

"Aldrik, please," she begged.

"Listen, Vhalla—let me tell you what I should've before you let the Empire's accursed monster into your bed."

CHAPTER 21

"THE WEST FELL, and most did not want it to go down gracefully," Aldrik began.

"The Knights of Jadar?" Vhalla asked tentatively, wondering if she'd finally fill in the curious blanks of the histories she'd been trying to sift through for months.

"Just so." There was the ghost of appreciation for her haunting his eyes. "They loathed my mother's family for kneeling before Solaris. Most of all, they loathed my mother for marrying my father.

"My uncle tells me that, in her way, she loved my father *for* his conquest. When he speaks of her, he tells me she was as beautiful as a rose with thorns twice as sharp. My mother had never been bested in combat before, which made my father enthralling, despite the unusual circumstances under which they met." Aldrik shook his head. "It wasn't until I was engaged to the Northern girl that I thought about how impossible my parents' love was.

"After the Knights disowned my family, they used their knowledge of the Caverns to prepare a plot to drive out Solaris, to purge the Western Court of all those who were no longer loyal to 'King Jadar's Ideals.'" Aldrik scowled. "They stole the Sword of Jadar. My mother's father had told her where he had hidden it, and she discovered it missing within hours of my birth."

Vhalla remembered her conversation with Ophain; the lord had mentioned the sword had gone missing, but he so carefully left out the truth of the matter.

Aldrik shifted uncomfortably and continued, "My mother left. She never even told my father where she was going. She disappeared into the night on the fastest Warstrider and raced without rest to the caves, despite still recovering from the pains and blood loss of labor."

Vhalla grimaced at the thought.

"She confronted the Knights before they could penetrate into the heart of the Caverns." Aldrik paused, blinking away shining tears. "She was alone, but she used the Knight's knowledge against them. She was a Western princess and had access to Mhashan's crimson history. She Bound her will with the crystals; she gave everything to block the Knights with a barrier of her magic. Even when they killed her, the barrier held."

"How do you know all this?"

"She left a letter," he answered. "When she went missing, my family went searching through the palace, keeping things hush before a search party was sent. I suppose there were places that she and her sisters would share, secrets with notes. My mother hid a letter in one such place. By the time they knew, it was too late."

"Why didn't she let someone else go?" Vhalla frowned. "Why did *she* run off?" Vhalla omitted what she really wanted to know. *Why had Aldrik's mother left her newborn son?*

But he heard it. "Who knows, really? I suppose she was magically the strongest. She knew she would be stopped by anyone she told. Perhaps she knew the route the best. Perhaps she had researched it best. If it had been me, and I had something I desperately wanted to protect, I wouldn't trust anyone else to do what must be done. The Knights were at all levels of Western society. She could have been assassinated by telling the wrong person while trying to mobilize a force, and then it would be far too late."

Aldrik paused and looked at her with sudden clarity. Vhalla realized that, for the first time, he understood what his mother had felt. She glanced at the paper she had clutched longingly, a mother, a father, and *their* child. Aldrik's eyes betrayed his resolve; he was prepared to do the same for her and a child who may never even come into existence.

"If your mother gave her life to form the barrier," Vhalla thought aloud, "how do you know about it? She couldn't have left word about what actually transpired in the Caverns."

His expression darkened, and Aldrik looked away, cursing under his breath. "Vhalla, I am sorry."

"Sorry? For what?"

"For taking your father from you all those years." He winced.

"What?" She blinked.

"For taking all those mothers, fathers, sisters, brothers from their homes. I didn't know, I wouldn't have . . ." He sounded like a boy pleading to a parent for forgiveness. "I didn't know how much it hurt to lose someone you truly loved. It was my fault."

"What was?" she asked gently, deciding arguing would be more stressful for him.

"The war." Aldrik swallowed. "The War of the Crystal Caverns was my fault."

"What?" Vhalla breathed, dazed and confused. "How? No, Aldrik, I'm sure . . . You're just guilt ridden right now. Everything isn't your fault. Even your mother. She didn't die because of you, she died because of insane xenophobes."

"It is!" The fire in the hearth flared, emphasizing Aldrik's wild emotions. "*He* told me that I was powerful, like my mother—that I would be great. I didn't know the whole truth, and I believed him. He told me that I could serve my country, help my family. That I would be loved, more than my brother ever was, more than any prince, king, or Emperor ever would be."

Vhalla opened her mouth, struggling for a word in his almost angry tirade.

"I was a fool, a boy. I was innocent, wide-eyed. And, like the idiot I was, I believed him." Aldrik cursed at himself. "I believed him because I wanted to. Because I did not yet know the world was full of liars and deceivers. But I should have known, I was too smart not to know."

"Who is 'him?'" Something sunk heavily in her stomach.

"Egmun."

"What did the bastard do to you?" Vhalla struggled to control her rage, her anger.

"Nothing I didn't ask for myself." Aldrik hung his head.

"I don't understand," she confessed, wishing she did so he would not have to endure another moment of the conversation.

"He didn't even choose me, not at first. I'm sure I would have been high on his list, but being the prince, I was a liability to his goals. Too many eyes on me, too much risk someone would find out." Aldrik fell back onto the pillows limply.

"Find out what?" Vhalla asked.

"He was fascinated by the Caverns, and he wanted to learn their secrets."

"For power?" she interjected.

"I don't think so . . ." Aldrik mused softly. "Egmun was never really like that. He was addicted to knowledge. It was beyond liking books or memorizing facts. He wanted to push the boundaries. He did not just want to know, he wanted to be the *first* to know. He wanted to discover, and each discovery was a drug stronger than any other. Even if he held all the power in the world, it would have bored him after the initial rush, I think."

Vhalla reclined on the pillows as well, too exhausted by the conversation to sit another moment.

"Egmun chose Victor."

"Victor?"

"Indeed. But because he was my mentor, I was eventually brought in on it, too." Aldrik sighed. "I thought—I saw the crystals as the pinnacle of what it meant to be a sorcerer: to handle them, to wield them, to control them.

"Egmun taught us both." The prince stared at his hands. "He put crystals in our palms, he took notes, and he taught us what he knew. Victor had been at it longer than I had, but I took to it like a fish to water. I knew power, and I did not want to relinquish it. Egmun was an amazing teacher, really. He was charismatic, enthusiastic, encouraging. He wanted to watch us excel and to learn from us. I had a taste, and I was hungry and wanted more; however much he gave me wasn't enough. It was never enough."

"But, crystal corruption?" Vhalla asked.

"He was careful, or tried to be," Aldrik addressed her concern. "He would only let us handle them every few days. Victor was the first to show signs of sickness, though. Then we turned into test subjects without realizing it. Victor was constantly pushed to the limit to determine how much he could endure. Looking back, it was wild, it was reckless, and it was amazing Victor did not end up corrupted with taint."

Vhalla remembered Victor's notebook. *It was all true.*

"Egmun knew. Of course, he knew. The man knew everything, even beyond what was written in books. If there was a secret whispered on someone's lips, it would find its way to him. Maybe that's why he's the perfect—in all the worst ways—Head of Senate now. He knew of my mother, of her sacrifice. He knew it was her magic that sealed the Caverns.

"He went to the Caverns and tried to unlock it himself. He was a gifted sorcerer, but he wasn't strong enough. The magic of the barrier rejected him."

"But it wouldn't reject you." She understood what happened with horrific clarity. Magic wasn't in the blood, but she remembered Gianna explaining how there was something about magic passed through families.

"Egmun had procured the sword, he had me. Victor was no longer needed." Aldrik clenched his fists, baring his teeth in anger. "He took me to the Caverns with our sacrifice. He paid the blood toll, but it wasn't enough. The man we killed was simply a Commons, so it was rejected.

"Everything went wrong. The delicate stasis of the crystals was thrown out of balance by my actions, letting the power seep into the world. It unleashed taint into our world, reaching out eagerly to corrupt as quickly as possible." Aldrik's voice weakened. "I rode back through the rain and told my father everything. That I'd damned our people and cursed our kingdom. He sent soldiers, but they were no match and became tainted monsters, spreading the taint further. I told my father, I told him I wasn't fit to be a ruler . . ."

Vhalla sat up suddenly, staring at Aldrik. The rainy night of a boy taking a knife to his skin made sense. "Don't say it. I know."

"It was my fault," he whispered.

"No," she said firmly. "It was Egmun's fault. You were only a boy."

"My father was of the same inclination." The prince sat upright again also, keeping his fingers intertwined with hers. "He told Egmun to seal the Caverns, whatever price had to be paid was not nearly enough. But should Egmun be successful, he would be pardoned. He went back to the Caverns, and he lived up to his word. At first, the lingering magic of my mother's barrier rejected him, and I ended up being forced to help him establish a new barrier in the structure of the old one."

"That's why he doesn't have magic anymore," she realized. The minister had given up his power to restore the barrier.

"After that, Egmun was awarded his life and a position on the Senate for holding his tongue about how the crown prince had started the War of the Crystal Caverns," he murmured.

"I realized I was a bad person to be around. I caused countless deaths. I let evil, true evil, into the world." Aldrik pressed his palms into his eyes. "My life, from then on, was built around a lie. A lie that I was not some monster who—had I not been the crown prince— would have been put to death. A lie that I was still a prince worthy of the crown that rested upon my head. So I became the prince of lies. I embraced being the black sheep. Perhaps I thought eventually it would make my father see I wasn't fit for the throne. I still have never been punished properly for the weight of my crimes."

He finally ran out of words, and the sound of his unsteady breathing filled the room. Emotions assaulted her one after the next: shock, horror, anger, pain. Half a dozen more rose in her as she stared at the man quietly suffering before her.

"You must hate me," Aldrik said softly. "Now that you know me, truly know me, you must hate me." He continued before she could get a word in, "I should've told you so long ago. But I was too selfish; I knew I'd lose you if I did."

"I'm still here," she whispered after a long moment. Aldrik stilled, his breathing becoming shallow so he could hang on her every word. "I do not hate you. And I know if you had told Baldair, he would have felt the same as I. He would not have hated you for this. You have punished yourself enough, more than enough; stop blaming yourself for crimes long past, whatever role you may or may not have had in them."

"Vhalla," he whispered weakly.

She gripped his hand tightly and pulled him to her. She wrapped an arm around his shoulders and pressed him close. "I could never hate you."

Aldrik buried his face back into her chest and upper shoulder, much like he had before. Though this time, there were far fewer tears, far fewer emotions wracking his body. *Then again*, perhaps too many emotions were coursing through him that he was simply stunned numb. Either way, she held him gently, trying to offer him as much reassurance as she could.

"I feel better," he confessed.

"Do you?"

"Better being relative," he sighed. "But yes."

"For a prince of lies, you seem to enjoy the truth." Vhalla smiled weakly. He huffed in amusement. She relished that somehow; he had found the eye of the storm.

"I'm tired."

"Me too."

"Come." He pulled them off the floor and out of the room.

The prince led her to his bedroom, and she joined him in his bed without a second thought. Singed, bloody clothes and red eyes, they became a tangled mess of limbs. Their chests alternated heaving with tears and feeling so empty that there was no more emotion from which to cry. He never explicitly asked for her to stay, but there was nowhere else Vhalla would've been. She eventually fell asleep with him tucked tightly in her arms as a storm brewed just outside the door.

CHAPTER 22

THERE WAS A knock on the outside door.

Vhalla rolled over in her sleep, and Aldrik's hands followed her. He pulled her to him instinctually, his body curling around her. She sighed softly. Everything hurt less when she was in his embrace.

Another firm knock roused her further. It must have been loud, or it would've been impossible to hear from across the large main room and his bedroom. Vhalla blinked her eyes, opening and closing them with a wince at the blinding light.

The knocking continued, and a soft call of Aldrik's name finally brought him to life.

"Who is it?" she mumbled, staring out the windows. It was just after dawn, so they couldn't have slept for that long. The sun's brilliant rays bounced off a thick layer of snow that had fallen on his balcony during the night. *The first snow of winter*, and Vhalla could feel no joy for it.

"I'm not sure . . ." Aldrik proceeded cautiously to the main room.

"Are you going to answer it?" she whispered, following him.

Aldrik held up a hand in reply and listened.

"Aldrik," a voice called gently through his main door. "I know you're in there."

Vhalla's head was sluggish with exhaustion. It was too gentle to be the Empress or Za. It wasn't melodic enough to be the princess's. She thought perhaps it was some cleric or staff, but none of them called the prince by his name. *Who could it be?*

"Aldrik?" More knocking. "If you're there, you don't even have to open the door, just say something."

"Elecia?" he called into the door.

"Aldrik." Vhalla heard the sorrow in Elecia's voice. She heard the grief, the guilt at having been too late. *If Vhalla could have just switched places with her, then perhaps Baldair would have lived.* She took a shaky breath. It wasn't fair to blame the other woman but, by the Gods, Vhalla wanted to.

"I want to talk to you." Vhalla realized why she didn't recognize Elecia's voice immediately. There was a quivering strain to it. A tension pulled out her words in an unfamiliar way.

Aldrik's fingers closed around the lock. Vhalla watched him as he was just about to turn it. She opened her mouth to object, considering her soot-stained clothes and obvious bedhead.

"Aldrik, do you remember that time when you and Baldair came to the West together?" Elecia said quickly. Aldrik stilled. "You both had an official meeting that I so desperately wanted to attend. I thought it was viciously unfair that I couldn't go."

Aldrik's hand fell away from the door.

"You promised me I could go. Baldair thought you were just telling another one of your lies, but you had a way, remember?" Elecia's story was slowly told, her words enunciated one by one as though she was in desperate need of him to hear them. "I thought you were so kind then. Do you remember what you wore?"

The prince took a step away, his face suddenly serious—a thin veil for the panic that lit his eyes. Vhalla didn't understand.

"I remember, I'm sure it's no surprise . . ." Elecia continued rambling.

Vhalla never heard the rest of the story. Aldrik spun on his heel and practically sprinted back toward her. Vhalla's hand was in his, and he tugged her into the bedroom, closing the door quickly behind them, taking care not to slam it or make any loud noises.

"Aldrik, what's going on?"

He threw open one of the large armoires in the room, reaching behind the familiar plate for a key.

"My father is waiting out there," he answered in a rush.

"What do you mean?" She couldn't fathom how he knew that.

"I hate that memory," he explained, taking her hand again and leading her into the secret hall between his room and the Tower. "We were kids. I snuck her in through a passage I'd discovered that people used to secretly listen to the conversations in the room."

"What?" Vhalla struggled to connect things in her head. *Why did this matter now?*

"He punished me fiercely for taking her somewhere she didn't belong. He said that if someone had discovered her presence, it would bring great shame to the crown for having a secret listener on official business. That I was lucky they didn't." Aldrik opened the door to the Tower, half-pulling her up it.

"So, your father is there?"

"I have no doubt. Elecia's being forced to be a puppet right now. No matter what she may think of my stealing you into my room, if there's one thing Elecia would hate more, it would be being someone else's puppet."

"What will your father do?" Vhalla's head hurt from all the crying the night before, from the grief, from panic.

"I don't know, and I don't have enough time to figure it out," Aldrik said with a curse.

If there was one thing the Gods did for them that day, it was keeping the hallways bare of observers. Though Vhalla had no idea how it would matter if someone did. Clerics had surely already been talking of the crown prince stealing away the Windwalker in a fit of grief. There were likely already rumors running rampant through the castle about the future Emperor's infidelity with his *favored whore*.

She grimaced at herself for even thinking what was certainly the gritty truth.

They stopped before the highest door in the Tower. Aldrik slipped the key into the lock and affirmed all her suspicions that these were the secondary quarters of the crown prince.

Braziers around the room sprung to life with a wave of his hand, casting long shadows beneath the sparse furniture. There was a table and two chairs placed toward the center. Along the back wall were, unsurprisingly, shelves of books and cabinets of curiosities. There was a small bed pushed to the left corner, a door next to it. Another door led off somewhere to the right of the room. The few windows were covered with heavy black curtains. It wasn't a large space, perhaps three of her personal quarters, and everything had a slightly stagnant and dusty smell to it.

"Your Tower chambers."

"Yes, and they only have one exit or entry." He pressed the key into her palm. "This is the only key. I need you to lock that door behind me and let no one in. If someone comes and knows you are in here, ignore whatever they say and ask them what is most beautiful just before it dies."

"What is most beautiful just before it dies?" she repeated, committing it to memory.

"A rose," he answered softly. "If they do not respond with that, do not let them in—even if it is me. No matter what else they do or say, *do not open the door*." Aldrik swallowed. "And if someone forces entry, jump."

"What is going to happen next?" Vhalla tried to anticipate his thoughts and plans, to make some of her own. Everything was moving too quickly, and the world was still in flux from Baldair's death.

"I don't know." Aldrik pulled her to him suddenly. "I wasn't thinking. I haven't been thinking. I don't have a plan. I don't know what will happen. I haven't calculated how likely certain courses of actions are. I don't know, Vhalla, so I will plan for the worst."

"Let me help you." She pried herself away from the warm safety of his embrace.

"I will, but first I have to go and find out how the pieces are moving." His palms were on her cheeks. "I will take you away myself, if I must. For now, just hide."

"But—"

"Elecia will run out of that stupid story soon, if not already. When she does, she may be able to buy more time but, damn it, they may be knocking down my door already." Aldrik shook his head and pressed his forehead against hers. Vhalla swallowed. *All this because he took solace with her in his moment of grief?* Would his father really go so far? "Stay here, stay safe. I will come back to you as soon as I can."

The door clicked closed behind him, and Vhalla was left alone in the room.

She shivered as her bare feet stumbled across the stone to the door. Vhalla turned the lock with her shaking fingers and drew an unsteady breath. The world kept spinning, her head was thundering, and her heart would not relent in its panicked flutter.

Vhalla sunk to the floor, staring at the small room. *She was trapped like an animal backed into a corner.* Even Aldrik was terrified, and he'd brought her to what was possibly the most secure place he had. He relied on his skill, the Tower, and time to keep her safe. But if all that failed, she had no idea what fate awaited her.

"Baldair, this is all your fault." Vhalla squeezed her eyes closed and refrained from shouting at ghosts. She curled into a ball and buried her face in her knees, just focusing on breathing.

Her eyes were jolted open again when a knock sounded on the door at her back. Exhaustion had somehow won out, and she had no idea how long she'd dozed. Vhalla struggled to rouse.

"Open the door?"

The voice gave her pause. "What is most beautiful before it dies?"

"A rose," Fritz answered, barely loud enough for her to hear.

Vhalla scrambled to her feet and snapped the lock open. Fritz entered quickly and stopped just within, his eyes adjusting to the dim light, as Vhalla closed the door behind him. The small sack he'd brought fell to the floor as Vhalla pulled him in for a tight embrace.

"Vhalla, Gods. Vhalla, what . . ." He couldn't seem to find

words. Her perpetually enthusiastic, ever-talkative friend couldn't find words.

"Fritz, everything is a mess." Tears burned her eyes again. "Baldair, Baldair is dead, and then Aldrik, he, we, we didn't—I mean." Vhalla shook her head. "He needed me, Fritz . . . It shouldn't be this way."

"Vhalla," he whispered gently. "You're covered in ash and soot *and blood.*" He put his palm on the crown of her head. "When was the last time you brushed your hair?"

Vhalla blinked at him. *Had he not been listening to her?* This was hardly the time.

"Is there a washroom here?"

"I don't know . . ." Vhalla couldn't decipher her friend's actions.

Fritz chose one of the two doors, and picked wisely. It led into a bathroom that was small, yet still befitting a prince. Fritz assessed things for a moment before beginning to draw a bath.

"Sit here." He placed her on the edge of the tub and began to scavenge through the drawers and cabinets. He located a brush and some soap before returning to kneel before her. "Will you let me help you bathe?"

Vhalla blinked; he was asking her to undress for him.

"I don't want to leave you alone right now, Vhal. I want to help you. I grew up with all my sisters and can assure you that you won't surprise me with anything. Plus, it's not as if you'd have anything that could entice me." He grinned half-heartedly.

Was he right that it didn't matter? Vhalla couldn't foresee Aldrik being particularly pleased at another man seeing her naked. She was fairly nervous with the idea. But she'd bathed with other girls. Did it make any difference that he simply had something different in his trousers than she? What was more important, how he was in her mind, or how he was in his body?

Vhalla slowly peeled off the singed and stained clothes.

Fritz didn't even bat an eye at her naked form. Concern and compassion were written across his face, and he focused only on hers. He exhibited no spark of want or desire. Vhalla saw Larel's spirit in her friend as he helped her into the steaming tub.

He hovered beside her, lathering soap into her locks with a

soothing touch. Vhalla stared at her palms. The water was already a dingy color from the soot and grime that was on her. A small voice counseled that she should feel guilty for her part in staying with Aldrik, but Vhalla couldn't evoke the emotion. *He had needed her.*

"Has the Emperor come into the Tower?" The hot water had calmed her enough to think rationally.

"No." Fritz placed some hair over her shoulder as he began to brush the next section.

"What have you heard?" She needed to know if she was going to calculate what was next. "Tell me true, Fritz."

"That Prince Baldair has died. That the Windwalker and Prince Aldrik ran off together in a fit of grief," he listed.

Vhalla laughed softly. "It's actually true, for once."

"They say the North will be up in arms about it." Fritz sighed. "Though, most people seemed to be more amused or surprised, but not upset."

"Should I find consolation in that?" *It was interesting, however, that the people seemed to consent to the crown prince and the Hero of the North being together.*

"You should find consolation in anything you can," he answered honestly.

"How did you know I was here? Aldrik?"

"Elecia." Fritz surprised her. "Aldrik told her because she can move more easily than he can right now. She sent me though, rather than coming here herself because, well, eyes are still on her also."

"Is Aldrik okay?"

"I'm not sure." Fritz shook his head. "Elecia left to go back to him, to try to help him with things. Rinse your hair."

Vhalla did as he instructed. She washed her body next, and the conversation died during that act. Vhalla emerged when the bathwater began to cool, Fritz dutifully wrapping her in a towel. The cloth smelled as though it had been hanging for too long but there was still a lingering, comforting scent of Aldrik to it.

She was forced to rummage through his drawers until she found a stash of clothes. Vhalla didn't have much to choose from, so she just picked what looked the warmest. As to be expected, it swam on her, and the waist of the trousers fell around her hips.

"What happened?" Fritz asked as they sat at the table. He grabbed the sack he'd dropped earlier from the floor and produced three rolls with meat.

"You have most of it already. Baldair died, I was there." She stared at the food blankly.

"Eat," Fritz insisted.

Vhalla forced herself to oblige. "After, it's just as they say. Aldrik ran, he took me with him. We hid in his room."

"Did you . . .?" Fritz asked slowly.

"We were a comfort to each other, but not in *that* way," Vhalla said firmly, proud she could look her friend in the eye and say it.

"Good." Fritz seemed equally pleased as he stood. "Try to get some rest. You look dead on your feet."

"You're leaving?" She stood also.

"I have to. It's not good for me to go missing too long. Grahm agreed to be an alibi if I need one." Fritz gave her a tired smile. "But it's still not a good idea to push things. No point in rousing suspicion within the Tower."

"Right." Vhalla grabbed his hands. "Fritz, thank you, for everything."

"Of course, Vhal. It will work out, I'm sure it will." Her friend's confidence sounded false, but the final squeeze he gave her before leaving certainly wasn't.

With the metallic sound of the lock sliding back into place, she was alone again in the room. Vhalla sighed heavily. There were books, but she didn't want to read. There was some kind of closet or storeroom through the other door. But it was dark, and she didn't feel too inquisitive.

In the end, Vhalla collapsed onto the bed, her face buried in the pillow. But she didn't cry. She didn't like feeling isolated and alone. Her mind was already churning with plans for what she could suggest when Aldrik returned.

For the third time in one day, a knock awoke her. The trend was exhausting, and on her way to the door, she peeked out the curtains, discovering it was nearly sunset.

"What is most beautiful just before it dies?" she asked through the door.

There was a long pause. "A rose."

Vhalla twisted the lock and looked at a familiar set of dark eyes. She breathed a sigh of relief. "Aldrik."

"Vhalla, we have to go." His voice was strange, some kind of tension pushing it up an octave.

"What's happened? Is it your father?"

"It has to do with none of that." He shook his head. The day competed with itself to get worse. "It's Victor."

"Victor?" The world stilled.

"I went to ask him for help and found him gone." Aldrik cursed. "All the crystals were gone, the notes from when we were boys open on his desk. I think he's heading for the Caverns."

"He, we were going to destroy them," she said hastily, hopefully.

"Not from what I read." Aldrik frowned. "He was lying to you, Vhalla. He wants the Caverns for himself."

"What, no—"

"We have to go stop him," Aldrik barked roughly.

"What about the barrier?" Vhalla inquired.

"The barrier?"

"The one set up by Egmun, after you . . ." Vhalla danced delicately with her words, suddenly wondering if she had misunderstood Aldrik's history.

"Victor was trained by Egmun," Aldrik answered quickly. "They're both Waterrunners, so I'm certain his magic would be attuned to Egmun's."

"What do we do?" Her encounters with the minister had grown stranger and stranger. After Fritz's cautions and knowing Aldrik's story, it wasn't a far leap of logic to think that Victor had gone off the deep end when it came to crystals. Horror raked itself across her heart. *It was her fault; she had handed him the axe.*

"We make haste for the Caverns." Aldrik started down the Tower, motioning for her to follow.

She nodded, grabbed a random cloak off a nearby peg, and shut the door behind her. Aldrik made no motion to tell her to lock it, and she completely forgot in her panic. She fell into step behind him, and he didn't even turn to look at her. *At some point, he had found time to fix his hair.* She wondered what really had gone on with the Emperor.

No, there were more important things to worry about than Emperors and hair, she reminded herself. Her chest tightened. Victor was headed to the Crystal Caverns with an axe that could sever souls.

CHAPTER 23

ALDRIK'S STEPS WERE fast, and she struggled to keep up. Her feet felt heavy, her mind sluggish with exhaustion and the mental strain of the past few days.

"Wait!" She stopped at the door to her room.

"Vhalla, we don't have time," he responded briskly.

"I know, but I will freeze if I go out like this."

"Quickly," he begrudgingly agreed.

Vhalla darted into her room and rummaged through things, not caring what fell out of place. Piling on layers, Vhalla was a mismatch of clothing: the gloves that went under her gauntlets, two pairs of socks, a rope belt to secure his oversized pants around her waist.

In her rummaging, Larel's bracelet fell

from its place of honor on the stack of Aldrik's notes. Vhalla paused, considering taking it, but left it instead. She didn't want anything happening to the last token from her friend; who knew what would transpire before the dawn.

Vhalla raced down the Tower behind Aldrik once more, throwing her cloak over her shoulders. It had been well over a year since she had last seen her prince as tense and shut-off as he was now, though she could hardly blame him given the circumstances. Two floors down, the door to the vessel room opened, and Vhalla almost ran head-first into the Eastern man who emerged.

"Vhalla?" Grahm blinked at her.

"I have to go." She glanced at Aldrik, who was now ten steps ahead. He did not so much as glance in her direction, simply expecting her to keep pace.

"What? Where? What is it?" He squinted at the prince she followed.

"I can't-can't explain." She took a few steps backward and called over her shoulder, practically running to catch up with Aldrik. "I just have to go."

A very confused Easterner was left in her wake. Aldrik pulled open one of the outer doors and ushered her inside. Vhalla caught a glimpse of Grahm on their heels as the door closed.

"Vhalla, that—" Grahm called

Aldrik slammed the door and locked it.

"We can't have distractions," he cursed gruffly. The doorknob turned as someone tried to open it. Vhalla stared at it uneasily. *Aldrik had never met Grahm*, she told herself. He didn't know the Waterrunner pursuing them. "Come."

He led as they plunged through the palace side door. They raced through the outer halls, avoiding the major arteries of the palace. Whenever someone would pass by at an intersection, they would duck behind a column or into a doorway to hide.

Vhalla panted softly. *They were sneaking*, she realized. What had his father told him? What would happen if they were seen? *Surely no one would stop them from trying to prevent tampering in the Caverns*, she insisted to herself. But that also depended on someone being willing to listen to the real reason why they were sneaking off in the night.

The person in the hallway passed, and they were off running again. Vhalla focused on her prince as they spiraled down stairs within an outer wall of the palace. She couldn't fathom the darkness that was determined to creep back into his mind. There was no doubt in Vhalla's mind that he considered his current circumstances as some sort of delayed justice, given how his mind worked.

Her chest ached for the man she followed out onto the snowy ground of the stables. They ran through the white moonlight. Colors were bleached from the world, and her toes already felt cold. A stablehand was startled into action by their presence.

"My prince?" The young girl blinked at him. Her eyes drifted over to Vhalla and they widened. Her mouth fell open.

"We need two horses; they should be already tacked in those stalls," Aldrik demanded, pointing.

"Not your mount, my lord?"

"No, I need those," he affirmed impatiently.

The Western girl's dark eyes looked between the two of them. She closed her mouth and a sly, knowing smirk spread across her features that she couldn't successfully hide as she departed to do Aldrik's bidding.

Vhalla panted softly, cursing the girl. She thought it was some scandal, the prince and Windwalker running off in the night.

"Mother, what's taking her so long?" Aldrik squinted in the direction the girl departed.

"Aldrik," Vhalla whispered gently. She placed a palm on his upper arm to reassure him. The fabric of his shirt was coarser than she was used to, and it moved strangely in the moonlight. He practically jumped away at her touch.

"Don't!" His sudden and intense anger directed at her was startling. "Now isn't the time, Vhalla."

She frowned, preparing to tell him off for his tone when the girl came back with their horses. They were tall with long legs and lean, ropey muscle. Aldrik checked the saddlebags on his mount, fumbling inside them a moment before swinging into his saddle.

Vhalla followed suit, deciding to let his snappishness slide given the pressure they were under as they rode out into the snowy night.

Vhalla glanced over her shoulder. She saw the castle ethereally shimmering in gold and white moonlight. She wished she had the ability to enjoy the beautiful scene that stretched before her, sparkling with the first snow of winter. But now was not the time for enjoyment.

Breath from the horses and humans let out small white puffs of steam into the night-time air. The houses passed in a blur. On occasion, some late-night wanderer or drunk would be startled as the couple raced by. But for the most part, potential observers were safely tucked in their beds.

They rode the most direct route down through the city and out the main gate. The dense buildings of the capital faded as they proceeded down the mountain. Aldrik turned north at the fork and, after a short stretch, they veered off for a more western headway.

A thin layer of clouds blotted out the moon, shifting and rolling the shadows of the world into a fluctuating state of darkness. Vhalla blinked her eyes, squinting through the dim twilight. Aldrik continued without fear or hesitation.

The barren trees fractured the sky above them like the lead of a macabre stained glass. Silence was their only company, moonlight their only guide. The world darkened again, and snow began to fall.

"We're lucky," he finally spoke.

"We are?" Vhalla asked, slowing her horse alongside his to give the animal a rest.

"With this much snow, our tracks should be covered," he explained.

"Does anyone know where we are going?" she thought aloud.

Aldrik looked startled a moment. "Yes."

"Then why would we want our tracks to be—" she began softly musing.

"Because we only want the *right* people to know," Aldrik spoke over her. "I can't just tell anyone we're headed for the Caverns, given their history."

"Of course." She glanced over at him. His jaw was clenched tight. "Aldrik, don't worry."

"Worry?"

"Well, yes." Vhalla shifted the reins in her hands. "I know that since it's the Crystal Caverns, you must be worried. But this isn't your fault. Last time really wasn't either. But this truly is not."

"I know," he said thoughtfully. "This is Victor's fault. But then again, I shouldn't have let such a powerful sorcerer go so unchecked."

"You couldn't have known."

"I should have." Aldrik frowned. "He was my mentor. We experienced the same thing as boys. I should have known. I should have put a stop to you working with crystals with him."

"I should've done it myself." Whatever Victor truly intended, she'd enabled it. Vhalla began to question everything the minister had ever told her. "Doesn't he see? All that's there is death."

"No, all that's there is power," Aldrik corrected. Vhalla considered the strange comment as the prince continued. "Neither good, nor evil, it's the hearts of men that turn a weapon into the tool of a knight or a butcher."

"How far is it?" His manner was making her abnormally uneasy, and Vhalla was eager to change the topic. Something about the night air and the stillness was starting to get to her nerves.

"It can take slow riders two days." He remained fixated on a distant point of the horizon.

"Two days?" They didn't have rations or supplies for a journey of that length.

"But these horses were bred for speed and endurance in the mountains. We can push them. I hope to arrive before dawn."

"How long ago did Victor leave?" She tried to remember how Aldrik said he'd known the minister had ridden off to the Caverns.

"Only an hour or two," he answered confidently.

"Perhaps we could intercept him before he gets there," she mused hopefully.

"Perhaps."

Vhalla resisted the parrot comment in the wake of something dawning on her. "Wait, how could you have known when Victor left? Didn't you only just go to his office before coming to me?"

"Someone else had mentioned seeing him."

Something still wasn't settling right. "But if Victor only left an hour or two before us, shouldn't we see trac—"

The reverberation of a low horn echoed through the mountains, sounding through the still forest. Vhalla turned. The palace and capital city was out of sight, but the sound was unmistakable.

"They know," he whispered. "Damn it, we should have had more time!"

Aldrik snapped his horse back to a run. Vhalla followed suit, her body tense. *If they were trying to save everyone from the Caverns, then why did it feel like they were fugitives in the night?*

"Can't we wait for more help?" she called, catching up to him. "We should be close to Victor now!"

"No!" Aldrik barked. "If they catch up to you and me, what do you think will happen?"

"I don't—"

"Think!" He waited for her to fill in the blank.

"Your father?"

"Who else?" Aldrik frowned and looked forward, pushing his heels into the horse.

"What will he do?" Vhalla wondered if she would ever be able to return to the palace.

"I don't know, Vhalla." Aldrik's voice was high and tense.

"He said nothing?" she asked, baffled the prince could go back into the company of his father and not know. The Emperor always seemed to be proud of his proclamations when it came to pulling them apart or conceiving some ill-designed fate for her. She had fully expected him to torment Aldrik with the knowledge.

"I don't know, and I don't want to speak on it!" He glared at her. "We have other things to worry about."

"What's wrong with you, Aldrik?" she exclaimed as they dashed through the night. "What did I do to make you lash out at me so?"

Aldrik stared at her, his mouth parted slightly. He closed it, and a gentle expression overtook his brow, even if his eyes still seemed guarded and distant. She relaxed some just seeing it, feeling a twinge of guilt at being so aggressive toward him in the wake of his grief.

"I'm sorry, Vhalla," he sighed. "Too much has gone on, and I need to do this. I need to focus right now."

Vhalla understood what *this* could be, what it likely meant for him. This was his chance to redeem himself. To protect the world from an evil that he had once aided in setting free. They were grieving, tired, and now hunted. Nothing made sense in the world anymore.

"I'm sorry for snapping," she apologized as well.

"I need your trust." He caught her eyes. "Please, tonight, just trust me."

"Always," she replied easily.

"More than anyone?" Aldrik asked.

"More than anyone." She forced a smile, hoping to encourage him.

Aldrik nodded, and they rode on through the soundless woods.

Eventually, the trees grew thinner as they began to ascend out of the valley. It was a slow slope upward, and Vhalla hardly noticed they were heading up a mountain until it was already upon them. They had ridden hard through the night; the horses were beginning to struggle with the pace.

Aldrik had not said a word for hours. He hardly even looked at her. There was no sign of pursuers, and yet they rode as if a pack of wolves were on their tail. The heavily falling snow was slowly covering their tracks. Even if the Emperor had caught wind of his only remaining son running off with the Windwalker, he wouldn't assume that they'd head for the Crystal Caverns.

Her horse lost its footing for a moment as its hoof slipped on some ice. Vhalla couldn't stop a call of surprise, and she tugged hard on the reins to right the steed. The mountain path was thin with a sheer edge on one side. Vhalla looked down and realized they had already ascended quite far.

"Are you all right?" Worry marred Aldrik's brow.

"I am." Her racing heart indicated differently.

"Let's take it a little slower. This path is not well maintained, and it can be a little treacherous in good conditions." He pulled back on his mount's reins. "We're close now; it's not much farther."

The sun began to rise. The concealing snow clouds finally began to lighten and fade into gray patches across the blood-red sky. Vhalla took a deep breath.

"There!" He pointed up ahead. "There's his horse."

The path curved around the mountain and eventually reached a small cliff area. Set into the mountain face was a large, pointed archway, carved directly into the stone. It was a gaping hole that was taller than thirty men on each other's shoulders. Vhalla squinted and made out a horse standing before it in the hazy dawn.

"We have to hurry!" she called back.

"Carefully!" Aldrik replied, and they increased their pace as much as possible, inching around the mountain wall.

The massive entrance to the Crystal Caverns made Vhalla feel even smaller as she pulled her steed to a stop before it. It felt like the gaping maw of a dragon that was ready to swallow her whole. The stone sculptures of wyrms and gods that guarded the archway had to have been ancient, and yet they looked as though they had been polished to perfection that morning. Vhalla dismounted in awe.

Aldrik grabbed a pack from his saddlebag after dismounting, slinging it over his shoulder. "We need to go. We're close now."

"Right . . ." Vhalla was frozen in place. There was an epic and wild power and it sizzled against her magic. A primordial essence hung heavy in the air and warned her about crossing the threshold between her world and the Gods'.

Aldrik paused, something out of the corner of his eye catching his interest. He dashed over to the edge of the cliff and looked down. Raising a hand, he shielded his eyes from the rising sun, squinting at the horizon. Vhalla followed his stare. Six riders were barely visible at the edge of the valley.

"We need to go!" He turned and started running for the entrance.

Vhalla dashed after him, plunging herself into the Crystal Caverns. The darkness was dizzying after they entered. The advent of the sunrise could not penetrate the heavy atmosphere that now shrouded her.

Aldrik was one step ahead of the darkness and produced a crystal. Vhalla lost the opportunity to ask how or why he carried such a thing as it flashed a brilliant turquoise. He placed it carefully in the center of the pathway where they had been walking. Like water, magic rippled outward from the small stone and into the floor they stood on. Its glimmering pulse stretched forward, branching out at points and creeping up the walls like magical vines.

The Caverns had to rival the palace in size. A pathway had been cut into the center that led forward through another smaller gateway. Giant towering crystal columns lit up the space. The roof glowed the same pale greenish-blue.

Vhalla was reminded of the ruins from which she had pilfered Achel. It was a cosmos of magic, sparkling infinitely before her. The shining colors bled from one crystal to the next in magical conversation. Vhalla could see dark pockmarks from where men had tried to claim powers from the cavern.

"There's no time." Aldrik strode forward, and she fell into place behind him.

Vhalla clenched her fists, opening her Channel. The crystals surrounding her compounded her magic, making it greater than she had ever felt. She tried to brace herself for any surprises that could lurk around any corner, and she prayed she would be ready.

CHAPTER 24

VHALLA SHIVERED. IN the dim light, the puffs of air marking her breaths almost looked magical as they dissipated through her cracked lips. It was a long night after long days, but she felt awake and alert.

"Are you all right?" Vhalla asked. "Are the crystals affecting you?"

"They are, but I will be fine. We won't need much time." His voice was low and garbled; the light shifted strangely over his shoulders.

They crossed through a small archway into a different antechamber. The glowing light followed their movement, and the crystals responded to her footsteps in silent welcome. Vhalla searched for the place where Victor may be hiding, but she couldn't find anything. It seemed a straight shot, almost like how a temple would lead to the Mother's pyre.

Vhalla stretched out her magical hearing, but she couldn't even hear breathing.

Aldrik stopped before a massive door. It radiated a similar power to what Vhalla had felt in the North, though deeper and stronger. Crystals had grown overtop it, resisting the glow that had been following Vhalla and Aldrik in shining protest.

"I need you to open those," Aldrik ordered.

"Why?"

"Do you want me to risk touching crystals further?" he snapped.

"Oh . . . of course," Vhalla mumbled. She started for the doors, her feet heavier with every step. Vhalla paused, her hand a breath from the crystal.

"What are you waiting for?" Aldrik growled. "Open it."

"This-this is the barrier, isn't it?" She turned and took a long, hard look at the man who had taken her to the threshold of fate.

He froze.

"Victor couldn't have gone farther than here. He hasn't . . ." Now that she was here, the idea that Victor could open the barrier because he was a Waterrunner like Egmun seemed asinine. *This was a greater magic.* "Let's go back the way we came." Vhalla tried to sound casual. "Maybe we missed Victor along the way. We can wait outside."

She took a step, which he met with force and speed. His hand closed around her bare wrist, painfully tight. An agonizing feeling sunk through her suddenly shaking bones as her stomach plummeted from her body.

"Aldrik, your hands are cold," she whispered in horror. She had relished in the hot lightning of his touch too many times to be mistaken when the fire was suddenly absent. She had learned to love her prince for all he was, for how the fire in his veins gave light to his passions and an inferno to his anger. *Nothing about him was ever cold.* "Let me go."

He began to laugh slowly. The unfamiliar icy fingers bit deep into her flesh. The noise echoed disjointedly from his body, not belonging to the lips they emerged from.

Vhalla tugged hard against his grip. "Let me go!" She withdrew a hand, frozen in horror as Aldrik's face rippled, dissipating like steam.

"No, I don't think so, my little Windwalker." Victor's voice, cool and calculating, it echoed through her worst nightmares come to life. "Do you know how long I have bided my time? Waiting, *waiting!* Everything has been going according to plan, and you will not take this from me now."

Victor cast away the last of his meticulously crafted illusion like a snake shedding its skin. The man grinned triumphantly, revealing a malicious glee.

Vhalla screamed and raised her hand. Victor produced a crystal from his pocket, slamming it into the base of her neck, setting her to sputtering. Ice crackled around it, making a collar around her throat, alight with Channel-blocking crystal magic.

She coughed at the shock of the cold. Her magic may be gone, but her fight wasn't. Vhalla raked her nails across his cheek.

Victor took the hit, laughing gleefully. "Is that any way to treat your mentor?"

"You are not my mentor!" she screamed through the ice biting her neck.

"Petulant bitch." He shoved her against the crystal barrier blocking the door.

Light exploded behind her eyes as the crystals forcefully extracted power from her. Victor's magic assaulted her Channels, and Vhalla felt like nothing more than a funnel for his will. His abilities as a Waterrunner shone through, and he pushed the magic out of her, into the crystal barrier at her back, beseeching it to open for his dark desires.

The world shattered, and Vhalla collapsed limply, her skin awash in the magic of crystals. Victor braced her as he watched the doors swing open before them.

"You dumb child," he hummed, throwing her numb body over his shoulder. It felt as if part of her had been ripped out, and all that remained was frayed seams. "Did you really believe he, of all people, would bring you here?"

The world buzzed, and Vhalla's eyes lost their focus.

"Only his magic would lower the barrier. Magic that Egmun had to use to restore the barrier because of his lovely, late mother." Victor threw her onto the ground. Vhalla's head cracked against the stone, and she groaned, attempting to roll onto her knees. "Oh, don't even try it."

Ice coated her hands and feet, holding her in place.

"You see, I had no idea how I was going to get him here given his disposition toward the place. But I had you, at least, and from the moment I knew what you were, I made sure the Emperor would only really trust *me* with your care. That meant promising him whatever he wanted to hear, but if you tell the man the sun shines from his ass, he will love you." Victor dropped the pack and began rummaging through it.

"But then, while I waited and tried to sort out Aldrik, you gave me the greatest gift of all." Victor laughed wildly. "A Bond! A Bond with the *crown prince*! You had his magic in you all along, it was right there, ripe for the taking."

"You-you lied to me . . ." she wheezed weakly, struggling to regain her awareness.

"You love the prince of lies and yet are surprised by them?" Victor roared with amusement. He produced more crystals, laying them carefully around her prone form.

"What you are doing will fail; it always fails."

"Don't lump me in with the incompetent fools who are so hungry for power that they are blinded by it. I am of a far greater stock. Egmun thought he could take this power, but he didn't have you." Victor caressed her cheek.

Vhalla spit at him. "I will kill you," she swore through chattering teeth.

"Will you?" Victor grinned. "I would certainly love to see that."

"I will." Vhalla's lips were beginning to turn blue and tremble. "*I promise.*"

"That would be impressive, as this place will soon become your tomb."

Vhalla looked around, her eyes finally focused enough to take in the space. She recognized the floor instantly. Spiraling out from her body were markings, and embedded into the stone was what she once thought were shards of glass when she had witnessed them in Aldrik's memory, but now knew to be crystals. *She was in the same spot Aldrik had made his first kill.*

Her fingers and toes screamed in pain from the ice surrounding them. She knew the next step would be numbness, and then they would turn black and die. Vhalla fought against the crystal around her throat, now burning her magic.

"You should be pleased." Victor produced the axe from his bag, the axe she had cleaned for him so that no other magic would interfere with his diabolical plan. "You're going to help bring in a new world order. Didn't we say we believed in the same things? Didn't you say you wanted peace? To not be hunted."

"You can't buy peace with war!" she screamed.

"Kill everyone who opposes you; what other peace is there?" Victor set down the axe by her and returned to the bag.

Vhalla struggled futilely to break the ice around her hands. *If she could just get the axe.* She stilled as she saw Victor produce a shining crown made of pure crystal. The last tool he had brought with him.

"What is that?"

"Beautiful, isn't it?" Victor held it up in appreciation. "The crown of the first king of this continent. It's traded hands quite a few times and was the hardest thing for me to track down. Honestly, harder than finding a Windwalker. King Jadar had it for a while, and the Knights are good at making crystal artifacts fall off the face of the earth. But, eventually, it returned South thanks to one of the old Southern Kings. No one thought to look in the most obvious place for it! A few dozen records back and I only had a few treasure halls to sift through."

"You're mad."

"Oh, Vhalla." He returned to her side. "The line between genius and madness is so very thin. Really, it all exists in the same grey area." Victor boldly placed the crown upon his head. "I fear, my dear, that you must die without ever seeing my new world order. But know that your death will build a society that favors sorcerers for eons to come."

Vhalla heard the echoes of stones bouncing down the

mountainside. A horse's whinny echoed through the Caverns. Victor stilled, looking through the doors she had opened and down the long stretch of crystals to the main entrance.

"I think we will have an audience for my ascension." Victor smiled, turning.

A tall shadow stood in the entryway, the sunlight burning at his back. Vhalla struggled to lift her head, squinting to prove without a doubt what the frantic beats of her heart already knew.

"Aldrik!" she screamed at the top of her lungs. Her high-pitched, desperate call carried across the walls and out to her prince.

"Vhalla!" he roared in tortured and broken agony. His voice was as deep and dark as midnight, and Vhalla wondered how she could have fallen for Victor's pathetic impression of it.

"It seems you shall be the first Solaris to die by my hand!" Victor beamed and turned to face the inferno that roared toward them.

The Caverns were quickly illuminated with the burning rage of the crown prince.

CHAPTER 25

STEAM FILLED THE Caverns as Aldrik's flames met an ice barrier and vaporized it. He threw out an arm, sending another blaze in quick succession. Victor blocked it with a surge of magic, the crystals in the crown on his head flashing brightly to amplify his powers.

"Are you not happy to see me?" Victor japed.

"Let her go!" Aldrik skidded to a stop, bracing himself, and Vhalla pressed her eyes closed for the next wave of heat. The fire was so great that it sent explosive shockwaves through the Caverns.

"You always were the wild one! Running in head-first, not thinking, letting your emotions and that unstoppable rage of yours get the better of you," Victor bated.

Aldrik reacted quickly to the ice that formed beneath his feet. A spiral of flame swirled about him, blocking any further attempts to freeze him in place.

"Aldrik!" Vhalla cried, hoping he would hear her over the din of the flames. "Free me!" She struggled against the ice that held her. If she could get free, she could get the axe and remove the crystal blocking her sorcery. Victor was strong and bloated on magic-altering crystals, but Vhalla doubted he would be able to handle them both at once.

The prince's fire vanished at her words, and Aldrik looked, really looked, for the first time past Victor. Vhalla witnessed his rage deepen upon seeing her entrapped. He threw out a hand.

At first, his fire was a welcomed warmth. Like the familiar caress of an old lover or well-known friend. It weakened the ice and melted it around her. *Victor wasn't the only one who was trained to leverage the crystals*, and Aldrik's magic could stand toe-to-toe with the minister's.

But warmth quickly turned to heat and then to agony as Vhalla was burned for the first time by Aldrik's flames.

The ice vanished from around her, removing the barrier between flame and skin. She rolled on the floor, trying to snuff out the blaze. Every nerve in her body screamed in unison, alerting her to a blisteringly hot agony that seared across her flesh until it bubbled.

The moment her screams echoed through Aldrik's ears, the flames vanished. Victor turned curiously, and both men seemed to be stunned out of their assault upon each other by the woman sobbing and rolling on the floor. Vhalla tried to catch her breath, but her skin was alive with red-hot burns. Everything hurt; it was a pain beyond all previous thresholds, and she saw stars behind her eyes.

Victor a few steps toward her. He stared down at her writhing form. There was interest alight in his eyes at her pain.

"Vhalla, *Vhalla!*" Aldrik began running once more. He sprinted through the first archway into the antechamber just before the inner-most sanctum of the Caverns. Vhalla opened her eyes weakly. In a moment of desperation, she reached out to him. Victor stepped upon her hand, crunching her fingers with a twist of his boot and drawing a scream from her lips.

Aldrik was just at the doorway when a thick wall of ice covered it, stretching out from the crystals Victor had placed around the doorway. It was solid and almost perfectly transparent. Aldrik slammed into it hard, his momentum forcing him to collide. He bared his teeth, banging his fists against it. He tried to burn his way through but the ice repaired itself as quickly as he could conjure flames to expel it. Aldrik punched it with a cry of frustration, blood smearing against the wall.

"You fool," Victor chided darkly. "You would burn her alive in your rage." Aldrik's jaw was so tense Vhalla could almost hear his teeth cracking. "Everything you love, or that makes the mistake of loving you, dies. Doesn't it?"

Aldrik gave a cry and tried again to destroy the wall. Crystals around the doorway glowed with the same light as Victor's crown, responding to the madman's will and foiling the prince's best efforts.

Vhalla stared at the ceiling, trying to piece together the world as it crumbled and fell into the howling winds of change that now blew around them. *His fire had burned her.* "The Bond . . ."

"What?" Victor spun and looked at her.

Even Aldrik stopped his assault on the barrier for a moment. His shoulders heaved with his rough breaths from the magical exertion and stress.

The barrier had needed Aldrik's magic to open it. When the young prince had opened it all those years before for Egmun, he had certainly exhausted himself, but his Channel would have begun supplying him with more magic instantly so long as it hadn't been completely depleted. But, Vhalla did not have an endless supply as he had.

The Bond had given her Aldrik's magic, but Vhalla knew what power she had of his had been completely exhausted when Victor forced it out of her. Vhalla turned to Aldrik, tears welling up in her eyes. If a Channel could be blocked by exhausting a sorcerer's magic and a Bond was nothing more than a Channel between two people, then it *could* break if the magic was completely ripped out of one person all at once.

"Oh, I see." Victor blinked and tilted his head, glancing from Aldrik to her. He leaned in close to Vhalla's face. "Why, *Lady* Yarl, it seems I have done you a grand favor. I cannot find one ugly trace of the crown prince's magic on you."

With a cry, Vhalla ripped off the crystal at her throat, the ice taking strips of skin with it. Victor allowed her, confident to the point of arrogance that she would not be a threat to him, even with her magic. Vhalla shifted her vision and stared at her hand, knowing what to look for. It was void of any of the brilliance that Aldrik was swathed in. The one shining hope that Vhalla had was that she could see traces of her magic still within him.

"Aldrik, why don't you have a look for yourself?"

Aldrik glared darkly at the minister in reply. She was not sure if she had ever seen him look so bloodthirsty before.

"Oh, wait, that's right. Magical sight was yet another thing that you just couldn't excel at wasn't it?" The minister laughed and turned away. "You think you are so strong, but you are just a wildfire. You destroy everything in your path without restraint—"

"I will destroy you!" Aldrik proclaimed, suddenly looking behind him. "Za, Sehra!"

An arrow with Za's fletching pierced Victor's barrier. Runes like Vhalla had seen in the North spread out from the arrowhead and fractured the crystal-magic infused ice. Aldrik's flame burst through behind it, shattering what had kept him out.

Vhalla rolled away as Aldrik lunged, an inferno. She clenched her fists, feeling for scraps of her magic. She was still exhausted, and the abuse of opening the barrier was raw, but she wasn't letting herself sit helpless.

"You damn the world for a throne!" Aldrik shouted.

"Not for a throne." Victor dodged a flaming fist and shifted the air around him, the illusion hiding his movements as he got the upper hand on Aldrik's next attack. "For the world, for *our* world. It will be a new order; the Commons will finally see that we are not ones to be put beneath their feet to lift them higher in status. Never will a sorcerer be mocked or feel the need to hide. No, our magic comes from the Gods themselves! Commons will kneel before us and cower at our wrath."

Vhalla's eyes fell on the axe. She scrambled to her feet and reached out a hand, summoning the wind to bring it to her.

Another arrow pierced the air and sunk into her shoulder. Vhalla stumbled and fell, her magic faltering in the shock of pain. Vhalla turned to see Za notching another arrow from farther back in the Caverns. *The woman was shooting to kill.*

"Traitor!" Aldrik turned his fire to the Northern woman.

Sehra held up a hand and blocked the flame with a glittering of sigils in the air.

Victor capitalized on the confusion, grabbing the axe for himself. Vhalla struggled to her feet, ripping the arrow from her shoulder with a cry. Victor moved before Aldrik, Sehra, or Za could turn their attention back to their real enemy.

The axe cut effortlessly through her, severing Vhalla from shoulder to sternum. She coughed up blood, spitting it onto Victor. The axe shone brilliantly, as if satisfied its purpose was finally being fulfilled.

The crystals that Victor had carefully placed on the floor sparked to life, and the minister gripped her, holding her impaled on the weapon. Vhalla blinked blearily, blood pouring from the mortal wound. *Aldrik had said she would die.*

Magic lit up Victor's arm, arcing from axe to crown. It was the same feeling as the barrier, a leeching, a pull. But this time, it was on her magic itself. Victor drained her of the well of power that existed within her. He siphoned it off, storing it into the crown that shone brightly on his head.

By the time the axe finally dimmed, Vhalla was one shade away from death, and he dropped her husk to the floor. The crystal weapon turned dark, like obsidian, and fractured under its own weight. The room was alight, every crystal shining brightly in the same hum as Victor's crown.

"It is done," Victor spoke in the aftermath, his words echoing through her fading consciousness. "It is done!"

Aldrik raced to her side, scooping her up into his arms. Vhalla's head rolled against his shoulder, unable to support it any longer.

"Flee, flee!" Victor laughed, picking up a crystal. He crushed it in his fist, the magic coursing through his flesh with a flash of light. The Caverns yielded themselves to him. "But there's nowhere you can hide!"

The large stone doors began to close, and Aldrik slipped through them, leaving Victor behind. Vhalla tried to bring her eyes to focus, the world racing around her.

"Sehra." Za supported the magically exhausted princess, calling her name.

Aldrik ignored them and continued for the exit.

A loud explosion burst from behind them as Victor emerged from the doors without effort. Aldrik stumbled and slid behind a crystal, holding her to him.

"Aldrik, I'm sorry, I'm sorry . . ." she sputtered.

"Quiet," he begged with terror-filled eyes.

Vhalla watched as he grimaced and gripped the crystal next to him. His eyes flashed an unnerving red as Aldrik used crystal magic to build a stone cocoon around them. Vhalla closed her eyes, leaning against her prince for what she expected to be the last time.

The crystal shone as Victor departed, the magic fleeing as if being drawn into its master. A deep rumbling began to echo up from the depths of the Caverns. The crystals' brilliance began to fade, spiderweb fractures overcoming their pristine surfaces.

"Vhalla, don't do this," Aldrik pleaded, ignoring the world ending around them. "I need you. Don't leave me, my lady, *my love*."

She didn't respond, and the prince opened his mouth to let out the sound of his heart breaking.

CHAPTER 26

THICK FURS WERE piled atop Vhalla, and bandages were wound tight around her chest and shoulder. There was pain, but none too great, and sleep sat heavy upon the tops of her closed eyelids. She stirred in the hazy dawn she should not have been able to greet, pulled from sleep by the long fingers weaving themselves gently through her hair.

Aldrik stared down at her. A silent, relieved breath huffed across her face as a disbelieving smile crossed his mouth. His warm fingers stroked down to hold her cheek. He leaned forward.

It was a dream. She had died and walked in the faraway lands.

His lips pressed firmly upon her forehead. They were hot and soft, and his breath ruffled her hair as his body shifted closer to hers beneath the blankets. It was too wonderful a feeling to be real.

She forced together her last memories. *The Crystal Caverns, the fruition of Victor's plans, Aldrik's rush to her side.* Vhalla inhaled sharply and felt an aching in her ribs. The wound that severed her from shoulder to chest, the wound he had foretold would kill her. Vhalla remembered the warmth of his body holding her as she slipped away from the land of the living.

"Vhalla," he whispered, just barely audible. "How do you feel?"

"I'm dead, aren't I?"

Death was fitting. It had been because of her foolishness that Victor accessed the Crystal Caverns. The taint would be unleashed upon the world once more. Men and beasts would be twisted into monsters in addition to whatever great powers Victor had so clearly gained. She regretted so many of her actions, but the greatest ache was knowing that she had brought death upon the world and would never have the chance to fix it.

"My Vhalla, open your eyes and look at me." She obliged, trading her guilt for the visage of the crown prince. "You are not dead."

"But I . . ." She moved her good arm, wincing at the lightest touch on the bandage over her shoulder. "How?"

"You gave me life once; I gave it back," Aldrik breathed, nuzzling her neck lovingly.

"I don't understand." Vhalla frowned.

"Quiet." Aldrik glanced across her. "Or else you will wake them up, and I will be forced to share you prematurely."

"Them?" Vhalla asked. Her body was stiff and ached as she tried to lift her head. Fresh skin pulled taut under the bandages, and Vhalla was careful of her healing body.

It was a small room occupied by five others sleeping cramped upon the floor. On the other side of Aldrik, the feet of the ever-tall Jax poked out from under the blankets that he had effectively cocooned around his head. Elecia slept with her mouth open, her limbs spread wide and her breathing heavy. Cuddled closely to the woman and to Vhalla's immediate left was a messy-haired man; words could not describe the immense relief that filled her at the sight of him.

However, huddled in the corner were two people that Vhalla had never expected to see: Za was propped up against the wall, the princess clutched tightly against her. Vhalla scowled, remembering the arrow that had been shot for her heart.

Aldrik's arm tightened around her, and Vhalla allowed him to pull her back down onto the straw and woolen pallet that covered the floor. She looked to him in confusion.

"What happened?" she rephrased her demand, keeping her voice low. There was seemingly no possible explanation for how she was alive or in the company she now kept.

Her eyes scanned the room once more. There was one window, though it did not appear to have glass. Shutters were pulled over it, which did little to keep out the icy cold. The walls were well made, but a rough construction of cut logs layered upon each other, with river clay packed between to keep out the draft. There was no ornamentation. Nothing showed the careful hand of a craftsman. Even the small table and wardrobe looked to be slightly off-level, the rough edges having been smoothed from the oil produced by the rubbing of fingertips over sandpaper.

"Grahm found Fritz after he saw you leaving with Victor."

"But Victor—"

"As a Waterrunner, Grahm saw through the illusion," Aldrik preempted her question. "Fritz got Elecia, who went to me." His dark eyes glanced toward the corner, his voice dropping again. "They were unexpected and insistent additions."

"But Sehra knows about the crystals," Vhalla filled in logically.

Aldrik nodded, continuing," When Victor left the Caverns, he collapsed the entry, leaving us for dead. Luckily, Elecia was waiting with Jax and Fritz. Fritz could hide them with his own illusion, and Elecia managed to reopen the Caverns."

"But, how did I . . ." Vhalla could piece together the events that led Aldrik to the Crystal Caverns and how *he* managed to escape alive. *But he hadn't had a wound from shoulder to chest.*

"You were weak, dying."

"I was dead," she corrected morbidly.

Aldrik didn't argue that point. "Elecia couldn't heal you; there wasn't enough life left in you for her magic to mend. So I returned to you the life you gave me."

"The Bond," Vhalla breathed, realizing while his magic had been taken from her when the barrier fell, her magic had still lived on within him.

"It was enough, thank the Mother, for your body to accept her healing." Aldrik's hands were back to touching her, as though he needed to reaffirm each second that she was real.

"Aldrik, giving me back the magic I used to form the Bond with you could've killed you." Vhalla gripped him with her good hand. "What were you thinking?"

"That I wouldn't be able to face the world without you by my side." The prince's proclamation held no hesitation or thought beyond instinct. "Vhalla, I—" His words stuck. "I need you to know that how you are now has no bearing on what I feel for you."

"How I am?" Vhalla repeated, the moment too serious to merit a parrot comment.

"Victor took all your magic. It blocked your Channel like an Eradication . . . The magic of the Bond was enough to give you a spark of life and get Elecia's healing to take. But it was only a spark . . ."

"I'm a Commons now, aren't I?" Aldrik's pained expression told her everything.

There was a time when that was all she wanted, and now the knowledge threatened to crush her. She remembered the pull of achel, of Victor using his magic as a Waterrunner combined with the crystals to steal her magic. *It was all gone.*

Panic welled up in her and threatened to burn her eyes. She wanted to scream and shout and rave like a lunatic. Her magic was gone and it now sat in the hands of the most wicked creature she'd ever met. The thing that had been the catalyst for so much in her life over the past two years had vanished as though it had never been there. It was so unfair.

Vhalla pressed her lips together and let the moment wash over her. She let the panic fizzle and die without being given life by escaping between her lips. Her heart shattered into pieces that would be put back together in a new shape. She had lost her magic. But she lived to fight another day.

"Victor—" Aldrik spat the word with an instant malice. "Victor took everything. That bastard stole your magic from you. Curse him, damn him, fu—"

"Aldrik," Vhalla cut off his justified tirade. Nothing could be solved with his rage or her panic; all it would result in was waking everyone else. He conceded, the anger vanishing just with a look. "I understand. And you have yet to tell me, are you all right?"

"What?" Aldrik blinked.

"Are you all right?" She moved her own fingers to touch his beautifully high cheekbones. Her hands were now in further contrast to the flawless alabaster of his skin. She had raised and ugly scars covering her fingers, the skin stretched thin to the point of shining. *Burn scars from his fire.* "The Bond, the magic, when you gave it back, did it hurt you?"

"Vhalla." His brow softened, and his eyes widened. "How, why, *why* do you worry for me when you have lost so much?"

She smiled softly into the morning chill. He didn't understand the precious thing that still clutched her.

"Will my magic return?"

"Not without enough of your own magic to call to your Channel and activate it once more. Usually, it would take a vessel. But, we never made one for you. The only ones you ever created were unintentional and sent to me, and that magic has been exhausted. I'm certain Victor had a hand in seeing that overlooked, I should have—"

She spoke again, stopping him before he fell back into anger and self-hating, "Then that's that. And the Bond can never be reformed."

Even if she still possessed her magic, that fact would likely remain true from what she now knew of Bonds. It was not worth their lives to try to rebuild it. Sorrow threatened to consume her again and Vhalla vowed not to let it. The Bond may be gone, but he was still her prince. She did not need to feel his emotions magically to know he blamed himself when that was the last thing he should be doing.

"But I live," she breathed in disbelief. "I live, and you live, because of you. Aldrik, you are amazing."

"Aldrik," came a sharp whisper. "Are you awake?"

"Yes, Elecia."

"What's the . . ." Fritz rubbed his eyes, sitting. He looked at Elecia first, but it only took half a second for his head to snap over to Vhalla's and his eyes to become twice their normal size. "*Vhal!*"

With a straight arm, Fritz gave a shove to Aldrik's shoulder to push him aside. Fritz's hand fell across Vhalla's stomach, his palm on her pallet. He was sitting next to her before the flurry of blankets had time to land across the room. Fritz completely ignored the offended scowl coming from the prince. His bright blue eyes were glued to hers.

"You're alive!" Fritz almost shouted after a long moment of staring at her.

"You doubted me?" Elecia huffed in mock offense.

"I am." Vhalla struggled to sit, scooting up under Fritz's arm. "How do you feel?"

"Like I just had an axe in my shoulder." Vhalla brought her left hand across her chest, lightly massaging the bandages that lurked beneath the oversized shirt she wore.

"Sleeping beauty wakes." Jax roused and sat up on the opposite side of Aldrik.

Vhalla's eyes fell on the two Northern women in the corner. They had been woken by the commotion and regarded the Imperials with guarded attention. Vhalla's lips pursed at Za. Vhalla knew that if Za posed a direct threat to her life, Aldrik would allow the archer nowhere near her. But that only made the woman's presence all the more confusing.

"Let me see, Vhalla." Elecia walked over. It was now Fritz's turn to be unceremoniously shoved aside to make room for Elecia to access Vhalla's chest.

"Yes, why don't you take off your shirt and let us see?" Jax cocked his head to the side with a crooked grin. The action caused a cascade of perfectly straight black hair to slip over one shoulder and fall just below his pectorals.

"Jax." Aldrik gave a low growl.

He smiled sweetly. "What, my prince?"

"You know what."

"I don't think I do." Jax snickered.

"Boys." Elecia clicked her tongue. "I was serious; I wish to check her. All of you, out."

"*All* of us?" Fritz pouted. It was his turn to earn a warning—and slightly confused—stare from Aldrik.

Vhalla bit her bottom lip as she tried to hide a tiny grin, remembering her friend's delicate hand in helping her wash up after Baldair's death. The memory wiped any levity from her face fairly quickly. Like ice in her veins, the younger prince's untimely demise sobered her.

"*All* of you, yes." Elecia sighed and shook her head.

Aldrik stood, as if to lead by example. Vhalla was relieved when the two Northerners followed him as well.

"Now, off with the shirt," Elecia demanded the second the last of them had vanished through the curtain that served as a door into the unknown room beyond. Vhalla blinked at the other woman, startled by her directness. "I know you're hardly modest, and it's nothing I, or the older girls, haven't already seen."

"Older girls?" Vhalla paused, halfway done with unbuttoning the front of the oversized shirt, a shirt she had never seen before. Her movements were still painfully slow.

"Fritz's sisters," Elecia elaborated. "After Aldrik was a reckless idiot and nearly killed himself giving you the magic back—"

"Nearly killed himself?"

"Yes." Elecia scowled. "I will never forgive you for making him the reckless fool that he's been."

Vhalla had no retort.

"When I saw the mountain wall sliding to close up the Caverns, I thought you all were dead. But, no, you were alive and, despite dodging fate once more, Aldrik was determined to save you. After Aldrik gave you the Bond magic back, he collapsed, and I could do *nothing*. The princess was equally spent doing . . . whatever she does with her Northern magic. We couldn't ride back to the capital in such a condition." Elecia's words spilled out. "Luckily, Fritz could navigate us here. You were a bloody mess, more than anything I had ever tried to heal, and Aldrik wouldn't wake for a whole day, leaving me to guess if he would ever wake again—I thought he was dead because of you!"

"Elecia . . . I'm sorry." The other woman's pain was sudden and intense.

"First, it was Baldair, and I couldn't, I wasn't fast enough to get there." Elecia balled a fist in the blankets. "Then I thought I lost the man who has been like my brother. I shouldn't forgive you!"

"You shouldn't," Vhalla whispered, looking down at her hands. "For Aldrik, and for Baldair. I couldn't save him either."

"Shut up," Elecia said sharply. "Just shut up, I won't tolerate you feeling sorry for yourself and moping around. Aldrik, gods know what will happen to him when he gets back to the capital, *if* we get back. After how he left, I have no idea what the Emperor will do."

Vhalla stared at where Aldrik and the princess had departed. *What would the Emperor think?*

Elecia started on her bandages in heavy silence. They fell away, and Vhalla followed the woman's eyes to her chest. The moment softened as Elecia's fingers fell on the hideous deformity that now marred Vhalla's skin. "It's going to stay."

Vhalla swallowed hard.

"Healing you with magic alone wasn't very graceful, and we do not have any proper potions or salves. It's hard to make them when every plant is covered in snow." Elecia actually sounded somewhat apologetic. "It *is* healing . . . I will do my best to leave you with as small a mark as possible."

"It's fine. Thank you for doing everything you have already." Vhalla had learned to live with scars. "It will remind me what I work toward now. It will be my badge and my mission."

Elecia stilled. "What do you think you can possibly do?"

"A wise man once told me that something very small can cast a large shadow when it's close to the sun." Vhalla cast her heart in stone, her mind already churning around her next move. She pushed the loss of her magic down into the depths of her heart. There was no solution for that pain and she would just have to smother it until it died. She had an Emperor and a madman to deal with. But first, she'd start with the princess in the other room.

CHAPTER 27

THE CHAREM FAMILY home was a well-sized log construction. The tall pines dictated the dimensions of the structure more than any architectural plans the original builder may have created. One third was a loft, with a private room below that normally belonged to Fritz's parents; that is, until the random assortment of nobility showed up on their doorstep. The family had lived there for over four generations, and each person to inherit the house seemed to add their own touch. The first person built the home, the second added the insulating mud and clay mix between the logs, the third added a wooden shingled roof, the fourth added the wooden floor inside, and so on.

That was how Fritz's father explained it. Orelerienum Charem, Orel for short, was a large and muscled man. His bicep was wider than Vhalla's thigh. He had broad shoulders and weathered skin with smile wrinkles around his Southern blue eyes. His hair was cropped short, but Vhalla did not have to wonder who Fritz inherited his wild locks from.

Tama Charem was a full-figured woman with messy, light blonde hair. When it wasn't in a thick braid down her back to her waist, it was a mane around her face and shoulders. She was a kind and generous hostess with a round face and melodic laughter that complemented her husband's full-bellied guffaws.

"Gwen! Get up!" Cass, the eldest, called up to the loft. Her hair was short, cut like a man's and she looked to be the female version of her father—sturdy and unmoving.

"She's not getting up," Reona, the third child, remarked from by the hearth. She was a pretty girl with a button nose and a faint dusting of freckles across her nose and cheeks. "Not without food started."

"She needs to help with that food!" Nia rolled her eyes. She was cutting some salted meat and root vegetables to be put into a large pot. Nia was the second youngest, and she had already hit her growth. All legs and arms, she was a slip of a girl with fantastically wild hair to her shoulders.

"Gwen, if you don't get down here, I'm gonna tan your hide, miss!" Tama called. "You know we have guests." She looked back at Aldrik with a small, apologetic bow.

"Your hospitality is already more than enough," Aldrik said gracefully from a chair at the end of the table where he sat.

Vhalla gave him a small smile. She knew this life must be very odd for him, but he handled it like a gracious ruler. Aldrik caught her eyes, and his lips curled into a small smile in return. Vhalla looked away quickly, frustrated that after all this time, her cheeks could still feel hot near this man. They both seemed to be on a mutual elation just at the sight of each other, especially after all that had occurred.

The feeling sobered when Vhalla's eyes turned across the table, meeting the Northern princess's. There were many words unsaid, and she couldn't let the lull of normalcy distract them for too long. Vhalla caught the prince's eyes once more, and he nodded in agreement, able to read her obvious thoughts.

As much as Vhalla wanted to just kick everyone out, she knew why it hadn't been done yet. Fritz's family remained oblivious to the real reasons why they had arrived, knowing nothing more than there were injuries in the party. Vhalla resented the girls slightly for their ability to remain ignorant of the horrors in the world, but not enough to want to shatter it for them.

"Fire is going," Jax announced from the stone hearth that dominated a large portion of the wall to the left of the main entrance. He sauntered over to the table, leaning between Elecia and Nia. "My stunning lady, might there be the slightest thing I could do to assist you? I hate to see such beautiful hands being taxed with such labors." Jax took the knife from the open-mouthed girl's palm.

"I-I-Hi, hi, how are you?" she stuttered dumbly. The girl clearly had limited experience with men, and encountering Jax was akin to being thrown into the deep end. "What's your, name? Yes, that's, something, forgot, what's your name?" She smiled widely at the charming look Jax was giving her.

"My name." His hand cupped her cheek boldly. "Fair lady is—"

"Jax!" Fritz snapped, carrying in a load of lumber from the yard. "Away from my sister!"

"I do not think your brother approves." Jax grinned, passing the knife back to Nia.

"Let her be, Fritz." Cass rolled her eyes. "It's not like you're around to protect her normally; she's gotta learn."

"And oh, the things I could teach her." Jax snickered at Fritz.

"Jax!" Fritz practically jumped at the man.

"Fritter," his father boomed with a laugh, scooping up the scrawny sorcerer with just his arm. "Leave the girls be."

"I'm trying to help protect them!" Fritz frantically tried to keep the stack of cut wood in his hands as his father carried him, heavy load and all, over toward the hearth.

"Oh right, we need protecting?" Reona rolled her eyes as she helped with the lumber. They did not need wood to burn with sorcerers about, but Orel seemed to move out of habit. "Just like that time we got you out of the tree when you climbed too high up and wouldn't stop crying?"

"I was five!" Fritz whined, his father putting him down.

"Or the time when you got stuck in the smokehouse playing hide and seek and wouldn't stop wailing until Cass got you out?" Nia motioned with her knife at her brother.

Elecia sniggered, shooting Fritz a sideways glance.

"Let's not forget, girls, the time he was so scared by a nightmare he wet—"

"Enough!" Fritz cut off his big sister with a red flush. "There's a reason I don't come home!"

"You love us." Cass hooked her arm around Fritz's neck and ruffled his hair.

"So you're really the Windwalker?" Nia asked from her place by the hearth.

"Nia, that's not—" Fritz was quick with an apologetic look directed at Vhalla.

"I was." Vhalla attempted a brave smile. She had to brace herself to endure the wave of emotion that came with those words.

"Was?" Nia tilted her head. Cass began listening, too.

"There was an accident." Vhalla raised a hand to her shoulder.

"The one that made you all come here a day ago?" Cass asked.

Vhalla nodded.

"Sorcerers can lose their powers?" Reona asked sincerely.

As Vhalla opened her mouth to explain, there was a commotion from up in the loft. The patter of feet started from the middle and rushed toward the edge. A girl, who could not be older than six, holding a blanket like a cape about her shoulders, jumped off in clear disregard of the ladder nearby. Aldrik, Jax, and Elecia were all on their toes. Vhalla stuck out her hand instinctively to stop the girl's descent but no magic came to her palm, and she was forced to feel ashamed and awkward. Fritz just rolled his eyes.

"Papa!" the girl squealed, kicking her feet in the air.

"Good morning, my little Gwen!" Orel boomed. He crossed the room in five large strides and caught the bundle that was his daughter.

"Good morning, papa!" Gwen kissed his nose lightly. "How are you?"

"I am well, and how is my little princess?" The giant man poked her nose lightly, drawing a giggle from the small girl.

"Good!" she announced. "I would like my breakfast now!"

"It is not ready yet!" Nia remarked.

"It would be if you had helped!" Reona said begrudgingly, putting the top on the pot before carrying it over to the fire.

"Let me assist." Jax was up on his feet.

"It's really fine." Reona glanced skeptically at the Westerner.

"Fair lass." Jax chuckled, taking the pot from the girl's hands. "I am a Firebearer, the flames are my brothers and sisters, so they cannot hurt me." He reached into the fire dramatically and placed the pot on one of the farthest hooks bolted into the inner mantle.

"Oh, I see." Reona stared dumbly.

Nia giggled next to her, twirling a lock of hair around her fingers. Bringing Jax into a house of young maids was an awful idea.

Vhalla pointedly ignored the Northerners sitting across from her throughout breakfast. She would only have a short time to pretend at normalcy with the Charem family, and Vhalla would savor each fleeting moment she could. Their banter was a momentary escape from the truths that stared Vhalla down.

At one point, Elecia leaned over to Fritz, whispering something in his ear. It made Vhalla realize with a dull ache that she'd lost her magic hearing. She wouldn't have used it on her friends, but there would never be a chance to use it ever again for anything.

As soon as the meal was finished, Vhalla didn't have to wonder what was said anymore as Fritz promptly engaged in a quiet conversation with his mother, and Tama began to give marching orders to her brood that conveniently involved all outdoor activities.

Jax stood as the room was clearing. "It looks like all the ladies are heading to the creek to do laundry. I think they may need some extra supervision."

"Jax, I am not leaving you alone with my sisters!" Fritz hurried out behind him.

It all too conveniently left Vhalla, Aldrik, Za, Sehra, and Elecia at the table. Vhalla turned to her friend, and Elecia arched a dark eyebrow.

"Do you think I'm leaving?" she asked incredulously. "I was the one who cleared the room for this awkward little chat that needs to happen."

"Thank you for that." Aldrik took the lead at the head of the table. "We have quite a few things that we need to cover."

"Indeed." Sehra showed her intent to participate in the conversation. "Now that your Southern idiocies have unleashed the true strength of the Crystal Caverns."

Guilt pulled on Vhalla's shoulders, but she didn't bother trying to hide or deny the fact. She met the princess's eyes. "What do you know about the Caverns?"

"More than you do."

"That doesn't help us." Vhalla frowned.

"Who says I have any interest in helping you?" Sehra narrowed her eyes. "You had no interest in my deals, in my wisdoms, before. What makes you think my offers still stand for you?"

"Because you don't have a choice," Vhalla spoke, silencing the table. "Victor is insane. He plans to make a new world order, built around idolizing sorcery. He's going to go to any end to achieve it; he's already demonstrated that much. While *you* may be magically special, that is not going to exclude the majority of your people from being rearranged to where Victor feels they belong."

The confident expression slipped off the girl's lips. Vhalla knew just what button she needed to push. More than anything, the princess was loyal to her home.

"Our best chance is not to divide our strength by allowing a civil war," Aldrik agreed.

"You want us to stand with Solaris." Sehra clearly didn't like the idea.

"You are Solaris."

Za snorted at Aldrik's proclamation.

"No one will stand at all if we can't figure this out." Vhalla sighed, the table quickly devolving before her eyes. "Sehra, what do you know about what Victor did?"

The princess finally relented. "The man is quite clever; I will grant him that." She sighed and leaned back in her chair. Vhalla briefly saw fear in her eyes and was reminded that the princess was wise beyond her years, but still only a girl. "The artifacts were left by the Goddess, the Caverns her point of departure into the other realms. Each artifact connected the Caverns across the continent, drawing magic."

"Why affinities come from different regions," Vhalla realized. "Each one pulled a different facet of magic."

"So we believe," Sehra affirmed. "Our ancestors came from the Crescent Continent, from the lands beyond, seeking shelter because they did not possess the ability to harness magic like the old races. The weapons to build our world and the Caverns were the Goddess taking pity upon us."

"You can't really believe all this?" Elecia looked to Aldrik.

"Elecia, you are not above being removed from this council." Aldrik frowned and motioned for Sehra to continue.

"Believe what you will, Southerners," the princess huffed. "Shaldan has not forgotten our roots to our ancestral lands."

"So bringing achel back to the Caverns, and the Crystal Crown, Victor reunited the power and tapped into the font of magic itself in the process?" Vhalla tried to piece it together.

"Indeed." The princess laced her fingers. "What was truly brilliant was how he paid the blood price to awaken the crystals while stealing your magic, giving him immunity to the crystal's taint."

"It's why I tried to kill you." Za scowled at Vhalla. "If you died. He could not win. But the crown prince loves you more than his people and has now let out a power that will consume these lands."

Aldrik slowly lowered his hands to the table, his eyes narrowed. Vhalla swallowed hard. *She couldn't deny it.* If Za had killed her before Victor could, they wouldn't be in this position now.

"Za." Sehra watched Aldrik when addressing her handler. "You are not incorrect. But there is little point in saying such now."

"Why do the crystals not taint Windwalkers?" Vhalla wanted to glean as much information as possible from the girl.

"Who knows?" Sehra didn't seem as though she was lying or avoiding imparting a truth. "Because Windwalkers can radiate out magic more easily than other Affinities, they dissipate the taint into the air? Because the Goddess likes them better? Maybe because they were the first from the Crescent Continent? The early groups of Windwalkers weren't very interested in sharing information with our clans."

"So what can the crystal magic really do?" Aldrik asked.

"Anything." Vhalla's heart sank at the princess's word. "It's not a magic defined by the conventions we know."

"It's a greater power like that of the Crescent Continent," Vhalla finished, remembering the Emperor's vision, to use her to unlock the Caverns to take war across the sea.

"In Victor, you have just given birth to a demigod," Sehra said solemnly.

"We need to go back and warn the capital." Elecia looked to Aldrik.

"The capital is gone." Sehra shook her head at the futility of Elecia's suggestion.

"Don't you say such things!" Elecia snapped.

"Elecia, calm," Aldrik ordered. The curly-haired woman sat slowly. "The capital is bloated with soldiers from the war. If there was ever a time to brace for an attack, now would be that time." The prince pinched the bridge of his nose with a sigh. "All that said, we should return as soon as possible. If Victor hasn't already launched an attack, we may be able to help warn them."

"Go on your suicide mission. Za and I will have no part." Sehra drew her line in the sand. Aldrik studied his child bride for a long moment, his gaze searching. "I think, in light of recent events, we can reach a mutually beneficial agreement instead."

"I am listening." Aldrik sat back in his chair. Vhalla had to blink twice. Despite being of basic construction, it suddenly looked like a throne.

"My mother sent me South for two reasons: to thwart the Empire's plans for the crystals and to protect our people." Sehra was clearly ready to lay everything on the table.

"And assassinate the Emperor." Vhalla scowled at the Northern women.

"Assassinating the Emperor would've supported both ends," Sehra said easily. "But circumstances have changed." The princess returned her attention to Aldrik. "You need my people. You need our knowledge of the crystals, our fighting prowess. Give me your word as a ruler that you will relinquish Shaldan from the Solaris Empire, and you shall have knowledge and arms for this fight."

"Impossible." Aldrik didn't entertain the idea for more than a breath. "As Vhalla so aptly pointed out, you need to fight or your people will surely perish. Why would I agree to something you will do anyway?"

"The sea is not so wide between us and the Crescent Continent. We could flee."

Aldrik considered this a long moment. "You are smart, princess. So you know that I cannot make Shaldan a free state once more. My people will rebel after the price we paid to conquer it."

Vhalla almost pointed out that she had already said such to Sehra previously.

"Shaldan cannot be bought with Southern blood!" Za interjected angrily.

"Za, quiet." Sehra wasn't about to allow negotiations to be interrupted. "I want my people safe. I want Shaldan's interests protected, now and in perpetuity."

"Tell me you will fight with us, give us your men, your weapons, your knowledge, and you will have my word," Aldrik agreed.

"Your word isn't good enough," Sehra said sharply. To Vhalla's surprise, the girl's eyes turned to her. "You speak highly of peace."

"I do." Vhalla wasn't afraid to say so. "Our land has seen too much turmoil."

"Will you be peace's champion in the battle to come?"

"I will be."

"Are you finally ready to pay the asking price for it, when the time comes?" The princess's words had a weight to them unlike anything Vhalla had ever felt before.

"I will be," she reaffirmed after a long moment.

Sehra took a deep breath. "I will return home, and I will tell my mother of what has happened here. She will heed my counsel, and I will tell her to fight with Solaris. To remain a part of this Empire and its future leaders who vow to fight for peace and the wellbeing of our people."

Vhalla's heart began to race. *It was too easy.* She braced herself for the princess to continue.

"Needless to say, I will return to inherit my birthright of leading the head clan of Soricium as a Child of Yargen." Her eyes turned to Aldrik. "I have no interest in mingling my bloodline with yours if I am guaranteed that my people will be looked after."

"You have my word."

Vhalla frowned at the fraction of relief in Aldrik's eyes. *It was too easy*, she wanted to scream at him.

"I told you, that's not good enough." Sehra smiled tiredly. "My people need assurance. And since I know you are one to value the life of one you love more than an entire people, I will ask for only one."

"You are not taking Vhalla from me." Aldrik scowled.

Sehra laughed. "Predictable, but no. She will stay to honor her words to me, to prove that the future Empress of this land is worth her word."

"Who then?" Aldrik let his unquestioning silence stand as affirmation to the princess's assumptions that he and Vhalla would wed when he was no longer promised to Sehra.

Vhalla's hand went to the watch at her neck. It had miraculously been spared significant damage in the caverns. Her heart was still beating frantically.

"Your heir."

Confusion ran quickly across Aldrik's feature, anger quick on its wake. Vhalla knew he was imagining the child he'd dreamed of. *Their child.*

"You would ask for my firstborn?" His voice had gone deep and threatening.

"I ask for your heir, future Emperor." Sehra remained resolute. "If Solaris keeps their word throughout the battle that you will honor Shaldan and do everything to rid the world of this abomination, we will lend our strength. To ensure a lasting peace, your heir, which I imagine will be conceived quickly to fulfill your duty as a ruler, will come and live as a ward of my family for his or her first fourteen years of life. This will ensure that Shaldan is protected in the formative years of becoming part of your empire and that the next Solaris will care for and love our people as their own."

Vhalla gripped the oversized shirt she wore. If she and Aldrik wed she would be conceiving his heir, the heir Sehra wanted. *They wanted her child.*

"Fourteen years?" Aldrik balked.

The conversation faded a moment as Vhalla retreated into her own mind. She automatically assumed it to be her child. But who knew what would come to pass? Every day was less certain than the last. Taint had been unleashed upon the world, and she was nothing more than a Commons now. Vhalla looked at the turmoil on Aldrik's face. He was being asked to choose between his Empire and the family he'd been idolizing in his dreams. He couldn't make the decision rationally, so she did.

"I think you should agree, Aldrik," Vhalla interjected, not even noticing who she interrupted. The look on his face alone affirmed all her suspicions on what he'd been thinking.

"That would be your child."

"I know." *As if she needed reminding.* "And even if it is, I still think you should agree."

Sehra met Vhalla's eyes, and the princess gave an appreciative nod. The girl wasn't gleeful. Sehra clearly wasn't relishing in the idea of separating a family. But she also wasn't backing down from what she believed she needed to do to protect her people. Vhalla would never verbally admit it, but if she did have a child, there would be worse fates than being raised in a culture with such deep knowledge and apparent honor.

Aldrik stood, pacing the room. Everyone remained silent as the crown prince visibly debated all his options. He was the only one who could make this decision, as he would be the one who would be forced to honor it as the future Emperor. He paused, staring at the fire, suddenly still after the momentary flurry of activity.

"You have your deal." Aldrik didn't look at anyone as he spoke. *"Now leave me."*

Sehra stood gracefully, leaving with Za's arm tucked around her. Elecia gave Vhalla a glare. Clearly the woman didn't approve of Vhalla's influence on Aldrik. Vhalla pursed her lips; she wasn't going to be made to feel guilty for doing what she felt was right.

"Not you, Vhalla," he ordered without turning.

Vhalla sighed softly and crossed to her prince. His shoulders were stiff and his eyes focused on the flames, as if he prayed for them to tell him the answer. To present him with an alternative to what he had just agreed upon. Vhalla wrapped her arms around his waist and rested her cheek on his back.

"How could you?"

"For the same reason you agreed," she whispered.

Aldrik gripped her hands, holding her against him. "Our child will go and live with them."

"If everything comes to pass." Vhalla was back to being a Commons, and it felt as though war was about to break out once more. She couldn't stop herself from subtly pointing out that she may not even live long enough to marry Aldrik, more or less conceive a child.

Aldrik didn't entertain the thought, but continued, "The child won't even know us."

"The princess has not barred us from visiting. If the child could visit us—"

"You think they'll let the Solaris heir out of their sight?" Aldrik scoffed.

"Not at first," Vhalla agreed. "But I don't think they wish us harm, Aldrik." She rounded to his front, reaching up to cup his cheeks. "We're all just trying to survive."

Aldrik pressed his eyelids closed. "This wasn't how it was supposed to be. I was going to wed you, and we would live and rule, fat and happy."

"What storybook do you think this is?" Vhalla laughed tiredly. "Aldrik, do you feel no joy for the fact that this new sorrow only exists because we can now wed?"

He looked at her for a long moment, as if considering what he had been assuming all along for the first time.

"If you still wish it." Vhalla's palms fell from his cheeks.

He caught them quickly. Aldrik pressed her fingertips to his lips. "My love, there is nothing more in this world I wish for."

"Then let us fight for that dream." Vhalla ran her hand over the plain clothing he'd been loaned. She smoothed the abundance of fabric down over his lean frame, finding every curve of him where she always knew them to be. *The prince was hers.* "Your father . . ."

"Will be convinced," Aldrik finished confidently. "I will never let you go again. You shall stay here, at my side, as long as your heart is content for it to be so." She studied his face as he spoke. There was pain that fueled determination. There was fear that powered a resolve that hoped against hope.

Vhalla tilted her head upward, her eyelids slowly closing. They no longer shared the Bond, and so she could no longer feel his mind's inner design as though it was her own. He would need to show her, just as she would need to show him. His breathing washed over her cheeks as he paused, timidly.

Vhalla rose to her toes, closing the gap and gripping his shirt. It was the first time his lips had met hers in months and, despite all that had happened, they still fit perfectly.

CHAPTER 28

VHALLA SPENT THE night securely tucked within Aldrik's arms, though it wasn't entirely comfortable. Any amount of pressure set her scarring shoulder to aching and reminded her where she was and why.

She listened to the wind as it whispered through the cracks around the window shutters. At times, she could almost believe that her magic was still there, that the wind was still calling only to her. But when she slipped her fingers out from under the heavy blankets, she felt nothing other than chill air. *Just the air had become torture.*

Even Aldrik's breathing kept her awake. She'd only ever been close to the prince Joined, and now his out-of-sync breathing sounded loud. She didn't cry, however. She didn't let herself shed a single tear. It would be giving Victor what he wanted. Mourning the loss of her magic and Bond would grant Victor far too much control over her emotions.

No, Vhalla pushed closer to the man behind her. She had found love in spite of fate's design and Victor's plot. She still had her knowledge and her will. With those things she would still be deadly.

The first light that cut through the darkness roused Vhalla. She'd spent the night plotting and planning her next steps, how they would manage the Emperor when they returned, if they could truly trust Sehra to keep her word.

The limp arm that had been wrapped around her waist most of the night tightened the moment Vhalla tried to wiggle free. Vhalla turned, carefully positioning her right shoulder against Aldrik's chest. A pair of dark eyes studied her, and Vhalla allowed herself a small smile.

"Go back to sleep," she whispered. "You need your rest."

"So do you."

"I am no longer sleepy." Vhalla rolled her eyes.

"Did you have a bad dream?"

"No." Vhalla averted her eyes so he wouldn't see the pain he'd sparked in them. She knew he had not meant to, but just the mention of dreams made her think of what was lost between them. Never again would she see his memories in sleep.

"Is it keeping you up?" His fingers rested lightly on her shoulder.

"The pain is manageable," Vhalla sighed. "Elecia said it will scar."

"And?" he murmured nonchalantly. Aldrik leaned forward, pressing his lips into the fabric over the mark where Victor had stolen her magic and nearly her life. "You're not one to worry about feminine notions of your complexion."

"I'm not," she agreed. "Are you?"

Aldrik laughed lightly. It was a throaty whisper. "You could turn green with yellow spots and I'd find myself uncaring. If I'd wanted a dainty court queen, I would have picked from my father's line-up."

"The Fire Lord with a dainty court queen?" Vhalla grinned playfully. "Now there's an image."

"Ah yes, quite the hilarious failure." Aldrik brought his lips to hers lightly.

"Will you two get a room?" Jax groaned from Aldrik's opposite side. Aldrik was pushed closer to Vhalla as a swift kick was placed on his lower back. "Tired of listening to lovers' sweet nothings."

"Jax!" Aldrik snapped, rolling over. "I did not realize you wanted accommodations in the dungeons upon our return."

"After all I've done for you?" Jax snorted.

Vhalla took the opportunity to stand, stretching out her stiff limbs. Being brought back from the dead took a toll on one's body.

"It seems your lady does escape, my prince."

"Boys, I swear, do not make me get up from this pallet," Elecia threatened without so much as a hint of movement.

Vhalla grinned and held up an index finger to her lips, motioning for the men to be silent. Jax gave Aldrik a satisfied smirk before rolling over. Fritz snored on as though nothing had happened. The two Northerners in the corner ignored their companions. Aldrik just shook his head, running a hand through his limp hair. Her eyes caught his, and they had one more moment before Vhalla crept out to the main room.

She was not the first to wake. Cass had already stoked a fire. The tall woman now stood at the end of the large table that dominated the space closest to the crackling hearth. Her cerulean eyes turned up at Vhalla's sock-muffled footsteps.

"Good morning," she said softly, clearly still mindful that most of the people in the home were still in the depths of slumber.

"Good morning, Cass." Vhalla smiled, meeting the other woman's kind and toothy look.

"Did you sleep alright?" she asked.

"I did," Vhalla affirmed. She assumed the space next to the woman as one of Cass's sisters would, beginning to slice some of the root vegetables. Vhalla winced as she tested out what sort of pressure her shoulder could withstand.

Cass noticed, but kept silent about Vhalla's pain.

"I hope we're not putting your family out too much." Vhalla noted the quantity of food they were being forced to prepare.

"Don't worry." Cass shook her head. "It's nice to have Fritz home. It's not every day that we have a prince with us either."

Smiling to herself, Vhalla slipped the knife through another potato. She remembered being awe-struck and dazed at the notion of being near royalty. There was a time when just proximity to Aldrik could fluster her. Now she spoke with him without thought. She had no qualms when it came to scolding him or encouraging him to do something he may otherwise not consider.

Then there was Baldair. He had flustered her also. It had been his flirtations, then his misguided protection, and somehow at the end he was as good as a brother. The idea that he was gone still rested cold in her core. Vhalla sighed softly, her knife paused.

"You've been through a lot." It was not a question. Vhalla looked up at the Charem girl. "We all know the story. We heard it not long after the Night of Fire and Wind. You were the lowborn library girl turned sorceress who rode with princes."

"Was I?" Vhalla asked softly. She supposed some of it was still true.

"You tell me." Cass laughed. "In any case, it is an honor to meet you. Gwen had a mouse she found in the spring that she named after you."

"What?"

"I think she lost it." The elder girl coughed and glanced away. "But for girls like us, you are the impossible dream."

"It still feels impossible," Vhalla mused softly. "In some ways, it was a dream."

"Reona and I were planning on heading into town today." Cass passed her another potato. "Would you like to join us?"

"That sounds nice." Vhalla nodded. She needed to see how she fared on a horse, and a small practice ride sounded like a smart idea before pushing to the capital.

"I'm going to get her up soon. We should leave early to make it back before nightfall. Reona can linger," Cass explained. "I wanted to get breakfast started before we went off."

"You're a good big sister, aren't you?" Vhalla grinned, dumping some of her chopping into the large pot that was used.

"I try." She chuckled. "Fritz left when he was young, so I knew I had to look out for the girls. Speaking of, I'll go rouse Reona."

Vhalla finished while Cass disappeared up the ladder and into the loft beyond. She hummed softly to herself, trying to remember the mix of spices that she'd seen Nia put in the morning before. A flap of canvas distracted her, and she was surprised to see Elecia emerge.

"You're up?" Vhalla arched her eyebrows in surprise.

"Thanks to the boys," Elecia grumbled.

"Sorry."

"I blame you completely." The dark-skinned woman crossed the room, placing her hands on the opposite side of the table. Her voice dropped, and she cut to something that had clearly been on her mind since their first night at the Charem's. "Did Aldrik share your bed at the palace?"

"No." Vhalla looked back to the spices. "He was engaged to someone other than me."

"That seems to have changed yesterday."

"Before yesterday." Vhalla touched the watch around her neck.

"Since the North? Truly?" Elecia put it together quickly. Vhalla nodded. "My, you two really don't give a damn about his father, do you?" There was an appreciative note to her words.

"Not really." Vhalla shrugged, instantly regretting the motion.

"How is it?" Elecia caught the look of pain.

"Not bad, considering," Vhalla answered honestly. "Thank you truly, Elecia. I would've died without you."

"Yes, you would've." Elecia shook her head dramatically. "You're unlikely to stay in one piece without me being near."

"Seems so." Vhalla glanced up at the loft when she heard the creaking of wood. "I'm going into town with the girls, to test out riding."

"Good idea." Elecia nodded, watching Reona and Cass descend the ladder. "Aldrik will regret it if he's not there to perform the Rite of Sunset for Baldair."

The thought hadn't occurred to Vhalla, but she instantly knew it was true. Aldrik would never let a Crone perform the rite. It would be his flames to send Baldair into the Realms of the Father.

"I hear you're coming with us?" Reona yawned.

"If you'll have me." She needed to ensure she could ride as fast as possible. If not, she'd encourage Aldrik to return home ahead of her.

"Reona, check the larder on the way to the barn," Cass asked her sister.

"When we return to the capital, I will see that the Ci'Dan family shows their appreciation to the fullest extent for what you have done for us." Elecia met the eyes of the eldest Charem child. "Were it not for you, the life of our prince would have surely been forfeit. If we were stuck out in this winter, it would have been the end of all of us."

"Truly, it has been our honor," Cass said, ever mindful of her place in the world.

"Dresses! And axes! We want dresses and sharp axes!" Reona chimed in eagerly from the doorway. Cass shot her a glare. "I mean, yeah, our honor," she coughed.

Vhalla followed Cass out to the barn, bundled in a spare riding cloak of Reona's. She didn't have the energy to dread returning to the capital as she likely should, she only felt exhausted. The world had spun so fast it'd fallen off its axis, and Vhalla felt like she would be chasing it forever to try to get back on, just to live.

A surprise waited for Vhalla when they reached the open-style barn that housed the family's horses and small pens of livestock. Each stall was packed fuller than it should have been to keep all the animals out of the heavy snow, but Vhalla could easily pick out a steed slightly larger than the others.

Lightning, the mount that had carried her across the continent, whinnied as she pet his nose with her palm. He had always been a smart horse, and while it may have been her wishful thinking, the steed seemed to remember her. The horse had been well taken care of. He was strong, and his trot was familiar the second Vhalla was once more upon his back.

For a time, she had wondered what had become of her Lightning after leaving the North. Now she had no doubt who had taken care of him. *Especially after Baston's death.* Vhalla glanced over her shoulder to the slowly shrinking home, left behind as she followed Cass and Reona toward town. She wondered if Aldrik had managed to go back to sleep.

Her eyes fell on the barn once more, and Vhalla picked out the mount she'd ridden alongside Victor. *Victor*, the name made her blood bubble so hotly that Vhalla could ignore the pain in her shoulder due to the jostling of the horse. He'd been planning to use her from the start. He'd seen her saved from the Senate, and then he'd turned the Senate's sentence into an opportunity to get the axe. He'd trained her himself upon her return. He'd prepared her as carefully as a prize hog for slaughter.

He was the greatest puppet master the world had ever known. He'd manipulated princes and Emperors for his own vision. It'd be admirable, if that vision wasn't a twisted and corrupt thing.

The woods were washed in white, and Vhalla tried to turn her thoughts away from lusting after the former Minister of Sorcery's death. There were no others nearby, and the snow was pure and unblemished. The girls chattered on about this or that which they could also pick up in town. At a quarter day's ride away, Vhalla had no doubt that going into town was indeed an affair. It had been the same for her as a child, and she remembered with fondness every time her mother would take her into Leoul proper.

Whistling through the trees, the wind whipped her cloak around her. Vhalla drew her hood. Holding out a hand, the air slipped through her open palm. It felt different. She was once more normal, no more special than the girls she rode with. Vhalla looked up to the sky, broken and blotched by trees; there was one man who now felt what truly blew in the wind and she hated him all the more for it. Her red-chilled hands gripped the reins once more.

They reached the outskirts of town in good time, and Vhalla pulled her attention back to the present. The town closest to the Charems' home, Rivend, reminded Vhalla very much of Leoul. It was a town indeed, but barely so. Houses gathered closer together than normal. There was an inn, a grocer, some general stores, cobbler, seamstress, and other life essentials. But that was where the similarities ended.

The buildings were basic log construction with shingled roofs. It was different from the river stone and thatch-work that was made in the East. People used what was available to them in places like this. Most did not have glass on the windows. Some had been wealthy enough at various points to afford paint—that was now chipping away—on their storefronts.

No one seemed to pay the girls any mind as they rode to the

grocer and dismounted. Vhalla realized with her hood drawn she was likely assumed to be Nia and was content to blend in with the girls as they went about their business.

"Welcome, welcome!" the grocer hummed from behind his counter as a bell alerted him to their entry. "Ah, Cass!"

"Hello, Daren," Cass said with a smile.

"What'll it be today?" The elderly man rested his elbows on the high counter.

"The normal, please."

"You usually don't return to me so quickly." He began to grab bags of grain, salted pork, and preserved food from around the store. Cass helped, knowing where things were from prior experience. "Is little Gwen finally eating into her growth spurt?"

"Maybe!" Cass laughed.

"Actually we have—" Reona began.

"We have Fritz home also," Cass finished for her sister with a glare.

Vhalla realized they were keeping their presence silent. She wondered if they had been coached by Elecia or Aldrik, or if it was simply Cass's keen insight.

"Do you? How is our mad sorcerer doing?" The grocer began to tally up the pile on the counter.

"You know Fritz." Cass smiled as she began to count coins from a bag strapped to her hip.

"The lad has never grown up." The man chuckled as they began to collect the groceries. Cass passed a bag of flour to Vhalla, and she noticed the man staring at her strangely.

"Nia?" He squinted.

"Please excuse us, Daren!" Cass herded them out.

"What are you doing?" Reona hissed as they were loading the horse's saddlebags.

"I don't know." Cass paused, glancing at Vhalla. "But I didn't see how we could explain having the prince or the Windwalker at our house."

Being called the Windwalker stung.

"What's the point of having a prince if we're not gonna tell anyone about it?" Reona whined.

"Hush." Cass rolled her eyes.

"Thank you," Vhalla said earnestly. She realized the foreign horse would likely give away that something was different in such a small town. But perhaps it could be explained away as Fritz's mount from the palace.

"We should head home." Cass noticed Vhalla considering her horse and had the same idea.

"We should."

They tied up the last of their supplies to the saddles, and Vhalla adjusted the hood on her head, suddenly conscious of her own existence. Reona huffed, annoyed that her big secret actually had to remain just that.

A scream rang out through the quiet town.

All three girls turned to the source of the sound. A commotion was being raised at the far end of town. Vhalla glanced to Cass.

"Reona, stay here with the horses," the elder sister ordered.

"I'm coming." Vhalla fell into step by the eldest Charem girl. Cass gave her a nod and did not question her.

A crowd was quickly gathering at the main entrance to the town. People of all shapes and sizes poured into the street to see the source of the commotion. Judging by the size of the group, everyone who lived in the area was likely there. Cass squinted over people's heads. Vhalla had no hope of seeing, even on her toes. They pushed around the side to one of the storefronts. Standing on some wooden boxes, they could finally see the source of the fuss.

It was then that Vhalla realized how true the princess's words had been.

"Jon, Jon! What, what is wrong, Jon?" a woman blubbered, stepping forward from the semi-circular crowd. A man had walked, judging by the footprints, through the mountain snow, and he had come a very long way. He wore the bloodied and torn uniform of a palace guard. Blood no longer oozed from the gaping wounds in-between his plate. It had crusted and frozen.

His head tilted to the side, weighed down by a rock that jutted out from his eye. *No, it wasn't a rock.* Vhalla's eyes widened. The crystal shone unnaturally in the light of the afternoon. Blood coated the man's face from where the magical object had been shoved through. His other eye shone red, and his skin had turned to leather. Whoever this man had been, he was no more.

"I have been sent." His voice echoed, raspy and hollow, across the silenced crowd. "As a messenger, from your new sovereign." The crystal glowed ominously as he spoke; everyone stared in horror.

"I fought for the old regime, for the wicked Emperor Solaris, oppressor of power. For my loyalty, I was justly put to death, as were all who stood with the dying sun." The man's body did not move as he spoke; it was as rigid as a corpse, save for his jaw. "The family Solaris is dead. The Emperor died a screaming death. He has been flayed, his entrails set out for the birds and his skin used to make our lord's first banner. His lady wife followed him after. The sons of Solaris perished to hand over their succession rights to our lord's divine right to rule. Their bodies have been quartered and fed to dogs."

Vhalla's hands rose to her mouth. *Baldair*, was her only thought. The idea of Victor disgracing the remains of the golden prince gave her a sickening mental image. An image that she would use as kindling to stoke the malice she held for Victor into a fever heat.

"There will be no quarter given to those who show a love for the fallen sun that is the family Solaris. They are all dead and rotting. Even the Windwalker was put to death for her well-known love of the late crown prince."

Vhalla blinked. *The man spoke of her.* Victor proclaimed Aldrik and her dead to the world. He did not know they had managed to escape the Caverns and found shelter from the winter. In all his over-confidence, he was so drunk on triumph that he missed their salvation at the hands of Elecia, Jax, and Fritz.

"Love your new lord for he is akin to the Gods, supreme king, our one true master, governor of this world, Victor Anzbel. Those who share a fraction of his power as sorcerers are to be heralded as his chosen ones. They are invited to the capital to swear fealty and live the life of nobility. Those unchosen, Commons, are to learn their new place and prostrate themselves before their magical overseers." The grotesque animation finished its speech.

Vhalla felt an awful wrenching inside of her. *This was the power she had unleashed.* This was the fate she had allowed to be brought upon the world.

"We need to go." Vhalla grabbed Cass's elbow. The girl stared, gaping at the nightmare. *"Now."*

"Right." The eldest Charem was finally pulled out of her trance. As subtly as they could, they retreated from the crowd.

"Jon, Jon, what madness are you speaking?" The woman stuttered her words with grief and disbelief.

"Kneel before me, so that he may witness your loyalty to this new world order," the man continued as though he did not hear the woman.

They were halfway back to their horses, but in the silent town, each word was clear across the snow.

"Jon, please, speak to me as you always did. You-you loved, you were so proud to serve the Imperial family," the woman pleaded.

Vhalla clenched her hands into fists instinctually, even though there was no longer magic to Channel. Grief was clouding that person's judgment, and Vhalla was hopeless to help.

"Kneel, woman. Let your King Anzbel see your loyalty."

"What's going on?" Reona asked.

"Get on your horse," Cass snapped at her sister.

Luckily, the girl was old enough and Cass was firm enough that she did not question her. Vhalla swung her leg over Lightning. She noticed that sitting on the horses, they were tall enough to see the scene off in the distance. Reona's eyes were already fixed upon the living nightmare unfolding.

There was another scream, then chaos broke loose in the crowd behind them.

"All who do not kneel for the Supreme King Anzbel will die!" the man shouted.

They used the commotion to their advantage and spurred their horses into the woods. Vhalla turned in her saddle, picking up the rear behind the Charems. There was a commotion, shouting, crying, screaming, a flash, and the sizzle of magic. The town's resistance was brief. Just before all were out of her vision, she saw the still living kneel in the blood of their fallen friends and family.

"What was that, what was that, what was that?" Reona was shaking her head. She had heard and seen enough.

"Hush, Reona!" Cass's voice was breaking.

"We will be fine," Vhalla assured the girls. Two sets of blue eyes looked back at her as they raced through the wood. "There was only one. If he catches up with us, Jax, Aldrik, Elecia, and Fritz will protect us."

Vhalla gripped her reins. If she had her powers, that guard—the magically reanimated monster of Victor's—would be dead . . . again. But all she could do was run, run and keep the two girls with her as safe as possible by getting them away. She could no longer fight with her magic and had no weapons. She'd been reduced to using the only tool she'd ever had at her disposal: her mind.

Vhalla looked behind them at the deep tracks in the snow. Despite the cold, sweat ran down her forehead. If she had her powers, she could cover those betraying dips in the white world. Cursing aloud, she snapped the leather in her death-grip, her heels digging into Lightning. Anyone would be able to see the path leading right to the Charem home.

"We need to split up!" Vhalla pulled hard on her reins. "Loop around in circles."

"What?" Reona was shaking, and Vhalla doubted it was from cold.

"Make a bunch of circles, loop back, and then we'll meet back up again in a bit. Stay in earshot," Vhalla ordered.

Cass picked up on what Vhalla was attempting, likely she was one of the hunters of the family, and followed Vhalla's orders. It wasn't a perfect solution, but the abomination didn't seem too intelligent, and it was better than nothing. They rode apart for a stretch, coming back together just as the Charem home came into view.

Orel was out chopping wood. Tama and the two Northern women were tending to something in the livestock pens. The horses were a fury of thunder that shattered the relative peace.

Vhalla met a set of emerald eyes. Sehra studied her face as if she was able to replay the horrors Vhalla witnessed from her expression alone.

"Daddy!" Reona launched off her horse, stumbled, rolled in the snow, found her feet, and ran to her father. Orel was confused, but wasted no time scooping his crying daughter into his large arms. "Daddy, daddy, daddy!"

The commotion drew the men from within the home, and a pair of dark eyes met hers. Vhalla looked at Aldrik, and her chest tightened. He knew instantly something was amiss.

Vhalla and Cass dismounted, and the older girl stumbled in the snow. Cass went instantly to her mother, saying nothing. Tama stared at her shaken daughter and took her child into her arms without question.

"What happened? Reona, sweetling, what happened?" Orel tried to console his hysterical daughter.

Vhalla stood in the snow, at a loss as to who she should turn to. Her arms hung limply at her sides as the information continued to sink into her. Aldrik's gaze was upon her, his boots crunched the snow. Vhalla raised her gold-flecked eyes to meet obsidian.

"Vhalla," he asked, *he demanded.*

She swallowed. Someone had to do it. One of them had to say it, and she was not about to make the girls who had accompanied her perform that duty. They were just girls, as she had once been. But her innocence had long since been lost. It was a fate she would not force, nor push, upon the Charem daughters. Vhalla's shoulder ached all the way to her chest.

"Aldrik." She did not care for the lack of his title before anyone anymore. Vhalla spoke only to him. "It's Victor."

He took another step toward her. Vhalla braced herself. She would find the words. Strength, she had to find the strength first. Her will would replace her magic; it would be just as strong as her winds ever were.

"What happened?" He kept his eyes locked with hers.

"The Emperor." No matter what the man had done to her, to them, he had been Aldrik's father. Vhalla's voice softened. "Your father, the Empress, they're dead."

"What?" Elecia stepped forward as if she had somehow misheard Vhalla.

Aldrik tried to reach out, but only briefly. The spark that brought his hands to life was gone, and they hung at his side. His lips parted, and she saw shock crash down on him. Her heart broke for the man she loved. First his brother, now his father, and who knew how many countless others were dead and gone.

Panic momentarily overwhelmed her at the thought of everyone she still loved in the capital, but Vhalla pushed through it.

"There was a messenger—a tainted abomination—sent from Victor. I can only assume one of many," Vhalla answered Elecia, though her gaze stayed on Aldrik. "He was dead, long dead. But there was a crystal through his eye, and it somehow kept him moving." She shook her head; it was magic beyond her understanding. Sehra had said as much. All the rules were gone now. This would be a fight unlike any they had ever seen. "He said Victor had become the supreme king of this world. That the old regime, the family Solaris and all who supported them in the capital, were dead."

Her words filled the forest clearing, and Vhalla could see the moment everyone understood their meaning. Aldrik visibly swayed a moment, taking a step to adjust his balance. Vhalla's hand rose to the watch at her neck. He was a prince without a throne. A man who had lost his mother, his brother, now his father, along with his kingdom and everything he had ever known. No one said a word. Aldrik stared blankly at her.

"I'm sorry," she whispered. With those words, she knew it became real for him. Her sympathy, her pain on his behalf made the rest of it true, just as it had with Baldair.

He opened and closed his mouth, trying to find words. Her prince, he had endured so much death, so much loss and hurt that she could not save him from. Now Vhalla feared he was on the point of breaking. She took a step forward, at the same time as Orel.

"There is only one true king, one true lord of these lands. It is not some man whom I have never heard of before," the head of the Charem family announced.

Aldrik turned to face the burly woodcutter, his eyes wide and expressionless.

"And that lord stands before me." The man dropped to a knee, bowing his head. "Long live the Emperor Solaris."

Aldrik blinked at Orel, still at an utter loss for words.

"Long live the Emperor Solaris," Tama repeated her husband's words dutifully, and the matriarch sunk to her knees.

"Long live Solaris," Elecia announced proudly. Jax echoed the same, and both Westerners dropped to a knee, their heads bowed.

One by one, the Charem children began to follow suit. Each proclaimed their loyalty before sinking into the snow. To Vhalla's shock, she witnessed the Northerners drop to their knees as well. The princess's eyes were fixed on hers, and they spoke silent volumes, reminding Vhalla that their loyalty was on contingency. That their deal now mattered more than ever.

Vhalla turned back to Aldrik.

It was not a grand coronation in the Chapel of the Sun. There were no Crones to lead oaths. The wind replaced trumpets and snow replaced confetti of gold. He did not stand upon the Sunlit Stage, swathed in gold and white. There was no blazing crown of the sun to be placed upon his brow.

His succession came washed in the blood of his father and all who dared support his name. His gifts, his prizes of leadership, were loss and hardship. There was no mantle of the sun to settle upon his shoulders, only pain.

But she had lived to see that day. Vhalla was there the moment her prince became her Emperor. He turned back to her helplessly. For the first time in the whole of knowing him, Aldrik looked utterly lost, shell-shocked. She tried to offer him an encouraging smile, but there was only one thing to be done. She had something more important to give him than her smiles.

Vhalla dropped to her knee before the Emperor of the realms.

"Long live Solaris."

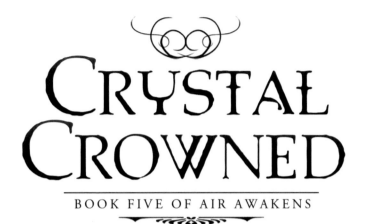

CRYSTAL CROWNED

BOOK FIVE OF AIR AWAKENS

Long live Solaris.

One bloodthirsty ruler has been overthrown by another,
casting the shadow of death over the Solaris Empire. Vhalla
Yarl stands upon the stage of fate, prepared to do battle one
final time. Fragile alliances will be tested and new bonds
will be formed as the world is reshaped. She fights as the
champion of peace, but when the night is darkest will she be
able to pay the price of a new dawn?

Get your copy today:
http://elisekova.com/air-awakens-book-five/

ABOUT THE AUTHOR

ELISE KOVA is a USA Today bestselling author. She enjoys telling stories of fantasy worlds filled with magic and deep emotions. She lives in Florida and, when not writing, can be found playing video games, drawing, chatting with readers on social media, or daydreaming about her next story.

She invites readers to get first looks, giveaways, and more by subscribing to her newsletter at: http://elisekova.com/subscribe

Visit her on the web at:
http://elisekova.com/
https://tiktok.com/@elisekova
https://www.instagram.com/elise.kova/
https://www.facebook.com/AuthorEliseKova/

See all of Elise's titles on her webiste:
http://elisekova.com/books/

Or her Amazon page:
http://author.to/EliseKova

THE AIR AWAKENS
SERIES

A library apprentice... A sorcerer princes... And an unbreakable magic bond. The rare elemental magic that lies in Vhalla Yarl will not only change the Empire's future, but the heart of its Crown Prince. Perfect for readers who want magic and romance!

Series complete!

"I read the full series in a just two days. The worlds was thrilling and the characters endearing... Recommend for fans of Sarah J. Maas and high fantasy"
- Kristen, 5 Star Amazon Review

Also in the Air Awakens Universe

THE GOLDEN GUARD TRILOGY

Three stories filled with mystery, romance, and adventure. Learn how the most illustrious fighting force of the Air Awakens world — the Golden Guard — came to be.

Series complete!

http://elisekova.com/the-crowns-dog-golden-guard-1/

THE COMPLETE SERIES

A sweeping magical adventure, filled with family, royals, romance, and sacrifice.

Series complete!

http://elisekova.com/vortex-visions-air-awakens-vortex-chronicles-1/

STAND ALONE
FANTASY ROMANCE

a DEAL with the ELF KING

a MARRIED TO MAGIC novel

Learn more at

https://elisekova.com/a-deal-with-the-elf-king/

NINETEEN-YEAR-OLD LUELLA HAD PREPARED ALL HER LIFE TO BE HER TOWN'S HEALER. Becoming the Elf King's bride wasn't anywhere in her plans. Taken to a land filled with wild magic, Luella learns how to control powers she never expected to save a dying world. The magical land of Midscape pulls on one corner of her heart, her home and people tug on another... but what will truly break her is a passion she never wanted.

LOOM SAGA

 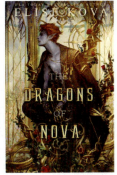 

What does an engineer with a dangerous past, a Dragon prince, and a trigger-happy gunmage have in common? One dangerous mission to assassinate a king. Perfect for fantasy fans looking for something different. Step into this dark and divided world today.

Series complete!

Acknowledgements

Jamie, Dani, and Iris—you three prove to me that true friendship doesn't know the limits of time and space. You three are all so important to me as an author and, just as friends.

Danielle L. Jensen—darling, you're wonderful. I don't know how you tolerate me some days, but I couldn't have asked for a better friend. From industry insights to simple encouragements, you really help me hold it together.

Nick—I can't wait to sit with you again and have you tear apart my manuscripts. You constantly make me a better author and take time to do it just becaue you are an amazing friend, so thank you.

My cover artist, Merilliza Chan—I can't believe we're almost at the end of this journey together. I feel like we've been through so much and have learned so much as creators. I hope you know how much working with you has meant to me.

My editor, Monica Wanat—your professionalism and understanding of my odd situations and way too regular manuscript delays has been invaluable on this journey.

The Tower Guard—each and every one of you are amazing. I hope you believe me when I tell you this. As of writing this there are 147 of you in our little group and I couldn't have asked for a better batch of people. Thank you for your support and for believing in me.